AFRAID TO LET GROW

A MARRIAGE SURVIVORS CLUB BOOK

ANNETTE NAURAINE

BEASLEY BOOKS

Cover Design: Lou Richardson, Ink Designs

❀ Created with Vellum

This book is dedicated to my wonderful husband, Peter, who has encouraged me throughout my writing journey, and to my two sons, Lincoln and Ulysses, who understand what my writing means to me.

This series is a Valentine to St. Paul's on the Green and all the people I've met who've become my friends.
Remember: if you don't want to see yourself in a book, don't be friends with a writer.

PRAISE FOR ANNETTE NAURAINE

In the Beginning: Marriage Survivors Club Prequel
...Readers will identify and empathize with the characters, who, in turn, will become readers' friends as well.

I enjoyed this quick and fun prequel to the Marriage Survivors Club series. You get to meet six women, who I assume will each have her own novel, at the moment their friendship begins. A great concept, and so refreshing to have a book about women older than thirty!

Short and funny novella about friends who meet at a funeral. This story sets up an entire series, so I can't wait for each novel about the women in the Marriage Survivors Club. Great banter. Looking forward to the rest!

About Do-Over Daughter
...I am looking forward to the rest of Annette's books in this series. The characters draw you in, and you want to find out what happens next!

...A nice, inspiring women's fiction read with lovely characters.

About Kissing the Kavalier
...This is the kind of wonderfully written book with several side plots and good character development that adds to the over all feeling of a well-written novel.

...Read this book if you love romance and the pain people must go through to get it.

...This is truly a great story that I found to be easy to read, fun and entertaining. I enjoyed the chemistry and the realisticness they brought to the story. I highly recommend this book.

...All the lush historical and cultural details and the rich textures woven through the story pulled me in and made me feel like I was right there, experiencing everything right alongside the characters.

AFRAID TO LET GROW

Annette Nauraine brings readers an emotional, funny, and heartfelt story that explores a mother's fears as she struggles to let her children go while facing her own fear of falling in love.

Olivia Maxwell is afraid of everything, including kittens. Determined to be a good mom, she does whatever it takes to keep her children safe. Eighteen years ago, her husband died, so she knows life can go up in smoke if you're not careful.

As a result, she's tried to anticipate every imaginable risk, warning her children about the dangers of food past its due date, kidnapping, bubonic plague, and planes crashing into the house.

Despite her pleas, her son drops out of college for a career guaranteed to put him in danger. Struggling to be allowed to grow, he pushes against all of Olivia's boundaries, even insisting his older sister, who has Down, should be allowed to experience love.

Can Olivia conquer her fears and let her children grow? Or is her reluctance to let them go about protecting them or herself? When an interfering fireman sets Olivia's menopausal desires aflame, will she risk falling in love?

Olivia's friends in the Marriage Survivors Club remind her that living a full life means embracing love and letting go. After all, it's never too late to grow.

From the Ionian Community

Dear Lord, please give me a few friends who understand me and remain my friends.

Addendum by the Marriage Survivors Club:

And who will tell me when I'm full of bullshit.

CHAPTER 1

You are the bows from which your children as living arrows are
sent forth.
   Khalil Gibran

Her arms weighed down with four heavy grocery bags, Olivia
Maxwell staggered up the steps to the front door.

The door was slightly ajar, which meant the alarm wasn't on.

Her heart took a dip.

She had dropped her daughter, Ariel, off only thirty minutes
ago because she had complained of being tired. She was twenty-
two and had Down Syndrome, but knew to lock both locks, turn
on the alarm, and not answer the door.

Olivia did everything she could to keep her children, Ariel,
and nineteen-year-old Taylor, safe from burglars, fires, floods,
thieves, airplanes falling from the sky, nuclear waste, lead in the
water, chemicals, kidnappers, drowning, earthquakes, and
molesters.

Why had she let her guard down and left Ariel alone?

Olivia shouldered the front door open and kicked the door closed behind her. She juggled the bags onto the kitchen table.

"Ariel," Olivia called. "You're supposed to keep the front door locked and the alarm on. Otherwise, it's not safe."

No answer.

"Ariel?" Olivia called again.

Maybe Ariel had fallen asleep in her room. Olivia trotted upstairs to Ariel's bedroom, but her bedspread lay neatly smoothed over the mattress with her collection of *My Little Pony* characters neatly arranged against the pillow. Olivia looked out the window and scanned the backyard.

Empty.

Olivia hurried to check her bedroom, Taylor's bedroom, and the bathroom. Her lip twitched the way it always did when she was nervous. She yanked open every closet even though she knew Ariel wouldn't hide in the dark.

Nothing.

Olivia felt like someone held her throat in an ever-tightening fist.

It was one of May's first lovely, warm days, so maybe Ariel had decided to take a walk. But she knew only to leave the house if she first asked Olivia or Taylor for permission.

Back in the kitchen, Olivia clawed her phone out of her purse and checked the tracking app she had installed on Ariel's phone. But the app showed Ariel's phone was in the house, so where in God's name was she?

Don't panic, don't panic. At least not yet.

Olivia speed-dialed Ariel. "Pick up, pick up, please, pick up."

Ariel's phone lay on the charging pad on the kitchen counter, ringing and ringing and ringing.

Ariel never left the house without her phone because if she

did, she was barred from watching America's Got Talent, and she lived for that show.

Olivia's mind spun into panic mode.

Olivia charged back out to the front porch. Shielding her eyes from the late afternoon sun, she looked up and down the street, hoping to see Ariel trudging down the sidewalk.

Nothing.

Someone must have convinced Ariel to open the front door and kidnapped her. Someone had been watching the house and knew a vulnerable person lived there. Olivia tried so hard to be a good mother, but she hadn't been paying attention and now it was too late.

Olivia was about to dial 911 when Taylor's Subaru pulled into the drive. Ariel sat in the front seat, eating an ice cream cone.

The knots in Olivia's stomach released. She closed her eyes, looked heavenward and muttered a curse, then a prayer of thanks.

Taylor climbed out of the car and waved. "Hi, Mom!"

She forced a smile despite her still thudding heart. "Where were you guys? I was scared to death when I came home to an empty house and an unlocked door."

Taylor adjusted his baseball cap, and the grin on his face hardened.

Oblivious, Ariel climbed out of the car. "Tay Tay buy ice cream cel-brate home." She held out a cone, ice cream dribbling down her hands. "Lick?" she offered.

Olivia said, "No, thanks, Honeybun. You forgot your phone, young lady, and you know what that means—no *AGT* this week."

Ariel stomped a foot. "Crap."

"Sorry, but rules are to keep you safe," Olivia said and gave her daughter a kiss on the temple.

Olivia wrapped her arms around her son's waist and pulled

him in for a real mom hug. She recognized his smell the way all mothers can identify their babies: young man, leather, and gym socks.

"Gotcha!" Taylor lifted Olivia off her feet and jiggled her up and down like a rag doll.

Her friends teased her about being the size of a twelve-year-old, which was about right. It was a mystery how she had given birth to a six-foot-three hulk like Taylor.

Feet dangling in mid-air, Olivia laughed. "No matter how big you are, I'm still the mom." She knocked his hat off and ruffled his hair.

Taylor set her down, picked up his hat, and settled it back over his lush curls. "Don't blame Ariel. She was so hyped to see me she forgot her phone."

Olivia straightened her clothes. "I'm glad you're home, but I thought you had finals for two more days, so I wasn't expecting you."

Olivia looked up at him with a chastising lift of her brows. "Next time you take her, please leave me a note or send me a text."

"I did leave you a note. It's on the kitchen table." He rested his meat hook fists on his hips and arched an eyebrow at her. "And my phone's out of gas, or I would have texted you."

Taylor looked so much like his father that it knocked her sideways. He was as strapping as Derek and had his dad's jumble of dark brown curly hair which sprang out from beneath his baseball cap. His angular face was defined by the fatless cheekbones of someone who played a lot of sports. Bulkier than when he had left for school after Christmas, she noted that he had an unfamiliar swagger.

Olivia was proud of him. Taylor was a good man. After he finished his medical residency, he would make someone a good husband. Until then, she just had to make sure his grades would get him into medical school.

Olivia tugged at her sleek ponytail, and her lip gave a final, residual twitch. "I was worried when I couldn't find her." Kidnappings happened all the time on those true crime shows, and it could have just as easily happened to Ariel.

Taylor easily hefted a pair of duffle bags out of the trunk of his car. "You shouldn't get so bent out of shape if Ariel's not home. She knows her way around."

His cavalier attitude made Olivia's jaw clench, but she resisted reminding him about Ariel's safety. He was a great brother, but clueless about what it felt like to be a parent. He would eventually understand when he was the one sweating bullets, waiting for a teenager to come home late or his daughter missed a period.

She said, "So why *are* you home early, anyway?"

Taylor's gaze slid away. "I finished up early. I'm going to take my bags in." He pushed the front door open and headed inside.

Frowning at his retreating—escaping—back, Olivia and Ariel followed him into the house.

Dropping his bags in the entrance hall, he headed immediately to the kitchen. He lifted a grocery bag on the kitchen table and pointed to a bright pink sticky note. "Here's the note we left you." He pulled it off and shoved it at Olivia. "All you had to do was look."

She read the note and tossed it in the trash under the sink. "I'm glad she's safe—and that she was with you."

"Mom, just admit you didn't find it, okay?" Taylor opened the fridge and pulled out three sticks of string cheese.

She sighed, regretting that they had already gotten off on the wrong foot. "All right, I'm sorry. You left me a note. Thanks."

"Stop worrying already." He grinned.

Oh, just you wait.

She couldn't not worry because it was in her DNA. She knew your entire life could change in an instant if you weren't careful.

Ariel sat at the table licking the dripping ice cream cone. Olivia said, "Wash your hands, honey."

"Okay." Ariel rose and laid the remnants of her ice cream cone on the counter. Over the sink, Olivia soaped up her daughter's hands.

"Mom, she can wash her own hands," Taylor said snottily.

Olivia shot him a look, but let Ariel finish washing her hands on her own.

When she had dried her hands, Ariel said, "I'm going in to watch *The Wiggles*."

"Okay, Honeybun." To Taylor Olivia said, "I'm making salmon for dinner. That okay with you?"

"Anything's fine," he mumbled around the cheese in his mouth.

She bit back the words, '*don't talk with your mouth full.*'

Olivia pointed to the fire alarm above the sink, its light glowing green. "Now that you're home, maybe you can change all the fire alarm batteries."

"Why? I did it at Christmas." He took a mug from the cabinet, set it under the coffee maker, inserted a plastic pod, and flipped the switch. "Why are you so safety-obsessed?"

"I'm not safety obsessed," Olivia said. "I like to change the batteries before they fail. People die of smoke inhalation, not fire. I taught you that."

"Oh, yes you did," he muttered. "And a hundred other useless things."

She frowned at his strapping back. Her friends teased her that she was afraid of everything, including kittens, but life was full of danger. Food past its due date, exploding lithium bike batteries, cars that could slip out of the park and roll over on you, avalanches on ski mountains, getting trapped you in your car when a bridge fell, cuts that could turn septic, and severe allergies to things you had no idea you were allergic to.

Or not listening to your mother.

He rapped the coffee machine with his knuckles. "Why isn't this dumb thing working?"

"You know I always unplug the appliances when I leave the house," she said.

He gave a noisy, irritated sigh. "God, Mom, you act like every day is Armageddon just waiting to happen." He plugged the coffeemaker in and flipped the 'on' switch again. "I'll bet you still carry that stupid window hammer in your car, don't you?"

She did, but she wasn't going to endure any more of his derision.

He leaned against the counter, and she flapped him out of her way. "I'm just cautious, is all." She set the slab of salmon in the sink. "How did your spring semester go?"

"Fine." The coffee machine hissed into his cup.

Fine? Fine? That was it? He had been gone three months, and all he could say was fine?

Olivia said, "You stopped texting or answering my phone calls, so I had no idea how things were going. I was worried."

She had briefly considered installing the tracking app on his phone, but her friend, Frankie, had said, "Are you crazy? He'll never trust you again. Is that the kind of relationship you want with your teenage son?"

Olivia's response had been, "Yes, if it means he's safe." Frankie's withering scowl made Olivia give up the idea.

Olivia felt Taylor's annoyance, like a cold front rolling in. She tried a softer approach. "I like hearing from you."

"Mom, I'm nineteen," he said. "I'm in college. You don't have to check on me every day. It's like you're the Gestapo or something."

She didn't try to disguise her hurt. "I am not the Gestapo because I like hearing from you."

If he texted, she knew he hadn't had a concussion in lacrosse, wrecked his car, and that there hadn't been a mass shooting on the campus. To make sure Taylor didn't take up his dad's hobby of cheating death.

Because one day Olivia hadn't been there and death won.

CHAPTER 2

A mother's arms are made of tenderness and children sleep
soundly in them.

Victor Hugo

As she had for years, Olivia woke at two a.m. She slipped out of
bed, dragged on her robe, and went to check on her kids.

Taylor had gone out after dinner to meet some friends, and
she had stayed awake until she heard his footfalls on the stairs.
After he had gone into his room, she padded downstairs and
double-checked that the house was safe. Her lecture must have
had some effect because, she noted with satisfaction, he'd
locked both locks and turned on the alarm.

Olivia was relieved to find Ariel fast asleep, snoring lightly
amid her cluster of stuffed animals. She tiptoed into her daughter's room and brushed the hair off her face. She leaned down
and gently kissed Ariel's forehead, then softly closed the door.

She had always loved looking in on her children. Her ritual
consisted of checking that the windows were locked, alarm on,

and fire alarms blinking. It was comforting to know they were safe in their beds, that nothing had happened to them while she was asleep.

She knocked softly at Taylor's door but got no answer, so she opened the door and peeked in, as she had so many other nights. It was something she had missed doing while he was at college.

He was sleeping on his stomach, his pillow bunched under his head. She smiled to see his feet hanging off the end of his XL queen-sized bed. It was a mystery how a colicky baby had grown into a young man who could sleep if a bomb went off in his bedroom.

Olivia reached out a finger and lightly caressed one of Taylor's chocolatey curls. His hair was springing every which way. She would have to remind him to get a haircut. She sent up a prayer of thanks that Taylor was home, safe and sound, in one big, food-budget-breaking piece. She had hardly slept for the first month he'd been gone, imagining hazing, drinking black-outs, and other terrible things.

Probably the worst thing that had happened was a bad case of athlete's foot, but it could have been much, much worse.

In her deepest heart, she still thought of her kids as her babies. She still wanted to protect them, to guide Taylor to a successful, fulfilling life as a doctor like his dad. This had been their dream since he had been a little kid. It would also ensure that he had the emotional and financial resources to take over Ariel's care when Olivia wasn't around anymore.

Her heart swelled with love and a sense of responsibility. Making sure your loved ones were safe was what good mothers did, and she'd be damned if, this time, she would fail.

She peered through the darkness at the clutter of shoes, clothes, notebooks, lacrosse sticks, pads, helmet, laptop, printer, empty soda bottles, and random bits of trash strewn all over the floor. Hopefully, his future wife didn't mind messes.

She nudged aside a pile of dirty clothes to check that the metal fire escape ladder was below the window, but it wasn't. Her annoyance flared. Did Taylor think he was immune to fire? Why did men believe nothing could hurt them?

Mothers and wives knew better.

A slice of moonlight shone through a gap in the curtains and onto a partly open bag on the floor. Spilling from the bag were coils of climbing ropes, climbing shoes, clips, and gloves.

Her mind screamed like a siren. She clenched her robe to stop her hands from shaking. Her breath came in stuttering, shallow gasps.

How long had he been rock climbing? Why not volleyball or badminton? Why something that might end with his skull smashed on a pile of rocks? She wanted to drag the gear out, put it in the trunk of her car and throw it into the ocean.

Olivia reached out her hand to wake Taylor and ask why he was rock climbing, but she stopped herself.

Olivia had always held up Derek as a role model to Taylor and, like every kid, he tried to be like his dad. If she told Taylor the truth, he might try even harder to imitate Derek. But this wasn't the way she wanted him to do it.

She closed the door softly behind her and went back to bed, where she didn't sleep a wink. The rest of the night, Olivia tried to figure out how to protect her son.

The way she'd failed to protect Derek.

CHAPTER 3

Children have never been very good at listening to their elders,
but they have never failed to imitate them.
James Baldwin

The next morning in the kitchen, Olivia's stomach was still
pretzeled with worry. She sat at the table trying to read the *New
York Times* home section, but the words swam on the page
because all she could think about was Taylor's bag of climbing
equipment.

He stumbled in, bedhead hair like when he was little, eyes
still blurry with sleep, in bare feet, his pajama pants dragging.
She used to love gathering him on her lap and nuzzling his
neck, which smelled like sleep.

"Good morning," she said, hearing the chill in her own voice.

"Morning." He gave a jaw-cracking yawn and took the milk
out of the fridge and a box of cereal from the cabinet.

His cellphone rang and, when he answered it, the smile on
his face made Olivia snap to attention.

"Hey," he said to the person on the other end of the line. His face turned moony as he shuffled into the living room.

A girlfriend. He hadn't mentioned anyone. Olivia rose from the table, careful not to let her chair scrape on the floor. She tiptoed to the door to eavesdrop and felt not a drop of guilt doing so.

His laugh was low, and the murmur of his voice was sweet and inquisitive. "Okay, I'll see you then. Bye." He clicked off.

Olivia slipped back into her chair and pretended to read a story about composting. When he returned to the kitchen, she asked, "One of your friends from school?"

One of your rock-climbing friends?

"Yeah, my girlfriend, Dani Karner," he said with a studied tone of nonchalance.

His eyes, as inscrutable as his father's, shifted from Olivia. It was as though he had window shades he could pull down at will, shutting her out. It had annoyed her with Derek and now with Taylor. Another example of how children inherited their parents' characteristics.

He poured cereal into a bowl and leaned against the counter to spoon it into his mouth.

She tried to match his nonchalance, but her Mom-Alarm was on Code Yellow. "You didn't mention you had a girlfriend."

He shrugged. "Yeah."

What sort of an answer was that? It wasn't that Olivia was surprised or didn't want him to have a girlfriend. He was nineteen, after all, and probably had the hormones of a bull. Sex in a relationship was a normal step toward adulthood. It was better he had a steady girlfriend rather than hooking up.

But what if he spent too much time with his girlfriend and neglected his studies? What if this girl was more serious than he was? It was better he had a steady girlfriend rather than hooking up. She was hurt he'd hidden the fact that he was dating. But the greater concern right now was his rock climbing and convincing him to stop.

She turned the page of the newspaper. "When did you...start dating?"

"Mm, like, last October. November. Something like that," he said.

Nine months without dropping a single hint. Not even the last time he was home. "How'd you meet?" She turned a page of the newspaper.

"Party."

She stared unseeing at the paper, biding her time. "What's her major?"

"Public health," he said.

His eyes had softened, and his eyebrows lifted as if he recalled something Olivia didn't want to think about. She could tell that this girl had her hooks in him. Time for a subtle hint. "She knows you're studying to go to med school, right?"

He huffed a derisive laugh. Milk dribbled down the front of his shirt. "Yeeeaaah, why?"

She held the newspaper so tight the edges crumpled in her hands. "Med school has a long timeline," she said. "You won't be ready to settle down until at least your residency. Even though we were crazy about each other, your dad and I waited until then."

She didn't want to say *don't get her pregnant*.

Olivia had given Taylor the condom talk every year since he was twelve. Red-faced and grinding his teeth, he sat through her factual explanations. They had these chats not once but twice a year, the week before his birthday and the week before Valentine's. She chose those dates because they were easy to remember, but she kept them written down in what she called her *Big Book of Safety Protocols*. There, she kept track of the annual dates when she warned him about drinking and driving, STDs, defensive driving, snakes, how to remove ticks, gambling, internet porn, internet addiction, internet cons and schemes, and when he was younger, a host of other things, like stranger-danger. The annual calendar hadn't changed much—only the topics of concern had expanded with elevating risk.

She had to worry enough for two parents since Derek was deceased. But she had forgotten to warn Taylor against getting a girl pregnant when you were pre-med.

Of course, he knew *how* girls got pregnant. If Derek were here, he would have taken care of all the manly discussions, but she prided herself on the fact that she and Taylor could discuss everything. Until last fall, apparently.

"Mom, I have zero interest in getting married, and neither does she." His voice dripped with derision. He slurped the milk from his cereal bowl.

"Sorry, I don't mean to pry or anything." But of course, wanted to know every detail about the girlfriend.

And she wanted him to remember what his priorities were. But first things first: the dangers of rock climbing.

"Last night, I—" Olivia broke off when Ariel trundled into the kitchen, making a beeline for Taylor.

She threw her arms around his waist. "Glad home, Tay Tay."

He hugged her back, producing a grunt of pleasure from Ariel. "Me too, Squirt," he said, bending to rest his chin on Ariel's head.

The sweetness they shared touched Olivia. She was immensely grateful that Taylor showed so much love, patience, caring, and understanding toward Ariel. A good thing, too, because one day, Taylor would be responsible for her.

Unless he killed himself in some stupid sporting activity.

Ariel wore electric blue exercise pants and a matching short-sleeved top. She smelled of vanilla soap and mint toothpaste.

She had managed to get her fine, straight brown hair into a messy ponytail, which Olivia would have to fix later.

"Go church, Tay Tay?" Ariel asked, her cheek still pressed to his belly.

"Not today, Squirt," he said. "It's not Sunday."

Olivia's eyes went to the small postcard on the fridge that was an announcement for the church barbecue. "St. Paul's is hosting a barbecue fundraiser for the LGBTQ youth shelter. I'd love it if you could come. Everyone would enjoy seeing you."

In the recent past, Norwalk had seen the tragic suicides of several queer young people. St. Paul's, where she attended and where she had raised Taylor and Ariel, undertook the establishment of a homeless shelter to help protect this vulnerable population. The dream had simmered for several years and was finally becoming a reality. Since Olivia was an interior designer, she had been hired to do the finishes at the Essex condo development. The shelter consisted of two units in the development that was conveniently located right across East Avenue from St. Paul's.

Olivia and her friends were leading the fundraising charge. The diverse group of six fifty-something friends called themselves the Marriage Survivors Club because they had each been blenderized by marriage in one way or another. They had uniformly sworn off reentering the age-old institution, but Frankie Carter had fallen in love with Cam Simpson, the condo developer. Hence, the two condo units for the shelter.

Olivia was the only widow in the Marriage Survivors Club. There was nothing they wouldn't do for one another. They'd met at St. Paul's Episcopal Church, where they were members, and together, they were a force to be reckoned with.

"I don't know if I'll be around." Taylor lifted his massive shoulders and let them drop. "Maybe."

"Who you talk phone?" Ariel asked Taylor. Apparently, she'd overheard him on the phone, too.

"I was talking to Dani, my girlfriend," he said.

Ariel pulled out her chair and sat next to Olivia. "She nice?"

"Yes, she's nice." One corner of Taylor's mouth curled into a smile.

"I want boyfriend," Ariel said. "Bitsy has Fred." Bitsy, who also had Down, was Ariel's friend.

"That's because Bitsy is thirty-five. You're still too young for a boyfriend," Olivia said.

That was one hurdle Olivia expected to deal with. Ariel would always be a child. She patted Ariel's plump pink arm and smoothed the hair around Ariel's ears. "Honey, get your brush, and I'll fix your hair."

Olivia's own ponytail was always sleek as the finish on a Ferrari. Her elegant, understated, classy look impressed her more well-to-do clients. She wore slim black pants, crisp white blouses, and sometimes pencil skirts, usually paired with gold jewelry. She always made sure Ariel looked attractive because she didn't want people to see only a young woman with Down.

"Hair looks fine to me," Taylor said, gently tugging Ariel's ponytail and making her giggle.

"Hair fine," Ariel parroted.

Olivia shot Taylor a frown, which he ignored. She'd always explained to him that Ariel would always need someone— Olivia or him—to watch her closely. To monitor where she went and with whom, and to ensure no one took advantage of her, that no one hurt her in any way. Dozens of little chores, like brushing Ariel's hair, went along with that. Some people with Down were a handful for even the most resilient parents, and Olivia was grateful Ariel was remarkably loving, sweet, and cooperative. It was nice to have her company at Olivia's shop,

Second Chance Designs, where Olivia gave her little jobs. Plus, having her daughter close made it easier to keep an eye on her.

"Pour cereal, Tay Tay?" Ariel implored Taylor.

Taylor said, "No, you get up and pour it yourself. You're not a baby."

Ariel scowled at him. "You mean."

"You gotta' learn to do stuff for yourself, Squirt," Taylor said.

This was something Olivia usually did because Ariel would make a mess, and Olivia would end up cleaning it up. Another small chore Taylor had to get used to doing for Ariel.

He handed Ariel a cereal bowl and the box.

She dumped half the box into her bowl. "Too many!" she whined.

"It's okay, Squirt." Taylor took the bowl and poured a little back into the box. "There, that's good," he said. "Now, the milk." He handed her the milk jug, which was heavy because it was almost full. It wobbled, and he steadied it, but Ariel sloshed milk on the floor, anyway. He took the jug back from Ariel and set it on the counter.

"Tay Tay! Milk spill!" Ariel cried, flapping her arms up and down.

Taylor rested his hands on her shoulders, bent, and looked into her face. He spoke calmly. "Ariel, it's no big deal. People spill stuff all the time, me included. Let's just wipe it up."

He pulled off a length of paper towel and kneeled with Ariel. Together, they wiped it up. "See what you did?" he said to Ariel. "You just got a new skill."

He gave Olivia a smug grin that reminded her of Derek right before he flung himself off a bridge tethered only by a bungee cord.

When you have kids, I'm going to remind you of that smug grin.

Ariel hugged him. "Thank, Tay Tay." She picked up the too-full cereal bowl and carefully shuffled her way to the table.

Taylor sat in his chair. The cleft in his chin—like Derek's—had deepened. When had his shoulders become so broad? When had his hands become the size of pie plates?

And when had he taken up rock climbing?

"Come church, Tay Tay," Ariel said with a mouth full of cereal.

Olivia said, "When I told Father Gabriel you were coming home, he asked if you could serve on the altar one Sunday and I said you'd be glad to."

Taylor scowled. "Mom, stop committing me to stuff, okay? I can make my own decisions."

"You used to like helping out at church," Olivia said, hurt. When and why had he started pushing back on her so hard? It was like he wanted to kick her in the shins every chance he got.

"Come," Ariel said. "Marriage Survivors Club hug you."

Taylor leaned back in his chair, extended his legs, and locked his hands behind his head. "I don't know. I might sleep in or something. You can stay home with me if you want, Ariel. I'll take you out for breakfast."

"I like church," Ariel said.

"I know you do, but you can do other fun stuff too," Taylor said to Ariel.

"Okay," Ariel said, as cereal clumped in the corners of her mouth.

Olivia lifted a napkin to wipe her mouth.

"Mom, she can do it herself." He snatched the napkin and handed it to Ariel. "Wipe your mouth with the napkin, Squirt."

Ariel grinned at her beloved younger brother and scrubbed at her mouth.

Olivia took a sip of coffee, which was stone cold and tasted like paint remover. If Taylor was going to turn everything into a battle, this was going to be a long summer.

CHAPTER 4

It is easier to build strong children than to repair broken men.
Frederick Douglass

Jack O'Grady nosed his car into a parking spot in front of Muro's where he could get coffee and one of the cinnamon crullers he craved, but only allowed himself on occasion. They climbed out of the car. Jack smelled the coffee and cinnamon all the way down the sidewalk.

Matt pointed to the store next to Muro's. "Do you think that store would sell my shirts?"

Jack looked through the front window of Second Chance Designs. The store was full of beautifully displayed furniture that belonged in million-dollar houses. Definitely not a T-shirt store.

"They don't look like a shirt store, buddy," Jack said.

"But you made me practice selling. We can practice again in this store," Matt insisted.

If Matt didn't have Down syndrome, the kid would probably have been the CEO of some tech startup. Every day he surprised Jack with his independence and creativity. Matt might have a disability, but he had his own kind of smarts.

Matt's mom, Jeannie, had been Jack's sister.

Despite their ten-year age difference, Jack and Jeannie had always been close. Matt had her smile, the sanding of freckles over his snubby nose, and dark wavy hair that cowlicked up in the center of his forehead. Sometimes, if the light was just right, or Matt turned his head just so, the sharp pain of her death hit Jack right in the gut.

Jack patted Matt's shoulder. "What say we have a cruller and some coffee at Muro's first, then find a different kind of store?" Jack said, in the hope of diverting Matt's singular focus on this store.

"Business before pleasure." Matt opened the back door of Jack's SUV and pulled out his Mattscrazyshirts.com branded tote bag with samples of T-shirts and the order forms. Matt was nothing if not optimistic.

Matt smoothed his T-shirt over his pudgy belly that was printed with one of his signature abstract designs. If you looked closely at the blue, purple, and orange swirls, you could see a landscape with a smiling face. Jack wore a similar shirt but with a different design under his jacket.

Matt asked, "Do I look good? Like a good guy who sells crazy shirts?"

"You look like a pro who sells crazy shirts," Jack said. He pointed down the street. Maybe there's a better store down there. Shall we go see?"

"No, I want this store," Matt said.

Sometimes Matt's determination looked an awful lot like inflexibility. Jack wasn't sure yet which was which, or how much to push back against Matt. But this was his dream, and Jack didn't want to be the one to squash it.

The minute they stepped inside the upscale store, Jack knew it was a colossal mistake. The store reeked of refined elegance. Soft classical music wafted through the place like smoke and the air smelled of roses and money. Curvy sofas, Lucite chairs, leather sectionals, arty lamps, and glass and chrome tables were tastefully grouped throughout the shop. Books of fabric samples were stacked on a shelf along the rear wall. Black and white close-up photographs of indecipherable objects and canvases with smears of color hung on the walls.

Not that he knew anything about art, but Jack liked Matt's paintings more than any of that stuff. Jack found the whole place pretentious and prepared to be thrown out.

"Matt, buddy, really, I think we should try another store. This one doesn't seem right," Jack said. But Matt was already halfway down the main aisle of the store.

Jack was in pursuit when a short, chubby girl with a wide smile ambled toward them. She had a round face, flat features, fine light brown hair, and wide-set blue eyes blinking from behind round glasses. Her age was hard to determine because she, too, had Down syndrome.

What were the chances?

In thick speech that could be hard to decipher, she said, "Hi, I'm Ariel. Welcome Second Chance Design."

"Hi ... I ..." Matt stared at Ariel with googly eyes. His mouth worked, but no sounds came out. He glanced up at Jack, then back at the young lady. "You're pretty," he said to her.

Ariel giggled, and her blue eyes sparkled. "Thanks you."

Jack glanced at a price tag on a sofa and nearly choked. "We're sorry to bother you. We were looking for another store." He laid a hand on Matt's shoulder. "C'mon, Matt."

Matt didn't move. Jack had never seen him with such a big

smile. He was smitten. Like every man at one time or another, he'd been laid low by a pretty girl.

If neuro-typical people fell in love so easily, the world would be a better place.

"No, I want to tell her about my shirts," Matt said, not taking his eyes off Ariel.

"You have a shirt," Ariel pointed at Matt's shirt. "Me, too." She patted her tummy.

"I sell shirts. Can you buy a shirt?" Matt asked.

"Maybe we can come back another day," Jack said, but Matt was already digging a shirt out of the tote bag. He dropped the bag on the floor and, just like Jack had taught him, he stretched out the shirt to better show the design.

"I'm Matt," he said, "and this is my Uncle Jack, and this is my shirt. I paint them."

"Pretty," Ariel said.

"Are you the manager?" Matt asked, sailing on with his pitch like a seasoned pro.

There was no stopping Matt now, so Jack stood back and watched his nephew. If only people could see past Matt's disability to his talent and ambition, they would be astonished. The same way Jack had been. Still was.

"Mom!" Ariel hollered toward the back of the store.

Now would come the heave-ho.

"Coming," a disembodied voice replied.

A small woman, mid-fifties, in trim black pants and a crisp white blouse, emerged from the rear of the shop. Her sleek blond hair was pulled back in a short, blunt ponytail that accentuated the fragile architecture of her face. A lot of women her age had frozen faces like TV anchors who had injected plastic or something into their faces, but this woman's face had well-used laugh lines. She was tiny, but her presence was as big as one of the over-stuffed sectionals. High-class all the way.

She would definitely show them the door.

But her blue eyes regarded Jack with both curiosity and gracious welcome. "Can I help you?"

Ariel pointed at Matt's shirt. "Matt paint shirts."

"Paints?" the woman asked, her confusion obvious.

"Hi, I'm Matt." He grinned his biggest smile. "This is my shirt," Matt said, and displayed the shirt he had on.

She was still smiling, but the woman looked questioningly at Jack.

"Hi, I'm, uh, I'm Jack O'Grady," Jack said. "This is Matt Wilson, my nephew and business partner. We sell shirts with his artwork on them. I'm sorry we bothered you." Jack gave a gesture toward the stack of boxes in front of the store sales counter. "I know you're busy, and obviously this isn't the right kind of place to sell shirts, but Matt wanted to stop in."

The woman extended her small hand, which was creamy and soft. "I'm Olivia Maxwell. This is my shop." Though she was small, her silky voice was not. It was packed with kindness, gloved in assurance. "I guess you've already met my daughter, Ariel."

Matt said, "Yes! She's very pretty!"

Ariel giggled again, and Jack couldn't resist a smile. Olivia smiled too and her blue eyes looked like sunshine on ice.

To Matt, Olivia said, "Thank you for stopping in to talk to me. You sell shirts?"

"Yes," Matt said with well-deserved pride. "I paint canvases, then we print the painting on T-shirts and sell them on my website, Matt's Crazy Shirts dot com, but I want to have my shirts in stores in Norwalk, so when people walk around, they can see them. Then they will know a man with Down painted them."

Olivia nodded and looked Matt right in the eye. "I think

that's a sound business strategy. I can see you've thought it through."

Jack could have kissed her feet for being so encouraging.

Olivia gestured to a sofa that looked far too expensive to sit on. "Please have a seat. I'd love to see your shirts."

"Look, it's really nice of you, but if you don't have time…" Jack started. But when she turned her gaze on him, he stopped talking.

Olivia said, "No, no, really. I like to encourage entrepreneurs, and I do want to see them."

Most people were always in a hurry to get away from people who were different from themselves. Jack had to admit that before getting custody of Matt, he was guilty of that himself.

Matt opened Jack to a whole different part of himself that he would never have known if it weren't for Matt. He taught Jack to be more patient and understanding of differences, which now, Jack could spot when he was out and about.

Matt plopped down next to Olivia and Ariel sat next to Matt, hip to hip. Jack eased down on the edge of an armchair that he was afraid might break under his weight.

"Ariel, honey, give Matt a little room," Olivia said with a flap of her small hand.

"No, I like it. She's so pretty," Matt said, shooting a smile at Ariel.

"Matt, the shirts?" Jack prompted.

"Oh, yeah." Matt laid his shirt out on the kidney-shaped coffee table in front of the sofa. "This is my painting." Matt said, "Show your shirt, Uncle Jack."

Jack sucked in his paunch and opened his bomber to display his shirt with Matt's design. Olivia's eyes widened, and Jack lifted his chest a little higher. He was a little old to be vain, but somehow, Olivia had inspired him.

"These are beautiful," Olivia said. "You paint these on canvas?"

Matt pointed to a painting with muddy purple smears hanging on a wall. "Like that, only mine are prettier."

Jack gave Olivia an apologetic look, but she was smiling. She had a daughter with Down, so she got it. On the other hand, Jack was still learning.

"You can buy my paintings, too, if you want to," Matt said, and Jack closed his eyes with a cringe.

"You know...," Olivia said. She tilted her head, and her gaze flew around the store, assessing the other artwork. "I think I might like to see your paintings."

"Really?" Jack asked, not even trying to hide his surprise.

"Yes. If they're as attention-grabbing and as beautiful as the shirts, I think I could sell some," Olivia said.

Jack leaned forward and said in a low voice, "You know, if you're just being nice, you don't have to do that."

"I know I don't," Olivia said. "But I think his paintings might be a perfect addition to my shop. When could you bring them by for me to see?"

This was turning out to be much better than Jack could have anticipated. Matt seemed to have an excellent radar for sales of all kinds. And if she bought the paintings, they would produce a lot more income than the shirts.

Jack waved his hand to get Matt's attention. "Earth to Matt. Would you like to sell some of your paintings here?"

Matt blinked at Jack. "Yes, and then I can see pretty Ariel," Matt said.

Olivia frowned slightly, and she shifted over on the sofa a bit. "Ariel, can you move down, please? I'm a bit squished at this end."

Ariel moved over only a smidgen, but Matt did likewise, so they remained glued together.

Trying to cover up his embarrassment, Jack spoke quickly to Olivia. "We could bring some by later in the week, maybe?"

Olivia was looking at Ariel. Olivia's brow was wrinkled with concern, and from Jack's experience, what looked like abject fear.

Olivia turned her headlight gaze on Jack. "That would be great. Bring me a couple of different ones so I can choose."

"Sure." Jack stood, not wanting to take any more of this perceptive woman's time.

"Mom, buy shirt," Ariel reminded Olivia.

"Of course!" Olivia said brightly. "That was why you came." She rose and went to the sales counter, and returned with a check. She handed Jack a business card.

"You're very nice to do this," Jack said.

"I'm a businesswoman. I know when something will suit my clientele," Olivia said with a knock-out smile.

Matt and Ariel were still mooning at one another. "Matt?" Jack said.

"What?" Matt answered.

Jack wished he could find a woman as willing to fall for him as Ariel was for Matt.

"Can you give Olivia the sales form we have?" Jack suggested.

"Oh, yeah." Matt dug into his tote and handed it to Olivia. "Fill this out and pay me this much and your shirts will come in one week. I have to print them first."

"Shirts come on truck?" Ariel asked.

"I want to bring them, can we, Uncle Jack? Matt pleaded.

"Yes, sure. And we'll bring some of your paintings then too, okay, buddy?" Jack said.

When the business transaction for the shirts was concluded, Matt said, "Now you get your cruller and coffee at Muro's, Uncle Jack."

"I show Muro's," Ariel said, and she shyly leaned against Matt's shoulder.

"Okay!" Matt said.

They launched themselves off the sofa and disappeared out the door before Jack or Olivia could stop them. They looked positively happy.

But Olivia looked positively stricken.

CHAPTER 5

Children are the anchors that hold a mother to life.

Sophocles

Olivia's lip twitched as she watched Ariel and Matt walk hand in hand to Muro's. It was only a few hundred feet, but Ariel was with a young man, which presented a host of risk factors.

"Will they be okay by themselves?" she murmured, more to herself than to Jack.

He'd heard her because he came to stand near her, radiating testosterone. "Matt's a good kid. He knows to call me if anything goes wrong."

She felt a hitch in her heart, like the jerk of a rope. "Do you think something could go wrong? Ariel has been to Muro's dozens of times, but never by herself."

Jack looked at her strangely. "I'm sure they'll be fine. She seems independent."

Olivia frowned. "She's not. Not really."

For the first time since he came in and she wasn't absorbed

in keeping an eye on Ariel and Matt, Olivia noticed what Jack looked like.

He was handsome in a rugged sort of way. His hair, toast-brown and scattered with gray, was buzzed short over a blocky skull. His taut-jawed face commanded respect, but his mouth was soft. His sable eyes stared at her with an unnerving direct-ness that made the tiny hairs on the tops of her arms prickle. He was strong, but there was something slightly befuddled about him, as if he was in over his head.

Anxiety barked at the back of her mind, a reminder to check, pull out her phone, and set a timer. "If they're not back in ten minutes, I'll go get them."

"Matt will bring her back, safe and sound," he said, his confi-dence not calming her in the least.

She went to her counter and bent over one of the boxes on the floor. "Pardon me while I get to work. Working is the best way to keep my mind focused."

Why had she told him that?

"Can I set that on the table for you?" he asked.

She hoped he wasn't being macho by making the offer. She didn't want him throwing out his back on her account.

At his age, he probably held a desk job that kept him off her do-not-date list, which included policemen, for obvious reasons, and electricians (electrocution), construction workers (limbs could get lopped off by a power). At the top of the list were skydivers, parachutists, scuba divers, paragliders, motorcyclists, and, of course, rock climbers. Any man she considered dating had to make a living tapping computer keys.

Jack slipped off his leather jacket and slung it over the back of a chair, and she instantly revised her assumptions about his job. Aside from an age-appropriate softening around his middle, he was in fantastic shape, with burly shoulders and a powerful chest. The wrists protruding from his long-sleeved shirt were like tree branches, and she couldn't help noticing that his jeans yielded a fine silhouette of his butt.

She might be post-menopausal, but she wasn't dead.

He picked up the box and set it on the worktable as if it were a pillow.

She sliced open the top of the box and pulled back the flaps. Inflatable packing pillows fluttered to the floor and barnacled to every surface.

"Let me get that for you," he said and reached into the box and pulled out the bubble-wrapped, custom-made lamp. He set it on the counter.

"You said Matt is your nephew?" she asked.

"Yes, I got custody when my sister and her husband were killed in a car crash." Pain crept into the fine lines at the corners of his eyes.

"I'm sorry for your loss," she said. "It takes courage to take on someone else's child, let alone one with the challenges that come with raising one with Down."

"Thanks. I'm finding parenting Matt is nothing like raising my own two daughters." He scratched the back of his bull-like neck, and she saw that befuddled look again. "I'm still figuring things out with Matt."

"You seem to have a lot of confidence in him." She glanced toward the window again, looking for signs of the pair. "But aren't you a little uncomfortable with him roaming the streets?"

It made her sound a little off-center, but Ariel wasn't as capable as Matt, and Olivia was a mom, after all. Moms were different from fathers.

She detected no condemnation when he said, "I decided to give him opportunities to grow, to not be afraid. Look at how determined he was to come in here and sell you your shirts. Took me a while to get him to go out and meet people, and now there's no stopping him."

"Ariel isn't like that with people," Olivia said.

He leaned casually against the counter and crossed his ankles. "She seemed pretty friendly when we came in. She greeted us, introduced herself, called you over."

"She's comfortable here in the store," Olivia said. And she was comfortable having her daughter here because then, Olivia knew right where Ariel was. "You seem to be on the right track with Matt."

Jack picked a wad of packing off the floor and stuffed it back in the box. "I think that people are happiest when they're not afraid. I figure if you're worried and scared all the time, you miss out on life, don't you agree?"

"Being vigilant is part of life, particularly when you have children." She picked at the packing tape, struggling to get the lamp unwrapped. "I think men are more tolerant of risk in general. All good mothers worry, no matter how old their children get."

"Even when they're grown?" he asked.

Hadn't he ever had this conversation with his ex? Had he forgotten whatever cautions the mother of his children had given him?

She gave him a smile. "That's when we worry most. When they're little, you can keep an eye on them. When they're bigger, they can do much bigger damage in a much shorter amount of time. It takes more energy to keep them safe because there are so many more options for danger to life and limb."

She knew she risked Jack thinking she was paranoid, but he'd just inherited a young person with Down syndrome, and he needed a gentle reminder not to let his guard down.

Ever.

She picked at the tape with her nail, and it started to come free. "People take advantage of others with disabilities. I think it helps to instill a healthy sense of fear in your children. And it helps remind you how fragile life is. Reminds you to cherish them and yes, stay vigilant."

He nodded and didn't laugh or mock her, so she hoped her message was getting through. Men loved their children as much as their children's mothers, but men could be a little naïve when it came to understanding the dangers of the world. Of just plain living.

"I don't want Matt to be afraid," Jack said as he lifted the lamp up so she could unwrap a length of the tape.

She glanced surreptitiously at the timer on her phone. Just five more minutes until she could go bring Ariel back. Leaving her with Matt wasn't the solution, it was a potential problem she had to manage. Matt might be a nice guy, but Olivia didn't exactly have the trust in him that Jack had. He wasn't dumb, but he wasn't a mom.

Another thought occurred to her. "What does your wife say about Matt and his being cautious?"

An outright grimace. "I'm divorced. Three years in September."

"But who's counting?" she asked.

Why hadn't anyone snapped him up yet? Kind, responsible, good-looking. Nice butt.

"You?" he asked.

She felt her face flush. Why did he want to know? She hadn't intended to make the off-hand question sound like she was asking if he was married or not.

He was waiting for her answer, looking at her with his direct gaze, which rattled her. And why was he having that effect on her? It was as though he saw something in her he liked. What was it that he saw?

She set her little shoulders back. "I'm widowed. I guess I worry enough for two."

He nodded. "It's hard, being alone."

That wasn't exactly what she'd said, but she let his comment go unanswered. She wasn't one to share her grief or guilt with anyone.

He unwound the plastic wrap from the lamp and set it on the counter. After he'd stuffed all the packing material back into the box, he stood back and eyed the lamp. He tilted his head one way, then the other. He moved his hands around in the air as if trying to reshape the admittedly bizarre lamp.

"Is this right side up?" he asked, and they both laughed.

Olivia said, "This client has, shall we say, exotic tastes." Her timer went off, and she couldn't help glancing out the window again. "They should have been back by now."

"You're worried. I'll go get the kids," he said.

He seemed trustworthy, so she didn't feel the need to lock up the shop and go with him to Muro's to bring Ariel back. And besides, Olivia could just look out the window and watch them coming back.

"Thank you," she breathed.

He really did have a nice butt. And nice eyes. And a nice chest. And he was nice. She hoped he took her words of motherly wisdom to heart.

"Let me take this box back to the back of the store for you first," he said.

She said, "That'd be great." Then she could see his butt again as he walked away.

Before picking up the box, Jack pushed up his sleeves to the elbows. There, on the back of his forearm, almost buried in the curly hair, was a wicked scar running from elbow to wrist.

A cold, dark, jagged pit with no bottom opened in her stomach. One by one, as if someone was hurling them in, she felt the pit fill with the stones of guilt, fear, and the primal need to protect those she loved from danger.

The day Derek got his nearly identical scar, it had been a

pristine day, cloudless but gusty, the air chilly and scented with spring rain. The rock-climbing guide, a young man with sinewy arms and legs, assured them the climb was well within their abilities.

He had been wrong.

She was terrified of heights, but like always, she went along to keep Derek safe.

The guide climbed first, then Derek, and her last, because they could pull her up easily if she got tired. They climbed slowly, carefully following every one of the guide's instructions. Her fingers cramped, and her legs burned, but she kept up. The wind picked up, trying to push her off the rock like a giant hand, but she swallowed her fear and kept going.

Derek looked down at her and shouted, "Isn't this a blast? We're so far above the entire world!"

"Yeah, a blast!" she shouted back. It was sheer hell.

Derek climbed a bit, then cried out.

Above her, the rope jerked, and she found herself dangling in mid-air a hundred feet above the ground. Pebbles fell on her helmet, making a *tap-tap-tapping* sound. When she looked up, Derek was holding his arm. She looked up again, and something wet fell on her face. She wiped at her cheek, and her fingers came away smeared with blood. Blood was streaming from Derek's arm.

She wouldn't let herself scream because she knew she had to help save Derek.

The guide calmly told them what to do. She reached out, found two small handholds, and pulled herself back onto the rock face. Derek climbed down with his one good arm. When they reached solid ground, she wasn't sure who she wanted to kill first, the guide or Derek.

At the nearest ER, they stitched up an eight-inch gash in Derek's arm. He said, "It wasn't fatal."

Not that time.

Jack returned to the front of the store, smiling a smile that could have melted stone.

She glanced at his arm, but he'd pulled his sleeves down again. Maybe he'd gotten the scar in some perfectly innocuous childhood accident. An accident that happened when his mom wasn't paying attention.

"Thanks again for being so nice to Matt," he said.

She handed him his leather coat. "And thanks for helping with that, uh, exotic lamp."

"Maybe when we bring the paintings back, we can all go to Muro's." He shrugged his brawny shoulders into his leather jacket. A leather jacket that gave him a dangerous James Dean sort of look. He said, "They have great crullers. What could a cup of coffee and a cruller hurt?

"Sounds good," she said, noncommittally. As long as Matt and Ariel sat on opposite sides of the table, what could a cup of coffee and a cruller hurt?

"And thanks for bringing Ariel back," she said.

He extended his hand to her, and she gave him hers. He held on for just a moment too long. His hand was big, callused, warm, and steady. A careful hand, no doubt. A risk-free hand.

"No problem. I have to get Matt home and get to work, anyway."

"What do you do?" she asked, looking for a bland closer.

He hooked a thumb over his shoulder. "I'm a fireman. Captain at the firehouse around the corner."

CHAPTER 6

Love does not begin and end the way we seem to think it does.
Love is a battle; love is a war; love is a growing up.

James Baldwin

Taylor came into the kitchen where his mom was cooking something that smelled fantastic. College food always had a generic smell, but his mom's cooking was excellent. He bent and hugged her around her waist. She glanced up at him, a surprised but pleased look on her face.

"Thank you. That was unexpected," she said, smiling.

"I was hypnotized by the smell of your cooking," Taylor said.

"I knew there was a reason," she said and laughed. It felt good to make her happy instead of having her scold him or act like he was so dumb he was about to walk in front of a bus all the time.

But she was going to be pretty unhappy in the not-too-distant future.

"Hi, Tay Tay," Ariel called from the living room where, in her gurgly voice, she was singing along with *The Wiggles* on the TV.

"Hey, Squirt," he called back, hoping she didn't invite him in to sit and watch the show with her. He understood how much she loved it, but it turned his brain to mush.

"I'm making your favorite: roast beef with potatoes, carrots, celery, and gravy," his mom said cheerily, but her shoulder blades were like a pair of stiff little chicken wings. Another of her tells.

He put a smile in his voice. "Good, 'cause I'm starving."

"Where've you been off to?" she asked, not in a Gestapo way, but in a friendly-mom way.

"Gym," he said, "They hired me part-time."

"Oh, nothing full-time for the summer?" she asked, disappointed yet again.

She'd been on his case about getting a full-time job, but because he needed time to study for the firefighter exam, he'd asked for part-time and gotten hired. "Nope, but it's okay," he said.

She had her back to him, but he could tell by how fast she was stirring the pot on the stove that she was upset about something. He started inching out of the kitchen when she said, "I was, um, straightening up your room earlier and noticed some—"

He interrupted her. "Mom, it's my room. I'll get around to cleaning it up. Just leave it."

Why did she think he couldn't do little stuff himself? That he needed her nagging him? It was so annoying.

"I noticed that—I saw ..." Why did she sound so weird and shaky? "What, you found a dirty sock?" he asked.

"You have a bag of rock-climbing equipment." She hardly knew the difference between basketball and lacrosse. How did she know what his gear was for?

He didn't want to get into it, so he just said, "Don't go through my stuff, okay?"

"I wasn't," she said. "I just, well, I ..."

He opened the fridge and swilled orange juice from the carton while her back was turned. Everybody—except moms—knew that OJ was always better from the carton. He swallowed a swig of juice, then said, "Dani turned me on to climbing. We climb with some other people from school."

One of the reasons he liked Dani was her free spirit vibe. She was easygoing. And, like him, she loved the outdoors. She also liked pushing the edge, which he didn't like, at least not for himself. She'd encouraged him to go for his dream of being a firefighter, which was another reason he was into her. She made him feel like the things that meant something to him were important and worthwhile.

His mother stirred the gravy like she was a little cement mixer. "Rock climbing isn't safe, you know."

He squeezed the juice carton too hard, and the sides caved slightly. He put the carton back in the fridge. "Mom, don't have a stroke. We're all careful. We wear helmets and stuff. Dani and two of the guys are really experienced. I'm just starting out, and it's lit."

Her voice still shaky, she asked, "What does 'lit' mean?"

"Fun. Great. A blast," he said.

She shuddered. "I'm only telling you because I love you."

She always said that when she didn't want him doing something. It made him feel manipulated, and that angered him. "I'm not cliff-diving or anything."

She spun around, her eyes huge and scared. Her voice was intense. "But you don't know how dangerous it is."

Why was she practically crying? It made him feel guilty, but not enough to give up something he loved. "I'll be fine. Don't sweat it."

"Can't you find something safer, like bowling or golf?" she pleaded, turning back to the stove.

Was she serious? He threw his arms out. "How about swimming in a baby pool? Or mini golf?" he said.

"Okay." She made a loud sniffle and wiped the back of her hand across her face. She really was crying, which made him feel miserable but mad, too.

She pointed over her shoulder at the dining table. "There's two letters"—*sniffle, sniffle*—"on the table. One from the university bursar's office and one from the City of Norwalk."

Shit.

He'd planned to intercept any mail that came for him. He could tell by her voice that she was dying to know what was in the envelopes.

"You can give the one from the school to me. It's probably the bill for next semester," she said.

Or it was confirmation that he'd missed his finals, and that, he couldn't let her see.

His strategy was to soften her up some and slowly work up to telling her that he wasn't going back, then drop the bomb about what he really intended to do. He didn't want to spend the next three months listening to her nagging him to go back to school. Mostly, he didn't want to let her down. It was only May, and he figured he could wait until August before trashing her dreams for him.

"Mooom, it's addressed to me. Don't worry about it." He slipped it into his pocket and turned away, relieved that he'd dodged that bullet for now.

"Why are you getting a letter from the City of Norwalk?" she asked.

Even though she had little raccoon circles around her reddened eyes, she could still get all up in his business. He frowned down at her. He didn't mean to loom, but it was hard not to because she was about the size of a Keebler elf.

"Are you going to be checking on everything I do now that I'm home for the summer?" he snapped. "My mail? Texts? Phone calls? I'm not in high school, for crying out loud."

She looked like he'd slapped her. But there was no way to get her off his back except to push her off.

Her lip twitched the way it did whenever she was nervous. "I just wanted to know what's up. Anything you want to tell me?" she asked.

"Not really. You know, having you check on me and stuff is getting on my nerves." He lifted his baseball hat and reset it on his head. "Kinda weird after I've been at college for a year."

She nodded and turned away. "Sorry, I don't mean to pry."

The university would probably have thrown him out next year if he hadn't already decided to quit. Being a urologist, dermatologist, or gastro dude held no appeal. He simply wasn't meant for school, let alone medical school. A year away from his mom's worries and not having to listen to her push him to be a doctor like his perfect dad and grandpa, Taylor's own ideas for his future had come into focus.

She'd insisted he volunteer as an EMT trainee during high school in case somebody got hurt and needed help, and of course, as a way of getting a leg up on being a doctor. He found that he loved the adrenaline rush of helping people and being useful. Blood and injuries sent most people into zombie mode, but not him. Once, he'd driven by the scene of a fire where the EMTs were guys he'd trained with, so he'd stopped to help. Watching the firemen was amazing. They were all over the place, chopping down doors, spraying water, scaling ladders, running into the burning building, carrying out pets and people. That was when he started thinking that a fireman, not a doctor, was what he wanted to be.

In his bedroom, Taylor tore open the letter and felt a door of possibility swing open. The letter outlined everything he needed to do—volunteering as a first step, registering for the course online, the physical test, applying, and interviewing.

He wished there was a section on how to keep your mother from having a nervous breakdown when you told her you wanted to be a firefighter?

CHAPTER 7

As iron sharpens iron, so a friend sharpens a friend.
King Solomon

Jack opened the door to his condo for Randy Connors, a fellow firefighter, who was Jack's best friend from the station. "Hey, come on in," Jack said.

Randy held up a bottle of Pinot Noir. "I brought some liquid courage."

"Since when do you need courage?" Jack laughed and set the bottle on the kitchen counter.

"Only need it when I come for my cooking lesson," Randy said. "It would be really embarrassing if I burned the house down."

"Hey, where's your designer stubble?" Jack pointed at Randy's smooth-shaven face.

Randy rubbed the back of his hand over his jaw. "This new guy said he kind of likes me without the scruff."

"Looks good on ya'," Jack said.

Randy was the size of a bull moose with the courage and spirit of generosity to match. He could have doubled for one of those models on a fireman's calendar. With his brawny physique, blue eyes, and blond hair, Jack couldn't understand why some guy hadn't already snatched Randy up. If he'd been gay, Jack would have snapped him up.

"Say hi to Randy," Jack said to Matt, who sat on the sofa, eyes glued to the TV set.

"Hi," Matt said.

"Hey, Matt, how are you? What'cha watching?" Randy asked.

"Ninjas. My favorite. Want to see this girl hanging in the air?" Matt pointed to the TV, where a dark-haired woman in a sparkly gymnast's leotard hung upside down from what looked like a ribbon.

Randy peered at the TV and said, "Looks scary! Give me three stories up with fire and your Uncle Jack at my back any day."

Matt pointed at the TV. "Ariel is prettier than this girl."

Randy raised an eyebrow. "Who's Ariel?"

"My new girlfriend," Matt said.

"You got a lady?" Randy asked.

"Yes. She's pretty," Matt said. "Her name is Ariel. She has Down syndrome too. We went on a date to the bakery."

"That's a great," Randy said. He grinned at Jack. "Maybe you can give your Uncle Jack here some dating lessons."

"Yes, I could," Matt said.

Jack motioned Randy over to his cramped, dilapidated kitchen. On the counter, Jack had arranged a cutting board, two knives, bread stuffing, onion, celery, a skillet, and a stick of butter.

Randy rubbed his hands together. "What are we making tonight?"

"Stuffed pork chops, salad, and rice pilaf out of a box," Jack said. "Basically, idiot-proof."

"That's me," Randy said.

On impulse, Randy had invited a guy he'd met online to his place for dinner, but he was a self-proclaimed terrible cook. The idea was that Jack would teach Randy a fairly simple recipe he could recreate at home to impress his date with his domesticity. Jack wasn't hopeful. Randy couldn't make toast.

Jack was the main cook at Station House Number Four and frequently, he gave some of the other guys cooking lessons during slow times. He loved everything about cooking: searching for new recipes, tracking down unusual ingredients, prep work, cooking, tasting, adjusting the seasonings. It relaxed him. There was no life and death pressure with chicken and dumplings.

Randy opened the wine. "Where are your wine glasses?"

Jack pointed to the cabinet where he kept two mismatched wine glasses. He dropped a chunk of butter into the skillet and set the burner on low.

Randy took the glasses down. "This your fancy set?" he asked with a laugh.

"Yeah, it's only me, and I don't care," Jack said.

"If you had a girlfriend, you'd care." Randy poured the wine and handed a glass to Jack. "So, Matt, how'd you meet this young lady?"

"She and her mom bought some of my shirts," Matt said.

Randy looked questioningly at Jack. Jack said, "Ariel is the daughter of the owner of Second Chance Designs over on Wall Street. Best part is, she asked to buy some of Matt's paintings for her store."

"Oh, yeah, I've seen that place," Randy said. "They have gorgeous stuff in the window."

"And the owner, Ariel's mom, is gorgeous," Jack said,

handing the onion, cutting board, and a knife to Andy. "Here, chop this, and don't cut your fingers off if you can help it."

Randy started chopping, but Jack stopped him. "Dude, first you peel the papery stuff off, throw it away, then chop."

"You should have told me." Randy followed Jack's directions and went back to chopping. "Second Chance does decorating, too, don't they?"

"What are you implying?" Jack asked in mock offense.

"Oh, nothing, nothing." Randy wiped away an onion-chopping tear. "You still have your bed on the floor in your bedroom?"

Jack said, "I like it that way. Then I don't fall so far when I roll out of bed."

Jack took the knife back from Randy and showed him how to chop the onion, then handed him back the knife.

Randy said, "Most people use this thing called a bed frame. When you got divorced, and we moved you in here three years ago, you said you'd get one." Randy used his knife to point. "And that brown plaid sofa? It looks like a Goodwill reject."

"What's wrong with brown plaid?" Jack crowed.

"Nothing if you're color blind."

"It hides stains," Jack said, then added, "Most of them, anyway."

"Not really," Randy said. "And what's with the books under the legs?"

"I know the sofa's a little rustic. The leg broke, and I ran out of time to get it fixed," Jack said. He took a celery stalk and a carrot and put them on Randy's cutting board. "Chop these next."

Randy raised his eyebrows and looked at Jack. "Have you unpacked those boxes we humped up here for you?" he asked and started chopping the vegetables.

"Uh, mostly. The other stuff I don't need," Jack said.

Randy paused and gave Jack a skeptical look. "Three years, and you haven't even done that?"

"I'll get around to it," Jack said, knowing that he probably wouldn't.

"The owner of that design shop might have some advice for you. Help you spruce the place up, so you won't be embarrassed to invite a date over."

Jack remembered Olivia's bright eyes like a pair of search lights shining on him. She had been so kind and generous to Matt. Though Jack had been staring at Matt's paintings for a year, she was sharp enough to see the value in it right away. Jack wondered about her nervousness when Ariel and Matt had cuddled up together. But she'd been a parent to a person with Down for much longer than him, so she knew things he didn't.

Randy grinned and shook his head. "You know how much I love you, man, but you could really use a woman's touch around here. That or a good decorator."

"When can I see Ariel at the store again?" Matt asked.

Jack hadn't thought he was listening. "We'll take your paintings over next week. I'll call and make sure Ariel will be there." Without thinking, Jack added, "I wouldn't mind laying eyes on the mom again."

Jack then pointed to the skillet of melted butter on the stove. "Put the onions and celery in here and sauté on medium until they're translucent."

"What's translucent look like?" Randy scraped the vegetables into the skillet. "Is the mom single?"

"Widowed," Jack said and took a swig of wine.

"See, you already know she's widowed, so that shows you're at least interested," Randy said. "You're not dead yet."

"She's way above my pay grade," Jack said, feeling rueful. "She's caviar and I'm hummus."

"You're not asking her to marry you, just to go out for coffee or brunch," Randy said. "Take a test run. See if you remember how to talk to a woman. All this time at the firehouse, you forget what women are like."

When he first saw Olivia, Jack had expected an ice princess —she'd been anything but. Gina, with dark skeptical eyes, a sly laugh, and thick chestnut hair, had been beautiful, too, though.

Randy sautéed the vegetables, their delicious fragrance filling the kitchen. "This woman at the shop, what's her name?"

"Oh-liv-ee-ah," Jack said, stretching her name out, so it sounded like French perfume or fancy wine. "But she would never go out with me."

"Never know until you ask," Randy said with the optimism of someone who had his pick of dates.

Jack hadn't dated since his divorce, and he was in no rush. Olivia was fourteen carat, but Jack wasn't ready to put himself out there. He wasn't even sure he had anything to put out there. He could be happy just seeing her at the shop when he took in Matt's paintings.

Jack unwrapped the pork chops in the sink and threw the wrapper in the trash. He kicked the shitty cabinet door shut harder than necessary, and it banged back open. He kneed it closed. "Someday, I want to replace this kitchen," Jack grumbled.

Not looking at Jack, Randy asked, "You still hung up on why Gina left you?"

"No," Jack said.

Randy made a great show of leaning back and looking at Jack's ass. "Your pants are doin' a three-alarm-fire."

Jack and Randy had ridden together for almost ten years. Randy could read him as well as anyone. Jack trusted Randy with his life and, more than once, that trust had proven well placed. He didn't mean to be touchy, but thinking about Gina sent his self-confidence into a nosedive. Since he'd missed Gina's signals, Jack didn't trust his ability to read any woman's signals.

Toward the end, he'd known Gina was unhappy, but he'd passed it off to growing apart, to having busy careers, to getting older. He'd never guessed there was someone else, let alone another woman.

Jack looked at the sautéed vegetables. "Now add a cup of this bread stuffing and stir some more."

Randy poured the stuffing into the pan and stirred in silence. Eventually, he said, "It's been three years since Gina came out, and you're still living like you're going to move back to your old house. Your stuff is still in boxes, and your furniture is a wreck. Maybe it's time you went out with someone."

Jack sipped the wine, which tasted of blackberries, licorice, and regret. "This wine is great," he said, ignoring Randy's well-considered, kind, and probably correct, advice.

"Buying matching wine glasses might be going too far in the getting-on-with-your-life department, but you could at least invest in a sofa or a bedframe," Randy said.

Jack looked into the skillet. "That's good. Now put that mixture into this mixing bowl and set it aside." Jack pointed to the pork chops on the counter. "Then, in the same skillet, sear these."

"Whatever 'sear' is," Randy muttered. He followed Jack's instructions, handling the skillet with the clumsiness of a man who didn't know it was a pan.

Randy said, "You might want to date before you forget how things work. I mean, look, you're a catch. You're healthy, have insurance, a 401k, a stable job, a condo—which admittedly, needs some TLC—no alcoholism, drugs, or felonies." Randy paused and grinned at Jack. "That I know of."

"Oh, yeah, I'm sure there's some sweet babe out there dying to go out with an old fart like me," Jack said.

"Old fart!" Matt cackled. "Old fart."

"Matt," Jack said, sorry he'd gotten Matt started. To Randy,

Jack said, "Why do I need anyone, anyway? Me and Matt are perfectly happy, aren't we, Matt?"

"I want to go on a date with Ariel," Matt said.

Randy turned the pork chops over. "Matt'll get a girlfriend before you. And you need a woman to keep you from living in squalor. Have you tried a dating website or anything? That's how I met this guy I'm seeing on Saturday."

"And why aren't you permanently attached?" Jack asked with broad sarcasm.

"Because I haven't met Mr. Right yet, but you'll never even meet Ms. Wrong if you don't try." Randy threw Jack a look that said, 'don't try to put one over on me.' "At least I'm putting in some effort."

Jack opened the rice pilaf and dumped it into a pan of boiling water. "Next, we take those chops out of the pan and let them cool a bit. Then we slice a little pocket in them and put the stuffing in."

Randy forked a chop out and promptly dropped it on the floor. He stabbed it and threw it on the cutting board. "Three-second rule."

Jack rolled his eyes and waved the pork chop away. "Okay, okay. So, let's say I did register on a dating site and did ask someone out. Once a woman got a load of this place, she'd never speak to me again."

Randy moved the chops around in the skillet. "That's why you need to ask the woman from the store for a decorating consultation. She could give you some pointers about how you could spruce up your crib."

One way to make sure Olivia didn't ever go out with him was to have her consult on his apartment. She'd think he was a total Neanderthal for owning a plastic folding table and four folding chairs for a dining room set.

"She'll just tell me to buy new stuff." Jack emptied his wineglass. "I haven't bought a new sofa because then I'd have to buy new carpet, then I'd have to redo this kitchen because it looks like crap. Then I'd want that cloudy sliding door on the balcony replaced so I could see out to the water. Then I'd want new paint and furniture and I don't know anything about that stuff and," Jack threw his arms out. "You see where I'm going with this, right?"

"That's total bullshit, and you know it." Randy poured Jack more wine. "It's time for you to move on from Gina. I mean, if you get upset just thinking about her, it's clear you're stuck. You're wasting your life pining for a woman who can't love you anymore."

When Gina told him she had fallen in love with her dental hygienist, a woman, Jack couldn't have been more shocked. He knew people came out later, but Gina had never given him so much as a hint that she was looking over the fence.

"I'm not pining. Do I look like I'm pining? No pining here. I haven't pined for years. It's just that I don't feel like having my balls run through a chainsaw again." Jack set the glass on the counter hard enough to break it.

"You can't play it safe forever, Jack, or you'll end up like Miss Havisham," Randy said.

"Who's Miss Havisham?" Jack asked.

"Never mind. Just ask the woman for a date," Randy said.

"I'm going to tell you to sauté the chops in varnish and turpentine if you don't cut it out."

Randy grinned. "I'm buying you a decorating consultation from Second Chance as a gift for teaching me how to cook this."

"Don't you dare," Jack said, stabbing an accusing finger at Randy.

But Jack hoped Randy would dare.

CHAPTER 8

Some people go to priests; others to poetry; I to my friends.
Virginia Woolf

The Marriage Survivors Club, which included Flicka, Bianca, Carolina, Frankie, and Olivia, already were on their third bottle of Rioja. They were still waiting for the perpetually late member, Hélène 'Frenchie'. As they did every other week, they were gathered for their regular Thursday evening dinner. They always met at Paella on Main Street in Norwalk because the owner, Jaime Lopez, didn't mind how rowdy they got. The table was spread with tapas, Spanish cheeses, and a basket of crusty, warm rolls.

Olivia noticed how her friend, Frankie Carter, was positively glowing. Frankie owned a successful contracting business called 'Women's Work' and she and Olivia frequently collaborated on renovation and decorating jobs.

She had fallen madly in love with Cam Simpson when

they'd met in a tussle over the property for the LGBTQ youth shelter. Now, they were tussling in bed.

Frankie's hundreds of tiny braids were twisted into a knot on her head and she wore maroon lipstick that accented her light brown skin. Tonight, she'd traded her usual work outfit of red work boots and jeans for brightly patterned leggings, a wine-colored shirt, and high heels. Frankie was happier and more relaxed than Olivia had ever seen her. Being in love certainly agreed with her.

Olivia said, "Frankie, I don't know if we can still let you come to the Marriage Survivors Club now that you and Cam have a hot romance going."

"Yeah, but they're not married. They prefer living in sin," Bianca said, as she straightened her Red Sox jersey.

Bianca Treviso was a divorce attorney and omni-sports fanatic. She carried a baseball bat in the back of her car, not for playing, but for self-defense. Known as a divorce shark, she'd faced down several enraged husbands. Bianca was who you wanted at your back if you got into a bar fight.

"And let me tell you, after all these years of being single, I like sinning as often as possible, and Cam is happy to oblige." Frankie waggled her eyebrows and laughed.

Olivia remembered how much she and Derek used to want one another, how woozy his kiss made her feel. How he could always lift her out of a funk with one of his lousy jokes. She missed their spirited discussions about art, politics, and healthcare.

Lying in bed at night, sharing the mundane details of her day, Derek listened raptly. It was as if he hadn't spent the day in the ER watching people die from gunshot wounds, patching up car accident victims, and telling people their loved ones didn't make it. She missed being the person someone wanted to get home to.

Olivia laughed. "You're making up for lost time."

"I know!" Frankie said, gleeful. "In the backseat of the car, in the office, on the kitchen counter—"

Bianca stuck her fingers in her ears and sang, "La, la, la, la, la!"

"All this talk about how much sex Frankie's getting is making me envious," Flicka said. "Let's talk about something more realistic for women our age, like hot flashes and sagging asses."

Frederica 'Flicka' Cole Williamson Strada Kolinsky Whitehall had a pouf of perfectly coiffed, flaming red hair. Her high cheekbones, surgically enhanced chest, designer clothes, and flashing green eyes projected the high-society persona of her former life.

Then she laughed like a truck driver and that persona evaporated.

The front door of the restaurant opened, and Hélène blew in. With her enormous eyes, black and white hair—a result of Mallen streaks—and her twig-thin figure, Hélène always looked like she'd stepped off a Paris runway. She taught piano to kids and a few college courses.

"Hello, everyone," Hélène said with her musical French-accent. She took the empty chair beside Carolina and peeled off her dark pink sweater. "Catch me up. What are we talking about?"

"Sex. What else?" Carolina poured Hélène a glass of Rioja. "Lack thereof, and in Frankie's case, the abundance." Carolina raised her glass. "The Lord maketh her cup runneth over."

They all laughed, which they did a great deal of when they were together.

Carolina Singh had married Flicka's third husband after she divorced him and then Carolina had had her marriage annulled. A bit shy, she was the most reserved of the Marriage Survivors Club, and with the faith of a saint, she was the spiritual center of the group. She never had a bad word to say about anyone. With almost black eyes and a hue of skin that spoke to her mixed Guyanese heritage, her features were mildly exotic. She wore her mahogany hair cut simply and her wardrobe tended toward conservative. Olivia suspected that Carolina's quiet demeanor disguised a brain like a vast library of information.

"Okay, enough about Frankie's love life," Flicka said, with the eagerness of someone about to share a juicy bit of gossip. "Let me tell you about the devastatingly handsome *gay* fireman named Randy Connors, who came into the store and bought a gift certificate."

Since Flicka's four large divorce settlements made it unnecessary for her to hold one of those depressing things known as a *job*, she frequently watched the shop for Olivia. Sometimes Flicka's 'help' worked out better than others.

Flicka leaned into the table and looked up and down with a conspiratorial grin. "I sold him a ticket to the barbecue. I'm going to introduce him to Father Gabriel."

With a hint of amused exasperation, Carolina asked Flicka, "Are you at it again?"

"Father Gabriel needs someone. I just know it," Flicka said.

"You've had *four* someones," Bianca said. "How does that make you an expert in finding someone special for others?"

So she could keep up the fiction that she never ate bread Flicka stole a pinch of Bianca's roll. "I'm telling you—Father Gabriel's sermons will get even better if he gets laid regularly."

"So that was a gift certificate you sold?" Olivia asked.

Flicka nodded. "I wrote it down in the book and in the schedule."

"I saw something," Olivia said, but trying to decipher your handwriting is like trying to read hieroglyphics."

"It's for another fireman. Some friend of his who's divorced.

Firefighter Randy said the guy's place needs major work," Flicka said.

"Did you happen to get a name of the person who the consult is for?" Olivia asked, because Flicka was as fast and loose with her record keeping as she was with her choice of bed partners.

Flicka squinted and stared into the distance. "Uh ... Jack something Irish."

Olivia's internal alarm made a stir. "Can you do a little better than that?" She lifted her wine glass to her lips.

Flicka snapped her fingers. "O'Grady. And if he's as hot as Randy, he'll be great eye-candy."

Olivia nearly choked on her Rioja. Bianca slapped her on the back, which nearly unseated Olivia.

Olivia set her glass down. "Are you certain?"

"Yup," Flicka said.

"You know this guy already, Liv?" Bianca asked.

"He came into the store with his nephew, Matt, who also has Down, to sell some shirts. He and Ariel were quite smitten with one another." Olivia topped off her wine glass, emptying the bottle. "It was all very... unsettling."

"Ooooh, Olivia's blushing!" Frankie chimed.

"I am not!" Olivia lifted a hand to her burning cheek.

"This Jack guy made you nervous?" Bianca said, smiling into her wineglass. "Like, afraid?"

"Not that I'm admitting," Olivia said.

"We'll take that as a yes," Frankie an arched eyebrow. "You're afraid of everything. Even kittens," Frankie said, repeating a phrase they all teased Olivia with.

"Well, you have a two-hour meeting with him next week, so prepare your delicate nerves," Flicka said. "And I wrote, 'no kittens allowed.'"

Everyone laughed again, but Olivia had to force herself to

join in.

Jack O'Grady did have a nice butt, but as a firefighter, so he was totally off-limits. Maybe she could distract Jack with the beautiful, ever-horny Flicka.

Olivia said, "You've got to go along with me on this consult, Flicka. You might like him."

"Is he hot?" Flicka asked.

Olivia tried to push the image of Jack O'Grady's butt out of her mind, but it had become stuck there like a bad dream. Or a good dream, depending.

"Did he ask you out?" Frankie asked, with the certainty that came along with being besties.

"Mm, sort of," Olivia admitted.

Bianca said, "You said yes, didn't you?" With her palm, she gave the table a smack, and the flatware rattled. "As your lawyer, I insist you agree."

Olivia flapped her napkin back in her lap and said, "I agreed to go for coffee, but that was before I knew he was a firefighter."

"I'll bet he could put out your fire," Flicka said in her most lewd tone.

They all laughed.

Olivia felt a flicker of heat in her lower belly. "I have no interest in even the hottest fireman. Too dangerous."

"Too dangerous for what?" Carolina said with a tilt of her head. "To give a decorating consult or go out on a date with?"

Bianca drew back in mock horror. "One might lead to the other."

"But the most dangerous thing would be falling in love," Carolina said quietly.

Who'd said anything about love?

Bianca pressed forward and, with a single brow lifted eyed each of them. She growled in her spooky voice, "Or he might have kittens."

CHAPTER 9

Adults are obsolete children.
Dr. Seuss

Taylor closed one eye, sighted to the hole on the third green, drew back his putter, and took his best shot. His ball skirted the windmill, bounced off the brick curb, and rolled into the hole.

"Yeah!" Ariel cried. "Got one hole."

"Yup, hole in one." Taylor grinned.

Hole in one wasn't tough to do on the mini golf course at Calf's Pasture Beach. They'd been playing since he could remember. Ariel used to get impatient and want to go home after the fourth hole, but now she made it through nine. Today, Taylor wanted to coax her to the eighteenth if he could.

His mom, who was exactly the right size for mini golf, set her ball on the linoleum tee. She whacked her ball, and it bounced off the windmill and flew into the rocks. She threw her head back, laughing that big laugh she had.

He wished she'd laugh like that more often. It was nice to do this with her. No pressure, no warnings, just fun. The way he felt when he climbed with Dani and his friends.

Ariel stepped carefully around the rocks to the fourth hole with the fake sand traps.

He went to her, picked up the tee, and moved it much closer to the hole. "This will give you a good chance."

Ariel tapped her ball so that it hardly moved.

Taylor helped her tap it again, and this time, it ended up six inches from the hole. With her putter, she pushed the ball in.

"Yeah!" he hollered, pumping his putter overhead. Ariel grinned and hugged him around his waist, and he hugged her back.

Their mom was smiling, her face soft and mushy, her eyes wet with tears. At least he knew how to do one thing right.

He made another hole-in-one when his mom sidled up to him. "When do you think your grades will come?" she asked.

Rocks sloshed in his gut. "I don't know. Soon, I guess."

She putted her ball up the green, and it stopped next to the hazard of a garden gnome. "Can you look online?" she asked. "I'm really interested to see how well you did."

I can tell you that already, like shit. "I could, I guess," he said.

"Do you think they might be better than last semester's grades?" she asked.

"I tried my best," he said, rattled that she was still harping about his grades.

Ariel picked her ball up and dropped it in the hole. "Yeah! One hole!" she crowed, raising her fists in the air.

He wished his mom was that easy to please. At the next hole, he drew his putter back a couple of times and tapped the ball, but this time it skipped into the rocks.

"That's okay," Ariel said. She bent, picked up his ball, brought it back, and set it on the tee again. "Go more, Tay Tay."

"Thanks, Squirt." He tapped it again, and his ball landed

behind the pot of fake flowers. His mom was totally throwing off his game.

Ariel hit her ball into the grass.

His mom said, "When I got your report card for the first semester, I wondered what exactly you were doing."

Even without taking his finals, he'd managed to make a shit-show of the last quarter. He went to classes, turned in his papers, went to the library, and studied, but the concepts didn't stick in his brain. He would have sworn that they leaked out when he went to sleep. The classes weren't just boring—they were like inhaling chloroform. He supposed lacrosse practice and the keggers at the frat houses hadn't helped either.

"I went to my classes, did all the assignments, went to the TAs, and asked for help." He squinted into the sun, which was lowering into the water. The air had begun to turn cold. "College is way harder than I thought it was going to be."

"Freshman year can be really hard. We can get you a tutor if you want," she said. Her eyes turned a smoky dark blue. "Did your new girlfriend have anything to do with your grades falling?" she asked.

Not that he was going to admit.

This game had started out fun, but now it was turning into the Spanish Inquisition.

"What are you talking about?" he asked.

"Huwee, huwee." Ariel motioned them on, and they joined her at the next hole.

"It can be hard—juggling school, a new girlfriend, the demands of a pre-med program—that's all," his mom said.

Ariel tapped her ball six times. "I got one!" she crowed.

"Hole in one," Taylor called out.

"Your dad cruised through his undergrad. It was medical school that really challenged him," his mom said. "But he ended up doing great."

Of course he did, because he was Superman, Batman, and Aqua-man, all rolled into one.

Taylor's next ball bounced into the trap for the hole.

How could he tell her to stop trying to turn *him* into his dad? Who could measure up to the late great Dr. Derek Maxwell, who deserved the Nobel Prize?

It was hard to say which was worse, her constant warnings about danger or having his dead dad held up as an example of who Taylor was supposed to be.

"When you weren't studying, how did you spend your time?" She nudged her ball. "I know kids like to party and stuff when they first go away."

He could tell that her mother's intuition—or whatever it was that moms had—was on high alert to sniff out something. That made his deflection shields go up.

He said, "I had a ton of lacrosse practices, and I only went to, maybe, three parties all year."

More like ten, but who's counting?

Time to drop some hints. "I think, you know, maybe I'm not cut out for college." Her face looked like he'd just stabbed a fork in her head.

"What are you talking about?" she said in her outraged voice, which for someone so small, was still like getting walloped upside the head. "Of course, you're cut out for college. We've always planned on you being a doctor. It takes a while to get your feet under you." She patted him on the back, which made him feel like a little kid instead of the man he was. "I'm sure next year will be great. You'll probably have to drop lacrosse to keep your grades up. You can take some online summer classes to prepare for the fall. Did you think of that? There might still be time to sign up for some required classes and get them out of the way."

His throat felt like it was caught in an animal trap, and he couldn't pry the words loose. "I was thinking of staying home next semester and taking a few courses at NCC."

She froze, and the soft evening air went cold as ice. "Why would you want to do that?"

Misery, like a wall of bricks, fell on him as though he'd been holding it up with all his strength, and he just couldn't do it anymore. "I don't know if I'm cut out to be a doctor, Mom. All the years of studying, the expense of medical school, all the debt I'll have." Her eyes were like ice bullets. Maybe I should do something simpler. I want to help people and everything, but there are other ways to that besides being a doctor."

Do it! Do it! Say it!

"But you loved being an EMT. Think of when you can help people get better, deliver babies, or transplant hearts." Her voice rose with enthusiasm. "When you were born, your father was so excited. Your grandfather was a doctor, your dad was, and he knew you'd want to be a doctor too. It's what we planned for you."

He hadn't planned on it. *They* had planned on it, and then just she had.

Ariel got in on the act. "Tay Tay be doctor?" she said, and he narrowed his eyes at her.

His mom smiled. "I picture him doing just that."

Ariel dropped her pink ball and putter on the grass. She was tired and out of patience. He should have paid more attention to her, but he was occupied with fending off his mom.

Ariel said, "Go home."

"I think that's a good idea. I have something I want to give Taylor," his mom said.

Driving home, dread boiled up inside Taylor. His mom wasn't taking the hint. Aside from just crushing her dream, he didn't know how to get her to hear what he was saying.

At home in the kitchen, he poured glasses of cold water for

all of them. He leaned against the counter and avoided looking into her eyes.

His mom pulled out a kitchen chair, patted the back and said, "Have a seat. I wasn't going to give you this until you graduated, but maybe it will give you some inspiration."

All excited, she left the kitchen, went upstairs, and came back with something behind her back. She had a giant smile on her face. "Hold out your hands and close your eyes."

"What am I, three?" he asked.

This was going to be some sentimental mom thing—he could just tell. Honestly, it was one of the things he loved about her. Other things he loved about her were that she was way more intelligent than he was. She was great at business and with design and decorating. Even though she went overboard, she did everything possible to protect him and Ariel. She worked hard to provide for them and be their mom and their dad. If she'd only stop treating him like he was a little kid.

Ariel cupped her sweet, pudgy, pink hands and closed her eyes. "Hold hands like communion."

He couldn't resist Ariel. She was pure love. "Okay, Squirt." He closed his eyes and held out his hands, and something metal and rubbery dropped into his hands. He opened his eyes and nearly fell off his chair. The back of his throat went thick.

His mom pressed her palms together and held them to her lips. "It was your dad's stethoscope." She pressed her hands over her heart. "He'd be so proud for you to have it."

Taylor stared down at the stethoscope, and all his hopes and courage bled away. He looked up at her. "Thanks, Mom," was all he could manage to say.

CHAPTER 10

Life is either a daring adventure, or nothing.
Helen Keller

With a glower of warning, Olivia turned to Flicka as they rode up in Jack O'Grady's condo elevator. "Look, your job now is to discourage him from hiring me."

"Why?" Flicka asked, all innocence.

Olivia knew her glower was basically ineffective against Flicka, but she had to try. "I told you guys the other night how nervous having his nephew around Ariel makes me."

Flicka gave Olivia a sideways glance. "You said it made you nervous to be around Jack, too."

She hadn't said that. They'd figured it out on their own.

Olivia said, "I want to keep this to the two hours on his gift certificate. I can probably get away with suggesting some paint colors, moving furniture around, and adding throw pillows."

"It's been a while since you've been in a single man's apartment, hasn't it?" Flicka said and laughed.

Olivia remembered the way Jack had looked at her and how it made her skin feel too small. She hoped he'd wear some nice jeans again. He really did have an excellent butt.

Olivia yanked her thoughts in line. "He's a very nice man, but like I said the other night, he's a firefighter, okay? Totally not datable."

"I'll bet he's hot and sexy." Flicka rolled her eyes up in her head, made puppy paws with her hands, and panted like a dog.

"Oh, be quiet," Olivia said, and she couldn't help laughing.

"You don't have to marry the guy," Flicka said, "you could"— she lifted one shoulder—"You know, have some fun."

Olivia stared at Flicka with horror. "He's a *fireman*. You can't have fun with a fireman."

"Have you seen the front of those firefighter calendars?" Flicka said and tugged at her skirt. "I could have fun with any one of them."

Flicka slipped her Louis Vuitton bag to the other arm. She wore her black Louboutins and a timeless two-piece suit. As always, her flaming red hair and her makeup were perfect.

"You're a little over-dressed, don't you think?" Olivia asked.

Olivia wore her usual dark slacks, a white blouse, and low heels. Easier to run if someone tried to mug her. Pepper spray nestled next to the notebook in her purse.

Flicka lifted her chin. "Every man appreciates a good suit on a woman." Breezily, she added, "Or off a woman. I even wore my thong underwear."

"You wear butt floss at your age?" Olivia asked, shocked but curious.

"Keeps me from remembering how old I really am," Flicka said.

They stepped off the elevator. Down the hall, Jack was waiting for them with the door open.

"Hi, Olivia. Thanks for coming." He stuck his hand out,

exposing the scar on his arm. This time, Olivia didn't shudder. She shook hands with him, and a *twang* went off inside of her.

Visible beneath his button-down shirt was his soft, small spare tire. He wasn't a romance hero of incomparable muscularity, but he was delicious just the same. He smiled and looked at her with that direct gaze, and her belly went wiggly-wobbly.

Fireman! Fireman! Fireman! No, no, no, absolutely not!

His 'I want to eat you up' smile startled Olivia. She fiddled nervously with her earring. "I'm here for your decorating consult." She laughed shakily. "Well, of course, I am. Why else would I be here?"

Behind her, Flicka made a sound somewhere between a cough and a giggle.

He held his hand out to Flicka. "Jack O'Grady."

Flicka stuck her hand out artlessly, not in the usual sinuous manner she used. Her voice was flat and dry. "Flicka Whitehall, sidekick, at your service."

He said, "Come in, if you dare." He stepped back, held the door open, waving them in.

Olivia felt the heat of his eyes on the back of her neck as she stepped into the room. Prepared for the worst, she schooled her face into a mask of non-judgment.

The living-dining room was a bachelor cliché. Empty beer cans on a scratched and stained coffee table, a pair of dirty socks on the floor, a basket of clothes waiting to be folded, a roll of paper towels unfurling across the floor, an empty pizza box on the sofa.

Thank God this is only a two-hour consult.

Flicka's eyebrows shot sky high. "Randy didn't say we needed hazmat suits. You definitely need Olivia's services."

"That bad?" Jack laughed.

Olivia could have kicked her. Fighting to keep her expression neutral, she said, "Ignore her. She has no taste whatsoever."

"Clearly, neither does he," Flicka said.

Jack laughed but looked at Olivia when he did so.

Olivia's plan of using Flicka as a decoy had not been well-thought out.

A brown and yellow plaid, legless sofa, with books for legs and sagging cushions, looked like he slept on it. Four folding metal chairs of various ages and a card table served as a dining set. The gold carpet was from the last century. The deck slider had an excellent view of the Long Island Sound, but the seal had failed, rendering the glass opaque.

Strangely, the place smelled like the inside of a fancy restaurant, redolent of garlic, tomato sauce, rosemary, roasted meat, and fresh bread.

"It's a nuclear waste dump," Flicka said with clinical detachment. "But Olivia can fix you up." Olivia tried to elbow Flicka, but she pivoted out of reach.

He laughed again, the low sound tickling the base of Olivia's throat. She said, "Flicka doesn't work with me. I only bring her along to provide the comic relief."

"I know it's a disaster," he said with a chagrined tone. "I meant to straighten up."

"It wouldn't have made any difference," Flicka said.

He threw his head back as he laughed again. He had a wonderful sense of humor, but Olivia still wanted to throw Flicka over the balcony.

Being near him was facing temptation up close and personal. Olivia fought her desire to bask in the warm glow of his smile and drown in his sable eyes. He wasn't possible. She had to protect Ariel from Matt and herself from Jack. That way lay certain disaster. Olivia pivoted away and swallowed hard.

Jack pointed out four of Matt's paintings on the wall. "I'd like to riff off those paintings."

Olivia hadn't noticed the paintings because of the mess, but she nodded authoritatively. Like Matt's paintings on the shirts, these were lively and electrifying, with abstract whorls of color and shapes. "We can do that," Olivia said.

"I can see why," Flicka said, the first intelligent thing she'd uttered since they'd arrived. "They're beautiful."

"What do you think? Is the place salvageable?" he asked.

"Exactly how much money do you have?" Flicka deadpanned.

He laughed again. Because the sound was infectious, Olivia laughed, too, before she caught herself.

He said, "I have a pretty good amount. I haven't spent anything since I was divorced."

"That's good, or you would have to rob a bank," Flicka said, arching a brow.

"I want to get new furniture in here, but the main thing is to redo the kitchen. I've wanted to do it for a long time, but never had the time." Jack's eyes met Olivia's, and his gaze hooked into her. She couldn't not look back.

He said, "Or a reason."

"Well, now's the time!" Flicka sounded like a used car salesman pitching a clunker.

This time Olivia's elbow connected with Flicka's rib and elicited an "Oof!"

Olivia crossed her arms in front of her as if that would protect her from the masculinity Jack exuded.

"Right this way." He held out his hands out like a maître d' at a fancy restaurant, ushering them to their seats.

Olivia stepped behind the counter into a small kitchen. It looked like he cleaned it with a toothbrush, but otherwise, it contained the original contractor-grade cabinets and counter-top. The cabinet doors sagged, and the drawers closed crookedly. She noticed some cookbooks tucked away in a corner. "Do you like to cook?"

His hands became animated and moved through the space. The scar on his arm rippled over the muscles of his forearm. "Anything," he said. "It relaxes me. Chopping, stirring, sautéing, boiling, broiling. I love to feed people. I do most of the cooking at the firehouse."

Flicka said, "Olivia loves to eat."

With her back to Jack, Flicka batted her fake lashes at Olivia. She wanted to reach over and rip those things right off Flicka's lids.

"I'd love to cook for you sometime," Jack said, looking down at Olivia like he wanted to have her for dessert.

He was so much taller than she remembered. Hunger plopped into her center, but it wasn't food she was craving. She tore her gaze away from him and looked out the kitchen window at the sun-glittered water of the Norwalk Harbor. "There's a nice view here. You might want to install a better window so you can see better."

"Great idea," Jack said. "Do you think the kitchen layout seems okay?"

Olivia said, "Oh, yes, it's a good workspace."

"No tearing out walls. You just have to replace everything," Flicka said. "That takes time, you know."

"How long?" He sounded more hopeful than discouraged.

He was playing along with Flicka, who was throwing Olivia under the bus.

Or into his bed.

"Oh, months at least," Flicka said. "Takes a lot of going back and forth, you know, lots of meetings over martini lunches, making decisions, consulting, looking at paint colors, new furniture for the living room, carpeting. Stuff like that. Olivia's really good at this."

Olivia felt her feet sinking into quicksand. This was supposed to be nothing more than paint and throw pillows. She couldn't be in the heat of this man's attention without turning into a puddle.

You don't do high-risk men anymore! You can't take losing someone you love again.

Losing Derek had knocked Olivia down in a way she hadn't known was possible. For a couple of years, she'd muddled around in a daze, wondering how she would get through the next day, much less care for and raise two children on her own. The Marriage Survivors Club and the parishioners of St. Paul's had pulled her through the muck of her grief until she could stand on her own two feet. She could not lose anyone else she loved, and, unlike Flicka, Olivia wasn't the type to have a fling. She had to find a way to extricate herself from this situation.

Olivia said, "Remodeling the kitchen, painting, new carpet, and furniture." She turned in a circle to take in the condo. "It wouldn't be a cheap undertaking."

"When she's done, you'll love it," Flicka countered.

She should have sold vitamin supplements on late-night TV.

"Let's sit down in my 'dining room' and talk ballpark costs," Jack said.

They sat at the card table, and Olivia took a notepad and pen from her handbag. "The kitchen could be redone with stock cabinets and tile flooring. The granite countertop will be the most expensive thing, but since you cook, that's an investment you should make."

"See! I told you she was good at this stuff," Flicka crowed.

"How much are we talking?" Jack asked.

Pretending to calculate costs compared with the risk of being in the heat of his hungry eyes, Olivia scribbled on her notepad. She tapped her pen. She needed the money for Taylor's tuition next fall. If she and Frankie took the job, it was inevitable that other people in the condo would hire them. But he really was a dangerous man, in more than one way.

She said, "The kitchen's a gut, plus appliances, paint, the living room with window treatments, carpet, and furniture." A thought came to her that she was sure would scare him. "Can you get a second mortgage?"

He paled.

Olivia was just thinking that she might have saved herself when Flicka's heel spiked the top of Olivia's foot. Olivia jumped and glared at her, but Flicka was studying her flawless manicure.

Flicka said, "Of course, you don't have to do everything at once."

Olivia stared at the notebook. "Well, you could save some money if you demo the kitchen yourself."

"No problem," he said in his smooth, confident fireman's voice. A voice that shook Olivia's insides. "Me and the guys could take it out in a day."

That wasn't what she wanted to hear. She wanted him to say it was too much trouble, too much money, that he'd changed his mind.

"You'll pick everything out?" Then he added quickly, "For your regular fee, of course."

"Of course she will. That's what a decorator does," Flicka said. "Don't forget the meetings. Takes lots of meetings."

Despite being irritated with Flicka, Olivia laughed. She was laughing more at this consult than she had in the last entire month. To Jack, she said, "Is she offending you because I can send her back to the car?"

He gave Olivia his heart-melting smile. "I think she's a good salesperson."

Flicka bobbed a nod. "Why, thank you."

Except what Flicka was selling was Olivia, not her services.

"So how much?" he asked.

Olivia totaled her fee, time, and a rough estimate of materials and gave him the number. His eyes flared, his Adam's apple bobbed.

"Give or take," Olivia added. She'd shave five percent just to look at his butt in his tight jeans.

"Of course, she'll find ways to save you money," Flicka said. "She always does."

Olivia stood, gathered her notebook and handbag. "Take as long as you want to think about it. Let me know if you decide to move ahead with some or all of it. We're talking about a lot of money, so I'll understand if you decide to shelve the project."

Flicka stood too. "But you know, her time fills up pretty fast, so don't wait too long."

Olivia planned to shove Flicka down the elevator shaft.

Jack crossed to the kitchen, yanked open a drawer and returned with a checkbook. He scribbled a check and handed it to Olivia. "Here's a deposit on your work. I look forward to working with you. How soon can we sit down and discuss everything?"

She took the check, and it felt like it might spontaneously combust in her fingers. This man was willing to renovate his condo just to spend time with her. It was like being trapped in a burning room and putting your hands toward the fire to warm them.

But despite everything, she heard herself saying, "Thank you. I look forward to working together."

CHAPTER 11

There are only two lasting bequests we can hope to give our children. One of these is roots, the other, wings.

Johann Wolfgang von Goethe

Taylor steeled himself as he and Ariel stepped in the front door. True to form, their mom met them at the door, all nerved up.

"Where were you guys? I was worried," she said, wiping her hands on a dishtowel.

"I sent you a text. Didn't you read it?" He brushed past and headed for the kitchen for a pre-workout snack.

She twisted the dishtowel. "You said you were going out, but not where."

"Tay Tay me job," Ariel said, so excited she couldn't get her words out. "I like–I work can ... I...I will go. I like."

"What?" his mom asked. Her face went whiter than usual.

Taylor said, "I took her to apply for a job at the grocery store, and they hired her as a bagger."

His mom stared, her mouth hanging open. She didn't say anything, which was a miracle.

"Mom?" Ariel said. "I can?"

"Hey, Squirt, get your clothes changed so we can go to the gym," Taylor said. "Huwee, huwee."

It was a silly word they'd used since they were kids because his big sister couldn't pronounce the word *hurry*. He wanted Ariel to hurry up, but he also wanted to beat it out of the house before his mom started a weepy meltdown. He opened the fridge, took out the gallon of milk, and poured himself a glass.

"I huwee, huwee," Ariel said as she labored up the stairs.

He could practically feel the frost of his mom's breath on the back of his neck. "What are you doing, Taylor?" she said in her pleading voice.

He leaned against the kitchen counter, drank slowly, and made her wait. "Drinking milk. Then I'm taking her to the gym. Ariel needs to get more exercise, or she'll turn into a pet turtle."

"That's ... that's great you're taking her to the gym," his mom stammered, "but I can't help feeling like you're using Ariel against me for some reason." Her blue eyes had turned the color of steel, a sign that she was preparing to deliver one of her tired monologues about the dangers of the entire world.

But after a year in college, he was prepared, ready to come out swinging. He shrugged and stuck his balled-up hands in the pouch of his hoodie. "I'm not using her against you. I just took her to apply for a job, just like she said."

His mom rested her hand on the counter, but he saw it was shaking. "But why did you do it without asking me? You know I need her to help me at the shop."

She sounded desperate, so he dialed it down. "Mom, Ariel needs to have a life."

Unexpectedly, she was cracking now, her lip twitching. "She has a life with me," she said.

He said, "You know that Down people live longer, healthier lives if they're more out in the community. More active. That's why I'm taking her to the gym." Taylor pointed at her. "Which you should have been doing."

She smoothed her ponytail. She had worn her hair that way for as long as he could remember. When he was a kid, he liked to lean into her shoulder to smell the fruity, flowery smell of her shampoo. When he was little, he liked feeling safe and knowing she was watching out for him.

At school, with his own thoughts, and without her warning him of this and that danger, Taylor realized he was way less afraid. He had started rock climbing with Dani and some of the guys and found it was a blast. He felt more powerful to push for what he wanted, what he thought was right, and that included what was right for Ariel.

"Ariel has a community," his mom continued. "She goes to Bitsy's house, to church, to socials at the Y, to the shop. She doesn't need a job, and now you've gone and gotten her hopes up. Don't you realize how much you're putting her at risk, trying to get her a job where someone might—" She choked out, "Why are you doing this, anyway?"

He was not going to give an inch. "Look, Mom, I know you think you're doing the right thing, but Ariel deserves a chance at a bigger life. You've kept her safe, and I get that you're worried about her because she is who she is. But when she's older, Ariel will never adjust to being without you if she doesn't learn some independence."

"She's perfectly happy at the store with me. She goes to Muro's bakery. She... she ...." Her eyes darted around the kitchen like she was looking for answers behind the coffee machine.

"See? You can't even say what she does," he said. "She might be chillin' at the store, but you won't be around forever. I won't be able to watch her every minute when that happens. There's a chance that neither of us will be around, and she has to be prepared for that."

His mom's face was red, and she clenched her little-kid fists. "You might not be here because you are doing stupid, risky things like rock climbing," she ground out. "Ariel is not your child. She's mine, just like you are. I know what's best for her."

"Leave my rock climbing out of it. That has nothing to do with Ariel," he snapped.

"You, you ...," she spluttered, "you don't know how dangerous the world is for her! For everyone. We have to be careful!"

He waited while she sobbed into the dishtowel. He felt bad for making her cry, but he pushed ahead. "You know I'm doing this because I love her too," he said quietly. "Mom, you have to get over the fact that I'm not a kid anymore. Neither of us are."

That shut her up for a second.

He took a deep breath. "Now that I'm home this summer, I can help drive her places, to her job, to the gym." He paused so she could collect herself before he dropped the bomb that would send her over the edge. "And I can take her out on dates with this Matt guy."

He didn't say, *"When the summer's over, I'll still be home."*

She lifted her tear-stained face out of the kitchen towel, and she had a fierce look in her eye. "There will be no dates with this Matt guy or any other guys."

She was like a badger. Once she got an idea in her teeth, she just could not let go.

He threw his arm out, disgusted. "God, why don't you just lock Ariel in her room? If I take her and go along on their dates, she'll be fine. Ariel won't ever live alone, but is freakin' happy when she talks about Matt. Maybe she won't ever be like you and me, but she is capable of love. I want her to have that," his voice rose until he was almost shouting, "and if you'd quit being so terrified of your entire life, you'd realize it too."

"Don't do this," his mom pleaded in a whisper.

Ariel came into the kitchen. With her eyes round behind her pop-bottle glasses, all hopeful, she looked at their mother. "I work grocery?"

Taylor glared at his mom. "I want Mom to say it's okay."

His mom clamped her arms to her sides like a tiny toy soldier. It would have been hilarious if she weren't such a hard ass. "I do *not* say it's okay," she said.

Ariel burst into tears, threw her arms around Taylor's waist, and buried her face in his chest. He wrapped his arms around her, and she soaked the front of his hoodie with her tears and snot.

His mom said, "It was completely irresponsible of you to build up her expectations. I'm only trying to keep her safe."

"It's a *grocery store*, not a strip club, Mom. She'll be okay." He patted Ariel's back and decided right then that he was going to ignore his mom. He said, "Never mind, Squirt. I'll take you. You can work at the grocery."

If Ariel working at a grocery store made their mom crazed, she would go off the rails when he told her his plans.

Olivia was shaking, so after Taylor and Ariel left for the gym, she made herself a cup of chamomile tea. She sat at the kitchen table and imagined every danger that could befall Ariel while working. Terrorists could storm the store and take hostages. She could fall. Get hurt on the job. Someone could assault her. She might get sick. Confused. A tornado could hit. Or a hurricane. Or fire. Someone might call her the R-word—retarded—and hurt her feelings. Olivia wouldn't be there to explain to Ariel, yet again, that some people were not nice, and it was not a reflection on her.

With shaky hands, Olivia lifted the teacup to her lips. She sipped her tea and inhaled the soothing aroma. Was Taylor right? Had she failed Ariel? Had she kept her from doing things she was capable of? Taylor didn't understand that good mothers protected their kids from things they couldn't see. Things their moms had lived through.

Since he got home, Taylor had pushed back against her on everything, and she didn't know how to reach him. Maybe he'd changed, and she hadn't. It felt like she was losing him. If he got hurt or killed, her entire world would fall apart—her heart would be irreparably crushed. It was why she couldn't let herself get close to Jack, or any man who might be hurt. She had to protect herself from being torn apart again.

Had she tipped the scales from protecting her loved ones, to protecting herself from losing them? Weren't they essentially the same thing?

CHAPTER 12

All children are artists. The problem is how to remain an artist
once he grows up.

Pablo Picasso

A few days later, Ariel was sitting in the front window of Second
Chance Designs when she cried out. "Look! Matt!" She clambered down eagerly out of the window and made for the front
door.

As she watched the pair cross the street, Olivia's insides went
into blender mode.

Jack is a *fireman*, she reminded herself. *With a firehose* came
the hilarious thought, and the image that flew into her mind was
definitely X-rated.

"They come, they come!" Ariel said, with enthusiasm Olivia
shared.

Jack carried some paintings, and Matt carried a bag. When
they stepped into the store, Ariel threw her arms around Matt.

Olivia went to pry her off. "Ariel, he's a stranger. We don't hug strangers."

"I'm not a stranger," Matt said. "I'm her boyfriend."

Ariel's face had love written all over it, but. Olivia knew Ariel didn't understand her feelings. Even if she did, Olivia would have been just as scared.

Heck, Olivia didn't understand her own feelings toward Jack. They wavered somewhere between the urge to lock the front door before he came in and wanting to stand in the heat rolling off him.

The safest thing would be to conclude the business and get the pair out as soon as possible.

Jack smiled, and just like that, the light seemed to dial brighter. He said, "You look even more beautiful than when you were at my condo."

No one ever told Olivia she looked beautiful, and the compliment warmed her down to her toes. "Thank you," she said.

Jack greeted Ariel with a smile and a handshake. "Hello, young lady, and how are you today?"

"I fine, thank you," Ariel answered.

Olivia felt a surge of gratefulness toward Jack's warmth and kindness to Ariel. Back when Olivia used to date, the minute a man found out she had a daughter with Down, they ghosted her. After a while, she stopped man-shopping. Most people didn't understand how much a special child had to offer, but she didn't have to explain this to Jack.

"I brought the shirts," Matt said and handed Ariel the bag.

Ariel pulled out three shirts, and one by one, held them up. "They bootiful. I love." She puckered up to kiss Matt.

Olivia laid a hand on her daughter's shoulder. "Ariel, you can just say 'thank you'—you don't have to kiss him."

With uncharacteristic belligerence, Ariel said, "I like. He boyfriend."

Olivia caught each word like a small arrow to her own heart. It was natural that young people wanted to be together and have feelings for one another. And it was just as natural for a mom to want to protect her child.

"They're okay, don't you think?" Jack asked.

No, she didn't not think so.

He was an observant man, but clearly, he didn't know how easily things could get out of hand.

Jack said, "Is this an okay time for us to stop by? Are you busy? Because if you are, we can come back later."

Oh, please, don't leave.

She glanced at Matt and Ariel snuggling up on a sofa, and Olivia's breath nearly seized.

Oh, please, do leave.

She remembered Taylor's insistence that Ariel have her own life. Against her instincts, Olivia didn't say anything to the pair, but she had to watch, to be careful that nothing happened. Matt and Jack wouldn't be back once she bought the paintings. Then, everything would be safe for her, and Ariel, and Olivia might give Ariel a little more rope.

But only a teeny bit.

"No, your timing's perfect," Olivia said.

"Great!" Jack said. His eyes hooked and drew her in. Something inside her trembled, as though she'd had an inner earthquake.

"I brought two of my favorite paintings," he said.

"Let's take a look," she said.

Jack stripped off the plastic covering the canvases. He propped them next to the pair of canary yellow chairs. "We didn't know what might appeal to you," he said, "so if you don't like them, I can bring different ones the next time we stop by."

Oh, dear. There would be a next time?

There would be a next time!

She stood back, rested her chin on her hand, and studied the paintings. She walked back and forth, studying them from all angles, but she already knew she would buy them.

They were bursting with splashes of swirling color and vibrant shapes throbbing with life. It was like looking at a safe, sunny, pain-free world full of boundless joy and laughter where children were never in danger.

She felt Jack next to her, and her world felt as if it was sliding, slowly, slowly, off its axis and she was helpless to stop it.

She swallowed and fixed her eyes on the canvases. "Why are these your favorites?" she asked.

Jack's expression shifted between shades of pride and introspection. "The color, the swirls. They make me happy. Hopeful. It's a little like looking into a whole other world where everything is okay." He lifted his shoulders shyly. "Guess that's dumb, isn't it?"

He wasn't only a caring uncle—he had a vocabulary of emotions, and he wasn't afraid to use it.

"Not at all. They make me feel the same way," she murmured softly. "Art is supposed to make us feel things." She stood quietly, soaking up his presence. "Do they remind you of anything in particular?"

"For some reason, they remind me of when I held my daughter for the first time." He laid his palm over his heart, his voice thick with emotion. "It was like this thing in my chest burst open, and I ...." His eyes grew misty and filled with what could only be love. She felt the space between them closing even though neither of them had moved. He said, "I felt like I'd landed in a place I didn't know existed before that very minute."

She could hardly top that. It was so tender she couldn't look at him for fear she might tear up. His willingness to reveal his feelings touched her. She snuck a look at him. His eyes were not in the least fireman-like. There was a different sort of heroism in his gaze, in the set of his jaw, and in the way he showed his soft and vulnerable underbelly.

"That's beautiful," she said softly, afraid of disturbing the connection between them.

He gently asked, "Now, your turn. What do they remind you of?"

She knew right away. "That burst of yellow reminds me of sun on new snow. Of jonquils popping out of the ground. Of lemon slices floating in a glass of water. That twist of purple reminds me of the blanket I brought Ariel home from the hospital in. I still have it. I remember how sad and how happy I felt, all at the same time. Like you said, the painting makes me happy, but not only happy. It brings up a whole set of emotions. Excitement, nostalgia, fearlessness." She didn't know what had inspired that last emotion, but she recognized the old, rusty feeling.

Jack crossed his arms and regarded the paintings. "I knew Matt was gifted, but I never thought he'd be selling his paintings in a swanky store like this."

Their eyes met, and something syrupy and warm filled her ribcage. She knew she should keep this all business, but a part of her wanted to fall into his liquid eyes and float away.

He asked, "Do you think it's just us, or will these move other people like they do you and me?"

"I'm counting on it," she said.

She noticed a patch of stubble where he'd missed shaving. She clenched one hand with the other to keep from reaching up and caressing that tender spot on his cheek.

She spotted the kids curled up together on a display sofa, and her mothering instincts roared to life. She couldn't let things get out of hand between them, but she didn't try to separate them. It would all be over soon enough, anyway.

Then, Jack smiled down at her, and she couldn't look away. She felt a flip in her stomach.

Her mind, body, and heart were simultaneously staging a revolt against everything she had ever believed.

Olivia tore herself away from Jack and moved to her desk. "We should get down to business."

"What's the rush?" Jack murmured. The soft edges of his voice made the hair on her nape prickle. She needed to get these two dangerous men out of here.

She said, "If I can find my checkbook, I'll write you a check." She shuffled through the papers on her desk. She always knew where everything was, but today, everything was topsy-turvy.

He handed her the checkbook, which had been sitting in plain sight on the corner of her desk. When his hand brushed hers, she was pretty certain his touch hadn't been an accident.

Accidents can lead to injury, to broken hearts, to a life turned upside down.

CHAPTER 13

A gentleman is merely a patient wolf.
   Lana Turner

When Jack let his hand brush against Olivia's, that one touch jumpstarted his old heart. He was glad it had happened. However, the shocked look in her eyes, a look he'd seen at accidents, car crashes, and fires, said, '*How did this happen?*'

He watched as she gathered herself and wrote out a check in scratchy handwriting that slanted off the lines.

She handed him the check and, in a wobbly voice, said, "I-I..." she cleared her throat. "I want to hang the paintings right up front so they're the first thing customers see. Let me get my toolbox." She headed toward a back room in a hurry.

Olivia had inspired him to talk about his memories and the feelings connected with them in a way he'd all but forgotten how to do.

He noted the things on Olivia's desk: colored pens, a pretty notepad, a lavender tape dispenser, and a silver pen holder. Her soft feminine touches were everywhere, and everything she did was artistic and creative. That was why she'd immediately recognized the beauty of Matt's paintings. But more than that, she was able to put words and feelings to the paintings in a way Jack hadn't been able to, but that he felt.

Jack glanced around and saw that everything in the entire store was designed to inspire emotions. Olivia's almost magical ability to identify and bring out emotions was one reason he was attracted to her. She possessed a soft, classy elegance without being pretentious. She was approachable, but still tough and savvy enough to own her own business. When she wasn't nervous, Olivia was warm and friendly in a way he hadn't experienced before.

He wanted more than friendly.

It gave him some insight into his relationship with Gina. Maybe it had been the busyness of life and raising kids, but he finally understood what they had been missing as a couple. What he'd been missing all his life.

Olivia returned with a small pink toolbox. She carefully laid the paintings face down on a soft towel and measured across the back. From the toolbox, she took eye screws and picture wire. He sat on a stool in front of her, watching her small, white hands move with quick precision.

She was screwing an eye screw into the wooden stretcher when her hand slipped. "Ouch." She winced and stuck her finger in her mouth.

"Need some help?" he rose from the stool.

"I'm usually pretty handy. I don't know why I'm suddenly all thumbs." She opened a drawer and found a Band-Aid but fumbled trying to put it on.

He puffed out his chest comically. "I can do that. I'm a fireman. We help injured people all the time."

She laughed—a big sound—and it made him feel like he'd cut her out of a smashed car with the Jaws of Life.

As he wrapped a fresh Band-Aid around her finger, he was near enough to see the pale blond wisps of loose hair behind her ear. This tiny tangle made her appear tender and vulnerable. She was like a castle surrounded by the moat of her fear. A moat he thought he might gently dismantle, brick by brick.

He kissed her injured finger. "There, all better."

She didn't pull her hand away. When their eyes met, it was like staring into two patches of sunlit sky, and he felt a bit like he might be having a stroke.

He was being stupid. Or was he just feeling things again? He decided to go with that.

She whispered, "Do you do that for all the people you rescue from fires?"

"Only the ones I really like," he said, smiling.

They stood like that for a moment—her letting him hold her hand. His gaze roamed over her face, studying her pale blond hair eyebrows, the down on her cheek, the sweet wrinkle at the base of her neck.

One corner of her lip twitched. On an inhale, she said, "Oh, dear," and withdrew her hand.

He smiled. "I can screw those in if you want me to."

"That would help." She held up her hand. "Now that I'm wounded." She perched on the stool and watched him screwing in the screws.

Screwing. He fought a smile. Now there was an interesting idea—something he hadn't done in a very long time. But he wasn't the friends-with-benefits sort, and he doubted Olivia was either. He hadn't thought he was ready to put himself out there again, but he had to convince her that he was worth taking a chance on, worth getting to know, worth trusting.

Who didn't trust a fireman?

In the back, Matt and Ariel giggled at something, and Olivia's eyes sparked with anxiety. Jack had almost forgotten they were there.

"It's okay," he murmured in his most comforting tone. "We're right here. Nothing's going to happen."

"But...I-I- Ariel has never had ... a boyfriend," she said.

He picked up the screwdriver and said, "I get it, but they're doing great, don't you think?"

"It makes me nervous," she said, her lip twitching.

"I can tell, but it doesn't have to," he said. "I promise if anything happens, I'll leap to her rescue like any good fireman would." He smiled at her, and that sweet little nervous twitch stopped. "Does Ariel live at home with you?"

"Yes." She handed him a tiny eye screw, which he promptly dropped because his fingers were so big.

She handed him another one, and he twisted it into the frame. "Matt lives in a group home in Greenwich called Ability House, but he comes to my place for occasional overnights. He's really very happy there."

"Oh?" she said, surprised. She handed him a length of wire.

He threaded the wire through one screw, then the other, and twisted the ends together. "I couldn't manage him living with me since I'm still working. As you might guess, he was pretty broken up when he came to me, but with the staff support at Ability House, he's become more social and outgoing."

"It's hard to believe he was ever anything but outgoing," she said.

He laughed and shook his head. He said, "I know. He's a real powerhouse. Some of the residents help him with the business, packing the shirts for shipping and so on. It's worked out great for both of us."

When he finished the painting, he hung it on a hook above the yellow chairs. "You're right," he said. "It looks great with these chairs. You have a great eye for this stuff. I can't wait to see what you do with my place."

For some reason, her lip twitched again. He wanted to kiss that little twitch away and put a smile there instead.

She gazed at the paintings. "I knew these were beautiful when I saw the shirts, but they're even more stunning in person," she said, sounding pleased. "These will sell right away. If they do, I'll have you bring in more."

He started in on the second painting, repeating the same procedure as the first. This one went quicker since he knew what he was doing.

He said, "Matt's grown since he moved into Ability House. Just like him barging into your store and trying to get you to sell his shirts. He wouldn't have done that before. Ariel might do well there, too. If you like, I could ask if they have any openings in the women's houses."

She shifted on the stool and crossed her arms. "Do you make it a habit to tell other people what to do with their children?" she said with surprising bite.

He'd poked her when he didn't mean to. Lord, he was out of practice with women. He hung the second painting, took a step back and straightened it. "I wasn't telling you to throw her into a den of wolves, just that you might want to look at Ability House. It might be good for both of you."

Posture stiff, she slid off the stool. "She just got a job bagging groceries, and that's about as much risk as I can tolerate right now." She smoothed her ponytail.

That nervous tick again.

"What's life worth if you don't take some risks?" He reached up, and with two fingers, tugged gently on her glossy ponytail.

She gave an embarrassed smile, realizing that he'd spotted her nervous gesture. "Thank you for your help," she said, less cross now.

"I have to get going," he said, reluctant to leave.

She handed him his jacket, and he slipped it on. She pulled the front together and patted his chest. "Thanks for your suggestion, but I don't think it's right for me."

He said, "Sorry, didn't mean to overstep."

She nodded. "I know, but like I said, risk, raising a kid with Down, keeping them safe. It's all part of my decision process."

Jack called to the back of the store, "Matt, we need to go, pal."

Matt ambled over. "Can we come back, Uncle Matt?"

Jack took Olivia's hand, bowed over it, and made a big show of examining her bandaged finger. He raised his eyes to meet her gaze. "If Olivia's not too scared, yes, we'll be back."

Her cheeks were bright pink. "I'm not scared." She swallowed. "I'm just cautious, is all."

Jack kissed her finger, lingering over her hand. "You don't have to be scared. I have only honorable intentions."

CHAPTER 14

I want my children to have all the things I couldn't afford. Then
I want to move in with them.
   Phyllis Diller

Sunday morning, Olivia listened raptly as Father Gabriel said,
"Jesus gives us the example of being adventurous. It is an
uncomfortable question, but are we, as members of St. Paul's,
brave enough to take the kind of risks Jesus took? To embrace
the risk of love?"

*Of course, Jesus could take risks: he would be resurrected! Ask
Mary what she thought about Jesus's risks!*

Olivia squeezed Ariel's hand. Olivia didn't feel brave letting
her have a job. What she felt was backed into a corner by Taylor.

He was sitting on Olivia's other side, scrolling through his
phone. She elbowed him and gave him a reprimanding scowl.
He scowled back, but returned his phone to his pocket.

Olivia looked around and saw the people she loved
throughout the church. Bianca, Carolina, Flicka, and Hélène sat
further down the pew. Frankie and Cam sat across the aisle with
her sons, Jordan and Javier.

It was like sitting in her living room, surrounded by people who knew her but still loved her. Warmth and caring wafted through the air like the curls of incense. The sunbeams streaming through the stained-glass windows felt like God was pouring hope into the sanctuary. The love and friendship that Olivia had at St. Paul's were as solid and reliable as the stone pillars holding up the peaked ceiling above their heads.

It was a place where Olivia felt safe and loved, where both of her children were accepted and loved. She was immensely grateful for this place and these people. More than once, they had saved her when she couldn't save herself.

The choir ripped into a joyfully high, loud anthem at precisely the moment Carol Baxter chose to hobble down the left aisle of the church. Instead of listening to the rapturous music, Olivia's attention was drawn to the *stump, shuffle, stump, shuffle* of Carol's cane resounding through the sanctuary.

Carol fell frequently, and she'd only just had her second knee replacement. She was using a cane because she refused to use a walker. Beneath her free arm, like always, she carried her dead Lhasa Apso dog, Ozzie. Through the miracle of taxidermy, Carol had ensured her pet would never leave her.

Today she wore a hot pink flamenco-style ruffled shirt and purple harem pants. No matter what she wore, Carol was not a subtle presence. Everyone looked out for her, visiting her at home or in the hospital, ensuring she took her medications, delivering casseroles, listening to her ramble on, and driving her to church when she couldn't drive herself.

It wasn't clear if Carol had always been a bit daft or if she had early onset Alzheimer's or another form of dementia, but she was a beloved parishioner. To the shock and surprise of many, Frankie's dad, Vic Carter, had taken over some of Carol's care, but this morning, he wasn't at church.

Olivia had just turned her attention to the choir when a crash and a squawk raised a commotion on the side aisle.

Ariel, closest to the aisle, gasped, her eyes wide with fright. "Carol fall!"

"Oh, Lord, again?" Bianca muttered, which caused Hélène to hiss, "*Shhh!*"

Taylor rose and pushed past Olivia and Ariel.

Olivia turned to Ariel. "You stay here with Bianca." Then Olivia followed her son.

A crowd had already gathered in the aisle. Ushers and other parishioners pressed toward Carol, but Taylor moved with an authority that made people back away.

Carol lay on her back, clutching her right arm and moaning. She had knocked over an easel containing an icon of the Black Virgin and her dog lay beside her, his unblinking glass eyes giving him a creepy, possessed look.

Carolina was already calmly speaking to 911 on her phone.

Olivia and Taylor kneeled on either side of Carol. In an agitated voice, she said, "I have to get to school."

Taylor patted her shoulder and spoke quietly. "Carol, just lie still. The ambulance will be here in a minute." Then he placed his hand on her pulse, counting the seconds with his wristwatch.

"But I can't be hurt. I've used up all my sick days," Carol moaned, her face twisted in pain.

Carol regularly forgot she'd retired as a special education teacher years ago. People had taken to humoring her because the facts only upset her.

Taylor said, "Don't worry about your sick days. I'll have a word with your principal and make sure it's okay if you miss a few days."

How had he known to do that?

He took out his phone and began to take notes. "Can you tell me what medications you took today?" He was impressively cool and in charge, while everyone else ran around like maniacs.

With all her fears and phobias, Olivia was amazed that she had given birth to, and raised, a man whose default mode seemed to be calm. She was used to being terrified by nearly everything he did. She was used to how messy his room was, how he ate everything that wasn't alive. But she hadn't known he could be so unflappable.

"I don't take medications." Carol blinked her blue eyes flirtatiously at Taylor.

Olivia took Carol's hand and patted it. "You can tell him, dear. Taylor was an EMT, and he's going to be a doctor, so you're giving him practice."

For some strange reason, Taylor threw Olivia a penetrating glance.

What did I say wrong this time?

He said, "We need to know what your meds are, so we can tell the paramedics when they get here."

Taylor's authoritative manner reassured Carol because she listed a few medications.

Olivia wondered if Carol had been taking her meds because, when she'd greeted Carol before the service, she had asked Olivia if Nixon would be impeached.

In the near distance, a siren sounded, and the hair on the back of Olivia's neck rose. Sirens and flashing lights cut to her core like a laser through snow. To her, the sounds signaled danger rather than rescue, an emergency she had failed to anticipate and avert.

Through an open window, Olivia saw a fire engine lumber into the parking lot. The siren and low grumbling engine set her heart racing with dread.

"Are you all right?" Carol said, frowning at Olivia with concern. "You look kinda white."

It wouldn't do Carol any good if Olivia panicked. She tried to block out the sounds by concentrating on Carol's face and forced a smile. "I'm fine," Olivia said. "You relax now."

Two firemen trooped up the side aisle carrying a medical bag and wheeling a tank of oxygen.

Olivia felt like she could use a few whiffs.

She rose and moved a few feet away to give them room to evaluate Carol. As they drew closer, she recognized Jack O'Grady, and blood rushed from her head to her core, making her insides feel like popcorn in a popper.

"What are you doing here?" She sounded rude, even to herself.

His eyebrows shot up, and he smiled, making her insides tickle. "We're right around the corner, so we took the call. The ambulance will be here in a minute. Is it you who needs to be rescued?"

Truthfully, she wouldn't have minded being rescued by Jack.

"Me? Oh, no, I, Carol—" Olivia waved her hands. When she realized she looked like a panicked chicken, she clamped her arms to her sides. "I'm fine. Talk to him." Olivia said, pointing to Taylor. Her lip twitched, and she pressed a fingertip to still it, but not before she saw Jack's eyes catch the quiver.

Taylor updated the emergency personnel with the information about Carol's medications, doctor, and vitals, all of which he'd written down on his phone.

Jack focused his attention on Taylor. By the way Jack listened and nodded, she could tell he recognized how bright Taylor was. When this was done, she would introduce the son she was so proud of to Jack.

Seeing how capable Taylor was only reinforced Olivia's conviction that he was made to be a doctor, just like his father and his grandfather. She knew Taylor had doubts about school, but with tutors and summer school, a few encouraging emails, and texts, she could make it happen.

Jack looked incredibly handsome in his turnout gear. As he shifted and moved, the gear and clips on his belt made soft clanking sounds. The red suspenders holding up his fireproof pants rested on his broad shoulders. His T-shirt showed a well-defined chest. Ropy muscles and a dusting of dark hair ran up his arm. She'd never noticed these before because her eyes had fixated on his ragged scar.

Now she knew why fireman calendars were popular.

The ambulance showed up, and the two paramedics strapped Carol onto a gurney and swaddled her in soft blankets.

As the paramedics worked, in a low voice, Jack said to Taylor, "I saw you working. You're good, calm. You asked all the right questions. You have medical training?"

Taylor beamed like a five-year-old at his birthday party. "I was a volunteer EMT trainee in high school. Loved every minute of it."

Jack said, "Norwalk Fire Department is always looking for volunteers with experience as EMTs. Best way to get hired full-time if you're interested. We could use someone with your skills."

Every nerve ending in Olivia's body felt like a hot poker. Her fingers curled into fists, and she ground her teeth. Whenever Captain Know-It-All-Fireman Jack O'Grady showed up, he kicked her life off course. First, pushing Ariel and Matt together, then suggesting a group home for Ariel, and now urging Taylor into a high-risk job, which he didn't want, anyway.

Why didn't Jack mind his own business? Why did he think he knew what was best for everyone else?

She elbowed her way past the other fireman to Jack's side and fixed him with a withering glare. "This is my son, Taylor," she ground out. "He's going back to college in the fall. He's not interested in volunteering. He's planning to be a doctor."

Taylor glowered at Olivia, then he turned to Jack. Taylor said, "Thanks for the tip. I'm totally interested. And I'm not going back to college in the fall, anyway. I was planning on applying to the fire department."

Olivia's chest felt as though a fire engine were sitting on it. Her fury at Jack O'Grady forgotten, panic wrapped icy fingers around her throat. Taylor could not possibly mean what he'd said. She couldn't lose Taylor like she'd lost his father. If she lost Taylor like she'd lost his father, it would crush her. If he put himself in danger, she would be powerless to save him.

She would fail him, like she'd failed Derek.

CHAPTER 15

Parents are the bones on which children cut their teeth.

Peter Ustinov

Carol refused to let go of Taylor's hand, so he walked beside the gurney until they loaded her into the ambulance.

"My hero, my rescuer, thank you, thank you," she burbled over and over.

And he did feel like a hero. Bigger than life. Not the paranoid kid his mom wanted him to be.

Standing on the church steps, he waved, and in the space between his ribs, he felt a sense of envy, almost physical longing, as the fire truck pulled out.

He loved helping people in crisis. It gave him a rush even as his brain lasered in on saving the person.

This. This is what I want.

Out of nowhere, his mom leaped and grabbed his arm. Her face was chalky. Her hand on his arm was shaking.

Maybe he should have sent her along in the ambulance.

She said, "Why did you say you don't plan on returning to school?"

He pulled his arm out of her little kid's grip. He'd always been careful around her. He'd never wanted to disappoint her, but she was a bulldog on his being a doctor, but he knew what he wanted. He knew the difference between living out her and his dead dad's dreams and having his own dreams.

He scuffed at the grass. "Look, I didn't mean for you to find out this way. I didn't mean to blurt it out. I tried hinting at it, but you just wouldn't listen, Mom." He looked at her, and she looked completely wrecked.

"Why, though?" she asked.

Her eyes searched his face, looking for some doubt she could drill into, but there wasn't a single doubt in his mind. He put a fist to his chest. "Because it's what I want."

Her voice broke, and tears spilled down her face. "Fire-fighting is dangerous. And your father would be so disappointed. He loved being a doctor, and you would, too."

He clamped his jaw shut. He would not let her kneecap him with the hammer of his oh-so-perfect dad. The guy was dead, for God's sake! Taylor had put up with her trying to turn him into his dad all his life. He'd had this year to think about what was important to him, a year in which to fail miserably at school but, oddly, to build his own confidence through rock climbing with Dani.

With all that conviction pushing him forward, he said, "I know without a doubt I'm not cut out for being a doctor."

"But when you left in the fall," she said, "you were completely focused on your dream of getting into med school. What happened?"

"Reality happened," he shot back.

Her chin jerked down, and her eyes became like a pair of laser beams. "Why did you come home early?"

She had him cornered. There was no going back now. He tipped his chin up. "Because I skipped my finals."

Her mouth dropped open, and it looked like she might faint. Seconds passed before she said anything. "What? How could you do that?"

"Because I knew I wouldn't pass them, anyway." His voice rose. "Don't you get it? I hate school. I *hate* it! It's terrible."

Trying to live up to his dad's legacy was like being strangled. Bitterly, he finally admitted out loud what he'd been feeling. His clenched fists beat the air. "I'm just ... I'm just no good at it."

"Oh, honey, you are good at it," she whispered. She was still not listening to a word he was saying.

His face felt hot with long-pent up anger he didn't know he'd been holding. "No, Mom! I'm not. And I don't care about it! Don't you hear me? I don't want to keep failing at school. I don't want to spend the next ten years studying to be a doctor while life is happening. I don't want to be chained to books and labs for the rest of my life. I like being the first one on the scene." He swung his hand back toward the church. "That kind of stuff is what I want."

Her voice got quivery. "It's not the rest of your life. Medical school will be over before you know it. Look how good you were with Carol. Think how satisfying it would be to save someone's life," she said.

"There's other ways to save lives." His voice was louder and harsher than he meant it to be, and she flinched.

He paced around, breathing hard through his nose until he pulled it together. He couldn't lose his shit at church, or she'd never forgive him for that, either.

He said, "I just don't have that kind of patience or brains, Mom. I want to be a fireman."

She actually clasped her hands together, begging him, "Please, write to your professors. Maybe you can—"

His chest tightened. "Why can't you just accept this?" *Might as go all the way.* "I've made my decision. I already put a deposit on a fireman's course."

She slowly sank onto the church steps like a deflating Thanksgiving Day balloon. "You can't throw away your dream of becoming a doctor," she said, her voice breaking.

"That was never my dream," he said. "It was yours, and Dad's, before either of you ever even knew what I was like. I'm sorry to disappoint you and wreck all your dreams, but I don't want to be a doctor like my dad, Mom. I just don't."

He was relieved to have told her. It was real now. There was no going back. He still loved his mom, but he didn't know if she'd ever forgive him.

It was the week before the barbecue fundraiser for the youth shelter and the Marriage Survivors Club was busy with last-minute preparations. Everyone had been assigned a task. Flicka and Bianca were, quite logically, on drinks. Hélène and Frankie were buying hot dogs, burgers, and buns, and Carolina and Olivia were on the dessert crew.

This evening, Carolina came over to Olivia's to make brownies, and she welcomed the distraction. She was still reeling from Taylor's announcement and furious that Jack had invited him to apply for a job as a firefighter. It felt like she'd lost her son and a potential romantic partner in one fell swoop.

Carolina lined up six boxes of brownie mix, two cartons of butter, and a box of eggs on the counter. Olivia picked up a box and examined it. "I thought we were going to make them from scratch."

"This is scratch-ish." Carolina washed her hands. "Two eggs, a stick of melted butter, a box of mix, and we'll have twenty-four brownies per batch."

Olivia raised her eyebrows and surveyed the boxes. "That's a lot of brownies for the barbecue."

"Father Gabriel will eat one pan by himself," Carolina said, drying her hands on a towel.

Father Gabriel's sweet tooth was legendary. Why he didn't blow up like a balloon was a mystery equivalent to the Virgin birth. Sometimes the Marriage Survivors Club took bets on how many cookies he'd put away at coffee hour before he thought anyone noticed.

After Derek had died, seeking to find some comfort, Olivia started attending St. Paul's. She wept openly during Mass, stared blank-eyed and stunned at the stained-glass windows.

At St. Paul's, as had many others before and after, Olivia found support, a measure of peace, and strength enough to carry on. She also found her chosen family and the Marriage Survivors Club was eventually formed.

If it weren't for St. Paul's, she wouldn't have her shop. While she finished her design certification, the parishioners babysat the kids. They brought her gently used furniture to rehab and resell. When the shop fully opened, they shopped there and brought their friends to the shop.

Carolina beat the eggs as Olivia stared at the directions on the box, her mind circling her fears. Taylor falling through a collapsing floor. A flaming beam falling on him. His getting disoriented in smoke-filled buildings, a lunatic shooting at him. His oxygen tank could run out or malfunction. He might fall off a ladder. A skyscraper might get attacked, and he'd die in the collapse. He might inhale poisonous chemicals. He could end up with scars like Jack's or his dad's, with blistered skin, be disfigured, or disabled.

Once, she'd been afraid of terrorists, kidnappings, bubonic

plague, tornados, rabies, and a host of other things. But now her fears had a basis in reality, and she couldn't get past them.

Carolina said, "Did you hear me?" She had stopped whisking and was staring at Olivia.

"What?" Olivia glanced up. "Did you say something?"

"Okay, what's going on? Since I got here, all you've done is talk in monosyllables. So, whatever's bothering you, spill it." Carolina poked her whisk at the oven. "But preheat the oven to three hundred fifty degrees first."

Olivia set the oven. "Taylor doesn't want to go back to school."

"Hmm. Why?" Carolina said. "Nuke a stick of butter until its melted."

Numbly, Olivia microwaved the butter into a bubbly yellow puddle. "He wants to be, of all things"—Olivia threw her hands in the air—"a firefighter!"

Carolina said, "Pour the butter into my bowl."

On auto-pilot, Olivia did what Carolina told her while she beat the eggs and butter together.

"That's very brave of him," Carolina said.

"Brave? Foolhardy is what it is," Olivia said.

"It's a three-sixty from med school, that's for sure." Carolina dumped a box of mix into the butter and eggs and stirred.

The oven beeped that it had reached the temperature.

Olivia sank into a chair. "Where did I go wrong?" Olivia said. "What else could I have done? I taught Taylor about danger, safety, hard work, and responsibility. How can I save him from being hurt or killed?"

This was the first time Olivia had spoken to anyone about Taylor's bombshell and it felt good to share it, but her dread remained.

Carolina scooped the gooey mixture into a baking pan and popped the pan into the oven. "Set the timer for twenty-nine minutes," Carolina said. "It's not a foregone conclusion that he'll die on the job."

Olivia set the timer on her phone. "I've spent my life teaching him to avoid dangers of all kinds, and now he wants to run into burning buildings. I guess I forgot to warn him about the danger of fire and smoke. About falling off ladders and ledges."

If she'd only been with Derek the day he died, maybe she could have saved him. Stopped him from climbing before the guide arrived. Failing to protect Derek had nearly killed her, and now she couldn't protect Taylor.

"C'mon, you have to help me, or we'll be here until morning," Carolina said.

Olivia hauled herself out of the chair. "I won't be able to live if Taylor gets hurt. Was it a mistake to have him become a volunteer EMT? I only did it so he could save our lives in an emergency."

Carolina continued stirring, mixing, pouring. "He knew what to do when Carol fell. He was very self-assured, and everyone was impressed with his skill."

Her acceptance that Taylor's decision was irreversible annoyed Olivia. She wanted her friend to join her outrage, not calmly take Taylor's side.

"He thinks he should follow his own dreams," Olivia said. "Until now, he never even had a dream except to be a doctor."

"Sounds like his dream's." Carolina put a pan into the oven.

Olivia said, "Of course, Taylor's never been all that ambitious, but I figured I was ambitious enough for both of us."

Carolina started another batch of brownies. "Asking someone else to be ambitious is like asking them to be hungry."

The aroma of brownies triggered a craving in Olivia for chocolate and fat coma that might momentarily blunt her misery.

Carolina said, "Taylor can't live to make you happy."

Olivia grabbed the spatula and licked the last of the batter. "I don't know why not," she said, half meaning it.

As if by divine miracle, the final batch of brownies were in the oven. Carolina put the teapot on to boil. "Firefighting is a noble career," she said. "And isn't Jack O'Grady, the guy you have the hots for, a fireman?"

"I do *not* have the hots for him, but yes, Jack O'Grady is a fireman," Olivia said a bit snippily.

Carolina lifted one eyebrow and gave Olivia a suppressed smile of incredulity.

Olivia wondered if she was that transparent. "He's a nice man," she said. *With a nice butt.* "But he thinks he knows everything. He suggested that Ariel should have a job, that she should live in a group home. He's pushing his nephew and Ariel together. And worst of all, he suggested Taylor join the fire department! How could I have the hots for a guy that ignorant of danger?"

How indeed?

"Those sound like perfectly reasonable suggestions, and Taylor had already decided he wanted to be a fireman," Carolina said in her placid way.

Olivia didn't really hear Carolina because she was paying more attention to her boiling blood. "If I didn't have a contract to do Jack's apartment, I don't think I would ever speak to him again."

Carolina sat across from Olivia. Her voice was solemn but pointed. "Don't you think maybe it's time you let Taylor make his own decisions? Did you ever think of that?"

Olivia looked at a batch of brownies cooling on the counter and felt doubt seeping into the cracks of her certainty.

"Well ... maybe," Olivia said, "I guess kids have their own ideas when they get a little older, but that doesn't mean they're good ideas." A thought tumbled into Olivia's mind. "Hey! Maybe you could talk to Taylor."

"About what?" Carolina's tone was a cross between disbelief and laughter.

Olivia bent forward, eager for Carolina's help. But first, she would have to convince her. "About how dangerous it is to be a fireman. He trusts you, and I trust you. You could suggest he reconsider that this might not be how he wants to spend the rest of his life."

"But he *does* want to spend his life being a firefighter," Carolina insisted. The tea kettle whistled, and she got up and poured two cups of tea.

Olivia wagged a forefinger. "He only *thinks* he does."

Carolina laughed. "You should hear yourself." She set the mugs on the table and sat again. "Taylor's like my nephew or little cousin. I wouldn't try to twist his arm into doing something he didn't believe in. You taught him to be responsible, kind, thoughtful, and hardworking, and he'll be all those things when he's a fireman. None of the things you taught him will disappear. You've been an amazing mom and raised him to be brave in many ways. He's got a generous heart and loves Ariel and you. He'll be fine, and so will you."

If anything happened to Taylor, Olivia would never be fine. She knew the suffocating grief of losing someone. The guilt of failing to protect a loved one.

Carolina squeezed Olivia's hand. "Promise me you'll think about what I said."

"Thanks," Olivia said. "I trust you, and thanks for listening."

"Maybe you should pray about it and see what God has to say on the matter," Carolina said.

"I already know God agrees with me," Olivia said.

Carolina laughed and shook her head. She rose and took out

the last pan of brownies and set it on the granite countertop to cool.

Olivia closed her eyes and inhaled the sweet aroma. "Do you think anybody would notice if I ate a whole pan of those brownies?"

CHAPTER 16

I only like two kinds of men, domestic and imported.

Mae West

Olivia had agreed to meet Jack for breakfast to discuss his plans for his condo. They chose to meet at Sono Bakery, an artisanal bakery with pastries, bread, and delectable lunches and breakfasts. They sat at a table with mugs of dark, rich, hot coffee before them, waiting for their breakfast to come.

Olivia was still nursing her irritation with Jack for encouraging Taylor, but she was determined to remain professional and stick to discussing her ideas. She needed the work. She'd signed the contract, and she had only once ever chucked a client who'd driven her nuts. This meeting would be all business.

But that meant not noticing the way his eyes seemed to eat her up. The way one side of his mouth lifted in a flirtatious smile. The tickle in her chest when he laughed.

Staring into his coffee, Jack looked like a dog who'd gotten caught stealing a steak off the grill. "First off," he said, "I want to apologize about suggesting Taylor join the fire department. I didn't mean to cause trouble between the two of you. I didn't even know you had a son."

It struck her that he cared how she felt, that he'd upset her. His empathy came as something of a surprise and the steam went out of her.

"Thanks," she said, and couldn't keep from giving him a warm smile. "I don't even know where he got the idea of being a fireman." She felt heat creep up the front of her throat. "Not that there's anything wrong with that, but our plans had always been for him to go to medical school."

Jack nodded. "At the scene, he was very in charge. You don't see that kind of self-confidence in young guys very often. He'll be a success whatever he chooses to do."

"Thank you," she said, feeling the last of her annoyance drown in a wash of pride. "I guess I'll see if he's really serious."

"If you're still upset about my shooting off my mouth and want to quit my project, just say so." But the look in his eyes said, *please don't.*

She didn't want to quit, either. Where had she ever found warmth and consideration like his? A smile that made her toes curl. She smiled and said, "I already cashed the check, so you're stuck with me."

"I wouldn't call it stuck. More like hitting the jackpot," he said, staring at her with his eyes full of lust.

Her entire body flushed with pleasure, leaving her tongue-tied. She couldn't remember the last time anyone lusted after her. It made her feel like a woman, not just a mom.

Luckily, the waitress appeared and set plates of steaming eggs before them.

Jack dug in and chewed thoughtfully. She loved watching a man enjoy his food. It was like watching them during sex, the gusto and sheer pleasure.

He caught her staring and grinned.

His grin jumbled her thoughts. "So, how do you decide how to decorate a room?"

She said, "I always try to create spaces that make people feel welcomed and comforted."

"Comforted, not comfortable?" he asked, fork paused in mid-air.

"Comforted, yes."

"That's sort of what I try to do when I cook for people. I want them to feel well-cared for," he said.

"It's sort of the same thing. I want people to feel like they're stepping into a safe, predictable space."

Two creases appeared between his brows. He asked, "I like to toss in the unexpected when I cook. Do you think everyone wants ... predictable?"

It was a relief to find themselves talking about something besides kids, risk, and firefighting. She hadn't talked to anyone about decorating in ages, and she liked sharing this aspect of herself. She liked that he valued and respected her opinion.

Olivia put down her fork and felt free to talk because all his attention was riveted on her. "I think they do. Predictability means safety. I put together different elements of color, design, and arrangement for a unified whole. No bumps or surprises."

"I have one request." He opened his burly arms wide to demonstrate size. "A giant plasma screen TV."

He made her laugh, and she liked that about him. She gave him a playful smile. "Okay, but if you're always watching TV, when will you have time to read all those books that are going to come out from under your sofa?" she teased.

He laughed.

Once they'd finished their breakfasts, the waitress cleared the table and refilled their coffee mugs.

He folded his hands and leaned forward on the table. "Tell me about your ideas for my condo."

The smooth way he said it indicated he had ideas that didn't have anything to do with his condo.

"I haven't worked out everything, but I have a couple of ideas." Olivia took her phone, notebook, and pen out and set it on the table. "True to my store's name, I like to try to reuse or upcycle. I keep an eye out for gently used kitchens or designer-display models." She took her phone out and handed it to him. "I sourced a beautiful set of cherry display cabinets that would work. If you're okay with used, you could get them for around two thousand, which is a steal."

"Those look great," he said.

He handed her back the phone, and their hands brushed. An electric charge tingled up her fingertips, up her arm, to the base of her throat.

Does Flicka feel this every time she meets some new man on some dating app?

She saw he was looking at her mouth. In case she had a piece of food on it, she licked her lower lip. His brown eyes took on a silvery brightness that made her brain go soft. A pleasantly dangerous feeling.

His voice was liquid and golden as honey, and he said, "I'm putting myself in your hands."

She was too old for her focus to get scrambled in a man's presence. But Flicka would tell her she wasn't.

Olivia swallowed. "Since you ... don't mind the second-hand cabinets, how do you feel about second-hand furniture?" she asked.

"How should I feel?" he asked. He wasn't looking her in the eye, but smiling vaguely. His eyes roamed over her face.

She opened her notebook and needlessly flipped a few pages just to have something to do. "You should feel like a good citizen.

I have a wealthy client who's changing her family room. She wants to pass on two gently used club chairs and a coffee-brown leather sofa."

"What, no more brown plaid?" He crossed his arms and sat back in his chair with a mock-insulted expression on his face.

She laughed again and said, "You hired me to redecorate, not keep the lovely decor you have." But that *wasn't* the only reason he'd hired her.

She rested her hand on the table, and he laid his over hers. She knew she should pull it away, but she didn't.

"Okay, if you're sure," he said.

She caught a whiff of him. Flannel and piney cologne mixed with the aroma of coffee and baked goods. Perfectly yummy. She nodded. "It's in pristine condition, and my client doesn't care, so you can have it for free."

His eyes darkened, and she was afraid she'd insulted him somehow. He said, "If you think it's the right furniture, I'll take it, but I want to pay her for it."

"I'm sorry," Olivia said. "I didn't mean to insinuate you couldn't afford it. It's just that my client has more money than God and she doesn't want or need the money. St. Paul's, where I attend church, is setting up a shelter for LGBTQ homeless youth. I'm involved in decorating it, choosing finishes for the kitchens, getting furniture, and raising funds. A donation to the fund will be sufficient."

He eased back in his chair and tucked his hands under his arms in a self-protective posture. "An LGBTQ homeless shelter for kids?"

The contours of his face shifted, and what she thought was misery rose into his eyes. It startled her because it was unlike anything she'd seen in his eyes before. Wounded, she decided. She prepared to tread lightly, but she was not going to give an inch of her belief that everyone belonged.

She stiffened her spine. "Yes, some parents can't get their heads around their kids not being straight, and they kick them out. It's inappropriate to put a kid in an adult shelter, so St. Paul's decided to start a youth shelter. There, the kids can feel safe and supported."

He sipped his coffee, considering something for a long while before speaking.

She braced for a salvo of homophobia.

He said, "It's great someone is helping to care for these kids. Makes growing up a helluva lot easier when they can be themselves from the get-go. Things are changing from when you and I were kids, but it's still got to be...," he sighed in a weary, heartbroken kind of way. "Hard."

"That's what we think, too," she agreed, relieved at his stance on a potentially prickly issue. "St. Paul's is having a barbecue this Sunday to raise money for the shelter."

He rested his forearms on the table, clasped his hands, and waited for the waitress to refill their coffee before speaking. "If it's open to the public, I'd like to come and support it."

The misery in his eyes lightened, and she wondered what had caused it to lift. For some reason, he cared deeply about the LGBTQ community. A lot of times, people cared only about those closest to them in his case, Matt, but Jack was broadly empathetic. That characteristic touched her.

"Everyone is welcome at St. Paul's," she said.

"Great! I'll bring Matt," he said with a grin. "He'll love a chance to see Ariel again."

Uh oh.

"And we'll get to see one another again," he added.

Olivia felt as though she was looking at two cars speeding head-on toward one another. She hadn't counted on his bringing Matt, but it was too late to rescind St. Paul's invitation of universal welcome.

She would simply have to be extra vigilant and make sure Ariel and Matt didn't get too friendly.

Olivia folded up her notebook and collected her things. "I should have some more ideas for you later in the week. I'll call you and let you know."

"I'll stop by the store, and we can have another chat," he said.

And his mouth, his luscious mouth, curved into the most dangerous, kissable grin.

CHAPTER 17

Some men see things as they are and say why. I dream of things
that never were and say why not.

Robert Kennedy

At the firehouse, Jack was mindlessly polishing some chrome on
the pumper. He didn't usually do these sorts of tasks, but today
he'd taken it up so he could think over his breakfast with Olivia.
Being with her made him happy in a way he hadn't been in a
long time. And he looked forward to being with her again, to
that feeling of coming home she gave him. She'd raised her kids
alone and run her own business at the same time. She was
smart, and for lack of a better word, durable. Maybe it was a
stretch to think she would take up with him, but with her
history, she could stand being partnered to a fireman.

The name of her store, Second Chance Designs, said it all.
She saw potential in battered things that needed fixing up.

He hoped she might even see potential in him.

He was putting away his rag when a strapping young man sauntered into the firehouse. Jack immediately recognized the kid as Olivia's son, Taylor. His brown curls stuck out from beneath his ball cap. He wore shorts that showed off tree stump thighs and a short-sleeved lacrosse tee shirt stretched across a powerful chest and biceps.

The kid was a moose, but Olivia was a pixie, so he definitely took after his dad.

"Hey," the kid said. "We met at St. Paul's when you came out on a call Sunday. I was helping, and you mentioned I should consider volunteering as a fireman." His face was open, friendly, but with a hint of nervousness in his eyes.

Jack held out his hand. "Jack O'Grady. I remember you."

"Thanks. Taylor Maxwell." The kid's handshake was firm, confident. No nerves there.

"Yes, I know your mom and sister," Jack said. "My nephew is Matt Wilson. He and Ariel are sweet on each other. Your mom's converting my man cave into an actual home."

Taylor smiled—his warmth was like Olivia's. "Oh, yeah, right," he said, "Ariel can't stop talking about Matt."

"Same with him," Jack said.

"I'd like to meet him sometime." Taylor grinned.

The glint in the kid's eyes was not unlike Olivia's. "I'm planning on bringing him to the St. Paul's barbecue on Sunday, so you'll meet him there," Jack said.

"That'll make Ariel happy," Taylor said.

But not Olivia, Jack thought

"But you didn't come in to chat about them. What can I do for you?" Jack asked.

Taylor's glance slid away. "Um, I wondered if you might have a couple minutes."

Jack motioned him into the firehouse and up to the second-floor break room.

Taylor took a seat at the long table, his leg jiggling a mile a minute.

Jack held the coffeepot out, his eyebrows raised in question.

"No, thanks, I'm good," Taylor said.

Jack poured himself a cup of coffee. He had a sinking feeling that he knew what the kid wanted. Jack had hoped Taylor would forget he'd ever mentioned volunteering.

Jack pulled out a chair and sat across from Taylor. "So, what can I do for you?"

The kid took a deep breath. "Like you suggested, I registered to volunteer, and I'm set to start the fireman's course. You've worked here for a long time, so I figure your word carries some weight. Since you saw me in action and stuff, I wondered if you would be willing to put in a good word for me." Quickly he added, "I mean, if I pass everything." His face had the hopeful look only a young person could have.

Oh, boy. One way to make sure Olivia never spoke to him again was to recommend Taylor for a job as a fireman.

Jack chose his words carefully. "Your mom mentioned you going back to school."

"When I said I didn't intend to go back to school, I meant it," Taylor said.

"I didn't mean to cause trouble between you two," Jack said.

Taylor's upper lip rolled up like he'd tasted a rotten apple. "I hate school, and I don't want to waste my mom's money. I'm not cut out for it. I loved being a volunteer EMT in high school, but the guys I really admired were the firemen." Taylor's cement-block jaw jutted. "That's what I want to do."

Jack scratched the back of his neck. "Are you sure about this? Firefighting is a big responsibility. A lot of risks. It calls for following orders and procedures. The first rule of firefighting is, get out alive. Not all the danger is in the fire. It's rare, and I've never seen it, but equipment fails, a hose could detach or rupture, ladders can collapse, a stabilizer could fail, an oxygen tank could run out. There's plenty of boring stuff. It's not all about smoke, fire, and heroic rescues."

"I know," Taylor said. "I've thought about being a firefighter for ages, and it's what I want to do. Just took a while to make up my mind." Taylor shrugged his Goliath's shoulders.

How the heck are you going to get out of this, blabbermouth? Jack thought.

To stall, he rose, refilled his coffee cup, and rummaged around in his brain for excuses and diversions. "I can see how your mom might not like you becoming a fireman. Not many moms do," Jack said.

"She's just got to get used to the idea," Taylor said.

Jack sat again and stirred his coffee. "What about doing a couple more years, say at Norwalk Community College? Maybe give yourself time to be sure it's what you really want, then take the fireman's exam."

The kid laid his meat-hook fists on the table. If all it took was size, he would make a stupendous firefighter, but balls had a lot to do with it, too. That and an unwavering sense of duty.

Taylor said, "I know what I want, even if my mom wants me to do what she wants. Will you help me?"

He certainly was driven.

Jack silently kicked himself. First, he'd encouraged the kid, but now he was trying to discourage him. He wasn't a man to yank back a suggestion, especially since he'd have to say something along the lines of, '*Sorry, I was wrong. You're ill-suited to be a fireman because I'm hot for your mom.*' Olivia had accepted his apology this morning, but if he agreed to help Taylor, she'd feel hurt and that she'd trusted the wrong guy. Jack had ruined things not just for himself, but probably for Matt and Ariel.

The best Jack could do was stall. "Let's see how you do on the exams, and then we'll see if I can do anything."

Jack saw his chances of a relationship with Olivia growing smaller by the minute.

CHAPTER 18

Danger gleams like sunshine to a brave man's eyes.
Euripides

An hour after Olivia called Jack to invite him to look at the rest of the designs for his condo, he appeared at the store.

Maybe he'd thought she was on fire. And sort of, she was. He kept popping into her mind in all sorts of scenes: stretched out on his leather sofa, cooking in his new kitchen, sprawled on his new bed on crisp, white sheets.

Before calling him, she took a bottle of cold water from the fridge and drank it in one go.

Now, she opened her design board with pictures of tiles, fixtures, samples of carpet, and paint colors on the worktable. They settled on stools on opposite sides of her worktable.

It was good to keep distance between them.

Jack hadn't brought Matt, and Ariel was at her grocery store job, so they could concentrate on the design work.

"I think I can save your condo from terminal bachelorism," she said.

"Okay, show me what you got," he said and laughed. That laugh was like the taste of chocolate on the back of her tongue. Like the trickle of warm water down her body. Like ... *Fireman!*

She swallowed and concentrated on the design board. "Take a look at these. I chose these tiles for the kitchen backsplash with this counter. Sleek, but with a modern look."

He said, "As long as they don't fall off the back of a truck, whatever you think will be fine."

She laughed. She liked that they made one another laugh. His trust in her to create a home where he would be comforted and safe meant more to her than it ever had with any other client. As though he was giving himself over to her.

He crooked his neck to get a better look at the board. "I'm going to come around the table and sit next to you. That way, neither of us has to look at this upside down."

He moved around the table and took the stool next to her.

She stroked a fabric sample on the board. "I like this fabric for the living room curtains. It's voluptuous."

He was so close it was like being in a force field that drew her to him. His body filled the space beside her with a suggestion of dangerous pleasure.

"I love voluptuous," he whispered, his breath feathering her ear.

Her finger trembled as she pointed to the paint color, a cool grayish blue called Ocean Air, which she'd chosen for the living room. "I'm taking inspiration from the ocean outside your balcony window. I want to bring the ocean and sky right into your home."

His eyes were on her, not the granite, when she showed him the sample for the countertops. He said, "I love all it. Hard, but with flecks of beautiful color."

She flapped her blouse away from her chest before she knew what she was doing. "This is ... the carpet ... the carpet sample," she managed.

Tenderly, taking his time, he caressed sample and murmured, "Whatever you want, whatever you want."

Oh, she wanted all right, and that was the problem.

She wanted to *not* want this dangerous desire. She wanted safety, not these risky roller-coaster, gut-dropping feelings for a man who put out fires for a living. How could she object to Taylor being a fireman when she was attracted to one?

Their shoulders bumped, and she felt the hard muscles beneath his plaid flannel shirt. Good God, why had she let him sit close to her? He sucked out all the oxygen and replaced it with something that made her lightheaded.

Out of the blue, he said, "You mentioned you were widowed. How long?"

This wasn't something she usually discussed with clients or with men whose eyes devoured her. "Eighteen years," she said.

"How did your husband die?" he asked. Then added, "If it's not too personal a question."

A tight fist of grief grabbed her behind her breastbone. "I don't like to talk about it."

"Sorry." He swiped his big hand over the carpet sample again. "You never remarried?" he asked in a gently probing tone.

She gave her canned answer. "No, I never met the right person. And you?"

"Same. Nobody right ever turned up," he said.

His gaze suggested that he expected her to ask more about his divorce, but she kept her attention on the board. Mercifully, he straightened on his stool, giving her room to breathe.

She launched into a recitation of colors, carpet, cabinet knobs, hardware, and floor tiles.

"I have all the time in the world to be with you," he said in a voice as liquid as red wine. "You can slow down, you know."

She smiled at him. "Was I talking too fast?"

"Like you were in a race." The corner of his mouth twitched up in a smile, and her thoughts rattled around in her brain like an earthquake had shaken them off a shelf.

She busied herself putting away the board and samples. "Sorry, I didn't mean to rush. That's everything, though."

"It's okay," he said and stood. "Once the renovation starts, will you be at my place a lot? Should I give you a key?"

She'd often gotten keys from clients to let herself in when they weren't home. With Jack, getting a copy of his key had a weighty significance that she wasn't ready to take on, but the alternative meant going to his home when he was there. She wasn't sure which was more dangerous.

"I'll leave that up to you to decide," she said, taking the chicken's way out. This time, she was willing to accept the label.

He reached into his pocket, and the scar on his arm flashed. His fireman's scar. The scar like Derek's.

Her belly clenched.

Did Jack have more scars? What did they mean to him?

He drew a key out of his pocket. "Even if I didn't trust you, what would you abscond with…my empty beer can collection?"

She stared at the key in his hand for a split second too long. She found the courage to look at him, and his smile—seductive, or was that her imagination—promised heat and pleasure. Pleasure that would be so nice to sink into. To allow herself to be made love to, to give pleasure in return. Pleasure she hadn't had for so very long. That her body, and her mind, was on the brink of giving into.

She cocked her head and smiled back at him. "How do you know I don't love empty beer cans?"

He laughed. "You don't seem like the type."

He made her forget what type she was. Slowly, she raised her open hand.

He placed the key, still warm from being nestled in his hip pocket, into her palm. Taking her hand, he closed her fingers around the key. His hand was like having a shot of sunshine wrap around her fist.

"I trust you," he said.

But she was beginning not to trust herself.

CHAPTER 19

And lead us not into temptation but deliver us from evil.
Matthew 6:13

Father Gabriel, rector of St. Paul's on the Green in Norwalk, gazed at the lawn of the Chittim-Howell house where his parishioners were spread out on blankets and seated in folding chairs.

Every night, he thanked the Lord for sending these people into his life. They were big-hearted, caring, compassionate, loved radically, committed, and generous. Except when the annual pledge drive rolled around. Then they seemed to have forgotten everything that had happened in the parish the year before.

Formerly the rectory, the Chittim-Howell house was a two-story, white clapboard house with green shutters and a deep wrap-around porch. The house sat next to the church and contained the church offices and a small art gallery. In front of the house was a massive oak tree with a tire swing. There was a long swath of lawn where, after their practices, choristers kicked soccer balls and played tag. Parishioners seeking advice came to sit in Gabe's second-floor office. There, he let them come to their own conclusions on how to solve their problems. The house was as much a beacon to the community as the spire of St. Paul's was.

Today, Gabe had worn his short-sleeved black clerical shirt, madras plaid shorts, and topsiders that made him look like a sixteen-year-old masquerading as a preppie priest. There didn't seem to be anything that made him look older or wiser.

On this Sunday afternoon in early May, the breeze was swift but light, like the brush of angel wings. The smell of smoke, roasting hamburgers and hot dogs wafted from the grill and made his bottomless appetite roar to life. The laughter and the squeals of children running around were music as sweet to his ears as any hymn.

This barbecue was another of the Marriage Survivors Club's tirelessly innovative ways of wringing money out of the community of St. Paul's and Norwalk at large. Today's event aimed to raise funds for the LGBTQ youth shelter. Several other organizations from all over Norwalk had joined the effort to raise money, and as a result, there were many faces that Gabe didn't recognize.

Gabe joined the line to the smoking grill that snaked across the lawn. A blue shade canopy stretched over a wood-fired grill where Sam Wanamaker and his husband, Darren, flipped burgers and hot dogs and squabbled lovingly.

"That's way too much wood. You'll turn everything to charcoal," Sam said, waving away the billowing smoke.

"No, it won't. It's fine," Darren squabbled back.

To Gabe, there was a great deal more smoke and flame than necessary to cook the meat, but he wasn't dumb enough to get in the middle of that marital disagreement.

"What'll it be, Father, hot dog or hamburger?" Darren asked when it was Gabe's turn.

Gabe gave them a rueful smile. "I would like one of each, but my waistline has been burgeoning a bit lately, so just make it a hamburger, no bun, please."

After Darren had loaded up his plate, Gabe made his way into the tent, where sides and desserts were temptingly laid out on two tables. He helped himself to some of Gracie's curried potato salad, and, instead of the hamburger bun, he grabbed a slice of Death-by-Chocolate Cake before it disappeared. Desserts were his personal temptation, and Satan usually won.

Gabe spotted Flicka headed his way, and by the mischievous glint in her eye, he could tell she was up to something. Flicka was exuberantly loving, and meddlesome. She was a great champion of the church, gossiping, loving, and fundraising. She pissed some people off and enveloped others into the congregation. Gabe adored her, though sometimes, he had the not-very-spiritual inspiration to dunk her head in the baptismal font.

She had in tow a hulking, drop-dead gorgeous guy in shorts and a green polo shirt. She was determined to see Gabe married off, but even after three years, his heart was in no hurry to move along.

Flicka swizzled up to him with a sly smile. "Father Gabriel, I want to introduce you to a new potential parishioner I invited. This is Randy Connors." She leaned in and theatrically lowered her voice. "He's a firefighter."

Gabe tried not to stare, but it was impossible. Randy was beefy and rugged, with a chiseled chin and biceps like he spent all his time lifting fire engines. Not at all Gabe's type, but excellent eye candy. It wasn't likely that Randy was inclined towards men who preferred prayer and dessert over sweating and exercise.

Gabe shook Randy's hand and said, "Nice to meet you. I'm glad you picked today to come. The food is great, and the company is better."

Showing his white teeth and a single, charming dimple, Randy smiled and said, "I've heard a lot about St. Paul's, but I've never been."

"Flicka's a great ambassador. Everyone is always welcome at St. Paul's, no matter who you are," Gabe said and pointed to the food table. "Help yourself. We're glad you decided to join us."

Flicka hovered behind them, eavesdropping, no doubt. After they finished chatting, she pounced. "Let me introduce you to some more people," she said to the firefighter.

She steered Randy off. Poor man didn't even have any food yet.

"Hey, Father, over here," Bianca called and waved him over to where other Marriage Survivors Club members––Olivia, Frankie, Hélène, and Carolina––had gathered on blankets spread on the grass. Bianca scooted over so he had room to sit on a corner.

Gabe settled himself on the blanket and took a bite of his cake, closing his eyes in chocolate bliss. The burger could wait.

Wat Crabtree, his organist and choir director, was sitting beside Carolina Singh. Wat said, "I'm thinking our next fundraiser might be a concert."

"What kind of concert?" Carolina asked.

"Classical piano. I was hoping we could get someone famous," Wat said, and he took a bite of hotdog.

Gabe was not a risk-taker. Thinking of the expense, the cake turned to rubber in his mouth, and he forced the lump down his throat. When he'd swallowed, he said, "A famous person will be expensive. That'll be a big risk. We'd have to charge a lot for tickets to recoup the costs."

"Oh, no, we'd ask them to donate their time." Wat turned to Hélène and said, "I know most of your students are kids." Wat circled his fork in the air. "But I wondered if you might know someone who knows someone who could do this. Or maybe you know someone yourself."

Hélène's delicate, already pale face drained of color, and she looked positively faint.

"Me? Oh, I don't know anyone," Hélène squeaked. "I need some more lemonade." She rose and scurried away.

Gabe frowned. Hélène never scurried. She floated like a song on the breeze.

To Wat, Carolina said, "The Marriage Survivors Club will look into it and see what we can do. When are you thinking of doing this?"

Gabe lost track of the conversation because Cam Simpson dropped onto the blanket beside his beloved Frankie.

"I never knew how much fun it would be to play basketball with my soon-to-be son," Cam said. Despite breathing hard, he was grinning.

Funny, what gave people joy. It wasn't big houses, money, or fancy cars, but love, a sense of belonging, a purpose, and family. St. Paul's was all about those things.

Cam lifted Frankie's hand to his mouth and kissed it like a love-sick teenager. Her smile was rapturous, and, leaning into him, she giggled.

That was a sound Gabe *never* thought he'd hear out of her mouth.

"Can you tell her to marry me, Father?" Cam pleaded. "She won't listen to me."

Frankie had been wearing a sapphire surrounded by diamonds for a while now, and it twinkled against the dark skin of her hand. She and Cam were well-matched and clearly adored one another, but Gabe understood her reticence. Marriage wasn't for everybody, gay or straight.

Gabe answered, "Much as I love performing weddings, I never try to convince Frankie of anything, Cam." Gabe laughed at Cam's frustration. "I learned that a while ago, and I encourage you to heed it as well."

Cam said, "I'm warning you, Frankie. I'm a very patient man." Smiling, Cam flopped back on the blanket. Frankie bent and kissed him, and Cam smiled even wider.

On the next blanket over, Olivia was sitting with Ariel. "Is Taylor here?" Gabe asked Olivia.

Olivia pointed to her son, chatting with Randy Connors over by the dessert table.

Gabe didn't know how he'd missed seeing Taylor. He'd grown into a big, broad, and brawny man. Gabe remembered when Taylor had been a shy high school kid waiting to grow into his awkwardly over-sized body and to find his own personality. He was a man now. When Taylor had sprung into action with Carol Baxter, he'd displayed self-possession and calm beyond his years. He was a fine person, and Gabe hoped Olivia was proud of having raised such a good son.

"Nice having him home from college?" Gabe asked.

Olivia gave him an eye roll that spoke volumes of exasperation, love, and annoyance.

Gabe laughed. "If I can help in any way, let me know," he said, but really, aside from having been one himself, what did he know about teenagers?

Olivia said, "Pray for me. I need all the help I can get."

That Gabe could do.

CHAPTER 20

You must trust and believe in people, or life becomes
impossible.

Anton Chekhov

From her spot on the picnic blanket, Olivia caught sight of
Gracie, pregnant with twins, waddling across the grass with the
elegance of a truck with two flat tires.

"We're meeting at your place next week, Carolina, to plan
Gracie's baby shower, right?" Olivia asked. Carolina's eyes nearly
popped out of her head when she saw Gracie. She nodded in
silent amazement. "We'd better hurry up."

"Hope she doesn't sit down," Bianca said. "We'd need a crane
to get her back on her feet."

Giggling, Carolina poked Bianca with her bare foot. "Yes,
we're meeting at my place. I've sketched out some ideas for food
and decorations."

"No stupid party games, though, okay?" Bianca said. Then
she added, "Except maybe beer pong."

Olivia stretched her legs out on the blanket and lifted her face to the sun. It was just cool enough that she pulled her sweater closer around her. Overhead, trees shimmered their bright green leaves, and the grass was thick and springy as a carpet. She loved watching everyone enjoy this successful event she'd help put on. After enduring several days of Taylor skulking around the house and avoiding her, it was a joy to be with the Marriage Survivors Club and her other friends from church.

The guttural roar of a motorcycle pulling up to the curb ran over Olivia's moment of pleasure. The riders dismounted, pulled off their helmets, and shed their leather jackets.

Olivia stared in disbelief. Jack O'Grady and Matt.

A fireman who owned a motorcycle? Did the man have a death wish?

A mass of red-hot emotions tangled in her chest. Jack said he would come, but she hadn't believed him, but she'd hoped he would. Jack, who was her design client.

Jack, who was encouraging her son to throw himself into the dangers of firefighting.

Jack, who was pushing her daughter and his nephew together.

Jack, who thought her daughter should live in a group home.

Jack, who made her feel as if electricity sparked in her veins.

Olivia wasn't sure if she wanted to strangle him or rip off his clothes and take a look at his fire hose.

Ariel, with her wobbly walk, was already making a beeline for Matt. Taylor was right in her wake, grinning and waving at Jack. They'd only met once, so why was Taylor acting as if they were old buddies?

Olivia jumped up from the blanket as gracefully as possible. To her friends, she said, "Excuse me, I have to keep an eye on Ariel," and she hightailed it toward her children.

Taylor, usually his sister's protector, didn't seem to notice that Matt and Ariel were in the early stages of canoodling because he was talking animatedly to Jack.

The bike, all chrome, leather, and power, looked to Olivia like suicide on wheels. She could barely stand it when Taylor first learned to ride a bike, and she grounded him if she caught him without his helmet. How anyone could tempt fate by riding a motorcycle was beyond her. It was yet another strike against Jack O'Grady, the hot fireman.

Jack smiled. "Hello, Olivia," Jack said, with a voice that caressed her ear like a feather on silk.

He sported a shadow of a beard, which gave him a rakish and lascivious appeal. His gaze was uncomfortably penetrating. It made her want to move back as though she'd stepped too close to a hot stove.

"Hi. I didn't know you rode a motorcycle," she managed to say.

Jack stuffed his leather jacket into a side bag on the bike. "I've had 'er for about ten years. I rode cross-country after my divorce."

"But motorcycles are dangerous," Olivia squeaked out.

"Not if you know what you're doing, which I do," Jack said with a grin. "And motorcycles can be fun on a warm, beautiful day like today."

Taylor was too involved in examining the motorcycle to pay attention to Olivia. She wanted to bat him away from the killing machine.

Jack rolled up his shirtsleeves, revealing the scar on his left arm. A scar like Derek's. Why were men so attracted to life-threatening activities? Was it bravery or stupidity that made them step to the edge of life and balance on the precipice of death? And why did it fall to women to save men from themselves and the idiotic things they did?

"Maybe you and I can take a ride sometime," Jack said coaxingly. Hopefully.

She waved her hands in a not-on-your-life gesture. "Not bloody likely. Way too dangerous."

"I wouldn't let anything happen to you," he said.

His voice seduced her risk-averse heart into submission. Instead of *no*, her mind said *maybe*. A short ride around a parking lot wouldn't hurt. It would mean putting her arms around his waist and holding on. Pressing her chest against his back. The idea reminded her how long it had been since she'd leaned against a man and listened to his heartbeat beneath her cheek. How long since she'd been kissed senseless. How dangerous love could be.

Jack smiled and said, "This looks like a great picnic."

"Yeah, and I met Randy Connors—another firefighter from your station is here," Taylor said, pointing.

Jack waved at the hulking man. Olivia looked at the spot where Ariel and Matt had been standing, which was now empty. Somehow, while daydreaming about a motorcycle ride, Olivia had lost track of Ariel. Her heart gave a lurch. That was what happened when she wasn't paying attention.

She looked around, panicked. "Where are Ariel and Matt?"

Taylor jutted his chin toward the swing on the Chittam-Howell porch. "Chill, Mom. They're over there. They're fine."

Ariel's head rested on Matt's shoulder, and they held hands like any young couple.

Olivia remembered the thrill she used to feel holding hands with Derek. The warmth of his long fingers entwined with her own, and how their hearts beat together in a mutual agreement of ownership. But seeing Ariel and Matt snuggling together was the equivalent of a flaming meteor smashing into Olivia's face. She took a step toward them.

Taylor said sharply, "Leave them be, Mom. They're fine."

"You don't—" she started.

"Leave them alone," Taylor insisted, his eyes throwing sparks. He seemed determined to follow his own crazy path and drag Ariel into danger as well. Olivia didn't want to create a scene in front of Jack. He might think she was overly protective.

Ariel was grinning. She was ... happy. A profound sense of pride and loss filled her. Olivia's eyes grew damp. Her children were growing up in unpredictable ways and if Olivia hated anything, it was unpredictability.

Jack must have noticed her staring at Ariel and Matt because he lightly touched Olivia's arm. Jack said, "I know you know more about people with Down than I do, but Matt hasn't stopped talking about Ariel since they met. He'd never hurt her. He's a kind person."

Olivia prickled. Why was he in such a rush to push the kids together? "I appreciate that you honor Matt's attraction to Ariel—"

"Their mutual attraction, you mean?" Jack said.

Did he always have to be right?

"Well, yes," she admitted reluctantly. "The consequences could be catastrophic if he hurt her. Disabled people endure sexual assault six more times than the general population. Anyone, even Matt, might talk her into something. What if she were to get pregnant?"

Jack gazed at Olivia with compassion and understanding that made her knees feel watery.

Gently, he said, "My sister and her husband had Matt sterilized because they didn't want him to be responsible for getting a woman pregnant."

Olivia was speechless for a moment. Olivia had long put off having Ariel's tubes tied or putting her on birth control because she had always made certain this kind of situation never arose. There was no pill for preventing heartbreak.

Olivia wanted Ariel to be somewhat independent, but not so independent that she fell in love.

Ariel knew to call 911 if something terrible happened. She knew every escape route out of the house in case of fire. She always wore her seatbelt. She knew not to talk to strangers, not to go in deep water even though she could swim, not to give her address to anyone over the phone, to lock the front door, and turn on the alarm when she was alone.

But there was no way Olivia could protect Ariel from heartbreak.

Jack nodded at the kids rocking gently on the swing. "Want to take a walk before you have a stroke over their mutual affection?" he said with that carefree voice of his.

She stared down at the palm of his big, solid, proffered hand. Jack, a motorcycle-riding fireman, had no concept of what danger was. He had no idea how you could be left with a hole in your heart if you didn't pay attention. He had no holes in his heart, nothing that made him wary.

"Don't worry, I'll keep an eye on them," Taylor said. "You have my word on it," he added firmly.

Jack tilted his head inquisitively. "We can't take a walk together unless you come with me."

She was a fool to trust him. She knew this down to her bone marrow, but she placed her hand in his anyway. It felt like the bravest thing she had done in ages.

CHAPTER 21

> The pursuit of truth and beauty is a sphere of activity in which
> we are permitted to remain children all our lives.
>   **Albert Einstein**

Olivia held Jack's hand as they crossed St. Paul's Way and went over to the Town Green. It felt ... right. Safe, even. They strolled down one of the wide brick paths toward the gazebo. Somehow, the air temperature had gone up twenty degrees. She paused to shed her sweater.

Jack stopped to loop the arms of her sweater around her neck. His warm, reassuring smile made her want to lay her palms on his chest, to let go of the anxiety quavering behind her breastbone. She wanted him to be her safe place, but as a fire-fighter, he couldn't be.

Jack pointed to the yellow daffodils and red and white parrot tulips circling the gazebo. "Aren't the flowers beautiful?" he said.

He wasn't just a danger-flouting, risk-taker. He noticed

things. He saw her. And she wasn't certain how she felt about that yet.

"Tulips are my favorite, and these are magnificent," she breathed.

"Do you have a favorite color?" he asked.

"The ones with two colors. They're called parrot tulips," she said.

"I'll remember that," he said.

"And it's such a beautiful day." She tipped her head back. "Look how blue and silky the sky is."

He moved in front of her and smiled down. She tried to fix on the tiny mole above his eyebrow, but his gaze hooked into hers.

He said, "I've never heard it described that way. I like the unique way you see things. How important is beauty and making others comfortable to you."

Surprised, she blinked. No one had ever said anything like that to her and it sent a liquid pleasure through her. "Thank you," she said.

He nodded to the gazebo. "Sit a minute?"

Once they were seated, Jack leaned forward and braced his elbows on his knees, his forehead wrinkled. She sensed him thinking deeply about something.

He asked, "How disappointed are you that Taylor wants to be a fireman?"

Why had he asked her that? It hardly mattered. But how she felt about it mattered to Jack.

She sighed. "It's like he drove a stake through my heart when he told me he didn't want to be a doctor. I can't help thinking that if I said the right thing, I could change his mind."

He reached over and took her hand again. She didn't remember when they'd reached a hand-holding level, but it was comforting.

He said, "You're scared of him getting hurt. I get it. All good moms are scared of letting go of their kids, but for some reason, you're more scared than others."

She knew this about herself because the Marriage Survivors Club teased and prodded her about it. Jack had noticed her fear and remained attracted to her. He really was brave.

"I don't know how to not be scared," she admitted. "I'm not brave like you. You ride that stupid motorcycle, run into burning buildings and face death all the time. It's not possible for me not to be afraid for Taylor." She stared down at her hands, fingers tangled together in her lap. "And I'm afraid Ariel will fall in love and have her heart broken."

"Who said firefighters aren't scared?" Jack scoffed. "If they're not, they're idiots. But we depend on one another—we know the others have our backs. We have our training. You've had nineteen years of training Taylor and twenty-two with Ariel before having to let them go. That's more than firefighters ever get." He swiveled his head back to grin at her. "By most yardsticks, you're an elite, fire-jumping mom."

She laughed, a little sadly. "I never thought of it that way."

He bumped against her shoulder gently. Very gently. "Every parent has to let their kids go, Olivia."

"A lot of help you are."

He gave her hand a squeeze, and she felt as bright and sunny inside as the yellow daffodils. Something about him had that effect on her.

"There's something else I wanted to mention," he said, more solemnly now.

"You sound serious," she said, worried.

"Well, I don't want you to get you upset," he said.

"I make no promises." She bumped against his shoulder gently.

He scooted closer to her. "Matt's group home has a room

coming open in the ladies' house in a couple of weeks. I know you like having her around and at home, but I thought you might be interested. I had them send you an application."

She glanced over toward the church and saw Matt and Ariel rocking on the porch swing. She felt a hard lump at the back of her throat, and it was a moment before she could speak. "I knew Taylor would go, but I never thought I'd have to let Ariel go. I thought she'd be with me until my last breath."

He nodded. "I know every staff member at Matt's house. They're great, and it's very safe. I have all their phone numbers, and they have mine. I can call anytime and talk with staff, and Matt can call me whenever he wants."

"It's scary to think of Ariel living somewhere that I can't check on her all the time," Olivia said, embarrassed to confess her fears to Jack. "I think I'm the only one who can keep her safe." He probably thought she was a little crazy, but she didn't care. She loved her children because she knew that your heart could get smashed in an instant. And that instant could shape the rest of your life.

"I can imagine," he said.

She squinted into the too-bright sunlight. "I don't know if it's ... the right time."

"For you or for her?" he asked. He had her there.

"Thank you," she said, and smiled at him.

"For what?" he said.

"For understanding and not making fun of me," she said.

"Sometime will you tell me why you're so scared?"

His eyes drew her toward him, and she leaned against his shoulder. "Why?" she asked.

"Because maybe I can help you not be so scared," he said.

He inclined his head down towards her, and his gaze dropped to her lips. He was near enough that she thought she smelled smoke lingering in his hair and clothes. He pulled her closer, lowered his face to hers and kissed her lightly, then with more insistence.

Her body felt alive and feminine, and much to her surprise, hungry. When she came up for air, she said, "Whew!" She blinked to find her own center of gravity again.

"I agree." His whole face smiled, then he grew somber. "I know we don't know each other all that well, but I want to know you better. I want to help you not be afraid and to comfort you when you are. To talk you down off a ledge. I want something substantial with you. It doesn't have to be marriage, but I want something long-term."

She felt her stomach tip sideways. She hadn't expected any of this. Not a kiss or the suggestion of a long-term relationship. She hardly knew anything about him.

Olivia got up and meandered around the gazebo. "I don't know. The whole firefighter thing ... I've made it a rule not to date men in dangerous careers."

One corner of his mouth tipped into a smile. "You should have warned me about that before I kissed you."

She wasn't exactly sure if he was joking or not. She turned back to him. "That scar on your arm. Did you get that in a fire?"

"This?" He pushed back his sleeve and displayed the dark-pink, waxy, eight-inch-long scar. A bolt of fear shot from the roots of her hair to the soles of her feet. He pulled his sleeve down as he said, "No, I got it years ago defending a young lady at a bar."

She wasn't sure if that was gallant or foolhardy. "You got into a bar fight?" She came back and sat next to his solid, reliable self.

"Not technically," he said. "This guy was harassing her, and I told him to knock it off, but he wouldn't. When I insisted that he leave, he broke a beer bottle on the bar and took a swing at me instead. Me and my buddy threw him out of the bar."

She detected a note of well-deserved pride in his voice. She relaxed back onto the bench next to him. "And the girl?"

"I married her. Gina Lacosta."

Something about the way he said her name made Olivia wonder how his ex had broken his heart. Jack twined his fingers through Olivia's. His hand was rough and warm and sure. But was it the kind of hand she could hold on to? Or would she hold it while standing beside a hospital bed and saying her last goodbye?

She said, "Why did you get divorced?"

"Because Gina came out as gay." His eyes revealed a pain lingering inside of him.

Of course, she knew it happened, but Olivia had never expected that answer. "I'm sorry. I wish I knew the right thing to say."

Jack said, "Listening is all that's important. I didn't have a clue beforehand." He sighed. "She stopped wanting to have sex and started staying late at the office. There were some weekend business trips when she didn't pick up her phone. After about six months, I finally asked her if she was having an affair, and she 'fessed up." He stared off into the distance. "We'd been good together, you know? Two girls, a house, a life."

"It must have come as a shock." She rubbed his hand between her palms.

"The shocking part was that she was in love with another woman. I know people come out at different times in their lives, but it knocked me sideways."

She asked, "Was the divorce a knock-down drag-out?"

He shook his head. "Gina was honorable. She bought me out of the house and gave me part of her pension. She'd always had a high-powered job and made more money than me. That never bothered me."

He was a man with many kinds of courage. He didn't shy

away from talking about the hard stuff. He made her feel desired, and for all the danger his job entailed, he made her feel safe.

He continued, "I felt stupid when it happened." Another admission that took courage.

"Why?" she asked.

He said, "Like I'd missed the obvious clues during our marriage. Like I'd been living one marriage and Gina a different one. After we split, I rode my motorcycle to California to clear my head." He sat back against the bench and propped one ankle on the other knee. "All I could think of was that my marriage had been one long joke. I felt like I'd wasted my life loving someone who didn't really love me back. That our love hadn't been real. Like everyone knew about Gina except me."

A whiff of smoke from the grill drifted over from the church. And something else, the sharp odor of plastic. That was the way your insides smelled when they were melting down.

Olivia felt his grief and self-blame, the loneliness that creeps up and gnaws at you before you realize that you are in the mouth of something lethal and can't extricate yourself.

Jack said, "We'd been together for twenty-five years, and I thought life was worthless without Gina. I kind of gave up living." His expression was one of rueful humor. "I guess that's why I let my house turn into a slum." He gazed at her with sparks of hope in his eyes. "I thought I'd had my one shot at love. Until you walked into my life, then everything seemed worthwhile again."

She let Jack gather her against him. She nestled her head into the curve of his shoulder. The light changed from wan to blazing May, and the sky was wider and higher than ever. The red and white of the tulips intensified as though they'd only just burst forth. The laughter of the children in the churchyard was like music.

Jack said, "There's one more thing I wanted to mention to you. Taylor came to see—"

A plume of swirling black smoke caught Olivia's eye. She jerked out of Jack's embrace. She couldn't speak. She pointed.

He stared across the street.

At the church picnic, fire danced against the sky. Black smoke billowed. Orange flames licked the canopy over the grill. The stink of burning nylon wafted on the wind.

Carried by the wind, sparks had alighted on blankets and trash in the garbage bin.

On blankets and lawn chairs, a dozen small fires had flared up.

Sparks landed on the roof of the Chittim-Howell house.

Screams shattered the laughter as people scrambled for safety.

Jack vaulted off the gazebo and ran.

She hadn't been paying attention. She'd let her guard down. The fist of her heart pounded in her chest. Adrenaline launched Olivia to her feet.

She had to save Taylor and Ariel.

She followed Jack at a dead run.

CHAPTER 22

Teach your children poetry; it opens the mind, lends grace to wisdom and makes the heroic virtues hereditary.

Walter Scott

Taylor saw Ariel and Matt snuggled up, swinging on the porch swing.

Directly over their heads, smoke spiraled into the sky.

Taylor vaulted out of his seat and screamed, "Ariel! Fire! Run!"

His legs ate up the lawn. His heart thundered, but oddly, his mind was a laser that could have cut diamonds. He heard nothing, felt only the ground beneath his feet, saw only the flames as though through a pinhole.

He knew precisely what to do.

Taylor saw Ariel grab Matt by the hand and, like Taylor and Mom had taught her, she took off as fast as she could. She led Matt to the farthest corner of the yard.

Good girl, Squirt! Once he saw she was okay, Taylor pivoted toward the blue nylon canopy, which was engulfed in flames. Jack was running hell's bells, and they converged on the canopy at the same instant.

Randy, Taylor, Jack, and Father Gabriel each yanked a canopy pole out of the ground. Without a word, in sync, they walked the canopy away from the crowd and over to the parking lot and dropped it on the asphalt.

Someone swept around the corner of the house with the hose and soaked the flames.

"That was close," Jack said, panting hard.

To Taylor's relief, people had stomped out all the small fires. Everything seemed under control when Father Gabriel pointed to the porch roof. "Oh, Lord, no!" he moaned.

Tendrils of smoke were curling up from the roof.

Taylor said to Jack, "Boost me." To Randy, Taylor said, "Once I'm up, pass me the hose."

Jack made a hand hammock.

Taylor clambered up and stood on Jack's shoulders. Taylor hoisted himself up onto the ancient cedar-shingled roof.

Randy handed a kinked hose up to Taylor.

Taylor took the hose, sprayed the roof, and extinguished the smoldering embers that could have burned the hundred-year-old house to ashes.

A pumper engine and ambulance pulled up, but they weren't necessary. Everything was done. Cheers erupted from the picnickers.

Taylor eased himself down from the roof.

Father Gabriel crushed him in a bear hug. "Thank you, thank you," he said. "Thank God you were all here."

Taylor and Randy slapped each other on the back. Parishioners shook Taylor's hand, congratulating him, exclaiming relief.

Taylor felt not exactly heroic, but more alive. Every cell,

blood vessel, muscle, and nerve ending were firing together. It was as if his life had snapped into place. He didn't have to think about being safe. He didn't hear his mom's warnings. In those glorious seconds, his entire life's purpose was to keep *others* safe.

This was why he wanted to be a firefighter. There was nothing like the rush of saving someone or something, of being first on the scene of an accident, of helping. It made him feel competent and capable.

He was meant to face flames.

Then, his mom came scurrying across the lawn, her eyes round as a scared mouse's. She was so out of breath she could barely speak. "Taylor, you ... could have been ... killed. You scared the––the living daylights out of me. You could have caught on fire, fallen off the roof, or inhaled too much smoke."

"Mom! Back off!" Taylor said. "I'm not a kid anymore."

She looked stunned and took a few steps back.

Bianca took Olivia by the elbow. "As your lawyer, I advise you not to say anything else until you've had a shot of tequila."

Thank God for the Marriage Survivors' Club.

Ariel came up and threw her arms around Taylor. "You hero, Tay Tay."

Taylor grinned down and hugged his sister. "It's cool, Squirt."

Matt put his arms around Jack. "Uncle Jack, I'm glad you're okay. You're my hero. I don't want you to get hurt."

Jack hugged Matt. "It's okay, buddy. Don't worry. I'm not going to get hurt. I couldn't leave my best pal."

"Don't leave your best pal," Matt said, staring up lovingly at Jack.

His mom was still standing there in shock. Carolina gave her a glass of something and Bianca made her drink it. That should stop her panic.

Randy came up to Taylor and slapped him on the back.

"Congrats. Jack mentioned you had stopped by the firehouse to talk to him. He said you wanted him to talk to the bosses about getting hired. I can see that you'll make a great firefighter. We'll both be happy to put in a word for you, too."

"Thanks, man. I appreciate it," Taylor said.

His mom's jaw dropped. To Jack, she said, "You didn't say anything about Taylor stopping by the firehouse or asking for your help." Her voice was an angry squeak.

With a guilty look on his face, Jack said, "I was getting to that when—"

"And to think I kissed you!" his mom said.

Ugh.

His mom kissing Jack O'Grady, or anybody for that matter, was not something Taylor wanted to think about. He had more important things on his mind, like following his dream.

CHAPTER 23

Good actions ennoble us, and we are the sons of our deeds.
Miguel de Cervantes

The next morning, Taylor was basking in the glow of talking to Dani. He'd told her about helping to put out the fire, how it made him feel. She'd praised him, but she'd seemed kind of distant, which wasn't how she'd been when they left school.

Since he'd returned home, they'd both been so busy it had been hard to connect except by text. He was looking forward to her support, for her to cheer on his goal of being a fireman. He didn't understand why she'd sounded kind of like she wanted to get off the phone.

Before leaving school, they planned for him to visit her in Charlottesville on Memorial Day weekend. They had firmed up plans, but she didn't seem too hot on the idea. On the other hand, he was totally stoked to climb some of the spots around Charlottesville.

And, of course, to screw their brains out.

He'd hung up and was lacing up his sneakers when his mom

appeared in the kitchen doorway. She'd been hovering more than usual since the fire, probably so she could ream him out some more. He was so over that.

She leaned against the doorframe, wiping her hands on a dishtowel. "Want to go get ice cream?"

He didn't look up but kept lacing his sneakers. "I promised to take Ariel and Matt bowling."

"Oh," she said, disappointment in her voice.

He had a radar for that: her voice dropped, she sounded all sad, he felt guilty. It was like a built-in response, but this time, he refused to do his thing and feel guilty.

"I didn't tell you because I didn't want a hassle." Taylor gave his laces a yank. "I've kind of had enough of you busting my chops about the fire at church."

She didn't say anything for a moment, and he gritted his teeth, bracing for a nag.

She said, "I should have told you how brave you were. I'm sorry."

Wow!

"Thanks," he said.

She twisted the dishtowel. "But about Ariel and Matt...." She just couldn't help herself.

He huffed a loud breath. He held his palm up. "Stop, okay? Ariel really likes Matt. When will she ever meet another guy she likes and who likes her back? You should let her have some kind of relationship with him. I'm just taking them bowling, not to the Justice of the Peace or anything. She's capable of more if you'll just let her leash out a little more."

"I do not keep her on a leash," she said, and slapped the dishtowel against her leg.

He raised his eyebrows at her. "I'm taking them bowling. End of story." She didn't say anything for a minute.

"Okay," she said. "We can always get ice cream over Memorial Day weekend."

He didn't say anything, hoping the moment would pass.

"You remember we're going to Providence as usual," she said.

Shit.

He'd hoped to get out of the house before they had this fight. He sat up straight and braced his hands on his knees. "I'm going to see Dani in Charlottesville that weekend."

She looked like she was either going to kill him or have a heart attack. Her face crumpled, and her eyes teared up. "But we go every year," she said in the voice she used when he'd crushed her Mom-ness.

Now Taylor did feel guilty. This wasn't just ice cream. He took off his hat and turned it around and around in his hands. "Listen, I'm really sorry, but it's a long weekend, and we're climbing with some of her friends. We've been planning it since we left school."

She eased down beside him on the bench and leaned back, her hands hanging between her legs. Tears trickled down her face.

Oh, God, don't cry! Please, for the love of God, DO NOT CRY!

"Why are"—her voice broke—"you doing this to me?"

"Doing what?" he asked.

"Pushing so hard," she said. "Everything. Taking Ariel for a job and pushing the relationship with Matt. Not taking your finals and not going back to school. Not going to Providence. Why?"

"None of this is not about you, okay?" he insisted. "Not the stuff with Ariel or me. Ariel needs a life and I have a life." He karate chopped the air. "I have someone I care about and want to see her. Why are you making such a big deal about this?"

She said, "But you know we always go to Providence on

Memorial weekend. We've gone since you were little. We've never missed a year."

He let his head sag back against the wall behind him and sighed. He would never be good enough for his mom if he didn't become a brain surgeon or discover a cure for cancer. Going to Providence every year only reminded him of how brilliant his father had been and how impossible it was to ever measure up to him. She talked about his dad like he was a god. Maybe if he'd known his dad, Taylor would have developed his own opinion. Seen his dad as human instead of superhuman, like his mom made him out to be.

"You and Ariel go. I don't need to anymore," he said tiredly. "It just doesn't mean anything to me, and it hasn't for a long time."

She said, "It's where your father's ashes are scattered." She sounded like he'd just cursed his dead dad's memory. "Every year, we go and see the places he loved. The ocean beach where we hung out. The park where he proposed. We eat at his favorite clam place."

Her eyes were pleading with him, but he felt like he could do what was important to him. He said, "Mom."

"Wh-wh-what?" she said between sobs.

"I hate clams."

Her face looked like he'd said *I like to eat puppies*.

He said, "I've done all that stuff. I know what a great guy my dad was, that he was like, a second cousin to Superman or something." He shook his head and felt his gut go into freefall. "I know I'll never be him. I know he loved you and all that stuff, but I'm done, okay? I'm just done."

She cried into the towel, then said, "It's what we do as a family." *Sob, sob.* "It's how I help you remember your father. He was such a remarkable man. I always thought if we went, you would be inspired to follow in his footsteps."

Taylor put his hat back on and stood. He looked down at her, brokenhearted and crying.

Good job, asshole.

"I know he was a medical genius," he said. "Mom, but I'm going to be a fireman.

She wiped her face with the towel. "Okay, okay. I get it. I'm overbearing and overprotective. But remember, it's because I love you and your sister."

That was always her excuse. 'I love you'. If she loved him, why did it feel like she had her hands around his neck?

CHAPTER 24

The soul is healed by being with children.

Fyodor Dostoevsky

Olivia stood at the stove, sautéing celery, carrots, and onions for a soup base. She boxed and froze it in case the grocery store ran out of food in the event of a major disaster like a tornado. They were rare in Connecticut, but anything could happen, and it was best to be prepared.

Ariel was sitting behind Olivia at the kitchen table. Out of the blue, she said, "I kiss Matt."

Olivia dropped her spoon on the floor. "When?"

The previous evening, Taylor had taken Ariel and Matt to the bowling alley with a group of other young people who had disabilities. Ariel had come home chattering endlessly about Matt and how much fun it had been, but she hadn't mentioned a kiss.

Panic surged through Olivia. She turned and looked at Ariel. "But Taylor should have been watching you. That wasn't supposed to happen." Her insides shaking, Olivia picked the spoon off the floor and washed it.

Ariel blinked. "Why?"

"Because ... you're not ready." The vegetables were sticking to the bottom of the pan, but Olivia's hand refused to stir.

"When I ready?" Ariel asked.

Never.

Ariel said, "I want Matt room."

"What?" Olivia asked.

"I go Matt room," Ariel said.

Oh, Lord, give me wisdom because I am totally not ready for this.

Olivia understood. Ariel wanted to go to Matt's room. Did they allow that at Ability House? Would Taylor sneak off and take her to visit Matt? Olivia and Jack had discussed this, but she hadn't expected this to hit her so soon. Or ever.

Was it Olivia who wasn't prepared for her daughter to have a relationship?

"You kiss Dad?" Ariel asked.

Olivia felt heat spread over her face. She took up a knife and cut more celery, slowly drawing the blade across the stalks.

Derek had been a mad kisser. His deep, possessive kisses curled her toes. Even when he was too exhausted for sex after a shift at the hospital, they necked and held one another until they fell asleep. Those had been two of the greatest joys of her life. It made her feel loved, desired, and appreciated. It made her feel as if he was keeping her safe in his arms.

Olivia blew out a slow breath. "Yes, that's ..." she squeezed her eyes shut. Opened them. "That's what married people—people who love one another—do."

"Matt house"—Ariel paused, searching for words as she sometimes did—"kissing room."

Olivia's knife slipped, barely missing her finger. "A room for ... what?" She swallowed hard.

"Special for ..." Ariel searched for the words again, "love."

"Oh ... I ..." Olivia wiped a tear away with her shoulder.

The Marriage Survivors Club joked and laughed all the time about sex—the dearth and the blessing of it. But Olivia never thought she would be discussing sex with Ariel.

"I go Matt?" Ariel asked, her voice filled with both innocence and longing.

Olivia put the extra celery in the fridge. "I-I don't—I don't know."

Tears backed up in her throat. How could she prepare Ariel for more than cuddling and kissing? Olivia had read all the books, blogs, and social media pages filled with advice for talking to your Down child about sex. But now that the moment had arrived, Olivia couldn't bring herself to accept that Ariel was in love. How could she keep Ariel's heart from being broken?

"Can live Matt, Mom?" Ariel asked.

"Oh, honey," Olivia whispered as she tried to keep her shoulders from shaking.

When Ariel was first born, Derek comforted Olivia and reassured her that, during her pregnancy, she had done everything right, that it would be all right. But Olivia had been paralyzed by fear and guilt. She struggled to get out of bed, to eat, to shower. All she did was look at Ariel and apologize to her over and over in her mind.

Her mother, Virginia, an iron-willed Southern belle, came up to help with Ariel. Virginia cooed over and cuddled Ariel, fed her, dressed her, made soup and tea for Olivia, and forced her to get out of bed and walk.

Virginia set Olivia down at the kitchen table and, in her inimitable way, said, "This isn't ever going to be over, Olivia. This is your child now and forever, amen." She tapped the table with a painted fingernail. "God gave her to you for a reason. It might not feel that way right now. You might feel like all your dreams have gone up in smoke, but this child needs you."

Olivia covered her face with her hands. "I don't ... what did I do wrong?" she sobbed. "I don't think I can do it. I feel so ..." She sucked in air between her sobs. "Scared."

"Honey chile," her mother said in her steel-magnolia voice. "You didn't do a single thing wrong. You will be a great mom, just not to the kind of child you thought you were going to have. But you are going to have to pull yourself together. You are this little girl's only chance at a good life. You cannot fold up and quit. I will be here for you, and so will Derek, but Ariel is going to depend on you for the rest of her life. So, get off your"— Virginia pressed her lips together before continuing—"fucking ass, quit grieving, and love this baby."

It was the only time Olivia heard her mother curse. She'd done exactly what her mother said. Olivia wished her mother was here to tell her what to do now.

Ariel got up from the table, put her arm around Olivia's waist, and laid her head on Olivia's shoulder. "Mom, no cry. I take care you." It was one of the longest sentences Arial had ever said.

Olivia turned around and hugged Ariel. "Oh, honey, you don't have to take care of me." Olivia didn't want her children to feel like their lives had to revolve around caring for her.

'Get off your fucking ass and love this child.'

Taylor was right. Jack was right. The Marriage Survivors Club was right. Ariel was ready. Olivia turned off the burner and set the pan on the counter. She dried her hands on a towel and took a tissue from the box.

Taking Ariel by the hand, Olivia led her into the living room. "Come, let's talk about me and your dad and you and Matt." She sat on the sofa and turned toward Ariel, who sat beside her.

"Honey, I adored your dad. When we fell in love, I thought I would die of happiness."

"Me, too," Ariel said, grinning. "I die Matt." Her eyes had a sparkle and glow Olivia had never seen before.

"I know, honey." Olivia tried to find words to describe the indescribable.

She remembered the warmth of laying in Derek's arms, the way he nuzzled her temple. She loved the way he caressed the front of her neck. His eyes smiling at her over his coffee mug. How he tucked her against his side when they sat on the sofa and watched TV. His silly socks and bow ties. Sunday mornings spent in bed, drinking coffee, and reading the newspaper. Making love a second time. His terrible jokes and puns. She'd even loved the way he snored.

God, even after all these years, she still missed him.

"Your dad was very sweet, and I loved him—I still love him," Olivia said.

"Matt sweet." Ariel closed her eyes and made an air kiss.

Olivia had been a surprise premature baby. The last of five, she'd struggled with precarious health for several years, and her mother insisted on keeping her close to home, keeping her out of normal kid's physical activities. She had absorbed her mother's caution, but it wasn't until her own children had been born that she understood her mother's anxiety.

Ariel wouldn't entirely understand what she was telling her, but Olivia wanted to explain how Derek made her a better person. "I learned things from your dad, too."

"To bowl?" Ariel asked.

"No, we didn't bowl. We did"—Olivia slid her eyes away—"We did other things together."

Ariel said, "Matt bowl."

"Did Matt show you how to bowl last night?" Olivia asked.

"Yes. Show bowl good."

"He showed you how to bowl better?" Olivia clarified.

"Yeah." Ariel closed her eyes and looked ready to float away on a river of happiness.

How could Olivia deprive her daughter of the same kind of happiness Olivia had shared with Derek?

"Your dad taught me how to make a perfect omelet," Olivia said. "When we went swimming, he showed me how to breathe with a tube so I could look underwater at the fish. I wanted to be with him all the time. He made me happy."

"I happy Matt," Ariel said.

Olivia moved to tuck a strand of loose hair behind Ariel's ear but stopped herself. "I'm glad he does."

"I want night Matt," Ariel said.

Olivia gave Ariel's hand a squeeze. "You know, sometimes people change their mind and don't want to be in love anymore," she said.

"Why?" Ariel asked.

"They change their minds. Someone moves away." Olivia waited a moment to let that sink in. "Sometimes they just decide they don't love the other person anymore. If that happens with you and Matt, you might feel very sad."

"Okay," Ariel said. "I go Matt."

Joy, not fear, bloomed in Olivia's heart. This moment felt wondrous, like seeing a star born in the midnight sky.

Perhaps this was what letting go felt like.

"I'm going to tell you what sometimes happens when you spend the night with someone you love." Olivia drew a deep breath and began.

CHAPTER 25

Each day of our lives we make deposits in the memory banks of our children.

Charles R. Swindoll

Jack pulled his Harley into a parking spot right in front of Second Chance Designs and cut the engine. Taylor climbed off the back of the bike. Riding a motorcycle was like the thrill of learning to ride a bike as a kid—like flying, taking off, being free.

Except his mom only let him ride in the driveway until he was ten. Taylor said, "Thanks, what a blast."

"Anytime." Jack kicked out the kickstand.

Taylor noticed his mom staring out the window at them with her eyes bugging out like she'd just seen a murder take place. Inside the store, Taylor saw that her face was chalk white. Get a grip, he wanted to say. He was not going to do CPR on his mom.

"Hi," she said weakly. "What are you guys doing here?"

Taylor said, "My car broke down at the firehouse. Jack

offered to drop me over here because it's closer. I can go home with you when you close."

Taylor was volunteering at the firehouse while prepping for his exams. Getting to know Jack, Randy, and the other guys was cool. They made him feel like his dream of being a firefighter was within reach.

She set down the scissors in her hand.

A good thing.

To Jack, she said, "Thank God you at least gave him a helmet."

Taylor set the helmet down, hard, on her desk. "Mom, I'm here. You don't have to talk about me like I'm not."

"Oh, sorry," she mumbled.

"I always carry a spare helmet," Jack said pleasantly. "And besides, by bringing him here, I get to see you."

His mom's face turned pink.

Taylor looked from one to the other. Something weird was going on between them.

Her lip twitched.

"Maybe you'll join me sometime?" Jack asked. There was a funny, coaxing sound to his voice Taylor hadn't heard before.

Her eyeballs practically rolled back in her head.

"You should go, Mom. It's a lot of fun," Taylor said.

"I can't do something that. I have to think of you and your sister," she said.

She was so small that she looked harmless, but she had a killer right hook. Those punches were becoming less effective since Taylor started going for his dream.

Jack grinned as he shed his jacket and tossed it on the back of a chair. "My kitchen looks amazing. Frankie and her crew—and you, of course—have done a fantastic job. Way faster than I thought. I can't wait to cook for you."

"Okay," Taylor said, "but I hate anchovies, liver, and eggplant."

Jack raised his eyebrows.

Taylor realized he wasn't included in the invitation and felt like a dope.

His mom's entire face smiled, and she had a glazed look in her eyes.

Then it smacked Taylor like a lacrosse ball between the eyes. Jack and his mom were attracted to each other! *Ew.* But they were so old!

Taylor recalled how, after he'd put out the fire on the roof of the Chittam-Howell House, his mom said something about kissing Jack, but it hadn't registered.

Didn't old people stop having those feelings? They had saggy asses and wrinkly skin and potbellies. How was that sexy? Didn't the equipment just run out of gas? He wiped all images of the two of them from his mind because it was too disgusting to think about.

And how would she date Jack if she was afraid of everything he did? And how could she give Taylor a hard time if Jack was a firefighter?

Women. They make zero sense.

His mom said, "I look forward to your cooking, but please, don't give Taylor any more rides on your motorcycle. He didn't have on any leathers."

Taylor felt his face get hot as a stovetop. Didn't she realize that treating him like a little boy in front of Jack was embarrassing? He was nineteen, for God's sake! He'd been an EMT. He owned his own car. He'd gone to college for a year. Why couldn't she back off?

Something in Taylor bubbled over and headed toward his mouth in a hot stream. "I don't need you deciding what I can and can't do."

Jack looked startled and said, "I didn't mean to cause—"

"I'm just protecting you," she said, her cheeks turning fire-engine red.

"That's what you call it, but I call it smothering," Taylor shot back.

Jack put out a hand as if to calm Taylor. "Hey, Taylor, it's okay."

"No! No, it's not." Taylor took a step closer to his mom.

Despite the shocked look on her face, Taylor's mouth kept going. "I've had enough of your warnings. Drunk drivers, food past the due dates, fire, floods, bubonic plague, robbery, falling buildings, paint fumes, drowning in a car wreck, rabid raccoons and dogs, STDs, getting girls pregnant, walking alone at night, getting stuck on top of a Ferris wheel, bee stings, snake bites, Lyme disease, drowning, spider bites, chemicals in cleaning products, making sure a cold doesn't turn into pneumonia. And of course—now that I love it—rock climbing!"

"You've gone too far, Taylor." Jack's voice was sharp.

The guys at the station respected him, so why couldn't she? He wasn't a kindergartner who needed his hand held. Her neck was all blotchy and red, and her eyes were watering, but Taylor didn't care. He was a grown man and deserved to be treated like one.

He spoke slowly, hard, nailing every word. "You've spent my life, and Ariel's trying to protect us from everything. I've fought like hell not to be afraid. You've kept us on a leash long enough. I'm an adult, and so is Ariel." Taylor flung his arm out toward Jack. "Jack said there's an opening at the Ability House for women where Matt lives. I'm going to take her to check it out."

"Taylor, I just mentioned that to Randy in passing. You can't twist your mom's arm. Whether Ariel goes there is your mom's decision," Jack chewed off.

Taylor said, "Sorry to drag you into this, Jack. But I'm going to be Ariel's guardian when Mom dies. I think I should have some say on where she lives. If there's a place where she'll be happy now, I think we should check it out."

"I-I-I don't ..." his mom said in a watery voice.

Taylor didn't let up. His breath came fast and hot. "Ariel is crazy about Matt. They can see each other all they want there. She might like it there. When I have full guardianship, I won't be able to take her everywhere I go. And it's not fair to me to expect me to. And you're not being fair to her, either!"

His mom said, "But Ability House is far away. No one can care for her like I can."

"Yes, they can! You're just controlling her," he said, "just like you're trying to control me."

His mom touched her tiny hand to the base of her neck.

Taylor pointed a finger at her. "You going to make an appointment to take her, or should I?"

"No, I don't ... maybe ...." She looked at Jack for backup, but he was glaring at Taylor.

"Do it!" Taylor barked. "This is a chance for her to have a life. Then maybe you can have your own life, too!"

There was a stunned silence.

Her chest rose and fell quickly. She looked like he'd ripped her heart out with his teeth. He didn't want to make her feel bad or hurt her, but he was going to pry Ariel out of her hands.

His mom didn't say a single word, but her eyes were shiny with tears. Jack moved nearer and put his arm around her shoulders, confirming Taylor's suspicion that they had a thing for one another.

She was shaking, trying to hold it together. "Don't speak to me like that," she choked out.

"Look, I think it's time I looked for a place of my own." Taylor turned to Jack. "Thanks for the ride. I'll walk home from here."

CHAPTER 26

Familiarity breeds contempt - and children.
  Mark Twain

After Taylor had stormed out of the shop, Olivia collapsed onto one of the overpriced sofas. Jack went and sat next to her. Taylor's explosion had torn her apart, but Jack understood Taylor's desire to be treated like a man. He let her cry, rubbing circles on her back the way he'd done with his girls when they were little.

"It's okay," he said over and over. "*Sh, sh.*" After seeing grown men weep as they watched their houses and everything they owned go up in smoke, crying women didn't bother Jack.

"I didn't mean to cause such a rift between you and Taylor. I thought it was nothing more than a ride," Jack said. "I was talking to Randy about the opening at the women's residence at Ability House, and Taylor must have overheard me. I know I mentioned it to you, but I wasn't trying to do an end run around you or anything."

"I-I-I know. It's just that he's pushing at everything." Olivia blinked teary eyes, took short, sipping breaths, and let them out between pursed lips. She looked up at him, and big tears slipped down her face. "It wasn't your fault. I guess I had it coming."

Seeing her cry was like watching a porcelain doll cry. When he took her hand, it was warm and buttery soft, and an amazed burst of light shot through him.

She whispered in a cracking, shaky voice, "I've tried so hard. Every mother wants to keep her kids safe. What's so wrong with that?"

"I know, I know." He pulled over a nearby box of tissues and handed it to her.

She took one and swiped at her tears. She was so vulnerable, and he wanted to soothe her.

"I admire how you've raised your kids by yourself," Jack said, "but Taylor is a man now. Your fear is getting in the way of your relationships with your kids."

And with him. But Jack would wait to say that.

"As a man, I understand Taylor's drive to be treated like one," he said.

"And you're saying I don't treat him like one," she said miserably.

He paused, not wanting to twist the knife. "Let's just say, no matter how hard we try, all parents can do better, me included. He wants to forge his own path in life. He can't do it if you're always after him about choices you feel are dangerous."

"I bet you were a perfect parent." She snuggled even closer, warm and soft, against his side.

The memories came flooding back, making him grimace. "Uh uh. Once, I sent my girls to school in their flimsy Halloween costumes. They refused to put anything on underneath, so I gave up and let them go."

"What was so wrong about that?" From her tone of voice, he could tell she was smiling.

"It was January," he said.

Her shoulders shook as she laughed. He loved the way her laugh was too big for how small she was. He loved making her laugh. Loved comforting her.

"Another time, I forgot to pick up my youngest from school when they had a half day. The principal called, and I had to go pick her up—" he said, and rubbed a hand over his stubbly chin —"in the pumper truck because I was working. I had to keep her at the firehouse all day." He laughed and so did she. "The guys never let me live that one down. And another day, I made one of them a sandwich with bread I didn't know was moldy. She ate it, and on the way home from a field trip, she threw up on another kid on the school bus. And those are just a few of my bad parenting days.

She was chuckling through her sniffling now. "Did your daughters ever get boiling mad at you?"

"My eldest wouldn't speak to me for three weeks when I caught her and her boyfriend in the back of his car," he confessed.

She sat up and turned to look at him. "How did you know where they were?"

He felt the embarrassment even now. "Because I, uh, followed them."

She pointed a finger at him. "So, you *were* a scared, overprotective parent once yourself."

He raised his hand for the oath. "Guilty as charged."

She gave a hoot of laughter. "You must have terrified the poor boy."

"Not so much. She married him. Turns out he's a pretty nice guy." Softly, Jack continued. "But sometimes, Gina and I weren't paranoid enough. We had a real scare when we found a stash of drugs in the closet of our youngest." On his chest, he felt the crushing weight of terror at how close they'd come to losing their daughter. He understood Olivia's fear down to his bones.

"She did a stint in rehab and stayed clean. After that, it was a balancing act between fear and trust." He sighed and pulled Olivia back against his side. "I guess we did okay because she's happy and settled now."

Olivia said, "Now, you know how I feel about Taylor becoming a fireman. About Ariel moving out."

"But we all survived," he countered. Jack tightened his arm around her, and she didn't resist. "Why are you so scared, Olivia?" She sniffled and shifted her weight.

"I don't think I can lose someone I love again. I'd rather bear the fear than the guilt," she said in a small, scared voice.

He wanted to kiss the tears from her cheeks, to tell her it would be all right.

"You need to try to stop being so scared," he said. He took her hand and kissed the place where her fingers met her palm.

She twined her elegant little fingers through his big ones. "Mothers worry until they're dead." Her laugh was both sad and self-deprecating.

"Yeah, but you can't keep kids from doing stupid things," he said.

"Like riding motorcycles?" she asked, a smile in her voice.

"Yeah," he said. "Gina had a high-powered job, and she always felt guilty that I carried the biggest load of childcare and cooking. That arrangement gave me a chance to keep a close eye on the girls, be a part of their lives, and watch them grow up. Not many men want, or get to do that, but it's something I'm proud of. But I was never terrified they would die of snakebite or a rabid raccoon."

"Taylor was exaggerating," she said, unconvincingly.

"Was he?" he challenged.

"Well ... maybe only a little." She gave a small chuckle that tickled against his ribs. She let out a long, ragged sigh.

He said, "You've been a good role model. In a sense, the only person you have to blame is yourself that he's so determined."

"What do you mean?" she asked.

He rested his cheek on the crown of her head and smelled the flowery scent of her shampoo, the feminine-ness of her. She was soft, with a core of iron. A very attractive combination that could keep a man interested for a very long time.

"It's one of the many things I love about you. Despite being scared, you raised him and Ariel alone. You built a successful business," he said. "That all takes determination."

"I wasn't always so scared of everything until Derek died." She kicked off her shoes and folded her feet up under her. "Now I see death and danger everywhere."

Jack didn't want to upset her anymore, but he wanted to know how Derek had died. The way she'd avoided talking about it made him think there was something she was hanging on to. He pressed his lips into her hair. "You know, you've never told me how he died."

She was quiet, and he could practically feel her emotions churning through her.

"He was rock climbing and fell." She drew in a quivering breath. "It was one of the few times I hadn't gone with him."

He drew back and looked at her. "You used to rock climb?" The image of her scaling a rock wall was incompatible with the tiny woman curled up against him. He said, "That was pretty ballsy."

She grinned. "Thank you, but I didn't actually climb very fast, and I was terrified of heights, but I did it anyway, so I could keep an eye on Derek."

"Another example of your determination," Jack said. "Your

ass may be little, but it's hard as a rock." He laughed, and she did too.

Then she grew quiet again, and he waited until she was ready to go on. She said, "The time he fell, he hadn't climbed for a while. I couldn't go because I was still nursing Taylor. Ariel was only three." She pulled away, sat up, and looked at Jack.

He saw the pain in the deepening color of her eyes, in the pauses between her words, in her shaky breath. He took her hand and rubbed his thumb over her knuckles.

"Derek ... was supposed to climb with a guide, but the guide was late, so Derek started without him. They think he wasn't even very far up when he fell. They think his camming device— a climbing tool that's supposed to expand in a crevice when you pull on it—that he hadn't seated it properly in the crevice." She squeezed Jack's hand tighter than he would have thought her little hands could squeeze. Her voice was raw, as though she'd had to claw the words out of her throat. "He wasn't experienced enough to ever have climbed alone."

Jack couldn't hide his disgust. "Wait, are you telling me a guy with a toddler and a newborn was rock climbing? I'm sorry, but what kind of a dumbass does that?"

Her blue eyes took on a look of certainty, which he was becoming familiar with. A 'don't question me' stare.

"I would have made him wait if I was there," she said." "She pulled at her balled-up tissue. "If I'd been there, he might be alive today. It's my fault. I would have been able to convince him to stop."

"And you've felt guilty about this all this time?" Jack asked.

She nodded.

"It wasn't your fault he died," Jack said, furious that Derek had wrecked three lives because he couldn't wait fifteen minutes. "Anybody who climbs knows the risks. He compounded them by climbing alone and because he was inexperienced. That was plain foolhardy. Why did he take up climbing, anyway?"

"He was an ER doc. Dangerous sports made him feel alive because he saw so much death in the ER." Olivia's eyes took on a desolate gaze. "I thought we'd raise our kids together. Grow old. Travel. But there's been only me, so I have to worry for two."

"No wonder you're afraid of Taylor climbing. And it's a little boneheaded that he's doing it, given that is how his dad died," Jack said.

She met his gaze with an embarrassed expression. "Well ... about that ...." She cleared her throat and her lip twitched. "See, um, I never told Taylor and Ariel exactly *how* Derek died. I only told them he died when he fell and hit his head."

He kept from rolling his eyes, but only just. "Why not?"

"I've always been afraid Taylor would imitate Derek's risky behaviors instead of becoming a doctor." She ducked her sweet head. "So, I just ... I fudged the details."

As a firefighter, he'd seen death and destruction. He knew people were affected by a tragic loss for the rest of their lives, but his job was over once the fire was out. He rarely saw people afterward. Her heart had been scorched by guilt and loss. She was trying desperately to hold on to those she loved, but it wasn't working for any of them.

"No wonder you've been scared." He drew the warm little bundle of her against him again. "But you need to tell them the truth," he said, taking the risk of being a know-it-all.

"But I've kept it a secret for so long. Taylor's bound to be angry," she said, softly.

Jack suppressed a laugh. "Well, he won't be any less angry if you wait another ten years to tell him. And if he quits, you'll have one less thing to be scared about." She squirmed against his side, the way she'd tried to squirm out of the truth. "I'm so used to being afraid for my kids, I don't know if I can stop. Now, if Taylor really does move out, I won't know what he's doing at all."

He caressed her silky blond hair. "He's a man, Olivia. You don't need to keep an eye on him."

She hummed defeat.

Jack said, "He can stay with me for a bit if that helps. He can sleep in Matt's room."

She sat bolt upright and stared at him wide-eyed. "You'd do that?" she asked.

He cupped her face in his hands. "I do feel a little responsible for causing all the problems between you and Taylor. After all, I suggested he join the department. I gave him a motorcycle ride. I didn't tell you he'd stopped by the firehouse. And I let it slip about the opening at the women's Ability House."

Jack was used to taking care of people and helping them. It was why he loved cooking for people. It made them happy, which made him happy. It was why he was good with Matt and enjoyed helping at Ability House. And he wanted to take care of Olivia and try to help her get over her fear of the world.

"Maybe ... Taylor's right about Ariel living at Ability House," she said slowly. Doubtfully.

Jack cheered inwardly. He said, "You don't have to decide right now. Just see what you think. Someone will watch Ariel 24-7. You don't have to keep being scared about your kids. You're brave. You just forgot you were once, and you can be brave again."

She raised her head to look at him, and her blue eyes sparkled like a pair of icicles in a sunbeam. "You really think so?"

"Of course," he said.

She looped her arms around his neck and pressed her mouth to his. Her lips were soft and hungry. Their first kiss had been a doozy, and he'd wanted more of the same. He'd imagined holding her, making love, but this felt wrong, like asking somebody whose house had just burned down for a loan. She was too vulnerable.

"Olivia, Olivia," he whispered against her lips. Gently, he disentangled her arms from around his neck. "I don't want to take advantage of you when you're upset."

She quirked an eyebrow. "I know a way you can make me less upset." She rose, went to the front door, and turned on the *closed* sign. She flicked off the lights and returned to where he sat. She extended her hand, and he stood.

She put her hands on his chest. "Want to test out that second-hand sofa Frankie dropped off for you in the back storeroom?"

Yes, dear God, thank you!

"I'd like nothing more—if you're sure," Jack said. Who would have thought talking about letting go was an aphrodisiac?

Her smile was trusting. "Let me show you how sure I am."

And he let her lead him to the back room where she made his wildest—for a middle-aged man—dreams come true.

CHAPTER 27

Everybody knows how to raise children, except the people who have them.

P. J. O'Rourke

After her fall at church, Carol went to rehab, so Olivia volunteered the Marriage Survivors Club to clean Carol's house. Others from St. Paul's had offered to deliver meals, visit her, and mow her yard, which looked like a meadow gone berserk. It was what the people at St. Paul's did: they took care of one another, the way they had taken care of Olivia when Derek had died.

Regretting her offer, Olivia tentatively turned the key to the door of Carol Baxter's house. Olivia took a step back. "I'm a little afraid to go in there."

Bianca peered in over Olivia's shoulder. "She doesn't have kittens, so you should be fine."

They all laughed, and Olivia gave her friend a poke in the ribs.

Frankie said, "It's likely to be a disaster."

Hélène said, "With six of us cleaning, it shouldn't be too terrible." For someone so beautiful, she certainly had a practical side.

"What if there are mice?" Olivia squeaked. She hated mice. And anything that crawled, crept, slithered, flew at night and a million other small things.

"Here, let me," Bianca said in a heroic voice. She edged past Olivia into the house and turned on the light.

Bianca let out a bloodcurdling scream.

Olivia jumped. "Oh, my god, what is it?" She gasped and backed into Frankie, who caught her so she wouldn't stumble off the porch.

With an evil grin on her face, Bianca stuck her head back out the door. "Nothing. I'm just freaking you out."

"Bianca!" Olivia huffed, her heart racing..

"You are so bad," Flicka said to Bianca.

Bianca gave a proud grin.

They all trooped inside and surveyed the mess that was Carol's living room. Watching where she put her feet, Olivia squeezed between a gallon bucket of plastic Halloween eyeballs, a baby stroller with a giant stuffed panda strapped in, a bag overflowing with newspaper clippings, and a stack of textbooks. There were plaster garden elves, animals that had lost their stuffing, boxes of puzzles, three old coffee makers, a child's toy plastic wheelbarrow, two rolled-up rugs, four pairs of rubber boots in various sizes, dead plants, stacks of paperbacks, aluminum pans, a bicycle tire, rusted tools, fifty or so snow globes, stacks of newspapers tied with twine.

"A veritable smorgasbord of crap," Flicka said.

Olivia shuddered. "I don't see anything moldy or cobwebs."

"Those are probably in the refrigerator," Hélène said.

"I'll shoot you for the bedroom or the kitchen," Flicka said to Hélène.

"No, you cheat." Hélène dragged Flicka by the elbow into the kitchen. A second later, they screamed in tandem. "AHHHHH! KITTENS!"

This time, Olivia doubled over in laughter.

Frankie, who had missed her calling as a Civil War general, said, "I'll try to get the stuff off the floor so we can vacuum."

"You think there's an actual floor under all this junk?" Bianca asked, nudging a flat soccer ball out of the way.

Olivia, Bianca, and Carolina took the bedroom, where they quickly changed Carol's sheets, threw the dirty ones into the wash, dusted, and vacuumed. Bianca dumped Carol's collection of Christmas and Halloween ornaments into an empty box and hauled it to the basement.

"Don't go into the basement," Bianca said when she returned to the bedroom, brushing dust and cobwebs out of her hair.

"It can't be worse than the living room," Carolina said, straightening a Mickey Mouse lampshade.

Bianca rolled her eyes and nodded. "Oh, yes, it can."

Frankie came into the bedroom. She said, "This looks good. Now let's tackle the living room."

The six took up different positions around the living room and tried to make sense of what was there.

"You think she'll notice if we throw out some of this stuff?" Carolina asked. She held up a Santa, his head lulling drunkenly on his chest.

"Nah," Bianca said. "She'll just think she came home to the wrong house."

Flicka picked up a pillow and shoved aside a stack of knitted afghans. "Hey, look! There's a sofa under here."

"No! Really?" Bianca peered past Flicka and turned to the others. "She's right!"

"We're all going to heaven for doing this," Flicka said.

"Not you," Bianca said. "You've been married four times. The cut-off's three."

Flicka slugged Bianca with a pillow, throwing up a cloud of dust and making everyone cough and sneeze.

Carolina snapped open a large black plastic garbage bag and dumped in a half-dozen dead plants.

Frankie said, "I was over at Jack's and saw Taylor. I should have asked him to come along to lift some of the heavier stuff." Frankie frowned. "What's he doing there, anyway?"

The thing that Olivia had tried to put out of her mind roared back like a forest fire. A sense of doom and helplessness made her knees go weak. "We had a disagreement. He moved out and is staying at Jack's until he finds his own place." A sob fought its way up her throat.

All the work stopped. Olivia felt every eye on her.

Flicka handed her a tissue.

Olivia examined the tissue closely. "This isn't one of Carol's tissues, is it?"

Flicka said, "I would never do that to you. To Bianca, yes, but you, no."

Bianca said, "Let me guess, the spat was because Taylor's not going back to school, and you don't want him to be a firefighter."

"In a roundabout way, yes. Jack brought him to the shop on his motorcycle, and I told Taylor I didn't want him riding on it." Olivia blew her nose and dropped the tissue into the trash.

Frankie said, "Nothing like belittling a young man in front of someone he admires."

Olivia cringed at the accuracy of Frankie's assessment.

Bianca dropped about a hundred unused chopsticks and soy sauce packets into the trash bag. She said, "I have an idea. Why don't you chain Taylor in his room and never let him out?"

"Well ... I guess it was a mistake. But motorcycles *are* dangerous," Olivia insisted.

"So is cleaning this place up." Hélène dangled what appeared to be the desiccated carcass of a small rodent by the tail.

Olivia squealed and cringed.

"Don't worry, it's dead," Helene said.

Carolina held open the trash bag, and in went the varmint.

Olivia said, "I wish he could have chosen something safe, like an actuary, computer programmer, or dentist."

"Being a dentist isn't all that safe. I bit mine once." Bianca dusted a bookshelf and stacked the textbooks there.

"Hope you'd had your rabies shot," Flicka said, handing Bianca another stack of books.

Bianca guffawed.

Carolina threw a roll of water-spotted, shriveled paper towels into the trash, which was filling up. "Taylor doesn't want to do those things because they're not in his heart."

Olivia picked up a metal toy car without any wheels. It was the sort that Taylor had played with as a child. She turned it over in her hands, remembering how he stretched his plastic track across the living room, sending the cars down the track again and again. Then, one day, he grew out of it.

Olivia let Carolina's words sink in. *They're not in his heart.*

Frankie said, "Taylor's dream is to become a firefighter. If you try to stop him, he'll only resent you, maybe for the rest of his life."

"Yeah, what Frankie said," Hélène said.

Derek had lived his life to the fullest until his passion killed him. And as Jack assured her, it hadn't been her fault. And if Taylor died doing what he loved, it wouldn't be her fault, either. She couldn't deny her son his joy and passion, even if it terrified her.

She tossed the child's car into the trash bag.

"Even if I don't nag Taylor about firefighting anymore, I'll still be scared," Olivia said.

"Nobody said you wouldn't be," Flicka said and dropped a pair of men's underwear into the trash.

"If you learn to tolerate your fears, you might build up a reservoir of bravery. Of not being scared of other things," Carolina said in her kind but pithy way.

"Like kittens," Bianca said dryly.

"Or Jack O'Grady," Flicka said and smirked.

"Taylor got Ariel a job at the grocery store, too, so he's totally pushing my bravery buttons," Olivia said. She swiped her finger over a shelf and came away with a handful of lint.

"You let her get a job?" Carolina asked, astonished.

"I went along with it because I didn't have much choice." Olivia folded one of the afghans and laid it on the heap.

"She's proving to be very capable," Hélène said. "When the fire started, she rescued Matt. You must be very proud of her."

"I am." Olivia sank down onto the pile of afghans and felt very old.

Carolina picked up a headless doll by one leg. "Think Carol will miss this?"

Bianca hooked her thumb over her shoulder. "Out."

Carolina dropped it into the bag.

Bianca put her hands on her hips and gave Olivia a stony stare. "As your lawyer, I have to ask: what plans do you have for Ariel if Taylor gets hurt and can't care for her or," Bianca said, "to put it politely, you happen to be dead?"

Flicka rolled her eyes. "God, Bee."

"What? What? What'd I say?" Bianca asked, arms thrown wide.

The others snickered, and even Olivia cracked a smile.

"I've been thinking about that." Olivia sucked in a shaky

gasp of air. "Jack says there's an opening at Ability House for a woman. I'm thinking about scheduling a visit."

"That sounds great." Frankie's face broke into a wide grin. "She could live in a group home with other people like herself instead of her old, decrepit mother."

Olivia laughed. "I'm no older than the rest of you."

"We're not old," Flicka said with a haughty toss of her red hair, a color not found in nature. "We're like aged, fine wine."

With one hand on her low back, Bianca arched backward and groaned. "I think I've turned to vinegar."

CHAPTER 28

I do not know You, God, because I am in the way. Please help me to push myself aside.

Flannery O'Connor

As he made himself a cup of coffee, Jack admired his nearly finished kitchen. Olivia had done a great job, and he wished she was here so he could pour her a cup of coffee.

Whenever they were here together, there were workmen around, and she made certain to keep things professional. At least he got to stand close enough to smell the scent of her shampoo, to see the tilt of her sleek little head, to see intelligence snap in her eyes. He wanted to be the one to remind her how strong she was, that she could meet whatever challenge life threw at her.

He carried his coffee to the balcony and stared over the gray water of the Norwalk Harbor. He wanted to sit here every morning with Olivia, looking at the boats motoring out to the Sound, to sit here at night, sharing a glass of wine while the sun sank below the horizon. If she objected to Taylor being a firefighter, Jack wouldn't have a chance at more than a bounce on a sofa in the store's back room. It had been thunder and lightning, but he wanted more. He wanted to spoon against her, to hear her laugh every day, to ask what made her happy and to try to give it to her.

Taylor stepped onto the balcony. "Hey, mind if I join you?"

"Sure, come on out," Jack said.

Jack felt terrible that the motorcycle ride had resulted in a rift between Taylor and Olivia. It had been two weeks since Taylor moved in. For both their sakes, he wanted to patch things up between them without alienating either of them. First step: get Taylor to face the realities of growing up.

Taylor pulled up the other deck chair and slouched into it. They said nothing for a few minutes, just watched the water.

Without looking at Taylor, Jack said, "Have you thought about moving back home?" Out of the corner of his eye, Jack saw the tendons in Taylor's bull neck tighten.

"I don't want her telling me how to live my life every minute," Taylor said.

Jack smiled into his coffee cup, then said, "Moms nag because they love their kids. Dads, too. You'll understand when you have kids of your own. I get that she's a little over the top."

Taylor snorted. "A little over the top? She's the Gestapo, man."

Jack laughed at the image of tiny Olivia as a soldier. "If you don't want to move home, maybe you should consider getting an apartment of your own."

Taylor stiffened. "I don't think I can afford a place of my own."

"Do you have a friend or relative you could move in with until you save some money?" Jack asked.

"Mm, not exactly." Taylor looked away.

Two red splotches appear on Taylor's cheekbones. "Being a

fireman, climbing up on that roof at church, and putting out that fire didn't freak me out, but thinking about getting my own crib makes me a little nervous."

Jack addressed him sternly, as he would have one of his own girls. "You're old enough to decide not to go back to school without consulting your mom. You decided you wanted to be a fireman. You got your sister a job. You have a girlfriend you're going to visit. Those are all grown-up things. I'm not going to throw you out on the street or anything. You got this. You can stay until you find a place you can afford, but you should consider the next steps in your life."

And if Taylor moved out, Jack could have Olivia over for a "sleepover", although probably neither of them would get any sleep.

CHAPTER 29

To me, there is no picture so beautiful as smiling, bright-eyed, happy children; no music so sweet as their clear and ringing laughter.

P. T. Barnum

Olivia and Ariel stood in the spacious entryway of the women's residence of Ability House. They had come for a tour. Bea Dewinter, the director of the Ability House, greeted them. She had compassionate eyes, pin-straight silvery blond hair, and a laughing voice. "How did you hear about us?" Bea asked. Even her blue eyes laughed.

"Jack O'Grady. He's sort of a friend," Olivia said, not wanting to suggest they were a couple. "He mentioned that you had a vacancy in the women's house. He thinks Ariel might be a good fit."

"Jack's a wonderful guy," Bea enthused and laughed. "He's done so much for us here. He and his firefighter friends reno- vated our bathroom upstairs. They host a visit to the firehouse every spring and a chili dinner fundraiser for us in the fall. He's a great uncle to Matt. Such a generous man."

Olivia wasn't surprised to hear her praise. Jack was a dependable, thoughtful, responsible guy. He also happened to be handsome and a fantastic kisser. When he looked at her in a certain way, the heat in his eyes made her want to throw herself backward on a bed and lift her skirt. But she didn't intend to give her heart and soul to a firefighter.

"How many residents do you have?" Olivia asked.

"We have eight ladies right now." Bea held up a finger and smiled at Ariel. "And room for one more."

"I'm one," Ariel said brightly.

Olivia put her arm around Ariel. Olivia said, "That's right, and we want to see if this place is right for you."

Olivia's stomach felt as though she'd drunk bleach.

If Ariel moved in here, who would remind her to eat her vegetables, take her medication, and go to bed on time? To brush her hair and put on clean clothes? Who would make sure Ariel didn't get too tired, that no one kidnapped her, or worse? Even if someone got paid to care for Ariel, nobody did those things, as well as Olivia.

"Jack Matt uncle." Ariel patted her chest with an open palm. "Matt my boyfriend."

"I know Matt!" Bea laughed—a hearty, comforting sound.

Ariel grinned and chuckled.

Olivia twisted her hands on the handle of her purse and wished she had put in a roll of antacids.

"Matt paint," Ariel said.

Bea said, "Yes, I know he does. I've seen his T-shirts. Aren't they lovely? I have two myself."

Ariel looked around expectantly. "Matt here?"

"No, he lives about three blocks from here," Bea said.

Ariel looked crestfallen, but Olivia breathed a sigh of relief.

"I want live Matt," Ariel said.

Olivia remembered a quote from Barbara Kingsolver's. Parenthood: the Möbius strip of torment.

"Let me show you around," Bea said and hooked her arm through Ariel's as if she was her doting aunt.

As they took the tour, Olivia was pleased. The house had been donated years ago by someone who'd had a disabled daughter. It was a sunny contemporary, with tall windows, wide staircases, and lots of gleaming blond oak surfaces. The rooms smelled of lemony furniture polish, laundry fabric softener, and last night's dinner. Olivia noted that there were fire alarms, neon exit signs, and fire extinguishers. The common areas were spotless, and so were the bathroom and kitchen. Residents shared cheery bedrooms, but each lady had added her personal touch to her room with things like an Elvis poster, a minion pillow on a bed, stuffed animals, or a Rainbow Sprinkles bedspread. There were several aides laughing and chatting with residents, playing Chutes and Ladders or Go Fish.

"What happens if there's an emergency at night?" Olivia asked.

Bea said, "We have aides here 24-7 and they're all trained to recognize an emergency and call 911. If anything happens, the aides call me next, then I call you. The ladies all have phones. They can call friends or relatives whenever they want. Likewise, relatives can call staff or their resident. I always carry a work phone so I can be reached in an emergency."

Somewhere, Elvis broke into "Love Me Tender", and a woman sang along in an off-key, quavery soprano.

With her wide, comforting smile, Bea said, "Ariel, some of the ladies are in the other room having music and dance hour. Would you like to join them while I chat with your mom?"

"Yes," Ariel said.

Olivia thought Ariel would stick close by, but without a backward glance, Ariel toddled off in the direction of the music.

Pride shot through Olivia as she watched her go. Her daughter was brave, so how could Olivia not be brave, too?

"Let's you and I go into the dining room," Bea said, and Olivia followed her.

Olivia wanted Bea to be a Nurse Rachette knock-off, for this place to resemble a dungeon, a place where Ariel would never want to go. But to Olivia's dismay and relief, it was warm, welcoming, and homey. And best of all, it was safe.

The sunny dining room had a long wooden table with ten upholstered chairs and a breakfront with figurines of fairies, angels, grinning kittens, snow globes, plastic prancing ponies, a vinyl doll in a Cinderella costume, and a coffee mug in the shape of Elvis's head.

"Somebody loves Elvis," Olivia said as she pulled her chair out to sit down.

"Oh, that's Pammy," Bea said and laughed. "She's a huuuuge Elvis fan. Watches his movies over and over on the TV in her room."

Olivia nodded. "Ariel likes *My Little Pony* and *America's Got Talent*."

Bea laughed some more. She seemed to laugh at everything. She would have made a good addition to the Marriage Survivors Club.

She said, "All our residents love those, too. I'm a fan of the *British Baking Show*, though I would find it challenging to bake a cake out of a box." She laughed again, and it put Olivia a bit more at ease.

"The residence is lovely," Olivia said.

Bea said, "Ariel seems very sweet and seems to be highly independent. She'd fit right in with the rest of my ladies."

"Ariel's sort of shy," Olivia suggested.

Bea lifted one eyebrow. She didn't laugh. "She went right into the living room with the others. I bet she's dancing right along. Does she have a job?"

Olivia stared at the Elvis mug, the shiny black pompadour, the hooded seductive eyes. "Her brother, Taylor, got her a job at the grocery, and she loves it." She glanced at Bea. "So maybe she's not as shy as I think."

"Maybe not," Bea answered.

Olivia directed her gaze around the room, avoiding Bea's wise, sympathetic eyes. "I'm just unsure she's ready."

Bea said, "Many families have a hard time letting their adult disabled children move out of the home. Families want their kids to have a safe, stimulating, comfortable place to live when they're no longer around or able to care for them. That's what Ability House was designed to do. But everybody has their own timeline about when they're ready to let their kids fly."

Perhaps Olivia had stifled Ariel's independence more than she should have. Maybe she had done too much for Ariel and held her back from her best self. Had she used Ariel's disability to justify her own fears?

A voice inside her—God? Taylor? Jack?——said, *"or maybe it's because you love your child."*

Olivia squared her shoulders and tried to look confident. She said, "As she mentioned, Ariel really likes Matt."

Bea looked serious and didn't laugh. "Lots of the ladies like Matt."

Olivia's Mom-Alert clanged in her head. "Does he ... you know ...?" Olivia's lip twitched.

It was one thing to have the condom talk with Taylor, but discussing her daughter's potential lover with a woman she'd just met was mortifying.

You're not a prude. You just want to protect Ariel. Olivia also wanted Ariel to live her best life, and that meant letting her go.

At the thought, Olivia felt shrapnel tear through her chest.

Bea must have seen Olivia's hesitation because she said, "You can say it. There's nothing unspeakable around here. We're very open and upfront about our residents' lives and friendships."

Olivia's mouth was dry as sand. "Does Matt, you know, sleep with lots of the ladies?"

"Oh, no!" Bea laughed. "He's friendly and respectful, but I will say he does like to dance with everyone."

"If Ariel moved here, would she and Matt have, like..." Olivia cleared her throat. "A relationship?"

"You mean a physical relationship? Sex?" Bea's calm frankness took the sting out of Olivia's hesitancy.

"Yes, sex," Olivia said.

Bea said, "We do have a relationship room. Our younger residents have sex drives just like neurotypical people. We try to normalize physical relationships as much as possible. We do make sure there's no coercion, no forced or unwanted physical contact, and that sex is in the context of a relationship." Bea laughed. "In other words, *not* like a hookup on Grinder or Tinder."

Olivia couldn't help but smile.

In the other room, Elvis launched into a rousing rendition of "You Ain't Nothin' But a Hound Dog."

Now that was appropriate.

"I'm worried about Ariel, not only from a physical point of view, but I'm worried about her heart." Olivia's voice cracked. She blinked back tears. "I don't want her heart to get broken by Matt."

Bea nodded. "Of course you don't, but sometimes hearts do get broken, just like in the real world. However, our residents tend not to fall out of love once they've fallen in love."

Sunshine skated across the polished wood floor. Elvis's voice mixed with the laughter and singing of the ladies. Something in the oven filled the air with the aroma of a nutritious, thoughtfully made meal.

This was the sort of place Olivia wanted for Ariel. She would have more friends and a busier social life. She and Matt could have a relationship. It was what all parents dreamed of for all their children.

Olivia turned to Bea. "Do you think living here would be good for Ariel?"

Bea answered, "I think it would be great for her, but you'll need to ask Ariel what she thinks."

Olivia hadn't thought to ask Ariel what she wanted. Olivia felt she knew best until Taylor reminded her that she wasn't the only one responsible for Ariel's future. All along, Taylor had considered Ariel's potential. In some ways, he was wiser than Olivia. Or just braver.

Ariel appeared, all out of breath. Her cheeks were red, her face glistened with sweat, and her shirt twisted around her middle. She motioned for Olivia to follow her. "Mom, come. Dance fun."

Ariel's excitement both broke and made Olivia's heart soar. Her daughter was stepping into a world Olivia hadn't imagined for her. Olivia was aware of Bea watching her, smiling.

Bea rose. Enthusiastically, she said, "We absolutely want to see the dancing."

Olivia blinked in the too-bright gloss of the day.

Bea paused at the doorway into the other room. "You don't have to decide today. She can come back for a social evening or a weekend overnight. You can both see what it's like."

Olivia stood. "Let's go see the dancing."

In a spacious living room, four ladies were stomping, swaying, clapping, hopping, dancing, hooting, swishing skirts, grinning, pumping arms, and bopping heads to Elvis blaring from a CD player. No one's movements were in time with the song, but it didn't matter because everyone was having a blast. Grinning, Ariel was right in the mix, dancing away.

Olivia felt the fizz of Ariel's enthusiasm in her own feet, the air pulsing around her with pure, unrestrained, unselfconscious joy.

It was positively breathtaking.

Was this what Ariel needed to be her best person? How could Olivia have denied this to her dear daughter for so long?

The music ended, and everyone flopped and sprawled onto chairs and sofas.

Ariel rejoined Bea and Olivia. Olivia said, "You mentioned Ariel spending a weekend with you. Is that offer open?"

Bea laughed. "Absolutely. We're having a special social night coming up. Ariel could come spend the weekend with us."

"Matt come?" Ariel asked, her ruddy face lighting up.

Bea laughed again. "Yes, he will. He never misses a social night."

Ariel clapped her pudgy hands. "I want Matt."

Bea went on. "Over the weekend, Ariel can see what living here is like and you can see how you feel about her being out of the house."

"Would you like that, honey?" Olivia asked.

"I come! I come!" Ariel looked up at Olivia. "Yes, Mom?"

Olivia gathered her bravery and said, "It's a good idea. Yes, you can come."

Excitedly, Ariel spluttered, "I dance Matt. Matt like Elvis?"

Bea laughed. "I bet he does, but you'll have to ask him yourself."

"When shall I bring her?" Olivia asked.

"Bring her Friday of Memorial Day weekend," Bea said.

Olivia felt as though she'd been shot with bullets of ice.

Ariel wouldn't make the annual pilgrimage to Providence, but instead, she would be tasting a new life. Taylor would be with someone Olivia had never met, but who he was quite taken with. The life Olivia had created for her children was crumbling, and she couldn't hold the pieces of that life together any longer. She didn't want to. Ariel and Taylor needed to leave her, and she needed to let them go.

"I'll bring her," Olivia said through her tears.

CHAPTER 30

Women now have choices. They can be married, not married, have a job, not have a job, be married with children, unmarried with children. Men have the same choice we've always had: work, or prison.

Tim Allen

Taylor climbed the stairs to an apartment over an Irish-style pub called O'Neill's. The apartment was a two-bedroom share and supposedly furnished, but the stairs smelled like piss and stale cigarette smoke. He tried to reassure himself that he could afford some place better if he got a second job. On the other hand, a second job meant cutting his hours as a volunteer firefighter, which was giving him the experience he needed to show he was serious and capable. He needed time to study for the firefighter's exam and to keep himself in top physical shape so he could pass the physical part of the exam.

Taylor knocked on the door.

An emaciated, barefoot dude with skanky long hair, his eyes

at half-mast, opened the door. A cigarette hung between his cracked lips. Tattoo sleeves ran down both arms. The ripped jeans hanging on his hips looked like they hadn't been washed in a decade.

Taylor checked his phone to make sure he had the right address. "Hey, uh, this 12 Palmerston, apartment B?"

He peered over the dude's shoulder to the grody apartment behind him. It looked like the guy had held the rave in his living room. The rest of the place couldn't be much better.

"Yeah." The guy's breath smelled like he'd been eating decomposing rodents.

Taylor asked, "You Diamond?" Like that was his real name.

"Yeah," the guy who wasn't actually named Diamond said. His real name should have been Crackhead.

"Hey, I'm Taylor. I called about the apartment."

Although he would rather live in his car than this hole, Taylor figured he should take a look since he was here. At least it would give him something to compare to. He had to find something because he'd be damned before he went crawling back to his mother.

"C'mon in." Crackhead left the front door standing open and shuffled down a hall.

Taylor followed to a bedroom with stained, stinking carpet and a mattress on the floor. Every one of the bathroom fixtures had a brown ring around it. Two cockroaches scuttled along the kitchen countertop. Taylor was careful not to touch anything or stand close to the counter in case a cockroach leaped onto his clothes.

Crackhead slouched against the kitchen counter. He lit another cigarette from the half-smoked one in his mouth. The butt sizzled when he threw it in the sink. A thin curl of gray smoke floated up.

"Seven hundred," Crackhead slurred.

"Thanks, but I have a couple other places to look at," Taylor said.

"Okay, five hundred," Crackhead countered.

Not even for free. Not even if you pay me seven hundred. "I'll let you know," Taylor said with a wave. He slipped out the front door, careful not to touch anything.

Back in his car, Taylor looked up at the guy's window. If that was how some guys ended up, he got why his mom was afraid of sex, drugs, rock and roll, booze, and parties. The only place that guy was going was down. Didn't he have anybody that loved him?

That afternoon, Taylor saw six more apartments but couldn't afford any of them.

This standing on his principles wasn't cheap.

Taylor sat in his car after seeing the last apartment and sighed. School, with three squares a day, dorm life, lacrosse, girls, friends, and parties, was easy street compared to paying his own way and becoming a firefighter. Problem was, it wasn't the street he wanted to be on.

He rubbed his palms back and forth on the steering wheel. The back of his throat felt tight. He had to ask someone for advice—but who would listen to him and not tell him to go back to following his mom's orders? He couldn't talk to Jack because he and his mom were making googly-eyes at each other when Taylor had last seen them together. He didn't want Jack to think he couldn't pull his own weight or that he wasn't man enough to be a firefighter.

Taylor turned on the car. He felt as though he was looking at a road where someone had stolen all the street signs, and he couldn't figure out where to go.

Jack lay as still as possible so he wouldn't awaken Olivia. After her visit to Ability House, they had lain down for what Olivia insisted would be only a few minutes, and she'd dropped instantly to sleep, snoring softly in an endearing way.

He'd pulled a light blanket over her and let her sleep, though he'd hoped for a different outcome. Tendrils darker than the rest of her hair curled at her temples and in front of her little kitten ears. He loved watching her sleep. She was completely unguarded and vulnerable, unafraid. He studied the lines around her mouth and corners of her eyes. She'd earned every one of those creases. They were a map of her resilience and fierce love, and he hoped that one day, she would have a few of those lines for him.

She had no idea how bowled over by her he was. Finding time alone for them was challenging because of his schedule, which included some nights. Tonight, Taylor had pulled the night shift, so they were at Jack's, nestled into the new sheets she'd ordered for his new bed. Jack looked forward to Taylor finding his own place—then Jack and Olivia would have more time together.

Hopefully, much longer, more permanent time. Jack wanted to wake up beside her every morning for the rest of his life, to have her curl up against his side every night. But there was still that firefighting thing between them, and he always felt that was the reason she held back a part of herself. If only she would realize how brave and resilient she was, they might have a future together.

For all the time they spent together, every time Jack brought up Derek's death, Olivia would only say that he fell and nothing more. For some reason, she still couldn't trust Jack not to judge her for something.

Her lids fluttered open. She smiled sleepily and stretched. "How long have I been asleep?"

"Mm, an hour," he said with his lips against her temple. "You were exhausted when you came home, so I'm surprised it wasn't longer. I take it the visit to Ability House was hard for you?"

She rolled over onto her back and lifted her arm above her head. He nuzzled the side of her neck and inhaled the scent of her skin.

"Did Ariel like it?" he asked.

The bright blue of her eyes dulled as though she were looking at him through foggy glass. "Loved it. But it's not home."

"Next best thing." He toyed with a strand of her hair. "I'm sorry, this is hard for you."

"I probably wouldn't have gone if you and Taylor hadn't pushed me into it," she said.

"Me? I only mentioned it. Taylor was the pusher, not me," he said defensively.

She sighed wearily. "You're right. He seems to be pushing every issue he can nowadays."

"He has Ariel's best interests at heart, just like you do." He traced her jaw with a finger. "But you have different ideas about what's best for her."

She didn't say anything.

He nudged ahead. "Now that you've seen it and you both love it, what's your hesitation?"

She pulled back to look at him. "Look, I said she could stay overnight for a weekend so, see? I am making progress in letting go." She poked him in the chest with every word. "Don't push me past what I'm capable of."

"I don't think there's anything you're not capable of." He was unable to stifle a chuckle.

She pulled the cover up to her chin, and she looked even smaller. "I'm trying to be the best mom I can be."

"I know you are, but there's not just one way to be a good

mom. All good moms and dads want their kids to grow up to be happy."

"Yeah," she said, her eyes flaring like a pair of sharp embers. "But dads think growing up is done by taking risks and dangerous chances."

He didn't want to fight, but he didn't want to be unfairly lumped in with men who chose selfish stupidity over real love. "I'm not Derek, Liv."

"Sorry," she murmured. Her lower lip trembled as she stared up at the ceiling. "What do you think is best for her?"

It was the equivalent of a woman asking, 'Do these pants make me look fat?' He didn't want her fears to drive her decisions. "Can I be honest?"

"Only if you agree with me," she said.

He laughed, and so did she, but he heard the pain in the tightness of her tone.

"If she moves to Ability House, you'll be thrilled, and so will Ariel," he said.

She threw the covers back, preparing to get up. "I still feel like I should keep her at home. If something terrible happens to her, I could never forgive myself. It would break my heart into a million pieces."

He threw his leg over her and pinned her to the bed, and she pounded playfully at his log-thick thigh with her fists. He took one of her hands and nibbled at the knuckles, and she relaxed again.

He pushed her blond hair back from her face. "Nothing's going to happen. I know Derek died and left you with two little kids, but you weathered that storm. I have no doubt that you can get through anything else life throws at you," he said.

"You're a fireman. You would say something like that," she said.

He leaned in and whispered into her ear, "You're my hero. I want to be like you."

She laughed. He raised himself up on one elbow. "Ariel can always come home if it doesn't work out, and she can come home for visits. It's not like you're throwing her in prison."

"I know," she whispered. "And thank you for understanding that this makes me a little crazy."

"You know, I think you have something in common with Ariel," he said, not rushing, letting her absorb his words. "She's a lot more capable than you realize and you're a lot more resilient than you realize."

She looked into his eyes for a long time before she said, "Take off all your clothes. I want to see you naked."

CHAPTER 31

> When we were children, we used to think that when we were grown-up, we would no longer be vulnerable. But to grow up is to accept vulnerability... To be alive is to be vulnerable.
>
> **Madeleine L'Engle**

At St. Paul's on Sunday morning, Taylor was on the altar serving wine during Communion. Parishioners queued up in the center aisle, split in the middle, and peeled off to the left and the right to receive Communion. He hoped his mom wouldn't come to the side where he was serving.

He wasn't sure how much he believed in God and Jesus, but the music, sermons, and rituals made him think everything would be all right. Being here felt like home. It felt good to be here where people knew him.

His five honorary aunts in the Marriage Survivors Club used to babysit him, bought him great Christmas gifts, loved him, cheered at his lacrosse games, were always glad to see him and insisted on hugging him no matter how old he was.

They, unlike his mom, believed in him.

St. Paul's, the Marriage Survivors Club, along with his mom, taught him to believe everybody was the same, no matter what. When you had a sister with Down, it helped to have reinforcements on your team.

Except for this morning, he felt himself staring into a black hole of being parentless, homeless, and any other -*lesses* he could think of. He wasn't looking forward to seeing his mom. He'd taken Ariel and Matt bowling on Thursday night, and when he dropped Ariel off, he hadn't gone in because he didn't want to fight with his mom.

It would have only made them both feel worse, and this was as crappy as he'd felt in a long, long time.

After church, he went downstairs for coffee hour. He wanted to see Ariel and eat stuff neither his mom nor Jack ever bought. The food table was a junk food smorgasbord with bowls of potato chips, plates of cookies, cupcakes, donuts, bowls of mixed nuts, a chocolate cake, and brownies. He'd taken the last donut when Ariel rushed up and threw her arms around his neck. The donut fell off his paper plate onto the floor.

The story of his life.

He picked it up and made a three-pointer into the trash can. He returned Ariel's hug. "Hi ya', Squirt."

Ariel said, "Take us movies?"

"You mean take you and Matt to the movies?" he clarified.

She nodded, grinning, and clapped her hands.

He laughed. "You're dating more than me." That made him proud of her, and himself. Having a relationship was a big accomplishment, and he'd contributed to that.

"Sure, I'll take you guys," he said, though he didn't know when he'd find the time.

Ariel was genuinely happy. For someone with Down, that was big. She was excited about her job and Matt. Ariel had her limitations, but he was proud to be helping her push those. Keeping his mom from crushing Ariel's happiness while maintaining his own dreams of becoming a firefighter alive was a little like juggling flaming knives.

Carolina appeared next to him. "Hi, Taylor. Hi, Ariel. How are my favorite nephew and niece?"

"I happy because ... because ..." It took Ariel a minute to formulate her thoughts into words. "Matt my boyfriend."

"It's terrific—you have a sweetie." Carolina hugged Ariel, making her grin.

Carolina threw her arm around Taylor's neck and gave him a squeeze. He was tempted to pick her up in a hug, but he wasn't sure that was right at church coffee hour.

Taylor liked all the Marriage Survivors Club members, but Carolina was the sweetest, with an angel-like air about her. Not that he believed in that kind of stuff either, but he always thought she could have been a nun. Calm and understanding floated around like sweet smoke. He'd grown up calling her and all the other Marriage Survivors Club "Aunt," but at nineteen, he was too old for that anymore.

Ariel's mouth pulled down at the corners. "But I sad. Tay Tay live not home."

The tendons across his stomach tightened. He took a long time choosing a chocolate cookie from the platter.

Carolina said, "Oh, dear. Do you mean Taylor doesn't live at home?"

Ariel nodded.

Taylor narrowed his eyes at her.

"Did something happen?" Carolina asked.

With a curt nod, Taylor indicated his mom on the far side of the Undercroft. "Yeah, mom happened."

His mom was never alone, but now, she stood by herself, face pinched, shoulders hunched, in a corner. She could come off as an ice cube when she was mad, but at church, she practically worked the room.

It was his fault that she looked so upset.

Carolina followed his eyes and pursed her lips.

Ariel said, "I go Mom." And she trundled her way through the crowd toward their mom.

Carolina drew Taylor to a quiet corner. Her loving brown eyes pinned him down. "Care to elaborate on what happened?"

Taylor spilled his guts. How he and his mom had fought about Jack giving him a ride on the motorcycle. How she was upset because he wanted to be a firefighter. The trip to Providence he wouldn't be making. How Jack asked him to find a place of his own, but he couldn't find anywhere affordable.

It was embarrassing to be bitching about his problems, but it felt like a fifty-pound barbell dropped off his back. He was relieved at the chance to talk to someone who knew both him and his mom. Talking to Carolina was different, like talking to an aunt. Carolina could see both his and his mom's positions. Maybe she could get his mom to be reasonable instead of acting all crazy.

"What will you do?" Carolina asked.

"I'll sleep in my car before I go home," he growled. "If I did, I'd never hear the end of her complaining about my not going back to school and about becoming a firefighter. I can't take it." He took another bite of the cookie, but it tasted like Styrofoam. "I don't get it. How come she can't be my mom without running my life?"

Carolina nodded.

He clenched his fists. "She takes every chance she gets to lecture me about something. I'm trying to stand on my own two feet."

"Mm, hm," Carolina murmured. Her face was sympathetic

and comforting, and he felt listened to for the first time since coming home from college.

"And you know, Aunt Carolina, I feel bad that I hurt Mom, you know, disappointed her."

He'd called her "Aunt," which felt good. Guess he hadn't outgrown that. He tossed his plate with the sugary junk into the trash.

"She doesn't love me unless I do what she says." His chest ached like he'd been elbowed in the sternum.

"Did you always feel like this?" Aunt Carolina asked.

He considered it for a minute. "Kind of. I've always tried living up to my dad's legend or whatever, but he was some kind of superhero, and I'm ..." he dropped his head. "I'm not."

Across the room, his mom's face was the saddest he'd ever seen.

"Why does it hurt her if I try to have my own life?" The next words flooded out of him before he could think. "I don't know where to turn, Aunt Carolina. I really don't." He trained his gaze on the hardwood floor as if the straight lines held an answer.

Aunt Carolina put her arm around his shoulder. "I can see you're upset that she's upset, but you have to live your own life. I can see both sides. I'm sorry you're both hurting. Letting go has been difficult for her."

He nodded. "If I don't stay around to make it happen, Mom won't let Ariel see Matt. You saw how happy she is."

"Your mom is losing both of you at the same time." Aunt Carolina sighed. "That's hard for a mother, especially after losing your father. She's never gotten over it, and that's why she's so scared about everything."

He hadn't thought of it like that. His mom only ever acted like he should be his dad's clone, but if his dad died, he saw how she might be afraid.

"But that doesn't mean you shouldn't have your own life or

follow your own dreams," Aunt Carolina said, and now he had to stop himself from picking her up in a bear hug.

He knew she wouldn't make him feel stupid, so he asked, "What ... what do you think I should do?"

Aunt Carolina's expression was practical. "Well, first, you should come and live in my extra bedroom. It's not fancy, but I will not throw you out until you can find a place or get a good job as a fireman."

Relief washed over him. He let his head loll back, and he looked up at the ceiling. *Thanks, God.*

"Getting you out of Jack's place will let your mom and Jack see if they have enough in common to have a relationship," Aunt Carolina said.

He hadn't thought of that angle. "They both deserve a chance."

"So do you and Ariel," Aunt Carolina said in the way he wished his mother would speak to him.

Then reality slapped him. "I don't have a lot of money."

She patted his arm and smiled. "Pay me what you can. You can help out around the garden and yard. Does that sound okay?"

His chest felt like an expanding balloon. Just like that, by telling someone, his problem was solved. He grinned. "Seriously?"

"Yes, seriously," she said, patting his arm.

Then his mom moved across his line of sight. She looked wrecked. He felt a frown lowering his brows. "But what about Mom?"

Aunt Carolina's voice was like a TV judge passing a verdict. "You let me and the other Marriage Survivors deal with your mother."

CHAPTER 32

Children are apt to live up to what you believe of them.
   Lady Bird Johnson

The Marriage Survivors Club was gathered in the living room of Carolina's tidy bungalow to organize the baby shower for Gracie's twins. Mostly, the shower was an excuse for the Marriage Survivors Club to throw a party.

Though they all knew it, no one mentioned Taylor had moved into Carolina's spare bedroom. Olivia was surprised how lonesome she felt for him. She imagined she could smell him like animal mothers could identify their babies.

Olivia felt a simmering resentment toward Carolina. It was the first time she'd ever felt truly upset with any of the Marriage Survivors, and it threw her off-center. The least Carolina could have done was talk to Olivia before she'd let Taylor move in.

While Bianca, Frankie, and Flicka were bickering about whether to serve mimosas or Bloody Marys, Olivia slipped out of the living room and down the hall.

She peeped into one of Carolina's spare bedrooms. What she saw shocked her.

The bed was neatly made, and the curtains were pulled back to let in the sun. There were no clothes on the floor and no lacrosse or rock-climbing equipment stacked in the corner. She tiptoed in and opened the closet door. Taylor's size twelve shoes were paired up on the floor, and his shirts, even some of his T-shirts, hung on hangers. The dirty clothes bin was empty, and the room didn't smell like Eau de Jockstrap. She peeped under the bed. No dirty dishes or underwear. This was totally unlike his bedroom at home. Did Carolina have more influence on him than his own mother?

Olivia lifted a clean shirt to her nose, but it didn't smell like Taylor or her laundry detergent. It smelled like adulthood. How dare he be so organized here, but not in his own home?

Flipping through his clothes, she found his high school lacrosse jacket. She buried her face in the folds of the fabric, wanting to leave behind a trace of her love.

Well, even she had to admit that was stupid.

He'd left her behind, but that didn't mean she was ready to give up her irritation with Carolina.

Olivia made her way back to the kitchen, where Carolina was busily assembling cheese and crackers on trays.

Casually, Olivia lobbed her bomb. "Why did you let Taylor move in without speaking to me first?"

Carolina didn't look up, but calmly carried on. "He's old enough to make his own decisions. And besides, he's lovely to have around."

I think so, too!

Olivia turned to see Bianca leaning against the doorframe.

"He's a great young man. Anyone of us would take him in. You should be grateful to Carolina instead of pissy," Bianca said bluntly.

Olivia's face felt red hot. "I am not pissy. At least she could have asked my permission," Olivia said indignantly.

"She doesn't need it, and neither does he," Bianca shot back.

Leave it to Bianca to pick a fight.

Carolina handed Olivia the plate of cheese and crackers. "Can you take this to the living room, please? If we don't get started, Gracie's twins will be in college by the time we're done."

Since Carolina wouldn't duke it out, and Bianca was taking Taylor and Carolina's side, Olivia took the platter and swept past them into the living room.

Hélène tangoed through the front door. "*Bonsoir, mes amis!*" she sang out in her usual melodious way. "Sorry, I'm late."

"Bone swoor, Frenchie," Bianca sang back in a croaky voice that made the rest of them cut up.

Olivia eased onto the sofa between Bianca and Frankie.

Carolina took a seat and settled her yellow legal pad on her lap. She always took notes at the Marriage Survivors Club meetings because she drank the least, which meant her handwriting was legible the next day.

"Now, for the mimosas, I have two bottles of champagne we can use," Flicka said. "Not the cheap crap, either. Veûve Cliquot."

"I'll bring the beer and peanuts," Bianca said.

"This is supposed to be a classy event, not like an afternoon watching a baseball game," Hélène said and laughed.

"Since I can't cook," Frankie said, "I'll bring the extra chairs from church and help Olivia with decorations."

Hélène tucked a strand of her black and white hair behind her ear. "I'll bring homemade macaroons and chocolate-dipped strawberries."

Olivia's emotions tightened around her throat like a fist. When it was her turn, she muttered, "Here we are, planning a celebration for two new babies coming into the world. If mothers had crystal balls to see their children's departures and destinations, the human race would cease to exist."

The chatter stopped, and she felt everyone's eyes on her.

"Aren't you being a little overreactive?" Frankie said gently. "Kids always grow up."

Of course, Frankie was right. Frankie put a glass of white wine in Olivia's hand and she knocked it back in one go.

Olivia blinked back tears. "Maybe the Marriage Survivors Club should invent a sort of ritual observance for kids leaving home to take dangerous, ill-advised life paths."

"Oh, Liv," Frankie said, wrapping an arm around her shoulder. "Moms practice saying goodbye in increments: first step, first day of school, sleep-away camps, birthdays, earning of driver's licenses, graduations, going away to college. A mom's hands get filled up with joys and goodbyes until they're too full to hold on to your children."

Since she'd fallen in love with Cam Simpson, Frankie had become much wiser and more introspective. Though she couldn't have said why, this, too, annoyed Olivia. It was like everybody was ganging up on her. But they were loving her, too.

"Okay, so what do you do when the most emotionally astute member of the Marriage Survivors Club has a breakdown?" Bianca pronounced.

After a bit, Carolina folded her hands and said quietly, "We listen. I think Olivia's upset because I let Taylor move in until he gets on his feet."

Olivia wiped her face and blew her nose. "Why can't he get on his feet at home?" she sounded whiny.

"Because, according to him, you're on his neck about everything. He feels like you don't hear him," Carolina said with infinite kindness when what Olivia really wanted was to kick over the coffee table and start a brawl.

"I hear him. I just don't agree," Olivia said.

"Mothers rarely do," Frankie said, archly. "That's why kids kick and scream to go off on their own." She bumped Olivia's shoulder with her own. "As is necessary in this case."

Olivia bumped Frankie back. They would do anything for one another, including taking one of their sons into their homes and helping to launch them in ways their mom might not be able to.

Hélène handed Olivia another tissue. "You raised Taylor well, so why don't you trust him to make good decisions?"

Olivia said, "Being a firefighter is not a good decision."

"It's his decision to make, not yours," Flicka said. "Jack O'Grady is a firefighter, and you're dating him."

"Go ahead—be snarky," Olivia said. "You don't know what it's like to be a mother."

Flicka turned her face away, but not before Olivia saw a shadow of hurt flit across her friend's exquisite features.

Carolina set aside the yellow notepad. "Do you want Taylor to have an unhappy life because he's doing what you want him to do?"

"But he'll be safe," Olivia argued.

"And fucking miserable." Bianca popped a cracker loaded with a piece of cheese into her mouth in one bite.

Flicka gave her a sardonic scowl. "Nice, Bee."

Bianca saluted her with another cracker.

Flicka said, "You can't spend the rest of your life with one hand around Taylor's neck and the other around Ariel's ankle."

Bianca picked up a block of cheese and examined it. Airily, she said, "Just because you're afraid of everything, including kittens, doesn't mean Taylor should be."

"I am not afraid of kittens," Olivia said between giggling and sniffling. "And for your information, I did visit Ability House with Ariel. She's going to spend a weekend there."

Hélène did jazz hands in the air and sang, "Glory to God in the highest!"

Even Olivia laughed and leaned against Frankie, who put her arm around Olivia's shoulders.

"Aren't you happy about how great the kids are doing?" Frankie asked.

"That's because I've warned them what dangers to watch out for," Olivia said.

Flicka poured herself her third glass of pinot noir. "You have to stop believing your own bullshit."

Bianca sang out, "Ding, ding, ding, ding! My bullshit-o-meter is ringing."

Olivia clenched her fists. "You don't know what it was like to lose my husband. I can't go through the grief and guilt again."

"Guilt about your husband's death?" Bianca said. "My bull-shit-o-meter is going crazy."

Olivia only ever told them that Derek had fallen while climbing. She'd never told them that she hadn't been there, that she should have stopped him going. That if she had, Derek would still be alive.

Carolina said serenely, "If you'd stop feeling guilty for whatever you feel guilty about, you could let go of being afraid. Living is full of risks, and you miss a lot of life if you don't embrace some of them."

Olivia found it impossible to be annoyed with Carolina. It was like being mad at the Virgin Mary. "Sorry, I was mad," Olivia said.

"It's okay," Carolina said. "I imagine letting go of your kids isn't easy."

"And if you're less afraid of life, maybe something would happen between you and Jack O'Grady," Flicka said in her smutty voice.

With everything that had been going on in her life, Olivia hadn't had a chance to let them in on her news. She grinned. Saucily, she said, "It already has."

And the Marriage Survivors Club hooted, hollered, clapped, and demanded details.

CHAPTER 33

Why is it that we rejoice at a birth and grieve at a funeral? It is
because we are not the person involved.

    Mark Twain

When Olivia arrived for Gracie's baby shower, Carolina looked
unusually harried. "Is everything okay?" Olivia asked. "What
can I do to help?"

Carolina blew out a breath. "Boy, am I glad you're here. We're
a little behind in preparations. Can you help Flicka set up the
food?"

Olivia patted Carolina's shoulder comfortingly. "Everything's
going to be fine." Olivia picked up two trays of food and carried
them to the already-laden table.

There were cheese and crackers, a three-layer dip, crudités, a
fruit platter, chocolate-dipped strawberries, cupcakes, cookies,
brownies, and, of course, wine and champagne.

Hélène, as usual, was late. Flicka was arranging a bouquet of
pink and blue daisies while criticizing Frankie, who stood on a

stepstool, hanging a crepe-paper swag across the living room window. Bianca busied herself setting the last of the folding chairs around the living room.

Olivia saw Gracie and Robert slowly navigating their way up the driveway. Gracie seemed to be moving even slower than usual. "Guests of honor are here," Olivia called.

Carolina rushed to the door and held it open. "Come in, Gracie and Robert."

Gracie braced her hand on her lower back. Robert held her elbow as she struggled enormously up the steps. Her dress could have doubled as a hot-air balloon and her feet were so swollen she wore flip-flops.

"The traffic all over town is terrible," Gracie said between huffs and puffs. "I was afraid we were going to be late."

Gracie's face was red with strain and damp spots bloomed under her arms, and it wasn't even all that hot outside. A spike of worry ran up the insides of Olivia's arms.

Carolina and Olivia exchanged worried looks. When they were out of earshot, Carolina whispered, "She doesn't look great. Do all pregnant women look like that?"

Olivia shook her head. She had loved being pregnant with both her kids, but she felt a welling of sympathy for Gracie. "Carrying one child was hard work, but two has to be a special agony."

Robert was in his own kind of agony. His eyes were bloodshot, with purple smears of sleeplessness below them. His skin looked sallow and sickly, and his hands trembled slightly.

Olivia pitied the poor man. He couldn't know it was only going to get worse.

Frankie said to Gracie, "Have a seat on the sofa. As soon as the guests arrive, we'll start opening gifts."

Gracie's eyes widened when she saw the flowers, balloons, and crepe paper festooning Carolina's living room. "It's beautiful. You went to so much trouble for us." She dropped onto the sofa with a wince and a grunt.

"It's no trouble," Carolina said. "We want to celebrate with you. It's not every day that St. Paul's gets two new members simultaneously."

Robert's laugh was a hysterical cackle, and Olivia was afraid he might lose it entirely.

Frankie whispered to Olivia, "Do you think we should slip one of Flicka's 'calming' pills into his drink?"

Olivia considered it might not be a bad idea. She said, "Can you blame him?"

Frankie shook her head.

To Gracie and Robert, Olivia said, "Would you like a glass of iced tea? I hope you're hungry because we have a ton of food."

Gracie took a tissue out of the pocket of her voluminous dress and wiped away the perspiration from beneath her eyes. "Just some iced tea, please. My tummy's a little rumbly right now. Maybe I'll have a little something later."

With her skin-tight dress and fiery hair, Flicka waltzed out of the kitchen with a tray of food, looking like Betty Crocker from hell. "Hello, darlings. When do those little buns of yours come out of the oven?"

Gracie patted her tummy and smiled painfully. "The doctor says another two weeks, but I wish it were sooner."

"Well, not today, okay?" Flicka said. She set the tray down in front of Robert, who inhaled cheese, crackers, dip, crudités, and mini quiches.

With the back of her hand, Gracie wiped sweat from her forehead. Olivia shot a glance at Frankie, who was frowning. She was clearly worried, too.

"Hungry, Robert?" Bianca teased.

Gracie patted his back. "I haven't really been able to cook for a month. He's kind of sick of frozen dinners and takeout." She asked Robert, "Could you please hand me a napkin?"

Robert handed her a napkin without pausing his eating or even looking at her.

Gracie blotted the folds of her neck.

The Marriage Survivors fluttered around, making certain everything was ready. Bianca nudged Olivia and whispered, "That's the third time Gracie has done that since they arrived. Do you think she's okay?"

"No," Frankie, who had two adopted sons, said. "That's why everyone should adopt."

Bianca scratched her head stupidly. "How's that supposed to work?"

"Go home and ask your mother," Flicka said and lifted one corner of her mouth.

Hélène, looking uncharacteristically rattled, wafted into the living room, carrying a bouquet of yellow, pink, and orange Gerber daisies. "My heavens, the traffic!" she exclaimed. "I thought I would never get here. Sorry I'm late, but this time, it really is not my fault."

Hélène presented the flowers to Gracie, who thanked her profusely. But her lips were pressed into a tight smile, which was nothing like her usual merry grin.

"Gracie doesn't look good," Hélène said as Olivia handed her a glass of champagne.

Frankie, who stood nearby, whispered. "We're all attributing it to the fact that her due date is near, and it's twins."

Between bites of cheese, Bianca said, "She looks like she's giving birth to a pair of water buffalos."

They all tried unsuccessfully to hide their snorts and guffaws of laughter.

Gracie asked, "Where's Ariel? I thought she'd be here. She's been so sweet every time she sees me. She always asks how long until the babies come."

"She has been unbelievably excited. Taylor took her and her boyfriend to a movie. He'll drop them off as soon as the movie ends," Olivia said. "She was torn between the shower and a date, but the date won out."

As she answered, Olivia felt every eye of the Marriage Survivors Club on her, gauging her nerves, but she served them up a smile and knew they understood. The explanation was almost painless. Olivia was astonished she had become used to Ariel's working and dating.

Her kids were growing up, which meant that Olivia, too, was growing in ways she couldn't have foreseen. She had more time to relax, to promote the store on social media, and to volunteer at church. It was a bit like being an hourglass that had been flipped. Her attention was pouring, grain by grain, into other things in her life, including Jack O'Grady.

It felt lovely to be cherished and held, skin to skin, by someone after so many nights alone. Of course, it wasn't a long-term thing. He was a firefighter, after all.

Guests, primarily St. Paul's parishioners, began arriving a little late. Everyone complained of the traffic snarls, backups, horn honking, ragged tempers, and people cutting one another off. Brightly wrapped gifts grew into a colorful mountain. Boxes of formula, a tandem stroller, cribs, and disposable diapers in graduating sizes had already been donated. Guests helped themselves to copious amounts of food, chatted, joked, and offered to help when the babies arrived.

Kurt and Lawrence Schmidt arrived with Ellis in his carrier, and for once, he wasn't screaming, but just the same, Olivia galvanized her nerves for one of his screech-o-ramas. The two dads imparted all their hard-won parenting knowledge to Gracie, whose clenched expression grew even more tense.

Gracie's smile wavered as she opened the gifts, as she occasionally winced.

Flicka leaned over to Olivia and whispered, "She looks sweaty and pale."

"How would you feel with two things the size of basketballs pressing on your bladder?" Olivia said.

Privately, Olivia agreed with Flicka, but she was working to keep her nerves from igniting unnecessarily. Things would wrap up soon and Gracie would be home, in bed, where she probably belonged.

"How come you're not worrying about Gracie?" Flicka teased. "That is so not like you."

Olivia tipped her chin up in a gesture of self-satisfaction. "I'm working on being proactive instead of worrying."

"Okay, I'll worry for you." Flicka rolled her eyes skyward and made a few whiny anxious noises.

Olivia laughed. "Stop it, will you?" she said.

Flicka pointed at Gracie with her wineglass. "Deal, but only if you go ask her if she's all right. Otherwise, I'll worry myself into another glass of wine."

Olivia decided that Flicka might be right. She perched on the arm of the sofa and whispered into Gracie's ear. "Are you sure you're all right? Should we cut this short and send people home?"

"Oh, no!" Gracie said with a half-mast smile as she dabbed at her neck with a wrinkled soggy napkin. "I've waited weeks for this. I'm so happy to be here. I'll be fine."

But Gracie did not look fine, and Olivia was beginning to hear the slow, low clanging of her internal alarm bells.

Gracie opened the pile of gifts to *oohs* and *ahs*. Bianca stuffed two trash bags with wrapping paper and Flicka refilled wine glasses until Frankie made a finger-slashing-across-the-throat gesture, the universal signal to stop. Flicka refilled her own glass and returned the bottle to the table.

Frowning, Hélène sidled up to Olivia. "Do you think we should ask her if she wants to lie down?"

Olivia shook her head. "We're almost halfway through the gifts. As soon as that's done, people will leave, but let's move this along. I'll cut and plate the cake."

Hélène glanced at Flicka, who was leaning against a doorframe so she wouldn't fall over. "And if Flicka's not too drunk, I'll get her to pass out the plates with the cake," Hélène said.

"At least that'll keep the wine glass out of her hand," Olivia muttered and the two of them laughed.

A familiar baritone called out, "Hello!" And Father Gabriel stepped into the living room. "I came to offer my blessings and drop off something for the babies. I would have been here sooner, but the traffic in town is terrible. Streets all over town seem to be backed up and rerouted."

Olivia loved his wide-open smile and the way he towered over his parishioners while maintaining the approachable demeanor of a Golden Retriever.

The nasty, unbeloved Bishop had sent Father Gabriel Ayeliffe to St. Paul's on the Green in Norwalk to shut the place down, but the reverse happened. Church membership and attendance soared and now St. Paul's was on track to be one of the largest, most active parishes in the Episcopal Diocese of Connecticut. All because of Father Gabriel, who looked sixteen but had the wisdom of a centenarian.

"Come in and have cake, Father," Carolina said.

He patted his waist. "I'd love to, but I'm going out tonight for dinner."

Flicka said, "Oh, a hot date? Maybe with Randy, the firefighter?"

Hélène elbowed her. "Flicka!"

"Just curious," Flicka said innocently.

Father Gabriel's grin didn't flag. "I'm meeting with members of the Vestry and Wat. We're planning our next big fundraiser for the shelter. We've decided to have a piano concert."

Abruptly, Hélène turned on her heel and left the room. As she passed Olivia, Hélène's face was nearly as pale as Gracie's. What had Father Gabriel said to provoke that reaction?

"Would you like a blessing for the babies, Gracie?" Father Gabriel asked.

Gracie shifted uncomfortably in her seat and looked up at him with a smile that seemed forced. "I'd love it as long as I don't have to kneel."

The room grew quiet as Father Gabriel laid his graceful, long-fingered hand on Gracie's belly and said a prayer for safe delivery and health for the baby and parents. Olivia was pretty certain that whatever Father Gabriel said, God would grant.

When he finished, Gracie seemed relieved and grateful. She shifted in her seat again.

"I'll get you a pillow for your back, Gracie." Olivia ran and grabbed one from the bedroom.

Father Gabriel left after he'd had a piece of cake, and Olivia wished everyone else would leave too. She wanted to get Gracie home safely. However, there was way too much food and wine, and as usually happened when the parishioners of St. Paul's got together, everyone was having fun.

Olivia was about to shoo everyone out of the house when baby Ellis chose that exact moment to scream. His room-clearing shrieks drove the guests from the house like an announcement of the plague. It was the only time Olivia was grateful for the kid's lung power. He'd make a great chorister someday.

The Marriage Survivors Club had begun to clean when Taylor showed up with Ariel.

"No party?" Ariel asked, clearly disappointed.

Gracie said, "No, you're just in time, Ariel. I'm so glad you could make it."

"I date Matt," Ariel said, beaming.

"Tell me about him while I show you some gifts," Gracie said, patting the sofa cushion beside her.

Taylor came to where Olivia was cutting the cake. He said, "Hey, Mom. Sorry, we're a little late. There's a lot of weird traffic."

His coolness had dissipated, but he kept his distance, wary of being snared by her.

"It's okay. We're just finishing up, but there's still cake. Would you like some?" Olivia asked, and she smiled at him, determined not to push something on him he didn't want.

"No, thanks, I'm good," Taylor said. He hooked a thumb over his shoulder. "I'm going to give Robert a hand loading all their stuff in their van."

Olivia was wiping the dining room table when she heard a suspect low moan, followed by a gasp. A charge or white-hot fear chased up her spine. She rushed back into the living room.

Gracie had lifted her skirt up. There was blood everywhere.

CHAPTER 34

Children are the hands by which we take hold of heaven.
Henry Ward Beecher

Taylor had noticed that Gracie wasn't looking good. Robert needed to get her home as quickly as possible.

"Robert, I'll help you pack up this loot," Taylor said, and gathered an armload of baby shower loot and headed out the door.

As they reached the car, Taylor heard Ariel scream. "Tay Tay. Blood!"

Taylor dropped the pile of gifts he was carrying and raced back into the living room with Robert close behind.

In the living room, Gracie lay on the floor, her knees bent, groaning. Blood and fluids were everywhere, spreading beneath her in a widening pool.

His mom had her fingertips pressed to her mouth, open in a gasp. This would send her right into full panic mode.

Even Carolina's ordinarily calm face was full of fear. She

clasped her two hands together like she was praying. "It all happened so fast!" Carolina said. "I don't know what to do!"

Taylor kneeled at Gracie's side and took her pulse. It was fast. "Have you called an ambulance?" he asked no one in particular.

"I already did," his mom answered. "911 said the firefighters and ambulances are all out at a six-car pile-up on I-95. They said it would be a while before anybody could get here. They're sending an ambulance from Westport."

His mom's face came into focus. She kneeled on the other side of Gracie and took her hand.

Something between confidence and fear shone in her eyes. She met his gaze and said, "I told them a volunteer firefighter was already here."

"But there's all that road construction on Westport Avenue. It'll take forever," Hélène said in a shaky voice, her hands on either side of her face.

Flicka came around a corner and shrieked, "Oh, my God!" With a *thud,* she hit the floor in a dead faint.

The last thing Taylor needed was for all these women to keel over. He turned back to Gracie and said, "Don't worry. The ambulance will get here soon. I was an EMT, and I'm a volunteer fireman. I can keep you comfortable 'til they get here."

Bianca said, "Shall I boil some water?"

"Should we put Gracie in someone's car and drive her to the hospital?" Frankie asked.

Taylor glared at them. "Chill, guys. The ambulance is on the way." Taylor gave Gracie's shoulder a squeeze. "Gracie, I know it won't be necessary, but I'm going to go wash up. You just sit tight."

"Guess I'm not going anywhere," Gracie moaned.

Taylor rose and stepped over Flicka's sprawled form. At the kitchen sink, he soaped up to his elbows. It was weird, feeling electrified, and yet calm, in control. This feeling was why he wanted to do this. When he was doing this kind of work, he felt capable, powerful even. All his mom's warnings vanished from his mind. All he thought about was what to do next, how to save this person, make them feel better, make sure they didn't die or bleed out. And he had all the skills he needed to do it. He just hoped the ambulance got here before the babies.

Carolina came into the kitchen. She was shaking all over.

He addressed her with an authority that seemed like a new part of his personality. "I'm sure the ambulance will get here, but just in case, I need alcohol, a sharp knife, and clean towels. Sterilize the knife in the alcohol. Bring me the bottle of alcohol when you're done." Eyes like saucers, Carolina nodded and scurried off.

He returned to Gracie and felt her pulse, and was concerned to find it faster than before.

Carolina returned with fresh towels, which they spread under Gracie. Carolina set a shallow dish nearby with a sharp paring knife sitting in a bath of alcohol.

Someone had mounded pillows behind Gracie's shoulders and back. She howled and groaned, her face crunched in pain. She blew air hard between her gritted teeth.

Robert had rolled up his shirt sleeves and crouched behind her shoulders. "The ambulance is coming! Don't push, don't push! Breathe, pant!" His voice rose above Gracie's wailing as if he could slow the whole thing down by yelling.

Gracie bent double and made spluttering growls when she exhaled. "They're coming."

"These are just Braxton-Hicks contractions, aren't they?" Robert looked anxiously at Taylor.

What the hell do I know?

Taylor ignored Robert's freakout.

Robert put his mouth close to Gracie's belly. "Hang on, you

guys! The ambulance is coming! It's coming! Just wait a little longer! It'll be okay, I promise!"

Taylor wished Robert would pass out.

Bianca looked up from her phone. "The contractions are down to two minutes apart," she said in a voice that sounded nothing like Bianca's usual trash-talking.

Taylor locked eyes with her and felt his brows shoot up. "You sure?" he said in a low voice.

Bianca nodded.

How could this happen so fast? Maybe because it was a doubleheader.

Taylor had always been under the impression that labor and delivery took a long time, with contractions that lasted for hours, or at least long enough for a woman to get to the hospital or for the ambulance to arrive.

"Don't push, Gracie, breathe. Breathe," Robert blathered, inhaling so his nose made a whistling noise.

Taylor told his mom, "Go scrub up and come back."

She staggered a bit as she got to her feet.

Dear God, don't let her faint too.

"I want to pusssshh!" Gracie shrieked.

"No pushing, no pushing!" Robert insisted in a panicky voice. "You have to wait. Wait, honey! Wait, babies! Wait!"

"FUUUCK YOOOOU! I'M PUUUUSHING!" Gracie roared, screamed, grunted, and strained. Sweat poured off her face, soaking the neckline of her dress.

Somewhere behind him, Ariel said, "I help?"

Flicka moaned, "Oh, deeear God, ooooh, dear Goooood."

Bianca answered, "Yes, you can help me, Ariel. Let's drag Flicka out of here."

Ariel took one ankle, Bianca the other. Frankie and Hélène took Flicka's shoulders and the four of them half-dragged, half-carried her out of the room. Taylor loved Flicka, but right now, it was a relief not to hear her moaning too.

His mom reappeared. Her face was pinched, but she wasn't going bonkers or anything. That would probably come when she saw blood.

"Gracie, I'm going to take a look here, okay?" Taylor said. He kneeled between her legs and lifted her dress.

There it was: a dark wet curve of scalp.

Adrenaline raced through him like a gasoline-fueled fire.

This delivery was a rollercoaster without brakes.

"I see the head," he whispered to his mom.

Her eyes widened.

Over Gracie's groans and cries, Taylor listened for the sound of an ambulance, but there was nothing. He was aware of everyone's presence, of their fear sucking the oxygen out of the room.

Most people did dumb stuff when faced with this kind of thing, but Taylor's mind became calmer. Things slowed down. The light got more intense. The pressure in his chest felt good. It wasn't an adrenaline rush but a sweetness coming over him.

He was embarrassed to admit it even to himself, but he felt like angels were floating around him.

He was probably drinking too much Communion wine.

Ariel, Bianca, Hélène, Frankie, and Carolina came back into the room.

Frankie, ever practical, said, "I've scrubbed in case you need more help."

He gave her a warning glance. "As long as you swear not to pass out."

"I swear," she answered, and he believed her.

Frankie was a brick. She was the hardiest of all the Marriage Survivors Club. Bianca was the toughest, but Frankie could do anything without the distracting jokes.

Bianca said, "The contractions are down to a minute apart. I don't think the ambulance is going to get here in time."

No jokes from her now.

His mom murmured, "What shall we do?"

He felt as though he was crawling out of a skin he'd been struggling to shed for a long time. For once, his mother was asking him, not telling him, what to do. She was letting him be in charge—for once, trusting him.

In high school, when he was volunteering as an EMT, a family drove up to the firehouse. In the back seat, a Hispanic woman was giving birth. She was illegal and afraid to go to the hospital. Luckily, one of her kids knew help was available at the firehouse. The family had arrived just in time for one of the firefighters to catch a beautiful, fat, brown baby with a rooster's head of black hair and the cry of a future rock star.

Taylor never forgot that defining moment. It was another experience that made him want to be a fireman. Being an EMT wasn't enough—he wanted to be a fireman. There was something God-like in that guy's confidence, and that was who Taylor wanted to emulate.

Gracie screamed and gave one great heave, and the entire top of the baby's head showed, glistening, threads of blood and mucus smearing his scalp.

But the baby's scalp was gray.

Terror sucked every molecule of breath out of Taylor. Did the gray color mean the baby wasn't alive? What if the umbilical cord was around the baby's neck, choking him?

Oh, Jesus, Jesus, Jesus, no, no, no, no!

Gracie lay back against the pillows, bathed in sweat, moaning, and panting. Where was the ambulance? Could he do this on his own? Looked like he had no choice.

"Keep pushing, Gracie," Taylor said. Was that the right thing to do? He had no idea, but it seemed logical since these babies were in the fast lane.

"No pushing!" Robert shouted.

In another second, Taylor was going to tell him to shut up.

Carolina and Hélène braced Gracie's shoulders as she grunted long and hard. "Huhnnnn," Gracie moaned.

The baby's forehead, eyes, nose, and tiny pink mouth appeared.

He was sunny side up, slippery, with pale hair and a squinched-up little old man's face.

Taylor loosened the umbilical cord from the baby's neck. He turned and eased the baby down, and a shoulder slid out.

This seemed like a very odd way for God to bring humans into the world. Why hadn't humans evolved so that babies arrived some other way, like under a cabbage, delivered by storks or Amazon Prime?

He caught his mother looking at him with amazement and pride in her eyes.

She held a towel, ready to wrap the baby. Her hands trembled, but she didn't move or shift, waiting. His calmness was keeping her calm.

This wasn't too hard! He could do this!

"You can do it, Gracie," Taylor said, encouragingly. "We're almost there. One more good push, and we'll have the first one."

Gracie roared, and a wet bundle of arms and legs landed in Taylor's hands.

"It's a boy!" Taylor's chest swelled as if he was the father. He fought back a lump of emotion building in his throat. He and his mom traded smiles.

"We knew the lower one was a boy, but it's the other one we're not sure about," Robert said in a quavery voice.

Frankie snapped the butt of the knife into Taylor's palm.

Right, gotta' cut 'im loose.

Taylor cut the trailing umbilical cord and looked at Frankie. "How are you with knots?"

"I do a mean slipknot, but I think a simple knot will do." She knotted the cord not far from the infant's navel, then leaned back to admire her handiwork. "That oughta' hold."

Taylor placed the baby in his mom's hands. Her eyes glowed like Christmas bulbs.

To Frankie, Taylor said, "Use a soft towel to clear his mouth and nose." To his mom, he said, "Rub his back gently until he breathes."

He didn't know how he knew to do this, but he did.

They did as Taylor directed, and the baby let out a squally cry.

"Look, he's breathing!" his mom said in awe as she watched the baby for a minute.

"Oh, my God, oh, my God," Robert whispered. "I thought I was ready, but didn't think it would be like this." Tears flooded his eyes and his chin wobbled.

Frankie passed Robert the towel-wrapped bundle. She said, "I hate to tell you, but the rest of parenthood is kind of like this, too."

Carolina wiped at Gracie's forehead with a damp cloth. She lay back panting, sipping water from a glass Hélène held to her lips. When she finished drinking, Gracie said, "I want to see him."

Robert held the tiny baby for Gracie to see, and she smiled wearily.

"Here he is. Number one," Robert said proudly, as though he'd done all the work.

Another contraction came on. Gracie squeezed her eyes shut and groaned in pain.

Robert handed the baby to Carolina, who cradled and cooed to him.

Where is the damned ambulance? This is going at warp speed.

"Okay, number two is in the chute," Taylor said. When he heard Bianca snort with laughter, he realized it was a trashy thing to say, and he mumbled an apology.

Gracie strained and pushed for only a few minutes before a tiny butt appeared between her legs.

This was not the head Taylor had expected.

His mom glanced up at him with cold terror in her eyes. "He's breech."

CHAPTER 35

What's done to children, they will do to society.

Karl A. Menninger

This one was going to be way more complicated and higher risk.

Yo, baby! Could you please back up, do a U-turn, and re-approach the exit?

Taylor said, "Okay, this guy's butt first, Gracie. I don't know how difficult it's going—"

"AHHHHH!" Gracie wailed and pushed. The gray-blue behind and legs appeared, dangling with the terrifying rubbery consistency of a toy doll.

Taylor wiped the sweat from his face with his forearm. His legs were starting to cramp, and his back was aching from kneeling on the floor. He wished Jack were here. He'd probably done this a dozen times.

Gracie gave a grunt and pushed. The arms and shoulders slipped out.

Taylor tugged gently to loosen the umbilical cord around the baby's neck.

"It's a girl!" Robert crowed.

Now to get the head out.

Another contraction bowed Gracie in half, her cheeks puffing out, her face red, sweaty hair matted to her head.

"Bear down," Robert coached.

Grunting, Gracie pushed again.

The baby's head didn't budge.

"Is it over yet?" Flicka called from the kitchen.

"NO!" was the unison shout.

Three contractions.

Three massive pushes.

The baby's head remained stuck.

"Where's the ambulance?" his mom hissed.

This time, Taylor heard the shake in her voice and worried she would crack. She couldn't crack. He needed her hands in here. He needed her to believe in him.

Bianca said, "Ambulance is on its way, but they're still ten minutes out."

Taylor ground his teeth. *Ten minutes? The baby could be dead by then.*

Frankie said, "I'm going out to wave them down." The front door slammed.

Bianca leaned down, hands on her knees, and peered between Gracie's legs. "What's going on in there?" She could crack a joke about a nuclear explosion.

Gracie lay back, panting, and growled at Bianca.

"He's stuck," Ariel said from across the room, where she sat on a chair, watching. Everyone, including Taylor, had forgotten she was even there.

"On TV, man put hand inside." Ariel raised her closed fist. "Pull baby out."

Everyone stared at Ariel.

Taylor looked at his mom. "What are you letting her watch on TV?"

"You're the one who said I need to let her be more independent," his mom retorted.

Bianca said, "Ariel's right. I saw the same show. Put your hand inside, lift the legs, and tug."

"So, you want to give it a go?" Taylor barked at Bianca.

She held up her hands in surrender and backed away.

"The show's probably on YouTube," Bianca said.

"I do not need YouTube," Taylor snarled.

But the baby's color was tingeing toward blue.

Taylor's mouth went dry. His heart raced so fast he thought he might be dying.

What if YouTube was the only source of help available? He should have gotten on the phone with some physician from the hospital. Why hadn't he thought of that? Because he'd thought he could do this on his own. But really, he hadn't done it on his own. Everyone except Flicka had helped—even his sister with Down syndrome.

Bianca held up her phone, showing a YouTube video of a breach delivery. "Try this."

"He's not delivering my baby by watching a YouTube video," Robert shouted.

"SHUUUUTTT UUUUP AND GET THIS BABY OUT OF MEEE!" Gracie screamed.

Taylor heard the siren and whispered a prayer of thanks. Finally, somebody who could finish the job without the help of YouTube.

Robert wailed, "Hang on, honey. The ambulance is coming."

Gracie panted through pursed lips and said, "I wanted a home birth anyway, but noooo! You said it wasn't safe. Taylor's doing all ri—" A contraction racked her. "AHHHHH!"

She pushed, but still, the baby didn't budge. Taylor didn't think they could wait until the ambulance arrived.

"Okay, let me see the video," Taylor said. His mom leaned close to watch, too.

Gracie lay back, panting. "I don't know if I can do this much longer."

Taylor wished the baby could kick its tiny feet, put its hands on either side of Gracie's vagina, and wiggle her way out.

The video played on and on until it finally came to a spot where it showed the baby in exactly the same position as this baby: butt up, arms and legs out, head stuck. He squinted at the screen and listened to the instructions.

Now he knew what to do.

Thank God for YouTube.

"Gracie, when I say push, you push." He turned to his mom. "Mom, when I tell you, lift the baby's feet up like in the video." Like in the video, he reached two fingers inside the birth canal. He found the baby's mouth and hooked his fingers into the baby's mouth. He put his other hand on the back of the baby's neck. "Gracie push. Mom, lift now."

He tugged gently, and the baby slid out like a wet baby seal.

Olivia overflowed with breathtaking wonder. The world had been expanded by not two, but three new human beings.

She had seen Taylor born as a person she'd never allowed herself to see before, even though he'd been right there all the time. She couldn't have been prouder of Taylor if the babies had been his. He had delivered Gracie's twins, and he wasn't even twenty. She felt the same limitless awe as when she had given birth to him all those years ago. When they placed him in her arms, all the amazing things she had done with Derek seemed like poor substitutes for living.

The ambulance took forever to arrive, but, siren screaming, they pulled in just as Taylor delivered the baby girl. Those babies had been impatient, rocketing down the birth canal like a pair of Olympic tobogganers.

The Marriage Survivors wandered around hugging one another, laughing, wiping away tears, and recounting their part in the drama.

After Gracie, Robert, and the twins were whisked off to the hospital, Olivia and Taylor washed up in the kitchen.

"I can't believe you did that," Olivia said to him.

He splashed cold water on his dazed, sweaty face. "Why not? Think I didn't know what I was doing?"

"Did you?" She handed him a towel. He smiled the smile she had missed and longed for since he'd moved out.

"Not a clue," he confessed, with a humble expression on his face, and chuckled.

So did she. "But you sure acted like you did."

Taylor said, "You weren't so bad yourself, holding the baby girl up like you did and helping me. And you were cool. You never freaked out."

"If it had been anyone but you, I think I would have freaked out and passed out on the floor next to Flicka," Olivia said. "You didn't need me. You could have done it solo."

Watching her son bring two new lives into the great, tumbling, stupendous world was a miracle. By delivering the babies, he'd launched himself out of the orbit of her anxieties and into his own universe, where he would find his own adventures and path. A path he would travel without her.

And that was right and good.

Olivia burst into tears. She couldn't help it. She stretched on tiptoe and threw her arms around her son's neck. "I'm so, so, so proud of you." She stepped back and looked at him, her heart full to bursting. "You were so calm and in control. I was a nervous wreck, but you were so cool. I can't believe I gave birth to such an incredible son. That I raised you, and you turned out to be such a terrific young man."

He looked embarrassed as he dipped his chin and mumbled, "Thanks, Mom.

Olivia took her son's extraordinary, capable hands that no longer reminded her of Derek's. Taylor's hands had a singularity, strength, and tenderness all their own.

"I think you'll be a wonderful firefighter."

CHAPTER 36

We find delight in the beauty and happiness of children that
makes the heart too big for the body.
   Ralph Waldo Emerson

When Matt rang the bell, Olivia hung back and let Ariel open
the door for him and Jack. As they put their arms around one
another, Olivia had anticipated a rending inside, but instead,
their happiness smacked her across the heart. Her daughter had,
at last, beyond all possible odds, found love.

As the Marriage Survivors Club said, God worked in myste-
rious ways.

Jack had suggested they all go out to dinner tonight to
Osteria Romana, a white-tablecloth Italian place. Olivia's hair
was loose, fluttering around her face in a shimmer of silver
blond. She had on her usual little black dress, necklace, and the
matching pearl earrings that Derek gave her when Ariel was
born. The ensemble was sedate, but underneath, she wore a
black lace bra and panties. Jack wouldn't know she wore them,

but she knew, and that made her feel sexy. Flicka would be proud of her.

Jack took one look at her, and his eyes widened. "You look ... you look—I-I, wow! Even more beautiful than I've ever seen you," he said in a voice weakened by awe.

She tipped her chin up and looked into his eyes, where his desire drew her in. Slowly, she stood on tiptoe, reached her hand up to the back of his bull neck, and pulled his face to hers. She paused for a split second, savoring the suspense, the atoms of desire in the space between their bodies nearly setting her hair on fire. When she closed her eyes and touched her lips to his, heat and warmth feathered down the front of her throat and plunged to the seat of her belly.

She pulled back. His eyes were swimming like a drunk's.

Those lacy undergarments were well worth what she'd paid for them.

"Oh, my God," he said on an exhale. He brushed the back of his meaty hand down her bare arm.

Hot prickles rushed up the backs of her calves as if someone had slowly drawn a fingertip up her leg. If it had only been the two of them, Olivia would have skipped dinner and gone straight to dessert.

Matt and Ariel stood oblivious in the living room. Ariel spread her arms and twirled. "New dress," she said to Matt.

Olivia had taken her shopping and had her pin-straight hair blown out and done with loose curls left around her sweet, chubby-child face. She clasped her hands under her chin. Her daughter was now a young woman, and Olivia felt the same aching pride she'd felt when Taylor delivered the twins. This was more than she could have hoped for.

Matt said, "I like it. It is Rembrandt green, and that's one of my favorite colors. It is good to use when you paint leaves."

"Like tie," Ariel said to Matt. "It's orange."

Ariel's face was charming and enchanted. A feeling like floating on a bed of clouds made Olivia light-headed for a moment.

Her children didn't need her anymore. It was as though she was watching them be born again. She wasn't sure who had changed more, them or her. Her life was a diamond with new facets and brilliant sparkling colors. Derek would have been proud of their children, too. He would have been proud of Olivia letting Ariel go to Ability House for the weekend. For letting Taylor become a firefighter.

Okay, it had taken the birth of a pair of babies, but still, Olivia had stopped fighting Taylor.

Of course, she would always worry about her children because that was what good moms did: they worried. It was one of the many ways they showed their love, and no one could make them stop. But she found her stomach in knots much less frequently.

Jack must have seen the effect the young people were having on her because he took Olivia's hand. "You okay?" he whispered into her hair.

She didn't want him to see the tears in her eyes, so she nodded. But he knew and kissed her temple. She leaned into him for a few minutes, enjoying the safety she felt there. It wasn't forever because he was a fireman, but for now, it was enough.

"Our reservation's for six. Shall we go?" Jack asked.

"Oh, let me just get my wrap. I forgot it upstairs," Olivia said.

She ran upstairs to her bedroom and opened the bottom drawer of her dresser. She found the black cashmere shawl she seldom wore near the bottom and under it, an undershirt of Derek's she always kept there.

Even though she knew where the shirt lived, its presence caught her by surprise.

White, folded neatly, the round, crew neck collar slightly frayed, the shirt was still unwashed after all these years. She kneeled on the carpet and skimmed the much-washed weave of the cotton fabric with her fingertips. She held the shirt to her nose, closed her eyes, and breathed in deeply. Somewhere she had read that scent was the longest memory retained in the brain. Even if the shirt no longer smelled, she imagined she could conjure up Derek's unique fragrance: rubbing alcohol, not unpleasantly of sweat, coffee, hospital laundry detergent. Danger. Sex. Risk. She pressed the shirt against her lips and kissed it.

Oh, oh, oh, my darling. I will love you always. I'll see you this weekend.

Lovingly, as if it were a precious icon, she refolded the shirt carefully and placed it back in the bottom of her drawer.

Then she went downstairs to go to dinner with Ariel's boyfriend, Matt, and his Uncle Jack.

Osteria Romana wasn't crowded because it was a Thursday night. The aromas of buttery garlic, fresh yeasty bread, and tomato sauce wafted through the restaurant. Forks and knives clinked softly against plates and classical music was the back-drop to chatter and laughter. In a tank along one wall, brilliantly colored tropical fish swam through bubbles and fake seaweed.

When they were seated, Olivia wished their table was slightly larger so she wouldn't have to sit so close to Jack because his masculine energy created a web across the narrow space between them. His smile, the way his eyes met hers, his care for her, illuminated a future she wasn't prepared to step into. The pull of her love for Derek occupied so much of her heart that she didn't think it would be fair to Jack to lead him on anymore. This recognition was like a pair of scissors piercing her heart.

Later, she wouldn't really recall the conversation or even if the food was good. What she would remember was how happy Ariel and Matt were and how their shared happiness was like a fifth person smiling serenely at all of them.

Matt said, "I sold two paintings on my website."

"Good," Ariel said.

"Uncle Jack did it," Matt answered.

"That's wonderful," Olivia said. She turned to Jack. "For a guy who said he didn't know anything about art, you've become quite the wheeler-dealer."

Jack toyed with his knife and smiled. "It's basically free to put them up, so it can't hurt." He raised his eyes to hers. "When you took the pair for the store, I realized the paintings were a source of untapped income. The shirts are steady income but require a big investment to produce. He already had the paintings, and they're getting a lot of hits online. Thanks to you." He squeezed her hand, and his touch made her breath rush out of her lungs.

Had Derek's touch left her with this kind of brain-rattling disorientation? She couldn't remember. Guiltily, she withdrew her hand and sequestered it in her lap.

Jack stiffened.

She recognized hurt in the way his eyes turned a darker shade of brown, the way the corners of his mouth turned down ever so slightly.

She was relieved when the waiter set down their plates: salad and a side of pasta for her, seafood risotto for Jack, and penne and butter for Matt and Ariel.

"I go Ability," Ariel said to Matt.

"Remember Ariel, it's just to see if you like it." Olivia sipped her wine to quiet the flutter of nerves running through her.

"And to see if you can stand it?" Jack teased, his smile gentle and understanding.

When had he become so adept at reading her? At knowing her. He read things in her eyes she hadn't known were so obvious: fatigue, curiosity, iron-focus, and of course, anxiety and worry. How long had it taken Derek to do that? Had he ever been able to, or bothered to, read her semaphore face?

"It might not be a good fit," she said.

"It will be," Jack said with his annoying confidence.

"Know-it-all," she said under her breath, but with a teasing smile directed at Jack.

Jack laughed and held up his hands in submission. He said, "You weren't too hot on the idea at first, were you, Matt?"

Matt shook his head. "No. I didn't want to leave my house or my Uncle Jack."

"But you like it now, right?" Jack asked.

"I like it a lot," Matt said around his pasta. "I have lots of friends. We do things together. I am an ente-prenoor at my house."

"Yes, you are an entrepreneur, buddy." Jack squeezed Matt's shoulder.

As Jack described some of the activities at Ability House to Ariel, Olivia's mind drifted. The entire Memorial weekend was turning out to be a hand grenade. Ariel was going to visit Ability House, and Taylor was driving hours to see a girlfriend Olivia had never met. Having her children along on the annual trip to Providence had always softened the impact of her sorrow. This time, she would be alone.

Her grief always convinced her that she'd experienced a once-in-a-lifetime love—the kind most people only ever dreamed about. Grief had always been the persistent background roar of ocean waves accompanying the rest of her life. But this year, without the children, she worried that her sorrow would take on a different shape she might not recognize. That she might not be able to handle it.

Jack leaned over and kissed the corner of her mouth. It was like having sunshine poured into the corners of her soul where her grief and love for Derek huddled, and made it disappear.

But how could she turn her back on Derek and the life they'd had together for a new, different life? How could she forget what they'd meant to one another?

Jack said, "Taylor mentioned he was going to see his girlfriend this weekend. With both kids out of the house"—he waggled his eyebrows—"do you have plans for the weekend?"

She hadn't told Jack about going to Providence because she didn't want him to know how deeply she still loved Derek.

She dabbed her mouth with her linen napkin. "I'm going to Providence. I go every Memorial Day weekend."

"Really?" Jack stared at her, baffled. He frowned and poured her more wine. "How come you didn't mention it?"

She accepted the refill, though she didn't need it. Her head already felt mushy, her tongue loosened, guard down. "Because I didn't want to hurt your feelings."

Which she'd done, anyway.

"What do you do there?" Jack asked. He extended his arm and rested it along the back of her chair, as though coaxing her to him.

She said, "The kids and I always went together, but I'll be on my own this year. I stay at the Waldorf, where my husband and I had one night of honeymoon before he had to get back to his residency. Then, Saturday morning, I go out to Narragansett Town Beach, where we used to surf."

Jack tucked his chin back in surprise. "You surfed?" he asked as though she'd said she could fly.

"Yes," she said, pleased she had surprised him.

"What's surf?" Matt asked through a mouthful of pasta.

"Riding ocean waves on a skinny board," Jack said. To Olivia, he said, "Will you surf this time?"

"Not on your life," she said, and laughed. "I have kids." But not ones that needed her so much anymore.

"Good, because you know how dangerous that is and I don't want you to get hurt," Jack said.

"Touché," she said, smiling into her wineglass.

"What else will you do?" Jack said.

She set her wineglass down. "I'll picnic in Chaffee National Park because that's where my husband proposed. I also go to Derek's favorite oyster bar in Matunuck. I'll attend services at Grace Episcopal Church on Sunday morning, where we were married."

One of Jack's eyebrows was raised, and one corner of his mouth curled up playfully. "Do you spend the weekend wearing widow's weeds?"

Instantly sober, she straightened in her chair. "No, I do not," she said tartly. "It's the way I remember the father of my children."

He frowned more deeply. "Sorry, I didn't mean to tease you about your annual pilgrimage. I get it," he said with a nod. "Every year on the anniversary of my divorce, I like to take a long motorcycle ride. Helps me forget."

"The trip helps me remember," Olivia said.

His eyes bored into her. "Remember what?" he asked.

"How much we loved one another," she said, not looking at Jack.

Every marriage had bumps and rough spots. Derek had loved her, even if he sometimes forgot to tell her. Even if he indulged in his crazy hobbies despite her begging him to stop. Even if he ignored her feelings and fears.

Jack set his fork down and scowled down at his risotto. "So, you're going alone?"

Before he went any further, she knew where he was headed, but this weekend was sacred. She would celebrate what she'd had, and mourn what she'd lost: a wonderful, exciting partner, a fantastic, satisfying lover, and a man dedicated to his work and his children. Someone whose life had been cut off in its prime before he saw his children grow to adulthood, before she and Derek had time to grow old together.

It was not a weekend she intended to spend in bed with Jack. They could do that when she returned.

Jack's gaze made her feel as though she could lean into him forever, but for all she knew, Jack might die in a fire or motorcycle crash tomorrow—then she would be mourning two men. And that would break her in two.

Matt and Ariel finished and asked if they could go see the fish tank. Olivia watched them go and said, "They're good together."

"So are we." Jack lifted her hand to his lips and kissed her fingertips, making her bones melt. He placed her hand resolutely back on the table. "But I can't compete with a dead guy."

Dread toppled into her.

He leveled his gaze at her. "If you're still going off on a trip to pay homage to a guy who took you for granted, then you're not ready for what I want with you."

The backs of her knees broke out in a sweat. "I'm not going to pay homage to him. It's something I've done for ..."

For eighteen years. Had it been that long since she had loved a man who was alive?

"All right. I'm off this weekend. I could go along to help with the driving." Jack spun the stem of his wineglass. "Keep you company."

Blood spread heat to the tips of her ears. Her words came out in a whisper. "No, no. I have to do this alone."

His eyes held an unswerving conviction. "Okay, but think

about the future you want. One with a dead guy or a live guy. If you want to keep belonging to him, you can never belong to anyone else." His eyes were fireman eyes; hard, forward-driving, implacable eyes. "I'm not going to compete with a dead hero."

The room felt cold, and the candlelight anemic. Somewhere in the rear of the restaurant, someone had the audacity to laugh. The wine had left a vinegary bitterness in her mouth. In the kitchen, something was burning. Voices of the other diners were loud and argumentative. A busboy dropped a glass, and it shattered on the tile floor.

When she recovered herself, she said, quietly, "That sounds like an ultimatum."

"It is," Jack said. He pushed his half-full plate back and laid his linen napkin on the table.

She wasn't ready. Too many things were changing all at once. She'd wrestled two of her biggest fears: letting Ariel stay the weekend at Ability House and accepting that Taylor would be a firefighter. But she couldn't let go of her love for Derek. They'd been everything to one another. Though Jack filled her blood with sparks, her heart with velvety comfort, he wasn't Derek. It was unfair for Jack to try to occupy the spot where Derek still lived.

When she came back, she would simply have to tell Jack it was over.

CHAPTER 37

The seeds of success in every nation on Earth are best planted in women and children.

Joyce Banda

Olivia smiled at seeing Ariel's excitement as she bounced up the front steps of Ability House.

Bea Dewinter was at the top of the stairs, holding the door. She waved at them and laughed. "Hi, guys! I'm so glad you could come to stay this weekend, Ariel. We're all going to have a lot of fun."

This was the weekend that would decide Ariel's—and Olivia's—future. She had accepted that the risks to Ariel were minimal, but Olivia still felt like she was skiing down a black diamond slope blindfolded. She'd never done anything like this before in her life, and neither had Ariel. Clearly, her daughter was more ready than she was.

Ariel was brimming with enthusiasm, but Olivia's lip did its nervous dance. Half of her pulsed with happiness and pride, the other half with loss and anxiety.

"Matt here?" Ariel peered around the entry foyer, love-struck hope in her eyes.

Bea laughed. "Not right now. The gentlemen will be over later, and I'm sure he'll be here."

"We hug." Ariel clapped her hands.

Imagining Ariel and Matt wrapped in one another's arms, Olivia felt a volcano of worry erupt—of anxiety.

"They won't be—you know—I mean, going in the ..." Olivia cleared her throat, leaned closer to Bea, and whispered, "The conjugal room?"

"Oh, the couple's quarters?" Bea laughed. "Probably not this weekend. We have lots and lots of plans for the weekend. We'll have a cookout with hotdogs and hamburgers for dinner, and afterward, we'll have a dance. Tomorrow there's a pancake breakfast with the Kiwanis, and Monday, we go see the Memorial Day parade and have ice cream sundaes." Bea laughed, and so did Ariel.

Olivia tried to laugh, but she just couldn't make herself do it.

Bea motioned Ariel toward a wide staircase leading to the second floor. "I think your mom looks like she could use a rest for a minute while I show you to your room. We've put you with Sarah. She's just about your age, and I'm sure you'll like her because she likes *My Little Pony*, too."

"You'll come back so I can hug her goodbye?" Olivia asked.

"Of course. I wouldn't think of your leaving without a hug," Bea said.

Bea showed Olivia to the living room, where she dropped into a comfortably tatty wing chair that might have been in her parents' house.

In the same way Olivia decorated to her client's tastes, everything at Ability House was set up for the comfort and needs of the residents. Stacks of well-thumbed comic books sat on end tables. Crocheted afghans draped the backs of chairs and sofas, giving the room a homey feel. In the garden outside, women toddled between beds of roses. Happy chatter drifted through the rooms. Somewhere in the house, Elvis's voice sang, "Love Me Tender." Sun streamed in through the window and warmed Olivia's wet cheeks.

This would be a wonderful home for Ariel.

Ariel and Bea returned to the living room. Olivia rose from her chair and wiped her face, hoping Bea wouldn't notice, but Olivia saw that she did.

"Okay, I think we're all set," Bea said. "I have your number, and you have mine. Call whenever you feel the need."

Feel the need. Would the end of the driveway be too soon?

Olivia took Ariel by the shoulders and looked her in the face. "I'm going to Providence. You know that, right?"

"Yes," Ariel said. "I fun."

"Yes, you will have fun," Olivia agreed. She reached up to straighten Ariel's messy hair, but drew her hand back. Messy hair was okay, and Ariel didn't need her to fix it.

Olivia released her death grip.

Olivia had a sense that after she left, nothing would ever be the same. Not Ariel, not herself, not their lives. Could one weekend change a lifetime of a mom's worry and a child's need?

"We'll take perfect care of her, I promise," Bea said. Her eyes suggested that she understood what Olivia was experiencing. The woman was impossible not to like or trust, so Olivia told her heart to stop hurling itself against the wall of her chest.

"I'm proud of you, honey," Olivia said to Ariel.

"Matt coming." Ariel made a flapping gesture. "You go."

Olivia must have looked stung because Bea patted her shoulder. "You should be proud of both of you."

Olivia nodded. She did feel proud, but she also felt a hole where her identity as Ariel's mother had been.

"Hug?" Olivia mustered a smile. She enveloped Ariel in her arms and squeezed.

Ariel squirmed. "Too tight, Mommy!"

Olivia turned her loose and, without looking back, Ariel headed off toward Elvis.

Olivia slapped her palms against her thighs so she wouldn't reach out to hug Ariel again.

Bea didn't laugh, but she made a soft hum of compassion.

"Okay, then," Olivia said with false brightness. "I'll leave you to it."

When she hit I-95 North, Olivia pumped a fist in the air like Bianca always did when someone scored a point, kicked a basket, or whatever it was that sports teams did. Olivia crowed, "I did it!"

She'd decided this weekend she would indulge in the guilty pleasures of sleeping in, eating dessert, ordering French fries at the restaurant, and walking on the beach. She wouldn't worry about either of her kids for the entire weekend. She turned on the radio to the classical station and smiled. She would not worry about anything. Not even the bubonic plague.

CHAPTER 38

What's the greater risk? Letting go of what people think - or letting go of how I feel, what I believe, and who I am?

Brene Brown

Saturday morning, Olivia lay in the king-sized bed, staring at the ceiling of her hotel room at the Waldorf Providence. When she'd arrived yesterday, she'd ordered room service: a lobster roll and fries, a bottle of wine, then raspberry gelato. She'd treated herself to a long bubble bath in the marble bathroom while watching a chick flick on her iPad and sipping wine. The room décor, in muted aqua with silver gilt accents, was a bit dated and rococo, but elegant. The high thread count sheets were satiny, the lofty pillows soft and luxurious. It was all immensely lonely.

Olivia brushed her fingers over Derek's T-shirt spread out on the pillow next to her. Jack would know just the right thing to say to comfort her if he were here. But he might not be there when she got back home. He wanted to move ahead, and she was still treading water. She wasn't even sure she knew where the shore was.

If she couldn't let go of Derek, she would have to let go of Jack. This seemed a weekend of letting go of many people, of the roles in her life, of her own identity. Jack was asking too much of her. She wasn't ready to give up everything.

She hadn't slept all night but lay awake, listening to the steady *tat-tat-tat* of the rain pelting the window. Memorial Day in Providence was usually bright and sunny, but last night's drizzle had turned into a torrential downpour. The holiday to kick off the unofficial start of summer was usually celebrated with a parade featuring high school marching bands playing off-key, firetrucks, flag twirlers, and Little League teams waving at people lining the sidewalks.

This year, because of the rainstorm, the parade was canceled.

She closed her eyes and remembered the times she'd brought the kids here. They would bounce on the bed, and she would let them have Fruit Loops in the hotel restaurant. She took them to the gazebo at Narragansett and, just like Derek had, she pointed out the yachts sailing by, and the kids chose which one they wanted to sail around the world on.

She told her kids what a great father they'd had. She wanted Derek to be a hero to her kids, for them to know how wonderful he was. They would be excited to hear stories about their dad, how he worked in the hospital ER and saved lives, and how he was a terrible cook but liked to eat and never got fat. She never told them how Derek often came home so exhausted from work that he slept twenty-four hours straight, turned around, and returned to the ER.

She left out the part that he sometimes drank too much. That she and Derek had surfed at Narragansett. That, to feel alive, he had to be moving every minute he was awake, pushing to the edge of danger. That he could be inattentive and irritable. She never told them how this risk-taking had tied her in knots.

She had drunk her own Kool-Aid and forgotten that Derek had put his own needs ahead of his future and his family.

Perhaps she wouldn't have loved him if he hadn't needed her to patch him up and to protect him.

His addiction had been to risk. Hers had been—was—to being needed. Now no one needed her anymore, and she was going through a kind of withdrawal.

She pushed the covers back, pulled on her robe, and went to the window. In the distance, the ocean roiled gray and brown, and waves churned up whitecaps. Slate gray clouds hung low in the sky, and the rain fell in great sheets that lashed sideways. Wind blew the leaves off as if it were autumn. Down below in the street, their umbrellas turned inside out, pedestrians in raincoats and rain boots dashed through puddles.

Narragansett Beach would be dismal today, but she wasn't about to break with tradition even though her kids had thrown the pilgrimage overboard like a corpse. She showered and dressed in a wool fisherman's sweater, jeans, and tugged on her yellow rain slicker and knee-high rubber wellies.

In the car, she streamed Benjamin Britton's "Four Sea Interludes" from the opera *Peter Grimes* to the car's sound system. The mournful thrash of the orchestra was a perfect accompaniment to the occasion. Creeping along toward the beach, she whiteknuckled it through sheets of obliterating rain as the wind rocked her car. There were few other vehicles on the road. Passing trucks threw up blinding sprays of water, which her wipers, even on high, couldn't contend with. She drove by an instinct deep in her marrow.

At Narragansett Town Beach, she parked as close to the breakwater as possible and sat in the car watching Mother Nature throw a magnificent hissy fit. Waves rushed in and crashed onto the shore, and receding, left sea wrack on the sand. The horizon was invisible in the beating storm as though the ocean was wrestling the sky to the earth. Thunder rolled overhead, and lightning sliced across the steel-gray sky. The sound of the relentless waves matched the rhythm of her blood rushing through her ears.

She and Derek had spent hours surfing and board sailing on this endless ocean.

Finally, she admitted it to herself: she'd hated surfing. She didn't even like boats, but God, she had loved Derek. She would have done anything for him, especially to try to keep him safe.

She put the car in reverse and headed back toward the road.

Going to Chaffee National Park for a picnic was impossible, so she opted to drive to the oyster bar in Matunuck, Derek's favorite lunch destination. The rain was letting up, but the wind still threatened to shove the car off the highway.

Derek liked slumming it at the oyster bar with its rustic wood-slab tables, smell of stale spilled beer, and crushed oyster shells all over the ground and floor. He loved the briny taste of the oysters, the buttery cheddar-bacon rolls, and the mayonnaise-drenched coleslaw. He would wash down two dozen oysters with an IPA while she picked at her wedge of salad of iceberg lettuce with blue cheese dressing on the side.

When she came with the kids, Taylor always had fried clams —which he never finished—Ariel ate clam chowder, and Olivia still ate a wedge of iceberg lettuce with blue cheese dressing. It hadn't been the kids' favorite restaurant meal, but she wanted them to know what Derek had loved and enjoyed.

Olivia pulled into the parking lot of the oyster bar. The windows were boarded up, and a sign on the door said: Closed by Order of the Health Department. Another scrawled and fading sign read: Permanently Closed.

How could something she'd shared with Derek be gone,

possibly for good? She felt as though something deep inside of her had been yanked out by the roots. A thing that was so entwined in her that she didn't know how she could live without. Who was she without her memories and rituals? Everything was changing so fast, and she didn't think she could keep up.

Olivia drove back to the hotel through another sluicing of rain. Even though she'd worn rain gear and rain boots, she somehow managed to get soaked to the skin. She took a hot shower and climbed back under the sheets. She was about to order dinner from room service when her cell phone rang.

Without preamble, Carolina said, "I called to see how you are."

Olivia bit the inside of her cheek, but a sob gushed out, anyway. She told Carolina about Jack's ultimatum, how he wasn't going to fight against a dead man.

"Make a choice: dead Derek or jumping Jack," Carolina said, with uncharacteristic cruelty.

"You sound like Bianca," Olivia said. "It doesn't even feel like a fair choice."

"It's not," Carolina agreed. "One loves you and the other one can't."

Olivia's laugh broke into a whimper.

"You know, you don't have to stay up there alone all weekend," Carolina said. "You could come home."

"I do this every year. I'm fine." Olivia wiped her cheek with the edge of the sheet.

"I can hear from your voice that you're not fine. Talk to me," Carolina nudged.

Olivia sucked in a stuttering breath. "I'm not sure Derek was really all that wonderful." She sniffled.

"Tell me what he was like," Carolina said.

Olivia sank back onto the pillow and stared up at the ceiling.

"He was compassionate and patient. He loved his work. He was a sensitive lover and funny and intelligent."

Hearing the diffidence in Olivia's voice, Carolina asked, "But that's not all, is it?"

"His work and play took everything out of him," Olivia said. "He did high-risk sports, even though I didn't want to and begged him not to." Anger reared up like a fire, which, at great personal cost, had been long deprived of fuel. Now it licked along her veins with a vengeance. "I know he was busy and overworked, but he could have turned down extra shifts. He never helped with housework, childcare, grocery shopping, or laundry. I did it all."

"That must have made you mad," Carolina said.

"In his defense, he did change diapers occasionally."

"Whoopee," Carolina said dryly. "Did you ever ask him to help?"

Had she? "Well, not often," Olivia said. "I felt like he was already doing the heavy lifting." She laughed.

"What?" Carolina asked, a smile in her voice.

"One time," Olivia said, "I left the kids with him to go out with friends, and when I came home, he was snoring on the sofa, and the kids were in their cribs smeared with food and poop."

Their laughter died out simultaneously in resigned sighs.

Olivia said, "I'm not sure the Derek I remember was real or one I invented."

"You know the most important thing: you loved him, and he loved you. That's what matters most," Carolina said. "But maybe it's time to stop idealizing him and move on. Give Jack a fighting chance."

Olivia said, "Jack could die tomorrow in a motorcycle accident or a fire. I don't think I could get over losing someone I love again."

"He's not dead yet," Carolina reminded her. "You could spend the rest of your life with Dead Derek, or you could have six months, a year, or ten with Jumping Jack."

"Quit calling them that. It makes me laugh and I don't want to laugh," Olivia said and laughed sadly.

Carolina said, "I think the names are perfectly appropriate. If anything happened to Jack, you would bend, but you wouldn't break. As your friend, I absolutely believe in your ability to live through a nuclear apocalypse."

"Like a cockroach," Olivia said, and laughed some more. The Marriage Survivors all possessed the ability to provoke that reaction in one another, no matter what the circumstance.

Olivia said, "But if I let go of Derek's memory, it will mean I don't love him anymore."

"No, it only means you'll stop believing Derek was a saint. It means you stop believing you don't deserve to experience love again. It means you're willing to take the biggest risk of all: letting yourself fall in love."

Carolina's loving words shot through Olivia and blasted away everything she was clinging to. With Taylor becoming a fireman, with Ariel moving to Ability House, Olivia had no more excuses for being stuck. She could look down the road of her future or she could look over her shoulder at the past. She had a choice.

A companionable silence settled as Olivia thought about what Carolina said.

"I couldn't stop Derek. I wasn't there to save him and that's why he died," Olivia said. "I've always felt that if I'd have gone climbing that day, he might still be alive. I've felt guilty about that ever since he died." Though she tried to hold it back, a sob, mixed with a sigh, escaped Olivia.

The admission—finally—to one of her closest friends felt as

though Olivia had opened a part of her heart that she'd kept hidden from the Marriage Survivors Club.

"Oh, Olivia," Carolina murmured. "You aren't responsible in any way for his death. You couldn't stop him anymore than you can stop Taylor."

Olivia blew her nose in a tissue. Carolina said. "Why haven't you ever told us you felt like this?"

"I felt too guilty and ashamed," Olivia said.

"Well, that was a waste of your heart," Carolina said with an impatient huff. "We love you unconditionally. We've all made mistakes, but this *wasn't* one. Derek died because he fell off a cliff, and you couldn't have stopped him. We would never change our opinion of you because of how he died."

There was a prolonged silence while, as though her heart finally gave a gigantic exhale, Olivia sobbed into the sheets. She felt as though she'd taken a giant leap of faith, and her friend caught her.

"Thank you," Olivia finally managed to say. "I should have told you all sooner, but I just couldn't bring myself to do it. I was scared."

Carolina said, "I understand. Guilt and shame are like a toxic substance that sometimes takes a while to come to the surface."

How was it everyone else was so wise while me, who is supposed to be the most emotional of the Marriage Survivors Club, didn't see this?

"Are you going to be all right?" Carolina asked.

"Yes," Olivia said, not certain that was true.

It was a relief to be honest about her feelings and be reassured of still being worthy. She'd come to celebrate Derek, but a part of her had cracked open and her guilt was leaking away. Who was she now that she no longer believed she'd failed her husband?

And who had Derek been? A selfish, foolish daredevil or a

brilliant, dedicated doctor who had loved her? Like Taylor, she was going to have to reassemble her memories and feelings into a new and different shape.

Eventually, Carolina said, "If you need any of us, you know we're here."

"Thank you for everything." Olivia clicked off the connection.

She picked up Derek's T-shirt from the pillow and pressed it to her nose. It smelled like the bottom of her dresser drawer. She couldn't remember how Derek had smelled, or how his eyes glinted right before he did something scary. How had it felt to want him the way she had when they were young and reckless?

Derek was becoming a formless collection of hazy memories, some probably truer than others. His insistence on living on the edge had been the kind of invulnerability that adolescents believe in.

She had imagined herself as powerful enough to protect him, but that had been *her* fantasy, not his. She laid the shirt aside.

No more. She wanted a live guy, not a dead guy.

She'd been lucky enough to have loved and been loved by Derek, to have had children with him. If he hadn't lacquered his self-confidence onto her naturally timid personality, she might have crumpled when he died. Their life together had given her the resilience to go on after he was dead, raise her children, start a business, make friends like the Marriage Survivors Club, and attend St. Paul's. Derek believed she was brave, and eventually, it became true.

She lay spread-eagled on the bed, feeling the cool, crisp sheets beneath and the light, warm comforter on top. After all Derek had done for her, here she was alone, far from home, away from the people who knew and loved her best. She was rejecting the fearlessness he'd taught her.

But Derek had one last thing to teach her.

She slept soundly and awoke before dawn the next morning, feeling rested, resolved, and at peace. She packed her bags and checked out of the hotel.

Contrary to the weather report, the rain had stopped. On the horizon, the sun was just beginning to rise in a strip of apricot. In the faint light of dawn, she drove north to Narragansett Town Beach with Derek's T-shirt on the front seat beside her.

At the beach, she kicked her shoes off and left them in the car. She climbed out, taking Derek's shirt with her.

She walked to the water's edge, the sand cold and wet between her toes. A fierce wind whipped off the ocean, swirling her unbound hair about her head and buffeting her cheeks. The rolling waves made the music of exhalation and inhalation. As she stood looking east to the horizon, frigid waves washed over her feet until she couldn't feel them anymore.

One final time, she put Derek's shirt to her nose, then she strode into the waves. The chill made her catch her breath. The surf lifted her off her feet, pushed her backward, and dumped her on her butt, soaking her up to her neck, plastering her clothes to her body and soaking her hair.

She struggled up and, using her hands to dig her way forward in the cold churning water, she forged deeper into the surf until she was in up to her waist.

Then she let go of the shirt.

She didn't watch it wash out to sea, but turned her back and staggered through the waves back to shore.

She felt freer than she had in her entire life.

CHAPTER 39

When you break up, your whole identity is shattered. It's like
death.

Dennis Quaid

Taylor lay on his back, staring up at the ceiling of Dani's
apartment. It was cramped and smelled like mold with a
microwave, a tiny kitchenette, a half-sized fridge, a rickety café
table, and this double bed shoved in a corner. Over his head,
ugly yellow paint intended to hide a web of cracks was flaking
off. Over the front door, was a fuzzy brown water spot that
reminded him of a rotten peach.

Since Dani was older than him, he'd thought of her as more
of an adult than himself, but this place reminded him of that
grody place he'd looked at above the bar.

Taylor chose his words carefully. "So, like, I was wondering,
when does this internship wrap and when do you think you'll be
back in Connecticut? You weren't real clear on that."

Dani yawned like a sleepy cat and stretched her muscled

arms above her head. "Oh, I don't know. It depends on how this internship goes. They might give me an extension or something. It's nice down here. I mean, I'm definitely coming back to finish my degree in the fall, but mm, maybe, I don't know, I might put it off until the spring." The shiver she made caused the bed to shake. "Winter in Connecticut is so cold."

It was the kind of carefree answer he was used to getting from Dani, but now, it felt like a blow off.

She rolled onto her side and looked at him. "I'm a sunny person, you know?" She ran her finger down his bare chest. "I don't always stick to the plans I make."

He was beginning to see that. "Are you glad I came down?"

She stiffened on the mushy, too-small mattress. They'd planned that he was coming for ages, but when he'd texted her, she'd taken her sweet time responding. When he knocked on her door, she'd acted surprised to see him. He'd imagined her throwing her arms around his neck and kissing like she'd been waiting for a month to see him. But when she opened the door, she kissed him like he had bad breath.

She rolled over onto her back. "Well, yeah, sure. I'm really into you, you know? We have a good time together. We like a lot of the same stuff. The same bands. Rock climbing, mountain biking, hiking. We both like Thai food."

He felt a sinking feeling in his gut. "Okay, but I thought, you know, maybe there was more between us than pad Thai."

She pulled the covers up to her chin and stared at the ceiling. "I'm a lot older than you are."

"Only a couple years," he said.

"You should ... date around," she said.

He wasn't really interested in dating around. He was crazy about her. He wanted to be with her all the time. He thought about her, dreamed about her, wanted her all the damn time. Sometimes he couldn't concentrate because she was all he thought about. That was what he thought love was like, but then she was his first serious girlfriend, so maybe love wasn't like that.

He should ask Jack because he sure wouldn't ask his mom.

Dani said, "I mean, I'm not ready to give up seeing other people or anything."

She wasn't? That was news to him.

He kept his voice even. "Yeah, sure I get it."

He was pissed at himself for being unable to tell Dani how he felt about her. The way he had thought she felt about him.

He was glad he'd worn a condom, like his mom had taught him.

Back at UCONN, she made him feel like he was someone special. He wasn't scared of caring about Dani and disagreeing with her. She wouldn't break, unlike his mom, who crumbled like a fortune cookie when she was upset. Dani made him believe he could make things happen in the world. That he could accomplish his dream of being a firefighter. That they would be together when those things happened.

Best start being brave now. He decided to leap into the flames. "I just—you know, have a lot of feelings about you. You mean a lot to me."

But he didn't mean a lot to her. Clearly, he'd read the situation all wrong.

"So, like, what are you saying?" she mumbled sleepily.

She wasn't making this easy. He said, "That I really like you. I want to be with you all the time."

His cheeks got hot, so he knew they were bright red. He hated that about himself—it was so childish. Except he'd seen Jack blush once around his mom, so maybe guys did blush.

"Oooh, it's super sweet you drove all the way down here to see me," Dani said. Her voice rose at the end of the sentence, making it sound more like a question, not like she was stoked to see him. She sounded more like his coming down was convenient the way pizza delivery was convenient. She sat up. Straps of muscles in her back flexed as she slipped on a flannel shirt and pulled up her panties. Her thick, wavy brown hair flowed down her back. He reached out and raked his fingers through her hair that flowed down her back to her waist. He loved doing that, loved the messiness of her hair, her casualness. It relaxed him.

She got out of bed and flicked on a dented electric kettle sitting on the counter.

He propped himself on one elbow and watched her move around the room. He liked the round, plumpness of her butt. He liked her self-assurance, her steady movements.

"So, how's the fireman thing coming?" she asked.

The fireman-thing? Like it was a hobby, not something he wanted to spend the rest of his life doing. Not something she had encouraged him to do. Not something that he'd staked his heart and soul on. Did she even *know* him?

Did he even know her?

She took down two mugs from a shelf over the mini-fridge and put tea bags in them.

He hated tea. After nine months, didn't she even remember he hated tea? He knew she liked decaf coffee with a lot of half-and-half, Earl Grey tea for breakfast, eggs scrambled dry, cotton underwear, anchovies on her pizza, studying late at night, driving long distances, and lilac perfume.

And she couldn't remember he hated tea?

He said, "The fireman thing is going well. Like I emailed you, I passed the physical exam and the online course. I'll take the written exam the next time it's offered."

"Oh, yeah, right, you did say that. Sorry, I've been busy," she said, not sounding sorry at all. "Guess I forgot."

She flashed the smile that usually affected him like he'd driven a ball into the lacrosse net while running full speed. Only today, it didn't. Her smile felt hollow and left a hungry spot in his insides.

"What's the next step?" she asked as she poured milk into both their tea mugs.

If he had to drink tea, he preferred it straight up, the way he liked the truth.

"I keep volunteering to show I'm serious, get some experience, get a good grade on the exam. I filled out the application online, and once I pass the test, hopefully, I'll get an interview. Jack said he'd put in a good word for me."

She squinted. "Jack, that's the guy who's got the hots for your mom, right?"

The hots. It was kind of retchy to think of his mother being the object of Jack's "hots." Or that his mom had the "hots" for Jack.

"Yeah, she's dating Jack. He's the guy I told you about. The captain at the station house where I'm hoping to get a job."

She set the tea mug on the bedside table next to him. "Hey, I'm going to shower, then I have to meet some people. You coming?"

You coming? His throat tightened. What the hell else was he supposed to do, stay here, and look at the peeling paint on the ceiling? She'd known he was coming for the weekend, and she made plans with other people? Why didn't she just tell him to get the fuck out and go home? How could he have misread her so badly?

He sat up, pulled on his shorts and T-shirt, and stood. "Who are these people?" he asked. He plumped the pillows, pulled the sheets, and covers up—a habit he'd picked up while living at Carolina's.

He tried to sound casual when he felt like punching a hole in the wall of this shithole apartment. "I thought we were going rock climbing."

She said, "A mountain biking club I've joined. We're going riding out to this state park."

He frowned. "Why didn't you tell me? I'd have brought my bike. Instead, I brought my climbing gear."

She got a pitying look on her face, and he knew what was coming, but he had no idea how to brace himself for the punch.

She tucked her luscious hair behind her ear and cocked a hip against the counter. "Listen, it's nice to see you and every-thing, but"—she waved a finger back and forth between them—"this. I don't think it's a long-term gig, you know?"

"Oh." He rubbed the stubble on his cheek. "Are you breaking up with me?"

"Yeah, I think it's best. Maybe when I get back to Connecti-cut, we can hook up again. Do some climbing, some biking. It's been fun." She padded across the room and kissed his cheek. A soft dry kiss-off. "I'm going to jump in the shower."

"Sure," he said, and wiped some crumbs from the counter into the sink.

He waited until he heard the shower running, then dressed and left like some pathetic, rejected dog.

As he drove home, he was surprised that he didn't feel worse. Getting dumped, he guessed, was part of being an adult. It was official: he was a grownup.

CHAPTER 40

> But the fruit of the Spirit is love, joy, peace, patience, kindness, goodness, faithfulness,
>
> **Galatians 5:22**

Father Gabriel and Olivia stepped onto the stone labyrinth behind St. Paul's. Her china doll face belied the concern weighing on her. She had called him this morning from Providence, and the urgency with which she asked to see him made him suspect she had a problem. For the first time since he'd known her, her pale blond, blunt-cut hair was loose, tucked behind elfish ears, and she wore jeans and a sweater, making her look like a too-old middle school kid.

Gabe said, "I thought we could walk the labyrinth together. Sometimes being in nature, walking and talking together, helps me think of a solution to a problem," he said.

"Good idea," she said. "It's lovely back here. I should do this more often."

Sam Wanamaker and his husband, Darren, had installed the

labyrinth a few years ago. Silvery soft-needled fir trees surrounded the labyrinth and provided a barrier to the noise of traffic. A memorial garden where departed saints had been laid to rest bended seamlessly into the pre-Civil War graveyard encircling the church.

Gabe took a deep breath. The scent of lilacs was positively intoxicating. Bees nuzzled the smiling faces of the pansies, darting from one flower to the other. Daffodils, tulips, anemones, pink creeping phlox, and columbine were all in flower and clouds of low, tiny, blue forget-me-nots bordered the labyrinth.

Gabe wished, not for the first and certainly not the last, that his beloved Oscar was alive to enjoy this bit of heaven with him.

Olivia gathered her thoughts as she and Gabe made a half circle of the labyrinth. Gabe waited for her to speak. He was good at waiting. It was his superpower.

Olivia said, "I've decided that I want to put up a memorial at St. Paul's for my husband." She pointed to the rows of brass plaques in the ground which were engraved with the names of the dead. "I don't want a plaque in the memorial garden, though. There's not a gravesite because I spread his ashes in Narragansett Bay."

Gabe said, "I notice you contribute to keeping the Presence candle in the Lady Chapel lit in his memory. That's been a thoughtful memorial to him. You're literally carrying a torch for him."

A zinger but delivered with love and kindness.

She made a soft, self-deprecating sound. A cross between a sigh and a moan. "I guess I never thought of it that way."

In silence, they trod the circular brick path as the sun beat down on his neck and head.

After a bit, Olivia said, "I like seeing his name in the bulletin once a month, but now, I want something more permanent." She knew she wanted to go but needed to know in which direction. He would let her find her way.

She said, "Every year, on Memorial Day weekend, the kids and I traveled to Providence to remember him. Except this year was different. I went alone." She stopped on the path, marshaling her reserve. "I decided this was my last trip."

He was touched by the catch in her voice. "How do you feel about that?" he asked.

She glanced up at him. "Honestly?" She blew out a long breath and the contours of her face seemed to grow softer. "Relieved," she said.

She was such a bright, dedicated, and resilient woman. For years, she'd hidden her sadness well. What a toll it had extracted from her.

Grief was universal, an inevitable part of life, and yet, people hung on to it for years, stuck in the twin cement overshoes of regret and loss.

Gabe was one to talk.

Even after three years, he often spoke to Oscar as he ate dinner. Sometimes while reading, he would come across a passage and say, "Listen to this," and he would read it aloud. Then he would look up and find himself alone. Many times during his day Gabe thought, "I have to remember to tell Oscar this."

Then he remembered Oscar was gone, and Gabe's heart broke all over again.

Olivia told him of her long struggle with guilt and fear. How it nearly destroyed her relationship with her kids. How fear for their well-being had ruled her life since Derek's death. She talked about a new man in her life, Jack O'Grady, and her fears of losing him.

She clenched her little hands into fists. "I don't want to be afraid anymore. Derek made his choices, and I couldn't have stopped him. Taylor has made his choices, too, and I'm still scared for him."

"That's natural because you're his mother, but he's a man now and has to live his life, as do you," Gabe said.

"All my life, I've tried to protect my children, the people that I love, but I just can't any longer," Olivia said. She stopped, uncertain. "I-I want to have a life in the now, but ... I'm not sure how to do it."

"By understanding your feelings," Gabe said. "You've made the first step toward living in the now, as you put it. But don't expect to start training tigers right away."

She laughed—too loudly for such a small person—and he saw a glimmer of joy in her that he'd never seen before.

She moved along the labyrinth again, her stride half as long as his own.

"I wish I'd have figured this out sooner," Olivia said with a long sigh.

Gabe pressed his palms together, trying to look sage. But at twenty-nine, with the looks of a gangly high school basketball player, that wasn't easy. He said, "We get to our revelations when we're ready. People expect personal transformation to come in the way Paul experienced, getting blinded by a light, and falling off a horse."

"Where's a good bolt of lightning when you need it?" she quipped.

They shared a laugh, something he did a lot with his parishioners. Olivia was an example of how grieving too long could steal many of life's joys—something Gabe should take to heart.

"Do you think God did it to punish me for something?" she asked, her brow furrowed. "For doubting? For some terrible thing that I don't remember?"

He dropped his hands. "No. God doesn't do that. God loves us unconditionally, and he's not to blame when bad things happen to good people. I wish I had a better answer, but sometimes, things just happen." He glanced around at the beauty of the garden. "When Jesus performed miracles or consorted with society's castoffs, he didn't scold them or tell them they were outsiders because they were sinful. He loved them, period—that's what made him a radical. God loves you, and he loved Derek. His death was a tragedy, but look at you. You've risen above it and raised two lovely children all on your own."

"I guess, in a way, I've felt like I owe it to Derek to—" she paused, thinking.

He decided not to wait, but to deliver another zinger. "To be sad for the rest of your life? To suffer and be alone? Never remarry? Never fall in love again?"

She turned to him, eyebrows to her hairline.

Tough love, but there it was.

Gabe said, "He was a man who dedicated his life to relieving suffering. I find it hard to believe he'd want you to suffer and feel guilty that he died."

The sun was blazing now. His short-sleeved black shirt, clerical collar, and dress slacks were sucking up the sun. He wiped the sweat from his brow with the clean, pressed white handkerchief his mother had taught him always to carry. He was afraid he would soon begin to sweat through his black shirt.

How embarrassing! That was one of God's tiny mistakes: sweaty priests.

A sparrow with a worm in her mouth flitted to a clutch of sticks and twigs deep in the tallest fir tree. There were so many miracles if people only paused long enough to see them. They continued along the labyrinth as they talked.

"There's an old spiritual which I love: 'His Eye is on the Sparrow.' Do you know it?" Gabe asked.

"Yes." In a light soprano, Olivia sang his favorite line. "His eye is on the sparrow, so I know he's watching me."

"That's the one," he said. "I think it means every death saddens the Lord, even that of a sparrow. I don't mean to sound callus or minimize Derek's death or your grief and loss, but put in perspective, he had a fine, exciting life. He had two children, a wife that loved him, friends that respected him, and work he loved, which sustained him. It was the kind of life most of us want to live."

The bong-a-tron, the electronic bells high in the steeple of St. Paul's, began to chime noon. Every life had darkness and lightness. Oscar had died at midnight, the precise opposite of now.

The sparrow chirped, her song mixing with the ringing bells.

Gabe paused on the labyrinth. "Every death is a tragedy, not only those of the rich, or famous, or the brilliant or talented, but also the poor, the marginalized, the rejected, the addicts or alcoholics. Jesus didn't rank people when they were alive, and I don't believe God does when they die. I don't think we should either. Derek's death was untimely, but ..." He paused at the turn of the labyrinth path. "The real tragedy is when we, the living, fail to live fully as Christ meant us to live with purpose and joy. It's a kind of sin, really, to fail to see the adventure of life, to accept his blessings."

Gabe was trying to open his arms to God's blessings. One blessing came in the form of Flicka trying to set him up, but his heart wasn't following his own spiritual advice.

They started off again, Olivia walking a few paces ahead of him, each step leading closer to the center of the circle where, hopefully, some revelation lay.

But often as not, Gabe walked away as dull-headed and confused as ever.

They reached the center of the labyrinth. She said, "So, I came to talk about a memorial to my dead husband, but you've relieved me of something I've carried since he died." She tipped her face to the sun and smiled broadly. "I feel lighter now."

He gestured to the glass-topped picnic table sitting on a patch of gravel. "Let's sit at the table, and we can talk some more about what kind of memorial you want for Derek."

Gabe pulled out a cast iron chair for her and one for himself, and they sat in the sun.

Olivia wiped her forehead with her forearm. "Oh, my God, it's so hot in the sun." She glanced guiltily at him. "Sorry, Father."

He smiled and dabbed his forehead again. "No harm, no foul. What this garden needs is a shade tree."

Her eyes widened. Her brows shot skyward. She blinked. Twice. Her blue eyes blazed with excitement. "You said Derek had a great life. That's it! I wanted to memorialize his death, but I should memorialize his life." She sprang out of her chair and bounced on her toes like a wood sprite. "I've always thought of him as *missing* so much of life: the kids growing up, traveling, Christmases, Easters, baptisms, birthdays, all those things. But he had a *life*." She pointed at the cloudless, sun-filled sky overhead, her face filled with the brilliance of hope. "I want to plant a tree right here. It will grow here for years and years. It will give people pleasure, beauty, and shade. It will remind them of Derek, of life, not death. I want one of those flowering cherry trees. One with the fat pink blossoms that drop their petals everywhere like pink snow."

"I know the kind you mean," he said, her enthusiasm catching him. "That's an excellent idea. And we could even have a dedication ceremony in his honor."

She was transformed as she rounded the table.

He stood and was surprised when tiny, reserved, refined, proper Olivia Maxwell stood on tiptoe and threw her arms around his neck—or tried to. He bent to accommodate her diminutive stature.

Boy! For a petite woman, she packs a wallop of affection and joy.

These kinds of hugs recharged his emotional batteries and kept him going for days.

"Thank you, Father, for everything," Olivia said. "I can't wait to tell the Marriage Survivors Club, but first, I have to run over to the firehouse."

He always felt humbled to have the opportunity to watch his parishioners find answers to their problems.

Now, if someone might come up with an answer on how to stop missing Oscar, everything would be right in God's world.

CHAPTER 41

Some of us think holding on makes us strong; but sometimes it is letting go.

Hermann Hesse

Olivia had one crucial phone call to make before leaving the church parking lot and heading to the firehouse. "Bea, this is Olivia Maxwell."

"Hi, Olivia. How are you?" Olivia heard the barely suppressed laughter in Bea's voice.

"How did Ariel like her weekend with you?" Olivia asked. She rolled down her window.

"Oh, she loved it." Bea laughed. "She had so much fun, and she got along so well with my other ladies. You don't have to be in a rush to pick her up unless you want to. She's working on a puzzle in the garden with some of the others."

A brilliance of sun fell across a tall rose bush that stood next to her car. The bush was rampant with blooms—every leaf and petal pulsed with life. Voices of rehearsing choristers floated out the choir room window. A breeze cooled the happy tears on her cheeks.

It felt as if she'd grown wings. There was so much life to be lived.

Olivia smiled and wiped away a tear. "Good. What do I need to do to finalize her moving in?"

Bea waited a moment before answering. "You're ready?" She sounded surprised.

"If she's ready, I'm ready," Olivia said.

"I think Ariel is very ready," Bea said and laughed. "We'll talk when you pick her up."

Olivia felt as though she'd grown wings.

As she drove to the firehouse, Olivia's insides felt like spun cotton candy. In her final trip to Providence, she had sprung the lock on the cage of her own making, but Father Gabriel's wisdom had coaxed her out into the open.

Waves of hope opened a future on which she had long ago slammed the door. She didn't have to spend the rest of her life paying homage to Derek with guilt and regret. The tree would be a reminder of the possibility of renewal through all the seasons of life, symbolizing all she wanted in her, and her children's, futures.

Letting her children go was the scariest thing in the world, but it was also the most obvious step toward letting them become their best people. The only way she could become her own best person.

How foolish she'd been to ever think otherwise. But love could make a fool out of a person.

Jack had touched her life in many ways, even before she let him care for her. He brought Matt and Ariel together. Helped Taylor put out the fire at church and encouraged him to become a fireman. Taken Taylor in for a few weeks. At each step, she reacted badly, but Jack stuck with her, not letting her fear drive a wedge between them, even as she used her fear to precisely do that.

Olivia gripped the steering wheel and drove too fast. She pressed the gas pedal down even more, swerved around a too-slow truck and squeaked through a yellow light.

It had been her assumption that another loss like Derek's would smash her to bits, that she would be unable to put herself back together again, unable to care for her kids, her business, and herself. But after Derek died, she persevered and thrived with the love and support of the Marriage Survivors Club and her friends at St. Paul's. She saw that, even after the gut punch of losing her husband, she was resilient, loved, and cared for enough to get back up again.

Derek's death had not been her fault. Ever. She'd wasted so many years feeling guilty, but that was over.

Loving and living were risks, but not taking the risk meant a long, cold winter of the heart. She was ready for sunshine. Jack was the kind of man who could catch her if she fell off her high horse face-first. He might die, but she wanted the blessing of every minute she had left to spend with him.

At the fire station, Olivia veered into the lot. She slammed the car into park, not caring that she was straddling two parking places. She took a moment to try to compose herself but gave up and hurtled out of the car.

One of the garage bays was open, and Randy and Jack sat chatting on the shiny chrome bumper of one of the engines.

Too maniacally, she waved at Jack, her gesture a cross between a "hello" and a "come here" motion. Her mouth spread into a goofy grin she didn't bother trying to tame.

Jack ambled over, a smile like melted caramel on his face, but a wary questioning in his eyes. He didn't want any more false starts, she knew.

He didn't kiss her and kept his hands in his pockets. "Welcome home. How was Providence?"

"Lonely." She snaked her arms around his waist, wriggled, and rubbed up against him like a puppy. She said, "I'm ready to retire that part of my life."

He raised his eyebrows, his smile familiar and sweet to her. "And ... what do you intend to replace it with?"

"Something long-term that includes a lot of hot, wanton sex." Grinning, she bumped her pelvis against his. "With you."

His face looked as though she had offered to give him a private lap dance. "Not that I have any objections to that, but what's gotten into you?" he asked with a twinkle in his eye.

"Life," she said.

She slid her palms up his chest, feeling the rough, springy hair beneath his shirt.

With a quiet chuckle, he bent down, wrapped his arms around her, and pulled her close. His sunburned neck smelled of car polish, starch, and wind. She cupped his cheek, stood on tiptoe, and guided his face to hers. She opened her mouth to him, their tongues darting and exploring. A siren sounded in the lower reaches of her body.

Randy's voice broke through their fog of lust. "Hey, Jack! Gotta' go."

It wasn't her body but the fire alarm calling Jack to duty. Jack pulled back, his expression stunned, as if he'd witnessed a holy miracle.

She gave him a slutty Flicka smile. "How about you cook me dinner at your place tonight?" And she sashayed back to her car, putting a little swing in her saggy, stretch-marked butt.

CHAPTER 42

Then the truth will set you free
John 8:32

Olivia was in the living room, surrounded by a sea of boxes containing Derek's old stuff. She wore a ratty sweatshirt and a new pair of jeans, and her hair was loose. She checked her watch again and frowned. She'd left a message on Taylor's phone asking him to swing by, but she wasn't certain he'd show. She was ready to give up when the front door opened, and Taylor stepped into the foyer.

She hadn't seen him since he'd gone to Charlottesville, and she'd gone to Providence. She was relieved he looked the same: big, solid, all in one piece.

She laughed at herself for the thought. Of course, he looked the same! Nothing had happened to him, and probably wouldn't. She'd been listening to her crazy internal voice of doom for too long.

Now when fear reared its ugly head, she thought of Jack's

smile, the way his kiss made the heat run down through her center, how safe she felt in his arms, how they said, 'I love you', every time they saw one another or parted. She wanted to make every minute with him count because he could die in a fire or another Nine-Eleven terrorist attack.

But if he did, she knew she would survive.

"Hi," she said to Taylor. "Thanks for coming. I wasn't sure you would."

"Me neither," he said.

"I have some things I need to talk to you about," she said.

"That sounds ominous," he said as he toed off his shoes and lined them up with hers and Ariel's.

He asked, "Ariel here?" He lifted his baseball cap, ran a hand through his tousled curls, and put it back on.

He needed a haircut, but she didn't mention it. See? She *could* stop nagging! She felt a spark of pride at how far—and for her it was far—she had come.

She said, "No, the store asked if she could come in, so I drove her over."

His eyes widened in exaggerated amazement. "What? You mean you're not too nervous to take her to work?"

She grinned at his well-deserved teasing. "I'm pleased to report that I no longer hyperventilate when she goes into the store."

He said, "I figured I was going to have to watch *My Little Pony* for the millionth time again."

"I couldn't have asked for a better brother for Ariel," Olivia said. "Any adult who can sit through endless reruns of that show deserves a medal."

He laughed and stood with one toe on his instep the way he had as a kid. His socks were dirty and mismatched.

Well, that wasn't her problem–dirty socks weren't lethal or a mortal sin.

"How was your weekend in Charlottesville?" she asked. "Did you have fun?"

He turned away, but not before she saw the hurt in his eyes. "Dani broke up with me."

Olivia heard the pain of rejection in his voice. She wanted to wrap him in a hug, to tell him he would find someone who appreciated everything about him. Determined to let him be his own man, she jammed her hands into her jeans pockets and stayed seated. "I'm sorry."

"Yeah." He sighed gustily. "I guess it's for the best. She's kind of unreliable, I guess."

"I know it must hurt," she said, gently.

"Yeah, I'll get over it," he said, and she detected a sort of grim determination in him.

"At the risk of sounding like your know-it-all mother, don't let your heart get hardened to your emotions, or stuck in one mode," she cautioned. "Take it from me– you'll miss a lot of life."

He looked at her quizzically for a long moment before nodding. At least he hadn't told her she was full of it, so that was something.

He spotted the boxes in the living room. "What's all that stuff?"

She waved a hand around and said, "A few old things of your dad's. I wanted to see if you want anything before I throw it out."

"A few? This looks like everything he ever owned." He frowned at the jumble. "Why do you even have all this stuff?" He kneeled, opened a box, and dangled a single green and chili pepper printed sock. His face screwed up in an expression of disbelief. "Socks? You kept his socks?"

"He liked funny socks." She laughed, remembering the expressions on people's faces when they saw Derek's socks. "He said it took people's minds off their pain for a split second. Gave them something to talk about besides a burst appendix or a gunshot wound."

"I didn't know that about him," Taylor said, thoughtfully. Then he looked at her. "But keeping them is weird, Mom." He dropped the sock back into the box and closed the lid. "I most definitely do not want my dad's old socks."

"Of course not, but you might like some of his other stuff." She opened another box and dug out two bow ties, one with dogs, the other with a skull and bone pattern. She held them up. "He liked bow ties, too."

Taylor rubbed the side of his nose with a forefinger and gave her a pitying look. She laughed and dropped the bow ties back into the box. She brought out a wool ski sweater.

"We bought this in Italy." She held it up to Taylor's chest.

He stared down at it as though it were infested with vermin. "Even if this was the right size," he said in derisive disgust, "I would *never* wear this. It looks like it belongs to some old guy with no teeth."

They laughed together, something she didn't remember doing for a very long time.

Together, they sorted through the boxes. There were research papers, notebooks, yellowed paperback thrillers, high school report cards, ballpoint pens with the names of pharmaceutical companies printed on the side, one entire box of green scrubs and white lab coats, three college pennants, a plastic bag of baseball cards, a bunch of Valentine's cards from Olivia, a snow globe from Val Gardena where they'd skied, a takeout menu from the clam place in Providence, ticket stubs to concerts, theater playbills, fourteen different kinds of Pez dispensers, fridge magnets from Yellowstone and the Grand Canyon, a moldy rabbit's foot keychain, T-shirts from different bands, six beat-up sweatshirts, eight pairs of shoes, a Matchbox car of the same model as Derek's first car (an Audi), eighteen

VHS tapes, a box of CDs for learning Polish, twenty-one comic books, eleven dress shirts, a brown tweed blazer with honest-to-god suede patches on the elbows, and a Whoopee cushion.

Taylor kept the Whoopee cushion.

He cocked one eyebrow. "Why didn't you get rid of this junk?"

She folded a sweatshirt and placed it back in the box. "I was too torn up after he died to get rid of them."

He gave a snort. "What, in eighteen years, you still haven't thrown this crap out?"

He had a point.

She said, "It's not crap." She glanced around at the boxes. "Well ... not all of it."

He curled his upper lip at her. "Mom."

"Okay, most of it is crap," she conceded. "I guess I didn't get rid of it because I didn't want to forget him. Now it seems a little—"

"Pathetic?" he interrupted.

She narrowed her eyes at him. "Like hoarding, I was going to say."

Had she been in mourning for eighteen years? Taylor was right–it was pathetic.

She moved a stack of papers from the sofa to the coffee table and sat. She patted the cushion next to her and he dropped down next to her. It was a joy to have him near her again. To look at his zig-zaggy hairline, his thick straight brows, his hairy, bouldery knees. A few minutes would be enough, and then she would let him go again. Not fearlessly, but proudly.

After what she had to say, he might never sit next to her again, but she would take that chance because he deserved to know the truth.

She'd dreaded this moment for years, but there was no putting it off anymore. Jack had offered to join her when she told

Taylor, but she knew she had to face him alone. Now, she peeled her heart open, ready for however Taylor reacted.

"There's something I need to tell you about your dad," she admitted.

He huffed in exasperation, his default setting. "Look, Mom, I know he was practically Albert Einstein and everything. I don't need reminding. You've done enough of that over the years."

She felt his words like a pinch at the back of her neck. "I deserve that."

Looking ready to bolt, he stared straight ahead. He opened his massive hands, clasped them again. "Okay, so what did you want to say?"

She said, "Aside from looking through this stuff, I asked you to come over and talk because I haven't been entirely"—she made one big fist with her hands—"honest with you."

She'd had enough of playing it safe with her kids. Pain was part of the package of being a mom. Losing Derek had been like walking into a flamethrower. But as Jack, Father Gabriel and the Marriage Survivors Club reminded her, she had lived through it. It was the prospect of losing her children that drove her protective instincts into hyperdrive.

Okay, so she was a little overboard, but she was improving. She knew Taylor and Ariel would be okay without her. It would crack her heart if anything happened to Taylor, but he was a man capable of making his own decisions. Even Ariel had chosen her future.

They'd grown up–now Olivia had to grow up.

She took a long, slow breath. "I wanted to talk to you about how your dad died."

Taylor pulled back, and his voice carried a hard edge of suspicion. "You always said he fell, but you never said how."

"He died in a fall while rock climbing." It seemed so simple to say it now. Such a relief to push the mountain off her chest.

Taylor's brows shot up, and his head jerked forward. "What! He died rock climbing?"

"Now, do you see why I was so upset when I saw your climbing gear?" she asked.

His jaw jutted. "I don't intend to fall."

She said, "Neither did your dad. He started his climb before his guide showed up. He wasn't all that experienced. I wasn't there, or I would have stopped him, and I've never forgiven myself for not being there that day. The guide, who was only ten minutes late, found him on the ground with his skull smashed."

She felt molten, all-encompassing, boiling up inside of her, rage at Derek's foolish selfishness. "It was incredibly stupid of him," she bit off.

It was the first negative thing she'd ever said to her kids about their dad, and the honesty, both with herself and with Taylor, had the effect of releasing a steam valve.

Too stunned for words, Taylor stared down at his hands nestled one in the other. "But why'd he do that? Every beginner knows you don't climb alone."

"He knew," she said, "but he needed the adrenaline rush more than he wanted to be safe."

"Was he, like, an adrenaline junkie or something?" Taylor asked.

"Yes," she said. "It was the way he felt alive after all the death he dealt with in the ER. He was trying to prove his immortality, like death couldn't catch him."

"But *you* never climbed?" he asked, his voice rising in question.

"Oh, yes, I did," she said.

His eyes flew open. "No! Seriously? You climbed? But you're scared of everything, including heights."

"Terrified. I went along only because I thought I could keep him safe. Until the one time I wasn't with him, and he died."

She waited for tears, but none came. She felt steady and true. Guilt-free.

She went on. "It's taken me a long time, but I know now that it wasn't my fault. He died because he did something totally idiotic and selfish."

"Why didn't you *tell* me this before?" Taylor growled.

She took Taylor's beefy hand in her own, feeling the calluses along the ridges of his palm. "Because I felt guilty, because I couldn't make him stop. Because you had to grow up without a father. I didn't tell you because I was afraid you'd take up risky sports to try to be like him."

"When were you going to tell me? When I was fifty?" He yanked his hand back from her.

"You're right. I should have told you sooner, and I'm sorry. I never intended to make you afraid of everything, to doubt yourself or your capabilities. I'm sorry about that. Try to understand how afraid I was of losing you and Ariel. I thought it made me a bad mother if anything happened to you."

"I'm nothing like my dad!" Taylor jacked up off the sofa, his face livid. "I'm not some adrenaline junkie. I would never, *ever* climb alone. I would never do anything high-risk of Ariel."

She didn't begrudge him his white-hot anger, but neither was she going to let it stop her. "I won't lie—that's a big relief, but I still worry. I'm a mom and you can't stop me."

"Worrying didn't help you save him, though, did it?" he said with a sneer.

His words were like an iron-fisted blow to the sternum. "Taylor, that's not fair!"

"I don't care if it is or not. It wasn't fair that you never told me how he died." He threw his arms in the air. "I mean, he was my father. I had a right to know."

She forced herself to look at him when she said, "You're right, you did, and it wasn't fair.

286

"You just wanted to keep me scared of the whole world, so I wouldn't do anything to make *you* nervous or scared," he said.

She was ashamed of the fact that he was probably right. But she had thought it was the only way to protect him. Instead, he hated her for that right now.

She'd hurt him, made him doubt himself. It must have taken herculean strength to develop his self-confidence and a vision of his own future. He, too, had more strength than she gave him credit for.

"All this time, you acted like he was a god or something!" He was up, stomping back and forth in the living room, fists balled, eyes blazing. "Like he was perfect. I felt like if I only tried harder, did what you wanted, that I could live up to him." He strode to the door and jammed his feet into his shoes. "Well, you know what? I'm not like him. I'm not selfish or an adrenaline junkie, or a risk-taker. I want to be a firefighter so I can help people. I might not be smart enough to be a doctor, but I'm smart enough not to do stupid stuff like he did or to hide the facts like you did."

She said, "I know, and I'm—"

He slammed the door on his way out, leaving a wake of anger vibrating in the air behind him.

"—proud of you for that," she finished quietly.

She slumped onto a box and wrapped her arms around herself. She had lost him. Her heart pulsed with a guilty ache. For so many years, she had wanted to tell him, but was afraid of just this outcome. In trying to protect him, she'd driven him away, and she didn't know if there was any way to bring him back.

CHAPTER 43

Never lend your car to anyone to whom you have given birth.
Erma Bombeck

Olivia and the Marriage Survivors Club were having brunch after church at the Family Diner. The old-style burger joint with its red vinyl banquettes, counter stools, and gray Formica made it feel like they'd walked into a set for a 1950s movie. It smelled of bacon grease, coffee, cinnamon buns, and nostalgia. They all knew the waitress, the cook, and many of the regulars.

Even though the diner felt familiar and welcoming, the words swam on the page of Olivia's menu.

It had been four long days since she'd spoken to Taylor. Her anxiety and feelings of loss were a dull ache behind her breastbone. She held back contacting him because she didn't want him to hang up on her or cuss her out. She had to let him come back to her in his own time, but she knew that could be years.

Or never. Flicka snuck a sip of mimosa from her travel coffee mug. She always objected to breakfast at the diner because they didn't have a liquor license, so she brought her own booze. "You're quieter than usual, Olivia. Everything all right?"

Olivia closed her menu. She wasn't really hungry, anyway. Coffee would do. "I finally told Taylor how Derek died, and he was, rightfully, irate. After a few choice words, he stomped out and slammed the door."

"Kids are so self-righteous," Frankie said. "They think they know everything, and we're complete morons. They only acknowledge we're right when we're dead, thereby depriving us of the satisfaction of saying 'I told you so.'"

The thought provided Olivia no comfort, but she chuckled anyway.

Hélène motioned for Bianca to pass the milk for the coffee. "Did you apologize for keeping it from him?"

"Yes, but I haven't heard from him since I told him. I feel like I'll have to keep apologizing for the rest of my life."

"Bullshit," Bianca said. "You already apologized. The hard part is waiting until he's ready to forgive you."

Flicka dropped her jaw then said to Bianca, "You sound almost wise!"

Bianca's smile was smug.

"That could take forever!" Olivia said and slumped against the banquette.

"Or just as long as you kept the truth from him," Flicka said.

"But I can't wait that long," Olivia said. "When he moved out and went to Carolina's, it hurt, but I knew I hadn't done something completely awful. This time I know I did something completely awful."

"Welcome to the bad mother club," Frankie said. To the waitress, she said, "I'll have my two eggs, rye toast, hold the butter, and Olivia will have a serving of crow."

"Oh, be quiet," Olivia said with a smile.

Taylor was still living at Carolina's. Olivia had hoped he

might move back home sometime soon, but she doubted that would ever happen now.

"Has Taylor said anything to you?" Olivia asked Carolina.

Carolina kept her eyes on her menu. "You know if he had I couldn't tell you because that would be breaking his confidence." She handed her menu to the waitress and ordered a short stack of pancakes.

"But what if he ... I don't know, dies in a fire before we reconcile, then what? I'll feel horrible for the rest of my life," Olivia said.

"You'd feel horrible, anyway. Keeping his distance is his choice, not yours, and you don't have to feel guilty about it," Frankie said.

Hélène added, "You were open with him."

"Finally," Bianca muttered.

Flicka gave her an elbow jab. She said, "Our honorary nephew is growing up. Look at what he's done so far: pried your mitts off Ariel, helped her go on dates, traveled to see his girlfriend, pursued his dream job, moved out—albeit after a fight— and he's stood up to you. This is one more step on his way to becoming his own man. I, for one, am proud of him."

Olivia twisted her mouth to the side. "I hate it when you're right. And you don't even have kids."

Flicka's brows dropped, and she stared out the window, her vibrant eyes shadowed with hurt.

Olivia felt sorry, but she wasn't sure what for. Maybe it was merely her newly permanent emotional state.

Hélène ordered two eggs and asked, "Can you ask Jack to have a chat with him?"

"That's not fair either," Olivia said. "Jack's his friend, too, and that feels underhanded."

But it wasn't as though she hadn't hinted around, but for once, Jack didn't give her any advice.

"Mm, good point," Hélène agreed.

The waitress soon returned with an armload of plates, and they passed their orders to one another.

After a few bites, Hélène asked, "Aside from the fact that you feel hurt, what's the urgency to get in touch with Taylor?"

"I have some photos he's never seen, and I want to show them to him." Olivia held her mug out to the waitress for another cup of decaf. "He stomped out before I had a chance the other day."

"What kind of pictures?" Flicka asked.

Olivia answered, "Derek and I doing crazy outdoor sports stuff."

"You sure you want to show him those?" Hélène asked.

"She has to," Bianca said around a mouthful of scrambled eggs. "Finish the job she started."

"You know, maybe he walked out because he doesn't want to know more about Derek." Hélène picked a wedge of toast off Bianca's plate and nibbled. "He had this image in his mind of this perfect dad—"

"Thanks to me," Olivia admitted.

Hélène went on. "—and now he's got to get his head around the fact that Derek was, well, shall we say ...." She glanced up, searching the ceiling for the word.

"—a bonehead," finished Bianca. She put another wedge of toast on Hélène's plate.

"I wonder if he's afraid of becoming a bonehead like his dad," Olivia said.

"Could be," Frankie offered. "But he's also maybe trying to figure out how to have a relationship with his mom, who pissed him off. He may want to be connected to you, but he doesn't know how with this new information."

"He's got to learn to trust you again," Hélène said. "And that could take time."

These were all new ideas that Olivia hadn't considered as reasons for Taylor's further withdrawal. And they were reasons that had nothing to do with her, nor could she do anything about them. Taylor had to work through those himself.

Olivia sighed. "Being a mom is so hard. Seems like nothing you do is right."

"It's not," Carolina said.

Even though she'd never had kids, she had a wisdom that was deep and still as a clear mountain lake. She never had an ulterior motive for saying what she said, and her words were always delivered with unwavering love and acceptance. She, unlike Olivia, was entirely trustworthy. No wonder Taylor had gone to her with his problems. He'd made an excellent choice and Olivia was grateful all over again for her friends.

Carolina said, "Being a mom is about loving, and love is imperfect. Moms are bound to ... mm—"

"—fuck up," Bianca said with a lift of her eyebrows.

Carolina chuckled. "I was going to say disappoint someone." She put her arm around Olivia's shoulder and gave her a hug. "It will come out all right. Don't worry."

But Olivia was a mom, and she had a sixth sense. In the back of her mind, old anxieties about Taylor getting hurt because she wasn't watching over him smoldered. She couldn't help feeling that if she didn't reconcile with Taylor soon, it might be too late.

CHAPTER 44

The first half of our lives are ruined by our parents and the second half by our children.

Clarence Darrow

Randy strode into the firehouse dining room, where Taylor sat at the long dining table, folding some sheets and towels.

Randy took one look at him and said, "So, what gives?" Randy sat down on the benches across from Taylor.

"What do you mean?" Taylor asked, knowing precisely what Randy meant.

"All week you've looked like someone ran over your puppy," Randy said. The guy was so handsome he belonged on the cover of a magazine, not in a firehouse.

"No, I don't," Taylor said, knowing he did, because that was exactly the way he felt.

Randy gave him a big brother look down his narrow nose. "Hand me that basket, and I'll help you fold while you tell me your tale of woe," Randy said.

Taylor slid the basket of laundry nearer to Randy. Taylor had known firefighting wouldn't be all racing to fires and rescuing people, but he hadn't reckoned with the mundane tasks required to keep the station running: cleaning the firehouse, changing the beds, doing laundry, washing up after meals, cleaning the kitchen, maintaining, and cleaning the trucks, and general housekeeping. As the lowliest volunteer, he got stuck with a lot of tedious chores.

But he wanted to feel more a part of the crew.

Randy folded a bed sheet by basically wadding it up.

"Dude, fold it right," Taylor said crankily. "Gimme that."

Hadn't Randy's mom taught him how to fold laundry? Taylor's mom had, and once you knew, you couldn't go back to sloughing it.

Randy stood and handed one end of the sheet to Taylor, and together they folded the sheet.

Randy said, "You know, if this firefighting thing doesn't work out, you could open a laundry."

Taylor ground his teeth. He put the folded sheet neatly on the pile with the others.

"Seriously," Randy said. "You seem like you're pretty upset about something. What's up?"

Even though Randy was funny, Taylor sensed he had a store of wisdom that he didn't.

"Well, let's see." Taylor gave a sigh and threw Randy a bath towel to fold. "I'm living with my honorary aunt, had a fight with my mom, my girlfriend broke up with me, and I found out my mom's been lying to me about how my dad died when I was a baby. Take your pick."

Randy gave his head a single shake. "That's a lot to process. Which one's bothering you the most?"

Taylor took a hand towel from the basket, but it had a greasy handprint. He set it aside to bleach it the way his mom taught him.

"The stuff with my mom not being honest about how my dad died, I guess. She always made him out to be something of a genius superhero, but she forgot to mention that he died doing something totally stupid."

His dad's stupidity and his mom's lies were like the tangle of charging cords in the bottom of his desk drawer. Pull one end, and the knot just got tighter. He couldn't figure out who he was more pissed at—his father for being so stupid that Taylor had to grow up without a dad, or his mom for making the guy sound like a miracle worker. What else hadn't she told him about his dad? What kind of stuff should Taylor watch out for in himself so he wouldn't become like his dad? What parts of his dad did he have and what did he want to keep or dump? What kind of dad would he be when he had kids of his own?

He'd spent his life being careful because his mom drilled it into him to be afraid of everything. He'd tried to live up to the man his dad was, and now he had to be sure to *not* be like his dad.

"Hm," Randy hummed, setting the towel on Taylor's stack. "And you're mad because she exaggerated his positive qualities, right?"

"Exaggerated is putting it mildly," Taylor said. "Wouldn't you be mad?"

"Probably," Randy acknowledged. "But being a parent is hard." He folded three white washcloths into neat squares.

"How do you know? You ... have any kids?" Taylor asked, knowing he couldn't assume anything about anyone based on gender or sexual orientation.

Randy grinned. "Dodged that bullet. Have you told your mom why you're mad?"

"Wouldn't it be obvious?" Taylor described how he'd stormed out of the house after her big reveal.

Randy rooted through the laundry basket and pulled out another towel. "Not necessarily. People feel hurt in different ways about different things."

Hurt.

Taylor tagged his feelings as mad, but Randy was right: Taylor was hurt. His mom had a radar for what people were feeling, but for years she'd ignored his feelings.

Well, at least about this one thing.

Taylor hefted another basket of laundry onto the table. "I've been super-responsible. I take care of my sister. I was a volunteer EMT in high school. I graduated high school with reasonable grades. But she still didn't trust me to be able to handle the truth. And now I don't know who he really was." Frustration clawed at Taylor, and he frowned. "I mean, I got no idea."

"Ask her," Randy advised.

Taylor shook another sheet. He spread it on the table, smoothed out the wrinkles and folded it. He set it in the basket with the folded stuff. The laundry smelled of the harsh detergent they used at the firehouse. He preferred the stuff his mom used that had a flowery smell.

Taylor said, "She'll probably make up something else." But he knew that wasn't true. She prized honesty and taught him to be honest, which was why it was such a slam in the face that she hadn't been honest about his dad's death.

"Maybe she feels ashamed she wasn't on the up and up with you," Randy suggested.

The thought honestly hadn't occurred to him. She had apologized, but they hadn't discussed how they both felt. He hadn't given her a chance. And he wasn't entirely sure how he felt. He was still shuffling the deck on all that.

"Parents don't always get stuff right." Randy folded a pillow-case in a half-assed way.

Taylor held out his hand for the pillowcase. "Like how?"

Randy passed him the pillowcase, and Taylor refolded it like his mom did.

Pain gathered beneath Randy's eyes. "When I came out, my dad was disgusted."

"Seriously? That's bogus." Taylor folded another towel. His mother's words came back to him: any job worth doing is worth doing right.

"I know, but my folks were doing the best they could. That was how they grew up. I couldn't change who I was, and they couldn't change what they thought so quickly. It took two years and my older sister speaking up for me before they were ready to talk again."

"And did you? I mean, talk to them again?" Taylor asked.

Randy shook his head. "I'm sorry to say it took me another year to speak to my parents. By then, my mom was really sick with colon cancer, and I'd missed a lot of time with her."

Taylor stopped folding and let his hands rest on the tabletop. He wasn't used to guys talking about their feelings. He realized that Randy was showing him a new way to be a man, and Taylor respected Randy. While not all the firemen were Neanderthals, Randy lived as an out gay man in a profession that thrived on macho chest beating. Any guy with those kinds of guts was worth listening to.

Randy went on. "They wanted to reconnect, but I held on to being hurt and pushed them away. If I'd have let that go, I could have played golf with my mom, taken long walks with her, and played poker with my dad." His smile was sad, and his voice dropped. "Learned to make her meatballs and her homemade sauce."

"But they rejected you. Why did you want to reconnect, as you say?" Taylor asked.

"Because aside from this one thing," Randy said, his eyes soft with love. "They were great parents."

The smell of ham baking in the oven caught Taylor's attention. His mom baked it with brown sugar and mustard. He missed her cooking. Jack wasn't on cooking duty this week, so the meals had been bland. He kind of wished he could go home and have one of his mom's meals. To pick her up and jiggle her until she laughed. But first, he'd have to get over being mad. He just wasn't there yet.

Randy said, "They loved my sister and me, gave us a home full of love and laughter, taught us to be respectful and kind, to take care of people who had less than us."

These were the same things Taylor's mom had taught him. And he had to admit, he was grateful for those lessons. Things he would teach his own kids. Things he was grateful for. And how to wash and fold laundry.

"They made me who I am today, and I'll always be grateful for that." Randy squinted one eye closed and wagged a single forefinger. "But this one thing they screwed up, and for three years, that was the only thing I judged them by."

Randy had backed him into a corner without Taylor even realizing it. He'd delivered a knockout punch without a lecture —a technique Taylor wished his mom would learn. What Randy said made sense. But all the stuff about his dad was banging around in Taylor's head like sneakers in a dryer, and he didn't know what to grab on to yet.

"I was glad that I went back and made peace with them. I'm a firefighter, and so was my dad. I could have died or been hurt, and the only thing they would have remembered was that they'd hurt me. That would have been hard on them." Randy opened his boxer-sized hands, brought them back together. He gave a one-shouldered shrug. "And besides, I love my parents."

Taylor set the basket of fresh laundry on the floor next to another one. There was still one more to go. "So, you're saying I should forgive my mom."

"When you're ready." Randy swept his hand across the surface of the wooden dining table.

It wasn't like there was a rush. Taylor felt like being mad was one way to maintain his independence from his mom and a way to form his own ideas about his dad. Their conversation about his dad opened his eyes to why she was scared about everything. It wasn't like he was in danger. As a volunteer, he wasn't even allowed to go into a building yet.

The first rule of firefighting was to come back alive, so he wasn't in any danger, anyway.

"You told your mom that you were accepted as a probie?" Randy asked, referring to Taylor being accepted as a probationary firefighter.

"Not yet. As to forgiving her, I guess I will ... eventually," Taylor said to Randy.

The alarm blared. Taylor's heart kicked into overdrive.

Randy jumped up. The firehouse filled with the sounds of everyone scrambling to their assigned positions.

As Randy slid down the pole, he called back, "Just don't wait too long."

Taylor followed him down the pole, sure that he had all the time in the world.

CHAPTER 45

Even death is not to be feared by one who has lived wisely.

Buddha

Jack's phone buzzed on the bedside table with an alert specific to a fire callout. He reached for it, but Olivia grabbed his hand and put it on her bare breast. Somebody was on fire.

"Hey, no fair," he said with a laugh.

"I know," she cooed. Her coy smile almost did him in.

He kissed her breast and levered up on one elbow. "Duty before booty. Just let me check it."

She laughed and brushed her palm over his chest. "Why? It's your day off, and you've already put in your hours this week. Let the younger guys take the overtime."

He wanted nothing more than to stay in bed with her. She'd gotten up to drop Ariel off at her job. When Olivia got back, she'd climbed back into bed and snuggled up against him. He was looking forward to when someone at Ability House had that job. Then he and Olivia could wake up, have sex, and fall back asleep.

But right now, he was still a firefighter and felt a duty to the guys and the job. He reached across her and picked up his phone. The text read: *Fire in South Norwalk.*

"I should at least call in," he said.

"I bought croissants at Muro's," she crooned enticingly.

He smiled and said, "You know my every weakness." Reluctantly, and feeling like a slacker, he gave in and went to make coffee.

As they sat down, his phone went off again. He picked it up. Sick foreboding swept over him as he read the message. *Three alarm fire, 6 Ely, South Norwalk. All hands.*

He felt her reading him. She paused, her coffee cup halfway to her lips. "That's the second time. Why don't they call someone else?"

"I am someone else," he said.

In all the years he'd been married to Gina, he'd never felt the pull between love and duty the way he did right now. He wanted to spend the day with Olivia, turn his phone off, take a walk with her, and look at the sun making bright spots on the grass.

He didn't meet her eyes as he slid his chair back. "It's a three-alarm house fire in South Norwalk. All those houses down there are made of wood. They're calling everybody to the scene."

Her coffee cup clinked in the saucer as she set it down hard. She didn't have to say anything for him to feel her disappointment.

He kissed the top of her head. "This is what it's like being married to a fireman."

"I know," she sighed. She got to her feet and gave him a look that almost made him take his pants off again. "But can we please have that conversation about you retiring, which you keep avoiding?"

"I promise," he said, kissing her for what he knew might be the last time, because every time could be the last time. "As long as we can have that conversation about getting married, too."

"I loooove yoooou," she crooned against his lips.

"Now, who's avoiding a conversation?" He lifted her off her feet and, into the side of her neck, said, "Love you, too."

CHAPTER 46

God looks after children, animals, and idiots.
   Lou Holtz

Taylor clambered into the cab of the ladder truck. He drew deep breaths to slow his heartbeat. If he was so high on adrenaline that he couldn't think clearly, he couldn't do anyone any good. He heard Jack's voice quizzing him on the order to do things. Taylor mentally ran through his equipment and his procedures, keeping focused.

The phrase *"your first job is to get out alive"*, had been drilled into him so often he heard the words in his sleep.

Since joining the department as a probationary fireman, he'd been out on a heart attack, two car accidents, and a cat up a tree. This was the first actual fire he'd ridden out on. He knew, and most importantly, trusted his fellow firefighters. Everything would be okay.

Taylor smelled the smoke before he saw it.

It was a windy day. That was a bad thing because wind blew sparks and smoke. Smoke could overwhelm the firefighters, and sparks could ignite another fire. When he saw the column of smoke, his mind settled, but his heart beat against his ribcage like a small, fierce animal ready for battle.

The fire was in a three-story wooden row house in South Norwalk. Engine Company Number Two was already on the scene, their pumper pouring water into the burning house. Darien Fire was on the way. The police had moved the rubber neckers out of harm's way. Traffic police were doing a good job of keeping cars out of the area.

The engine man pulled up behind Number Two's pumper. Jack and the other crew members jumped out and reported to the IC—the Incident Commander. He told them that no one was inside the structure, which meant none of the firefighters had to risk their lives to get anyone out.

Roaring flames shot out the windows and roof of the house. Taylor tasted the bitterness of ash and smoke. Sirens of incoming emergency vehicles ripped through the noise of the scene. Firefighters shouted, coordinating their approach, instructions, and warnings. Steam rose in the air when it hit the flames. Flakes of ash danced and spun. Ash-blackened water flowed from the house, spilled onto the grass, down the drive, and into the street.

It looked like chaos, but every firefighter had a specific job and they all worked together to put the fire out and save the neighborhood.

Taylor loved it. He was exactly where he was meant to be.

The house was a total loss, but they had to keep the fire from spreading to adjacent homes. This was an old low-income neighborhood of multi-family houses and spreading fire could mean a catastrophic loss for many families.

Heat had melted the vinyl garage door. Flames licked at the

shrubs surrounding the house. The front porch was ablaze. Two firefighters manned a hose from the pumper. EMS was already treating one firefighter for smoke inhalation.

Taylor put the chocks behind all the tires, then activated the mechanism to set up the four H-style outriggers. These stabilizing devices would keep the truck from tipping once Randy raised and climbed the ladder.

The fire was hot. That could mean there was unusual fuel besides everyday domestic items feeding the fire. More fuel meant more danger. Could be somebody had stored kerosine or gas somewhere in the house. If this was a meth lab explosion, everyone in the area would be in danger.

Taylor's mind was clear and sharp as he went about his tasks. As a probationary firefighter, he couldn't go into the house. All his jobs were support. He unfurled a hose and attached one end to the hydrant and the other to the valve on the truck. The water would run through the hose, through the truck, and up the ladder, where at the top, Randy would direct it into the roof.

Another firefighter—the hydrant man—cranked open the hydrant. 1,500 gallons of water per minute, twenty pounds per square inch, gushed into the yellow hose. The hose expanded like a yellow anaconda gulping down a meal.

Taylor was attaching the second hose to the truck valve when he heard a sound like cannon fire. He turned to see that the metal flange of the first hose had broken off the engine valve.

He was horrified to see that the other end of the broken hose was still attached to the hydrant. The loose end flailed wildly, spewing water. It whipped Taylor's legs out from under him and knocked him to the ground.

He tasted blood, water, sand.

He scrambled out of the way as thousands of gallons of gushing water tossed him ass over end across the pavement.

He screamed for the hydrant man to shut the valve, but over the noise, no one heard him.

The last thing he remembered was the metal flange of the hose hurtling toward his face.

CHAPTER 47

No one ever told me that grief felt so like fear.

C. S. Lewis

Under the watchful eye of Matt and Ariel, Olivia was hanging yet another of Matt's paintings on the wall of her store. She had sold six and had requests from clients to see more. His website, Mattscrazyshirts.com was doing a steady business selling shirts, paintings, cards, tote bags, and crazy socks.

The idea that Derek would have loved those socks sprang up and immediately disappeared from Olivia's mind.

Matt said, "No, Olivia, it goes the other way."

"What?" She tilted her head to the side to get a different view.

"You have it wrong." Matt turned the painting sideways.

Olivia stepped back and crossed back and forth in front of it. She laughed. "Of course! I should have seen her in there!"

"Yes, that's Ariel smiling." Matt wrapped an arm around Ariel.

The painting had splashes of red that reminded Olivia of a smiling mouth. The swirls of pale brown were the exact color of Ariel's hair, and the explosions of blue were the exact color of her eyes.

"I can see that," Olivia agreed.

Olivia found it adorably romantic that Matt had painted at least five images of Ariel. If there was any sign of Matt's deep and abiding love for Ariel, his artwork was it. Theirs was the kind of love every mother wanted for their child. Ariel and her heart were safe with Matt. Hopefully, Taylor would find a love as joyous as Matt and Ariel's.

Olivia was grateful she could trust Ariel's physical safety to Bea Dewinter and her caring staff. After all these years of being afraid for Ariel, it now felt as if Olivia could finally take a long, deep breath that she didn't know she needed. These were some of the last days Ariel would be living at home with Olivia and the hours were filled with a poignancy that provoked tears as often as they provoked laughter.

Even her anxieties about Taylor were loosening their grip on her throat. Jack assured Olivia that Taylor loved his work and would make a terrific firefighter. She still hadn't heard from Taylor since their blowup, and she missed him. She worried about him—not as much as before—but she was a mother, and no one could make her stop worrying at least a little bit. Not even herself.

Olivia straightened the painting. "Okay, guys, I'm hungry. Who's ready for some lunch?"

"Me!" Ariel chirped.

"And me. I'm going to have a donut," Matt said.

"Only after salad," Olivia said.

Matt scrunched up his mouth. "I hate salad."

"I know, but no salad, no donut," Oliva said. Her phone

jingled. She checked the ID and held up a finger. "One sec, it's Jack."

She picked up. "Hi, honey. Fire over? Can you join us for lunch?"

In the long moment of silence, she felt disaster bearing down on her like a rogue wave.

"Jack?"

Nothing. Just his breathing.

"Jack? Jack, can you hear me?"

A long pause where the backs of her knees went numb.

His voice was terse, frightened. "Olivia, there's been an accident."

Her throat felt as though she'd swallowed a million knife-like icicles. Her mouth refused to form words.

From a great distance, she heard Jack say, "It's ... it's Taylor."

She gripped the desk to keep from collapsing to the floor.

He said, "Meet me at the Norwalk ER."

Please, God, please, please, please let Taylor be all right.

Olivia rushed into the ER and straight into Jack's arms. "Where is he? What happened? Is he going to be all right?"

He sat her down and captured her trembling hands in his. But most of his explanation shot past her, stopped by the wall of her shrieking anxiety. "Hose ... failed ...1500 gallons ... jaw ... nose ... concussion ... surgery ... be okay ... sorry ... sorry ... sorry ..."

Shaking all over, she gulped the overheated air of the waiting room. She dug her nails into her palms to keep from screaming in panic. Her words came out in a disjointed jumble. "... never let him do this. I should have—I shouldn't ... let ... out of my sight."

Her brain was on autopilot, and silently, she screamed accusations at herself. *You're a terrible mother! What were you thinking? Derek died because you didn't protect him! You didn't protect Taylor! You were a terrible wife and you're a worse mother. You didn't protect your child!*

A kind nurse pressed a box of tissues into her hand. Jack led her into an elevator, then into a waiting room with a big plate glass window that looked out over the city of Norwalk. Somehow, a coffee cup appeared. Doctors in scrubs came in and spoke to other families who went to see their loved ones through a set of double doors marked recovery.

What if Taylor never recovered? She would have two special needs children to care for.

Alone. Alone because she hadn't stopped him.

"Olivia, I'm sorry." Jack tried to hold her, but she shoved him away.

If this could happen to Taylor, worse could happen to Jack.

She paced and paced and paced. She paused only to glance occasionally out the window. Firefighters who hadn't been at the fire stopped by to keep vigil, and when they departed, new ones arrived. They told her they were sorry. They sat and chatted quietly, some praying, trying to offer comfort. Their mouths smiled, but their eyes did not.

The Marriage Survivors Club and Father Gabriel came to the waiting room, desperate to offer comfort. For some reason, the women introduced themselves and Father Gabriel to Jack. They assured Olivia that Ariel would be cared for and not to worry about anything. Father Gabriel told her the entire church was praying for Taylor.

Nothing comforted her. Nothing eased her guilt.

Olivia watched out the window as the late afternoon sun faded, and darkness crept over the town. A necklace of streetlights came on. The waiting room emptied of everyone but Olivia and Jack.

Still, no doctor came to tell her that her son would be all right.

She clasped and unclasped her hands. "I shouldn't have let him be a fireman," she said with a throat was raw with panic. "Stupid, stupid, stupid. Should have made him go back to school. If he recovers, he has to find another line of work. This is imposs—"

Jack's solid bulk blocked her frantic pacing. He gripped her forearms and spoke into her face, forcing her to hear him. "Listen to me. The doctors said he'll be okay. It will take a while for him to recover, but he'll be all right."

She thrashed her way out of Jack's grasp. "And what about the next time? And what about you?"

"It was a freak accident," he said. His face was grave. "And as for me, I've been doing this for years, and I've never seen an equipment failure like this."

She sobbed and beat her palm against her own chest. "It's my job to take care of him. He's my son. I can't let him go do this again."

He put his face close to hers. "Olivia," he said in an intense, hushed voice. "You don't have a choice. He's a man and has to make his own decisions. You can't do that anymore. You can't stop him anymore than you could stop Derek."

The words crushed her brutally, like the physical pain of childbirth. "How dare you say that to me!" She balled up her fists and punched him in the chest as hard as she could.

He gathered her against him and held her until she had no more tears to cry.

CHAPTER 48

To be able to throw oneself away for the sake of a moment, to be able to sacrifice years for a woman's smile - that is happiness.

Hermann Hesse

Jack stood beside Taylor's bed, watching the machines blink, and listening to the quiet whirr. On the opposite side of the bed, Olivia sat holding Taylor's hand, her face sagging with exhaustion. The low light from the bathroom light cast her tiny, fragile figure in shadows. She hadn't said a word to Jack since she'd punched him, and she looked about to break from the agony she was carrying.

Jack would have changed places with Taylor in the time it took to breathe. Anything to spare Olivia.

Jack knew Olivia would refuse, but he tried anyway. "You're wiped out. Why don't you go home, and I'll stay. You can get a shower and change clothes."

She didn't even look at Jack. "No, I can't leave him."

She stood, brushed a lock of Taylor's hair off his face, and stroked his cheek with the back of her hand.

Jack crossed to her side and tipped her face up to look at him. "We'll get through this together, 'Liv. I promise. I'll be with you through every step of his recovery. I'll drive him to rehab—whatever either of you need. I'll be there for you."

Jack wanted to take her in his arms and hold her, but she went to the window and stared into the night. "I can't see you anymore. I can't lose someone else I love. After Derek died, I was never the same."

Jack's gut hit the floor. He moved to her side at the darkened window. "Olivia, don't do this when you're upset."

Don't ever do it.

"You're a fireman. You ride a motorcycle." She stepped away from him. "I can't sit up, terrified that when you're ten minutes late, you aren't coming home ever again. You could have a terrible accident and I'd be left with a disabled partner. Or you could die some horrible death, and then I'll be left alone with a smashed-up heart." She turned to look at Taylor. Her voice was raw. "Watching him, waiting for him to wake up, knowing he might be injured for the rest of his life is the worst thing that I've ever felt since Derek's death. If something happened to you ...." She sobbed, "I can't go through this ever again."

He tried to hold her, but she thrashed against him with the violent strength only a grieving, frightened mother could muster. He backed off.

Jack wanted nothing more than to convince her Taylor would be all right. But judging how Taylor looked, Jack didn't blame her for doubting he would. His face was a black-and-blue mess. He'd sustained a concussion. His nose, jaw, and three ribs had been broken. There were lacerations on his face. He had a dozen stitches in his chin. He hadn't lost any teeth, but his broken jaw would be wired shut for six weeks. The force of the water had thrown him forty feet, and he was lucky he hadn't been killed. The doctor said his superior physical condition had saved him from more severe injuries.

Jack said, "The doctor said he's going to be okay."

"What if he's not?" she said, her eyes wide with fear. "What if his concussion disables him? What if he's not the son I know?"

It was a reasonable fear that Taylor's concussion might lead to a disability. Jack wanted to share with Olivia, but she wasn't letting him.

Jack said, "Olivia, I know you're scared, but this is a rarity. A freak accident. Do you want to go back to being scared about everything all the time? You're strong, and you learned to let go of your fear. I can't imagine that you want to be that person again. Don't decide about us based on this." He gestured at Taylor, swaddled in bandages.

She was totally wiped out, but in her eyes, he recognized fear but also a Momma-Bear's protectiveness. She would still claw the face off of anyone who tried to hurt her kid, and right now, that was Jack.

She said, "You're right. I don't want to go back to being afraid, but every time you go out on a call, I would be. I just can't do that." She rubbed her temple. "I'll have to call Bea Dewinter in the morning and tell her I've changed my mind about letting Ariel move into Ability House." She looked at him with that Momma-Bear look in her eyes. "And you'll have to keep Matt away from her."

Jack felt like he'd swallowed fire, and his whole being was going up in smoke.

Until he was faced with losing Olivia, he hadn't realized how much she meant to him. She'd become part of his life and existence. He ended his days and nights thinking of her. He wanted to be with her when she wasn't near him. She had filled up something he hadn't known was empty and just like she couldn't face losing someone she loved, neither could he.

He bowed his head and pinched his nose between his thumb and forefinger. "Olivia, I've been lonely for so long, and I didn't even know it until you came into my life. I understand if you need to take a break from us, but I don't want to lose you."

"You said I don't have a choice about letting Taylor be a fireman, and you may be right." She paused. "But I don't have to keep loving another fireman."

He made his decision in a split second. He was ordinarily careful and deliberative, but now the answer was so obvious he didn't give it a second thought.

"No, you're right," Jack agreed. "You don't have to."

"Thank you for understanding," she said, and he felt frost rolling off her.

"I'll quit." It was the best decision he'd ever made in his life.

She jerked her tiny head back and blinked her red-rimmed eyes at him. "What?"

He said, "I'll quit. I won't give up my motorcycle, but I'll retire. I have my time in, and I've got my full pension. If it changes your mind about us, I'll quit."

She swallowed and seemed to sway.

She didn't answer. He didn't have anything else to put on the table. He was cashed out. He waited the way they did at a fire, hoping no one was inside. Hoping for life.

She reached behind her for the arm of the chair and dropped into it as though her legs had finally given up. The low light of the hospital room cast her face in shadow, but he saw her debating. She was as beautiful when she was exhausted as when she woke up beside him.

He kneeled in front of her chair and took her face in his hands, made her look at him. He wanted her to see how much he loved her. "Did you hear me? I said I'll quit. I want to take care of you. I want us to have a life together. I want a future with you."

She blinked at him. "I heard you ... I think. I'm ..." She rubbed her forehead. "You can't be serious."

"I'm totally and completely serious. I don't want to give up riding because I feel free when I ride, and I hope you'll share it with me one day."

"You're serious," she said, eyes wide with a different kind of shock. "You're willing to quit?"

"I'll hand in my resignation as soon as the department office opens," he said.

"I can't ask that of you. You'll resent me for it," she said raggedly.

"No, I won't. I'm not doing it for you. I'm doing it for me. I found you, and I don't want to lose you." He rose and drew her up with him, into his arms. "When Gina wasn't in love with me anymore, I should have recognized it. I couldn't admit to myself that it was over. I held on to her longer than I should have, and that wasn't fair to either of us. I don't want to fool myself like that again. I love you more than I love being a fireman, so I'll give it up"—he palmed his chest—"for me to be happy, not you. If it will make you happy for me to walk out that door and out of your life, then I'll do it. But I won't resent giving up my career for you."

She laid her hands on his chest and looked up at him. "You'd do that for us?"

"Yes, but you have to do something for me in exchange," he said.

He kissed her hand, but her eyes narrowed, and she stepped back from him. "What?"

"You have to remember that before this accident, you knew you had to let go." He gestured to Taylor. "You knew that fear and loss are part of loving, and you have to remember that. You have the fortitude it takes to live through hurt. Your strength is one of the many reasons I love you."

She squeezed her eyes shut and chewed her bottom lip and went to the other side of the bed and stood at Taylor's bedside again.

Maybe asking her to remember that life would never stop hurting her was more than she could give. She was quiet for so long that he prepared to pick up his jacket and leave her if that was what she chose.

She dragged herself around Taylor's bed and tumbled into Jack's open arms.

CHAPTER 49

The one thing I want to leave my children is an honorable name.
Theodore Roosevelt

Olivia knocked softly on Taylor's bedroom door and poked her head in. "You awake?"

"Yeah," Taylor mumbled through his wired jaw. "Come in."

He lay on his bed recovering from the injuries caused by the fire hose accident. When he was released from the hospital, it was decided that he should return to Olivia's because it was easiest to care for him.

Olivia looked at her son's bruised and bandaged, swollen face and wanted to cry, to tell him that he should still go back to school for premed, that he didn't have to be a firefighter. When she saw how vulnerable and hurt he looked, love, swift and breathtakingly painful, overran her.

This was everything she had dreaded her entire life, but it was also the result of his living life the way he chose. If he was taken from her too soon, she'd had him and loved him and raised him for nineteen years—God had only loaned him to her.

Instead of nagging him, she handed him the plastic glass with a straw in the lid. "I brought you pureed roast beef with carrots and mashed potatoes."

He rolled his eyes. "That sounds so gross."

She eased down gently onto the edge of his bed. "I know, but you have to keep up your strength. With your jaw like it is, this is the only way to eat."

He took the glass, sipped, and grimaced. "It's like baby food."

"Sorry, eat up," she said.

Since he'd come home with his jaw wired shut, she'd made him pureed chicken soup, protein smoothies, and peanut butter shakes. She was worried about how much weight he would lose during his recuperation. Whenever she came into his room, she brought something in a glass for him to drink. Nagging him to eat was something she'd never had to do, but she had no qualms about nagging him now.

"Randy stopped by to see how you were doing," she said. She set the vase of flowers on the bedside table. "He brought these from the firehouse."

"Tell them thanks, okay?" he mumbled through his wired jaw.

"Of course." She gave him an envelope with a card. His hands shook when he opened it, but she resisted the urge to open it for him.

He read the card, smiled, and handed it to her. She set it on his dresser with the dozens of others from the Marriage Survivors Club, Father Gabriel, the parishioners, neighbors, and his friends.

"Everybody at church is praying for you. Father Gabriel wants to stop by when you're ready," she said.

"Any time is okay. It was good to see the Marriage Survivors

Club, except Aunt Flicka and Aunt Bianca kept making me laugh, and that made my ribs hurt," he said.

She laughed. "Those two have a way of doing that."

"Randy, he's a good guy," Taylor croaked. He looked down at his meaty hands, opened and closed them. "He, um ... before we left for the fire, he told me to make up with you. That anything could happen on a call. But I never thought I'd get my butt kicked by a freakin' fire hose." He gave a single laugh and winced.

"Oooh, I'm sorry it's so painful." She wanted to pet him, but she wasn't sure where it didn't hurt.

He straightened out the covers, his expression one of shame and remorse. "About what Randy said ... I was kind of ... I was a jerk the last time I was here, and I didn't—"

"It's all right." She patted his hand gently. "Don't worry about it."

"No, really, Mom," he said. "I'm sorry I was such an idiot. I was just surprised, I guess. It was tough getting my head around how Dad died."

She nodded. "I understand. You had every right to be surprised and angry that I hadn't been truthful with you."

"Yeah, well, sorry," he said.

"Forgiven." She wanted to kiss the bruise on his chin the way she used to when he was little and came to her to kiss his booboos. She just smiled at him.

He slurped his drink. "I thought I heard Jack's voice this morning. Is he staying here?"

There was a temptation to feel embarrassed. But why should she be? She wasn't dead.

"Yes, he is," she said, chin lifted.

Taylor's tight smile revealed a Frankenstein mouth full of wires. "That's good, that's good. I'm glad."

"I have something to show you." She moved around to sit

beside him, propped a pillow behind her back, and leaned against the headboard.

While he'd been asleep, she'd brought up some photo albums. Now she opened one to a photo of a brilliant orange and yellow parachute floating high above a canyon.

He frowned at the photo. "Wow, who's that?"

"That's your dad and me paragliding," she said, rather pleased at his surprise. He didn't think his mother had ever had a life before or since his birth, as if all she'd ever done was wait for him and Ariel.

Taylor squinted at the photo. "You *what*? Like, regularly, you mean like all the time?" His voice rose in astonishment.

She turned the page. "That was just one of the things we did together. This is us scuba diving at an old shipwreck off Key Biscayne." She flipped another page. "And here we are after a skydive. This was when we went hot air ballooning, and this was taken just before we jumped off a cliff to go hang gliding." She turned another page. "Here we are waterskiing, and obviously, this was us surfing."

Taylor's eyes widened with every page. "You guys did all this stuff? This is lit!"

"Yes, it was totally lit," she said. "This is us skiing in the Italian Alps. Your dad loved skiing *off-piste*, the danger of the triple-black diamonds, skiing off ledges and stuff." She shook her head, still shocked that she had tolerated such stupidity. "He was such a daredevil."

Taylor leaned closer over the pictures as she flipped through and showed him all the crazy, dangerous, insane stuff she and Derek had done. He murmured, "Wow, wow," over and over.

Then she showed him the final photo in the book. "And this is just before he went for his final climb." She didn't even sigh when she said it. Instead, an unexpected whip of anger lashed through her. Jack was right: Derek had been selfish to put his thrills ahead of her and the children.

But her part was that she had been acquiescent. She had loved him and wanted him to be happy. Wanted to chase away his demons, but she couldn't. So she'd done the next best thing and gone along with him. She had been dumb, but Derek had been damned stupid.

Taylor's gaze had softened. She wondered how he felt to see his dad's final photo, but wanted to let him have his own thoughts.

"A neighbor snapped this as your dad was saying goodbye." She touched the image of Derek's face with its dimples and the look of desperate escape in his eyes. "His last goodbye, it turned out."

The silence between them was heavy with all the broken dreams of childhood, parenthood, marriage, a life cut short.

She said, "That's you in his arms. You were just six months old, and Ariel was three."

He quietly studied the photo. "You look tired in the picture."

She did, indeed. She stood in a slouch, her mouth cockeyed with sleeplessness, her eyes a pair of blue, unseeing saucers with dark circles beneath. Her jeans hung on the jutting triangles of her hip bones, and her milk-stained T-shirt slid off one shoulder.

She looked like an anorexic scarecrow.

She said, "You were a colicky baby and never slept more than a couple of hours. Ariel was running everywhere, getting into everything, and every cabinet." Olivia sighed. "She was exhausting." Even now, she remembered the bone-crushing exhaustion she'd had to power through. When she didn't think she could take anymore, it only got worse after Derek's death.

"Where was Dad?" Taylor asked.

"Working in the ER or doing sports," she said.

"Didn't he care how tired you were? Didn't he care about spending time with us?" He sounded like a hurt little boy.

"He did." She drew a finger over a photo of Derek smiling on a beach. "But now I think he was scared."

It was the first time she'd even thought this, and it felt like the most genuine thing she'd ever said about Derek.

"Of what?" Taylor asked.

"Of his own mortality. Getting older. Being trapped. Of not being able to save everyone who came in. He needed to beat death to feel alive."

"Sorry, Mom, but that's fucked up."

"Don't curse," she admonished. But of course, he was right. She had just ignored it until now. "He was overwhelmed, too, but in his own way."

Taylor's brows lowered. "I feel like I don't know what he was really, really like, you know? I only know he was a great doctor, but what was he like as a person?"

She adjusted her pillow and sat back again. "He was funny. He liked terrible jokes. The worse, the better. And puns."

He smiled. "Really? Tell me one."

"Mm," she sifted through her mind until she came to one. "It takes some guts to be an organ donor."

He groaned. "Oh, God!"

"Never lie to an X-ray technician. They can see right through you," she said and laughed.

"Stop!" he rolled his eyes. "Those are terrible."

She laughed. "I know, aren't they? Here's a joke. The patient says, 'Doctor, I get heartburn whenever I eat birthday cake.' The doctor says, 'Next time, take off the candles.'"

"Okay, stop, or you have to leave." Taylor held his ribs and pressed his lips together to keep from laughing.

Her own laughter tapered off with a sigh. "He was a good doctor. He saved a lot of lives, and the nurses and other doctors respected him." She paused as she prepared to break her son's heart. "Except for this one time."

His face solemn, Taylor closed the photo album and gave her his full attention.

"A young man came in with abdominal pain, and he sent him home." She remembered Derek's devastation, how it had thrown him into a funk, which drove him to take up rock climbing. She felt Taylor sink into himself.

"What happened to the guy?" Taylor asked, and she heard the uneasiness in his voice of discovering his hero was human after all. Like Superman falling out of the sky.

"He died later that night," she said.

"Oh, man," Taylor whispered. "Why?"

"There was an obstruction in his bowel. Your dad should have ordered some tests, but was exhausted at the end of a double shift. It was a disastrous mistake, and I don't think he ever really forgave himself for it." She leaned her head back against the headboard. "Doctors everywhere make mistakes all the time that cause a patient's death, but your dad just couldn't accept that was human."

"So, he made mistakes like everyone else," Taylor said.

Regret like a sack of stones rested on her heart. "Yes. I know I always made him out to be perfect, but he wasn't. I never meant to make you feel that you weren't good enough if you weren't just like him."

Taylor sipped his drink and set it aside again. "What were some of his bad qualities?"

"He could be testy and short-tempered," she said.

"And arrogant, selfish, and self-centered," Taylor added.

"Yes." She nodded. "And worst of all, he thought he was invincible." She clasped Taylor's hand. "You're none of those things. He loved you and your sister, and I wanted you to love him. I didn't mean to make him out to be a god."

"Thanks for telling me the bad stuff." Taylor sounded sad but relieved too. "All my life, I wished I'd gotten to know him. I wished he hadn't died."

Oh, my darling boy.

She had tried to fill the void of Derek's absence with hero worship, but that strategy only left Taylor more, not less, bereft. Just because he'd been too young to remember his dad didn't mean he hadn't yearned to know him.

"Me, too," she said.

"You know, it was hard not having a dad," Taylor admitted for the first time ever.

"I know. When did you miss him most?" She looked at him, but it was hard to read his face, what with all the bruises, two black eyes, bandaged nose, stitches in his chin, and jaw wired shut.

"I guess at my lacrosse games." He went on quickly, probably so as not to hurt her. "It was great having you and Aunt Bianca screaming from the sidelines, but I always wished my dad had been there." He bowed his head, and his voice went thick with emotion. "I wanted him to be proud of me. I wanted someone to be proud of me. To believe in me."

She blinked back tears. "Oh, Taylor, I was proud of you, and I'm sorry I didn't tell you more often. I'm sure he would have been proud of you then and now. I never meant to make you think I didn't believe in you. I was just scared of losing you. I'm sorry about that."

"Sometimes, I wished that you'd married again. Why didn't you?" It was the first time he'd ever asked her about that, and she wondered how long he'd considered thought about it.

She shrugged. "I believed all the same things I told you until I thought he was a saint." She marveled at her stupidity, which rivaled Derek's. "It's hard to find a man who can compete with perfection. I realize now that I was afraid to lose someone else that I loved."

"But Jack's a firefighter. Aren't you worried about him?"

Thinking of Jack's sacrifice, she smiled, gooey chocolatiness filling her chest. "He's decided to quit, not for me, for him."

"Huh?"

"He'll have to explain it to you. He'll be here for dinner."

Taylor's lips lifted in a half-grin. "This sounds like one of those reverse psychology things."

"I finally decided that if I want to have love in my life, I have to give up being scared all the time," she said, the honesty of the words fitting her exactly.

"Whoa, you *have* turned over a new leaf." He chuckled and winced.

She winced in sympathy. "A bit of a new leaf. But I'm still going to be worried about you because I'm your mom, and you can't stop me."

He held his hands up in a gesture of surrender and said, "I wouldn't even think of it."

"But I no longer worry about bubonic plague, kidnappers, snake bites, terrorists, or planes plowing into the house anymore." She pressed a hand to her belly as a knife point of anxiety dragged itself from the base of her throat to the depths of her stomach. "I'll always worry you'll get hurt again, but I want you and Ariel to have happy and fulfilling lives, to know great love. I want you to have purpose and to live a life full of the things you love and enjoy."

They sat together, each absorbing what they'd both shared. She felt prouder and closer to Taylor than she thought possible. At last, she felt like a really good mom. Able to love, give space and support, to not let fear control her.

After a while, he said, "Mom, I want to be a firefighter, not so I can be some kind of hero, but because I want to help people."

Of course, he did. Because he wanted to be just like his dad.

"I know. You're a good man, Taylor." She would never again try to change his mind.

His eyelids sagged, and he let out a long sigh. "Thanks," he said in an exhausted whisper.

She rose and held the covers while he settled himself slowly and painfully back down.

"Thanks for showing me the pictures," he mumbled, halfway to sleep.

"I only wish I'd have done it sooner." She put the album on the side table. "I'll leave it here so you can look at it again whenever you want."

From her pocket, she pulled a pair of socks that had somehow migrated between the sofa cushions when she'd been throwing Derek's things out. She dangled them up for Taylor to see. "Sure, you don't want some chili pepper socks?"

He smiled and croaked, "Over my dead body."

CHAPTER 50

It's not only children who grow. Parents do too. As much as we watch to see what our children do with their lives, they are watching us to see what we do with ours. I can't tell my children to reach for the sun. All I can do is reach for it, myself.

Joyce Maynard

With an excited smile, Ariel tottered up the front steps of Ability House where Bea Dewinter waved a warm welcome.

It was Ariel's move-in day, and she'd been chattering about it for days.

Olivia followed, lugging a laundry basket overflowing with Ariel's stuffed *My Little Pony* characters. Frankie, Carolina, Bianca, and Flicka were right behind Olivia, carrying various bags and bins. Hélène had texted that she was on her way, but would be late.

Bea gave Ariel a hug and Ariel's first words were, "Where Matt?" Bea laughed. "Oh, look, he's right behind you!" Bea laughed and pointed to Jack's car pulling up..

Matt jumped out of Jack's car, and he and Ariel rushed into one another's arms.

"They are so adorable together," Flicka said.

Carolina set down a bag of clothing. "I wish I could find a guy who loved me as much as he seems to love her."

"Me, too," Flicka said.

"You goin' for number five?" Bianca teased.

Flicka arched an eyebrow. "I didn't say anything about marriage."

"Tramp," Bianca muttered good-naturedly.

Flicka laughed.

Jack climbed the stone steps to Olivia, his smile warming her all over.

Jack bent and kissed her. "How's it going?" He took the basket of stuffies from Olivia.

"Now that Matt's here, everything is complete," Olivia said, smiling up at him.

After Olivia introduced the Marriage Survivors Club to Bea, they followed her upstairs to Ariel's room. Ariel would share with Sandy, a woman about her age. who had experienced a traumatic brain injury. The large bedroom was spotless, sunny, and bright, with white eyelet curtains and twin beds.

Bea said, "I'll leave you all to get set up and see you downstairs in a bit." And she quietly disappeared.

Jack set the basket of stuffies in a corner and returned downstairs to see what else needed bringing up.

Frankie set down Ariel's prancing unicorn lamp on a bedside table. "Wow is all I can say. The house is beautiful, but comfy."

"This looks like a great place, Olivia." Bianca glanced around the room. She set down the bag containing a new *My Little Pony* bedspread, which the Marriage Survivors Club had bought as a gift for Ariel's new bedroom.

"It is," Olivia agreed. "Bea is marvelous, and the rest of the staff is helpful and attentive. The other residents are very nice. Ariel has even been able to transfer to another grocery store right here in the neighborhood so she can keep her job."

"So, if everything's so great, why aren't you smiling more?" Carolina asked in her serene way.

Olivia's legs felt weak. She sank onto Ariel's bed. "I'm happy, but I'm a little sad, too. Happy she'll be here, but sad she won't be home."

Carolina rested her hand on Olivia's shoulder. "It's possible —and okay—to be both."

Olivia lay her hand atop Carolina's. Having the Marriage Survivors Club here was like being wrapped in a hug. They understood Olivia, knew her children, knew her fears and short-comings, and loved her still.

"You're a great mom," Frankie said.

"I couldn't have done this without you guys," Olivia said, her heart full of tears and joy.

Love was an inadequate word for what she felt for the Marriage Survivors Club, and she knew they felt the same about her. They shared one another's tragedies and joys, forgave, chided, and encouraged. Olivia could count on them to call her on her bullshit. They were the ones she could call any hour of any day for help. And she didn't even have to call them. They somehow knew when one of them needed the others, and they appeared like angels.

Hélène wafted into the bedroom. "I'm sorry I'm late. The traffic—"

"We know, we know," Bianca said with an eye roll, and Hélène laughed.

Hélène set down the bag with Ariel's new *My Little Pony* towels and bed sheets. "The house is beautiful. I expected something more clinical, not so homey. Ariel will be very safe, and you should feel great about her living here."

Afraid to Let Grow

Taylor appeared in the doorway. The bruises on his face had turned rampant shades of blue and purple and were now fading to dull ocher. The stitches on his chin had come out the week before, and he was sporting a scar that looked a bit like a smile. There were scabs along his cheeks, and he still couldn't carry anything heavy because his ribs were still healing.

He cracked a smile, and Olivia saw nothing of Derek, only Taylor's dimples, the lively light in his eyes, the calm steadiness of him. He was so young, but already his own man.

Through his wired-shut jaw, he managed to lisp, "Mom, Bea wants us all back downstairs for something."

They all headed back downstairs, where Ariel and Matt were cuddled up on the sofa.

Olivia met Jack's eyes. She knew he was checking to see if their physical affection made her nervous, but she felt an explosion of gratitude, unweighted by fear, that Ariel had found love. It was a miracle Olivia had almost thrown away. Thanks to Jack and her friends, she hadn't.

Bea laughed. "Come around the back, everyone. We want to share a little welcoming tradition with you all," she said.

They trooped to the back of the house, where the other residents gathered around several picnic tables. There were a bunch of balloons, a cake, and a homemade banner that read *Welcome, Ariel*, decorated with stickers and crayon drawings. The ladies cried, "Happy birthday," "Welcome home," "Have cake," "Home sweet," and "Merry Christmas."

Everyone clapped. All the residents wore Matt's T-shirts imprinted with a painting of Ariel's face. Matt handed around more and everyone, even Flicka, gamely pulled the shirts on over their clothes. They all sang "Happy Birthday," which was somehow appropriate because Ariel was starting a new life.

Olivia was touched by the exuberance of it all and finally realized why Bea always laughed. This day was turning out to be wave after wave of joy that left Olivia undone. She clasped her hands over her chest to keep her heart from floating away.

Olivia looked around at the Marriage Survivors Club, Taylor, Ariel, and Matt. She didn't think she could love any of them any more than she did right now.

Jack held her tucked against his side. "Is it what you thought it would be?"

"More," she said, the scene wavering in her happy tears. "And it's all because you suggested it."

"I've been waiting to hear you say that." He laughed his rumbly laugh, and Olivia sank into his strong arms as he kissed her.

CHAPTER 51

And the dust returns to the earth as it was, and the spirit
returns to God who gave it.

Ecclesiastes 12:7

On Sunday morning after church, Jack stood with Olivia and the
Marriage Survivors Club on the labyrinth behind St. Paul's.
Taylor was there with his new girlfriend. Matt and Ariel,
wearing matching shirts from his latest collection called "Loving
Ariel," were also there. Jack had brought two dozen red and
white parrot tulips, and the look in Olivia's eyes had been worth
every dime he'd paid.

They were all gathered to dedicate a beautiful, eight-foot tall,
flowering crabapple tree to the life of Derek Maxwell.

Two weeks ago, when the date had been set and all the plans
had been made, Jack had asked Olivia if she wanted him there.

"Why wouldn't I want you there?" She lifted her head from
the pillow and gazed at him. When she fixed him with her

steady, sun-filled blue eyes, he would have cut off his leg if she'd asked.

"I didn't want to presume you wanted me there. Derek was your first love, after all," he said.

She looked up at him. "He's my past." With a well-sated grin, she said, "You're my future."

He didn't ask what she meant by that. She had to be certain she'd rid herself of Derek's memory before she was ready to look ahead. She might want Jack to be a part of her life, or she might not, in which case, he would ride his Harley across the country a second time.

Every day with Olivia was full of minute rituals that cemented their lives together. He brought her tulips once a week, no matter how expensive. She knew he liked his hamburgers rare, and he knew how she took her coffee. He knew she withdrew into herself when she was upset, and he was learning the signs; to listen before offering solutions. She knew he sometimes had terrible dreams about being trapped in a fire. He knew she hated scary movies. She could tell when he was lonely for his daughters and encouraged him to call them. She knew he liked to secretly read romantic suspense novels. He knew she was reluctant to share her worries, and he reminded her she didn't have to carry them alone. She knew he overcommitted and was teaching him to say no occasionally. He knew not to joke about danger and not coming home. He now wore leathers every time he rode his bike. She knew he wanted her to kiss him whenever they parted.

Every time he woke up beside her, or she regarded him with her astute gaze, he felt like he'd died and gone to heaven. She was the embodiment of the phrase "small but mighty."

Now that he knew what love could really be, the kind of fusing of lives he had with Olivia, he understood what Gina had been missing with him. The last residue of his guilt and resentment regarding her dissolved. He'd called her and apologized for dragging the marriage out, told her about Olivia. Told her that she deserved joy, too. They had both cried.

This afternoon the sun was practically singing. The air smelled of the light sweet fragrance of the crabapple flowers. Laughter was everywhere and Jack had the sense that everyone there already knew him—not of him or who he was, but that they knew *him.*

They were in a semi-circle as the choir sang a short anthem that made Jack's heart feel as though someone had poured sunlight into it. Father Gabriel, who hardly looked old enough to have a driver's license, let alone be a priest, intoned the twenty-third Psalm, and everyone joined in.

Olivia bumped against Jack's ribs, and he sent up a prayer of thanks to the God he started believing in when he met her. He had never been one for church, but he loved St. Paul's message that everybody was worthy of love and that all were welcome. Those ideas struck home with him every time he heard them. He was welcome here whether he was a true believer or not, and her friends had absorbed him as if he had always been one of them. He thought it was a shame that Gina hadn't grown up in a church like St. Paul's.

Father Gabriel solemnly lit some incense in a round metal ball and walked around the tree, swinging it. Afterwards, he recited a prayer, and Taylor helped Ariel read a short poem, after which she returned to Matt's side. He hugged her, and Jack saw Olivia wipe tears from beneath her eyes.

He tucked her closer and leaned down to kiss the top of her head. Her soft, wavy hair, set loose from the restrictive ponytail she'd stopped wearing, shifted in the breeze against his mouth.

When it was her turn, he saw Olivia was nervous by the almost imperceptible twitch in her lip, something that rarely occurred anymore. But as she spoke, her voice was firm and unwavering as she read a Bible verse that even he was familiar with.

There is an appointed time for everything and a time for every affair under the heavens.

    A time to give birth, and a time to die; a time to plant, and a time to uproot the plant.

    A time to kill, and a time to heal; a time to tear down, and a time to build.

    A time to weep, and a time to laugh; a time to mourn, and a time to dance.

    A time to scatter stones, and a time to gather them.

    A time to embrace, and a time to be far from embraces.

    A time to seek, and a time to lose; a time to keep, and a time to cast away.

    A time to rend, and a time to sew; a time to be silent, and a time to speak.

    A time to love, and a time to hate, a time of war, and a time of peace.

    I recognized that there is nothing better than to rejoice and to do well during life.

She returned to Jack's side, and he saw she was spent but relieved. She seemed, at last, finished with the ghost of Derek Maxwell. Finished with the crashing hurt he'd given her when he'd selfishly, arrogantly done something he was ill-prepared to undertake.

When the dedication service ended, the parishioners descended on the table laden with cool drinks and baked goods.

Hand in hand, Matt and Ariel went to Father Gabriel. "We want a wedding," Matt said.

Jack heard Olivia's sharp intake of breath. He took her hand and pressed it to his lips. "Don't panic," he whispered.

"I'm not," she whispered back, looking up at him, her eyes bright with tears. "I'm just surprised, is all. I wouldn't have thought they would understand that."

All reports of Ariel and Matt were that they spent every minute they could together. Still, Jack was also a bit surprised that at a memorial service, marrying was what was on their minds.

"You do?" Father Gabriel asked Matt.

"Yes," Ariel said. "We love."

Father Gabriel, who didn't look like he was flummoxed very often, stammered, "I have to ... I need to think about that." He threw Jack and Olivia a questioning glance.

Matt moved closer to Jack, and Father Gabriel made his getaway to the cookie table.

"We can, can't we, Uncle Jack?" Matt asked.

Ariel kissed Matt. "We want to."

"Matt placed his soft, pudgy hand, with paint under the fingernails, on Jack's shoulder. "You should, too," he said, looking up earnestly.

"Should what?" Jack asked.

"Make a wedding," Matt said. He released his grip on Jack's shoulder. Matt turned Ariel's face to him so he could kiss her cheek, and she giggled.

"You could be happy like us, Uncle Jack. You could come to Ability House and use the special room for kissing," Matt said.

Jack and Olivia looked at one another and both burst out laughing.

Taylor strolled over with his girlfriend, a young college woman who was a special ed major. He frequently turned to Jack for advice, and that made Jack feel honored. Taylor was turning out to be an even better firefighter than Jack had guessed he would be. He wasn't a cowboy, took on grunt work without complaint, and followed procedures to the T and backed up his fellow firefighters.

His dad would have been proud of him.

"I want to buy Ariel a diamond," Matt said. "You should buy Olivia a diamond, too."

"Yeah, Mom," Ariel said. "You buy Jack diamond."

There were times when Jack was rattled by how clearly Matt understood his own emotions and how he had no trouble speaking his own mind. But the guy couldn't read a social situation to save his life.

"Oh, we're talking marriage now?" Taylor said with a grin.

"You love Olivia, don't you?" Matt asked Jack.

"Well, yes, but ..." Jack scratched the back of his neck.

Beside him, Olivia was red-faced, laughing that laugh that was too big for someone so small. She was enjoying his embarrassment.

Taylor said, "What are you guys waiting for, anyway?"

Jack would make Taylor polish every inch of chrome on all the fire engines next week.

"I just buried your father," Olivia objected.

Taylor narrowed his eyes at her. "Mom, you buried him eighteen years ago. You just finally said goodbye to him."

"He dead," Ariel said with a finality that sent them all into paroxysms of laughter again.

"You're right, Squirt." Taylor hugged his sister. "Well put."

Jack did want to marry Olivia, but he thought at least they'd get to make the decision themselves after some discussion. He glanced down at Olivia, a question in his eyes.

"Yes," Olivia said, her sweet, fierce face turned up to his.

"You're sure?" Jack asked, afraid she would change her mind.

"More than I've ever been about anything," Olivia said.

"You don't mind being asked to marry me at your husband's memorial service?" Jack asked her.

She grinned up at him with a new naughtiness in her eyes, and said, "He dead."

And they all laughed some more.

In front of everyone, Jack gathered her in his arms and whispered in her ear, "Thanks for taking a chance on an old guy like me."

She pulled back, and her eyes searched his face, a smile on her lips. "Don't you know by now that I don't take chances? I only go for the sure thing."

Then she kissed him, and he wasn't sure if the choir was singing, but every muscle, bone, and sinew in his body sang.

CHAPTER 52

Always do what you are afraid to do.
   Ralph Waldo Emerson

Olivia wasn't sure who she was looking at in the mirror. "I look like a Hell's Angel."

She was dressed head to toe in black leather, and her feet were encased in thick-soled, high-top boots embroidered with red roses. The leathers, youth-sized small, felt stiff and smelled like the inside of a new car. On top of everything else, she had stopped straightening and coloring her hair and the rampant curls were coming in at an alarming rate. The wavy caramel blond color was streaked with gray added to the Hell's Angel look.

"I can't believe I'm doing this." She looked at Jack in the mirror. "Why did I let you talk me into this?"

"I didn't talk you into it. You can back out any time," Jack said, which made the giant salesman look distressed.

"You're right." Olivia kissed Jack. "I can, but I'm not going to because I'm fearless."

She felt absolutely no pressure to join him on the back of his bike for any of the reasons she had taken up sports with Derek. She was doing this purely so she could nestle against his back and wrap her arms around his middle. She wanted to share something with him that he loved for the sheer pleasure of doing it.

The motorcycle clothing shop on Route 123 was next to Banksville Fabrics, where she had previously spent happy hours fingering the home decorating fabrics in damask, linen, and nubby silks. Now she was debating the different cuts of leather jackets and pants and deciding which made her look hottest.

The salesman said, "I think this one will fit you." He lowered a fire-engine red helmet that matched the red roses on her boots, onto her head.

The salesman had an upper body like a water buffalo and multiple tattoos slithering up his arms and ringing his neck. His mangled nose had met with more than one catastrophe, and his reddish-brown beard might actually have been a small dog he was carrying under his chin.

She caught herself. *Don't judge. You don't know his story, and he doesn't know yours. Treat every stranger like they're Jesus.*

But she couldn't imagine that Mary would have let Jesus get tattoos.

Jack leaned on the counter, his face like a kid at Christmas. "This is going to be so much fun. You are going to *love* this. We can spend our retirement touring the US on a pair of Honda Gold Wings."

She fixed him with a beseeching look. "Let's just get through this first ride before you have us riding off into the sunset."

She had trouble buckling the latch on the helmet, so the salesman deftly snapped the latch and adjusted the chin strap to fit her. Jack had ordered a special pair of extra-extra small red gloves for her. He slipped them onto her hands.

"They feel like I'm wearing oven mitts," she said, her voice sounding too loud in the helmet.

"They take some getting used to," Jack said.

The salesman pressed a button on the side of the helmet. "Now, when you're riding and want to talk to him, you just press this microphone button and tell him to slow down or speed up, whichever you prefer."

She said, "Or stop so I can go to the bathroom."

The tough salesman's cheeks turned a brilliant red, but when he smiled, he had a mouth of perfectly straight, white teeth. He said, "And now, you're all ready for a road trip, ma'am."

She peered out through the darkened visor. Wearing leather biking gear, her blond hair flowing out beneath the helmet and over her shoulders, she felt more like a chick than a 'ma'am'.

"You look like a perfect biker," Jack said. The only time she'd ever seen him so excited was the first time he'd seen her completely naked.

She couldn't help herself, so she said, "You're sure this is safe?"

"Nothing's safe. You know that," Jack countered.

Of course, she knew that. He had refused to take her on a ride until she had made her peace with that. That peace felt freeing, like walking into a brighter, more spacious world. She knew things carried risk and danger, but she recognized that she was helpless, and not responsible, to prevent them. Fear had kept her a prisoner in her own heart, but now she felt unfettered, filled with so much love it hurt sometimes.

She flexed her fingers in the leather gloves. She determined to do this, to prove to herself that her love had overcome her fears. This ride was for her, not for Jack.

The salesman said, "Watch some YouTube videos to see how

you need to roll in case he does crash, which he most likely won't." He tilted his pumpkin-sized head at Jack. "Right?"

"Right," Jack responded.

She punched one fist into the palm of her other hand. "And if he does crash, we go together."

Outside, she climbed on the back of Jack's Harley. He turned the key, and the engine growled to life, sending vibrations through her bones and rattling her teeth. Her wild heart purred.

Jack kicked out the kickstand and backed out of the parking spot. She wrapped her arms around his waist, holding tight. She trusted Jack to take care of her, to be careful with himself and her. He wouldn't do anything stupid or foolhardy.

The day was clear and cloudless, with a bachelor-button blue sky and endless visibility. They headed to the Merritt Parkway, where he took the northbound entrance ramp. As they reached the end of the curving entrance and as they merged into traffic, her excitement accelerated at the same speed as the bike.

In her headphones, she heard Jack ask, "You ready for a ride?"

She pressed the button and answered, "Yes." She gripped his waist tighter and took a deep breath.

He revved the engine. She gasped as the bike surged ahead, pressed through the wind, the asphalt racing beneath them. The brush and scrub on the embankment blurred, and the world sped past as they raced beneath a canopy of emerald trees. It reminded her of flying on a plane and looking out at the world passing away beneath you. She had a sensation of being loosened from every earthbound concern or responsibility. The only things that existed were the man in her arms, the sky above, and the road unspooling ahead of them.

"What do you think?" he asked.

"Wheeee!"

AFTERWARD

Dear Reader,

I was inspired to include characters with Down syndrome in this book because of a young man named John Cronin and his dad, Mark. John has Down syndrome. He has a website called Johnscrazysocks.com that sells the craziest socks you've ever seen. He donates a portion of his profits to Special Olympics. Please head over to www.Johnscrazysocks.com and buy some socks. We need to stop judging people with disabilities and see them as whole human beings and members of our diverse society.

Thank you for taking the time to read my book. It's for people like you that I write and rewrite until I feel I've created the best story I can that will touch your heart. Reviews mean so much to a writer, so if you have enjoyed this book, I would be immensely grateful if you would go online to your favorite retailer, Bookbub or Goodreads, and leave a review.

I've included a scene from the next book in the series, "He Brought Me Music: Hélène's story," which I hope will pique your interest.

Thank you again, and see you in the next Marriage Survivors Club book!

Annette

Sign up for my newsletter here.

www.annettenauraine.com to find out what me, my cat and dog, and the Marriage Survivors Club are up to.

Links to my other books:

Do-Over Daughter: A Marriage Survivors Club Book 1
  https://books2read.com/u/bMzKNB
  Kissing the Kavalier
  Historical romance based on the opera *Arabella* by Richard Strauss. https://books2read.com/u/mBoKry
  Kerry and Bobbie and the Dead Senator: A killer caper
  https://books2read.com/u/bQNxeE
  Freebie: In the Beginning: Marriage Survivors Prequel
  https://books2read.com/u/3nNg5o

Follow me on SM:
  https://www.facebook.com/annettenauraineauthor/
  https://www.instagram.com/anauraine/

Review Sites:
  https://www.goodreads.com/book/edit_photos/195241581-do-over-daughter
  https://www.bookbub.com/books/do-over-daughter-the-marriage-survivors-club-book-1-by-annette-nauraine

HE BROUGHT ME MUSIC

BOOK III OF THE MARRIAGE
SURVIVORS CLUB: HÉLÈNE

A sudden bold and unexpected question doth many
times surprise a man and lay him open.

Francis Bacon

"But Wat, my studio is full. I'd love to help, you know I would,
but simply I don't have room for more students. I'll give him a
listen but I'm completely booked up," Hélène hissed to Wat
Crabtree.

They were standing in her music studio, whispering so the
father and son waiting on the other side of the French doors
couldn't overhear.

Wat was the choirmaster and organist-extraordinaire of St.
Paul's Episcopal Church on the Green in Norwalk, CT. It was
where Hélène and the Marriage Survivors Club attended
church. They were Hélène's best friends, were a diverse group of
six single 50-something women who prayed, drank and cursed
in equal measure.

"Darius is eleven, a child prodigy. Played Chopin at five,"
Wat said breathlessly.

Fear coiled in Hélène's belly.

Wat wasn't a big man, but he vibrated with the energy of someone who brought out the best in others. He was a Charmer, Persuader and Pied Piper, and that made him formidable.

And in this case, dangerous.

She glanced through the French doors where Darius Harding, and his father, Bryn, waited on the parent's bench in her entryway.

The boy, with a shrub of mad, wiry hair on his head, was tall for his age, made mostly of bones, with the translucent complexion of a kid who spent all his time indoors. His somber, dark eyes stared fixed disinterestedly on the floor as if he was deep in another world.

"You don't have to decide today. Just hear him," Wat said in a manner intended to insist while not sounding pushy.

She nudged a wisp of her black and white hair—a result of Mallen streaks—off her forehead. Hair that had given her her nick name. She gave Wat her disarming smile. "I only teach beginner students but I can give you names of other teachers."

Everybody thought their kid was the next Lang Lang. Thirty years of fobbing off the students who were actually good had hardened her heart against the loss. She hardly even felt the pinch of regret anymore.

Or that was what she told herself.

Wat's brows shot up, and she turned away so she didn't have to see the skepticism smoking in his eyes.

"How did he come to you, anyway?" she asked, not really considering taking the boy but curious anyway. She glanced out at him again. He wore his shirt buttoned to the neck and wore khakies with a knife's edge crease. He looked like a little old man who needed a hug.

"His father moved to Norwalk for a job." The way Wat paused hinted at something more. Wat paused. She waited for the real truth.

348

Wat went on. "About a year ago, the kid refused to play. The dad called Father Gabriel, and he asked if I could take him on, but when I heard him on YouTube, I knew he was way beyond me so I thought of you."

Why would he have thought of her?

The hair at the nape of her neck prickled. "Then, he's way beyond *me*." She forced a smile. "I'm happy to listen to him and call around to the other teachers to see if anyone has room in their studios."

But she felt the stirrings of temptation as always happened when finding a student who was actually talented.

On the parents bench, Bryn's knee jiggled up and down at a *presto* tempo. Probably forty-something, with his knot of an Adam's apple, he reminded her of Ichabod Crane. He was a pale-haired, slightly balding man with an elongated, thoughtful face and an anxious, roaming gaze. Father and son sat next to one another, but there was a chasm between them. Desperation and loneliness swam around their ankles, threatening to pull them down. They needed a life preserver, not a piano teacher, and certainly not her.

She crossed her arms and turned back to Wat. "I'd love to help, but I'm not the right person."

"There's one other small thing that might change your mind." Wat squinched his nose, pushing his glasses up. "Darius is selectively mute. When he quit playing, he stopped talking too. He refused to speak to therapists or speak in school. His poor father is on his last nerve. He thinks getting him to play piano will get him talking again."

"Thanks for thinking of me," she said. "I love teaching children, but if he won't talk and he plays Chopin, what he needs is therapy. He's way out of my league." She moved toward the doors to let Wat out.

Wat raised a hand to stop her. "Look, you don't have to decide today. Just hear him. They're here. What can it hurt?"

A lot. It could hurt a like holding flame in my hands.

She shook her head. "I'd be doing him a disservice. And what about the mother?"

"When I mentioned it the way Bryn responded made it clear she's not in the picture for some reason," Wat said. "And I didn't want to pry."

Bryn rose and paced, hands shoved deep in the pockets of his rumpled pants, his big head tucked forward as if searching for something on the carpet. Engagingly shambolic, he had a stretched-out body, and the bones of his shoulders poked sharp angles in his goofy, short-sleeved Hawaiian shirt. He looked perfectly helpless, but helpless didn't mean harmless.

His movements almost steathly, Wat met her in the crook of her nine foot Bösendorfer piano.

He whispered, "Hélène, I know who you really are."